T0354852

Beloved Grace

~ Awakening ~

Keri Nanette Miller, Ph.D.

BALBOA.
PRESS

A DIVISION OF HAY HOUSE

Balboa Press books may be ordered through booksellers or by contacting:

Balboa Press
A Division of Hay House
1663 Liberty Drive
Bloomington, IN 47403
www.balboapress.com
1 (877) 407-4847

Print information available on the last page.

ISBN: 978-1-5043-8553-4 (sc)
ISBN: 978-1-5043-8555-8 (hc)
ISBN: 978-1-5043-8554-1 (e)

Library of Congress Control Number: 2017912283

Balboa Press rev. date: 09/25/2017

Contents

Dedication

This book is dedicated to the one
Who makes my soul come alive,
Every time he looks at me
With his aqua blue eyes.

# Chapter One

Mortified Once Again

MORGANA'S TIRES SCREECHED as she pulled up into the right side of the inclined Y-shaped driveway and jerked her car into park. Her hands gripped the steering wheel as she clenched her teeth. Only thirty days left of that hell, and then she would graduate. Her wavy brown hair covered her face as she laid her head down on the steering wheel and sighed. "Soon I will be done with high school, then get college over with, and then I can finally start living my own life," she said to herself.

She shoved open the driver's side door of her ten-year-old white sedan and gathered her purse from the passenger's side seat which had dumped over during her road-rage induced Tokyo drift. "That jerk cut me off no reason!" she shouted. "Don't people know how to drive!" She angrily threw the contents of her purse back into their cloth cave as she noticed her phone way down on the passenger floorboard. She went to reach for it and slid, knocking her rib cage against the handbrake on the center console. "Son of a bitch!" she cried out. She struggled to reach her phone as she cursed her arms and fingers for not being able to grab it. The phone caught the bulk of her tirade until she finally managed to hook the corner and gain control of it. Then it too, was thrown into her purse with the force of an All-Star fast pitch. With her purse and its contents finally back together, she exited the car rubbing her sore ribs and looked bleakly at the backseat full of books she needed to study for finals. She let out a desperate breath and reached for the rear door handle.

"Morgana?"

She heard her name being called from across the street. It was the kind elderly lady, Ms. Lane. Morgana had never really spoken to her before, except for the occasional exchange of niceties. Ms. Lane would bake little loaves of different kinds of delicious breads or succulent cookies for Morgana and her mother. But besides a wave now and then from the driveway, Morgana never really engaged with her neighbor.

"Oh, hi, Ms. Lane." Morgana pushed aside her long, disheveled hair, gave a weak smile and waved, and then was about to go back to minding her own business.

"Morgana, would you mind giving a hand?" Ms. Lane called back.

Oh, great, now what? Morgana exasperatedly thought. "Yes, ma'am," she replied.

Morgana shuffled in her flip flops down the inclined driveway, kicking at some loose gravel her tires had stirred up in her haste to get home. She crossed the street to Ms. Lane's driveway, where her old, deep maroon Cadillac Deville sat with its enormous trunk wide open. Inside, Morgana saw tons of woven tweed grocery sacks that exposed their prizes of milk in glass jars and an assortment of other foreign fruits and vegetables Morgana wasn't used to seeing at her regular grocery store.

"I just got back from the farmers' market. Have you ever had fresh milk straight from the farm?" Ms. Lane asked excitedly. Morgana smiled politely and shook her head no. She didn't drink much milk anyway, but the thought of drinking milk straight from dirty, smelly old cows turned her stomach a little bit.

"Josef usually helps unload my groceries on farmers' market day, but he sent me a text saying he was delayed." As Morgana scooped up the sacks, she snickered to herself at the thought of old Ms. Lane texting. "You remember my great-nephew, Josef, don't you?"

Oh, yes. Morgana remembered him.

Josef was about five years older than Morgana and he had spent a few summers with Ms. Lane. Morgana remembered the summer when she was thirteen and Josef had come to their door asking her mom if she would like for him to mow the yard for her. This was the first time Morgana had seen him up close and he was even more gorgeous than she had imagined. He had golden tan skin, sun-kissed blond hair, and the most beautiful deep aqua blue eyes she had ever seen. They were the

2

color of the tranquil oceans next to white sandy beaches she had only seen in pictures online.

Thirteen-year-old Morgana gasped a little when he looked at her. He took her breath away. She was hiding behind her mother, pinching at her to say yes and let this beautiful Adonis mow their yard. Her mother graciously accepted his offer, and he set to work on the front yard grass. Wanting to impress her gorgeous impromptu gardener, Morgana sprinted to her room and put on her most grown-up looking sundress and the sandals with the small heel. She struggled to style her hair, which couldn't decide if it was straight or curly and always just seemed messy to her. She put in a glittery barrette to pin it out of her face so he could look deeply into her eyes, which couldn't decide if they were blue or grey. She globbed on some extra shiny lip gloss, and then ran into the kitchen to make some fresh lemonade. Josef was already done with the front yard and was working his way through the backyard by the time she had finished gussying herself up. She poured the lemonade into a tall glass full of ice and carefully set it on a silver serving tray. Her fantasy was to deliver the refreshing drink, he would fall madly in love with her, and they would live happily ever after as Mr. and Mrs. Perfect-Aqua-Blue-Eyes. However, the reality of her delivery could not have gone worse. First, she spilled the drink a little on the silver tray as she tried to open the back door. He was pushing the mower and she didn't think he noticed as she grabbed the now slippery glass in one hand and shook off the excess liquid from the tray. *Maybe I shouldn't have filled the glass so much,* she thought to herself. She regained her composure as he came back around. Unfortunately, this time, he was looking directly at her as the heel on her sandal got caught in the grass and she fell to the ground, spilling sticky, icy lemonade all over herself. Ice flew everywhere, even down the front of her dress. She ripped the hem of her skirt and grass stained her knees and palms. She remembered those deep aqua blue eyes and that smile as he was laughing and running to her aid. She was mortified beyond existence and went crying into the house. She never spoke to him again, and his boisterous laughter still haunted her ears.

"Yes, ma'am, I remember Josef," Morgana grunted, as she lifted the woven tweed grocery sacks out of the deep trunk of the old Caddy. She followed Ms. Lane up the walkway to the deeply recessed front door. Morgana suddenly realized she had never been inside her neighbor's house and looked around to see if there were any witnesses to her going inside. She wished she hadn't put her purse with her phone on the backseat with all her books when Ms. Lane had called out for assistance. As Ms. Lane fumbled a little with her keys, the glass bottles of milk were getting heavier in Morgana's arms. She understood why the elderly lady would ask for help. With relief, Morgana finally heard the lock click, and Ms. Lane pushed open the heavy wooden front door. A strong, pungent musk penetrated Morgana's nostrils. She gulped a little from the smell and shifted the heavy bags straining her arms before walking into the dark, dank house. She couldn't see as the house was dimly lit, even though it was bright and sunny outside. Morgana's eyes struggled to make the shift from light to dark, and she bumped into a pony wall hidden behind her arms full of heavy sacks.

"This way, dear," Ms. Lane's voice called out from the darkness. As her eyes strained to adjust, Morgana could only see walls full of creepy dolls. She rounded the corner and got a face full of dried flowers that seemed to be hung from an odd place in the middle of the room. The musky smell was so heavy she was having trouble breathing.

"Just set those on the counter, dear. And would you mind getting the others out of the trunk?"

Morgana set the fabric sacks on the counter and raced back outside. The bright sun hit her eyes, blinding her, as she made her way back down the path to the large open trunk. She grabbed as many of the bags as she could to try to make as few trips as possible to quickly complete the tedious task. She took a deep breath, filling her lungs with the fresh air before she ran back inside, holding her breath, and setting the second batch of heavy sacks on the counter. *Good Lord!* she thought. *Are the whole cows in those bags? They weigh a frickin' ton!* She hurried back outside, the sun blaring in her eyes, and took a long deep breath. She panted as she rushed to the trunk, hoping she could get everything in this one last trip. She snatched up the last seven cloth bags and repeated to herself, *In and out. Just drop these last ones on the counter and you'll be done with it.* She took one last, deep breath of fresh air as she heaved the heavy sacks through the door, around the pony wall, past the shelves of creepy glass dolls, and dodged the dry, dead bunches of flowers hanging upside down like decrepit little vampires.

"Oh, my, dear!" Ms. Lane exclaimed, "Those are so heavy, you didn't have to get them all at once!"

As Morgana lifted the last of them onto the counter, her arm muscles were a little shaky, and her eyes were not fully adjusted from going back and forth between the contrast of light and dark. She was still holding her breath as she tried to leave in a hurry. And that's when she heard his deep, silky voice that stopped her in her tracks.

"God, Aunt Katherine! It smells like somebody died in here."

Morgana slowly turned to see his tall, muscular stature, sun-kissed blond hair, that gorgeous smile, and those deep aqua blue eyes. He was standing in the doorway, illuminated by the bright sun behind him. He was even more handsome than she remembered. Despite herself, she could no longer hold her breath, and she choked while trying to breathe. He was chuckling at his joke and then laughed even harder at Morgana's snort as she struggled to catch her breath.

"Oh, Josef. You're hilarious," Mrs. Lane said as she walked over for a hug and a kiss from her favorite nephew and a couple of his friends who followed him into the house. "I didn't think you were going to make it, so I had Morgana help me. Remember Morgana?"

He laughed and smiled as he extended his hand out to shake Morgana's. "Of course I remember her. How could I forget?" His silky voice oozed. Morgana was completely embarrassed and blood rushed to her cheeks as she assumed he was remembering the klutzy kid with the lemonade soaked dress and grass stained knees. She shook his hand and nodded politely.

"Well, since he's here now, I've got to get home," Morgana announced, desperately trying to free herself of the awkward situation.

"Thank you, dear," Ms. Lane called out. "Please come back tomorrow. I'm making some zucchini breads for you and your mother."

"Yes, ma'am," Morgana responded apprehensively.

She made her way back through the dried-up bundles of dead flowers and passed the wall of creepy glass-eyed dolls. She could hear his steps behind her as she scurried to the front door. *Just let me escape*, she thought to herself.

"See you around." Josef's smooth rich voice wrapped around her body like silk and sent delicious chills up her spine.

In spite of herself, she just had to see his glorious eyes one last time. She turned to glance back at him and tried to be coy to catch a glimpse, but instead her flip flop tripped on the threshold of the doorway and she stumbled out onto the sidewalk. The bright sun penetrated her eyes, so instead of seeing him all she heard was his boisterous laugh as she scrambled down the walkway once again mortified beyond all existence.

Chapter Two

The Secret Garden

THE NEXT DAY, Morgana returned home from another mind numbingly dreadful day at high school. When she walked in the door there was a note taped to the refrigerator: "Ms. Lane has some zucchini bread for the bake sale that I need you to go get please. Love mom." (Smiley face)

"Oh, Mom! I don't want to go through that mess again! Aghhh! Whatever!" This time she grabbed her phone and huffed down the inclined driveway. She shuffled her flip flops at some rocks her tires kicked up and chanted to herself, *In and out. In and out. In and out. I'm just going to get in and quickly get out.* She reached the recessed alcove with the large heavy wooden door and rang the bell. She noticed some fresh potted flowers that brightened up the dark alcove. *That's nice,* she thought, as she heard clicking footsteps reach the other side of the door. Morgana took a long deep breath, preparing herself for the heavy musk stench that awaited her. Ms. Lane swung open the large wooden door and Morgana was so caught off guard by the bright sunlight streaming from inside the house that she forgot she was holding her breath and exhaled. She breathed in, then realizing what she'd done, she mentally prepared for her olfactory sensors to be brutalized by the stank odor that had practically burned her lungs, but was shocked when instead they were tantalized by the most delicious aromas that filled her nose. She let out a slight "Ah." Ms. Lane welcomed her in and Morgana couldn't believe this was the same house she was in just yesterday. She walked around the familiar pony wall, passed the wall of porcelain faces, only this time with the sun's illumination she saw that they were the prettiest dancing fairies, beautiful porcelain angels, and the cutest cherub figurines she had ever seen. These were so precious and adorable! She tried to remember what it looked like before and how she could have confused it so much. She decided that her eyes had tricked her with contrast from the blaring bright sun outside and the blacked out darkness inside.

Today she noticed the beautiful heavy cranberry velvet damask curtains tied open with a gold braided rope exposing the huge floor to ceiling glass doors. An open, white bookcase separated the formal dining room from the sunken living room. Morgana surmised the bookcase is what had all the dried flowers affixed to it somehow, but today she could see it was adorned with fancy crystal goblets, beautifully framed photos, and a gemstone rock collection that was kept in an open box of cream velvet with each stone in its own designated bed. Beautiful, elegant keepsakes and antiques, and fresh pink flower bouquets were nestled on the shelves. A huge round white marble pedestal dining table had a massive centerpiece of fresh cut pink and cream flowers. It was flanked by thirteen high-back floral chairs in the perfect shades of cranberry, cream, and pink that coordinated the whole room. The open concept kitchen with a matching, equally immense, white marble island connected to the dining room. Dark cherry wood cabinets, some with glass doors exposing their beautiful sparkling crystal goblets and glasses, grounded the professional grade stainless steel refrigerator, double oven, and six-burner stove top with a range hood that had a gardenscape scene hand painted on it. On the marble island sat another sweet pink floral arrangement, as did baskets of dozens of mini loaves of fresh baked bread.

This must be what smells so delicious, she thought. "Your home is so sweet and beautiful, Ms. Lane," Morgana complimented.

"Why, thank you, dear. It's full of all the things that make me happy," she replied with a lovingly proud little smile. "Do you have time to join me for some tea, Morgana? I find that fresh baked bread and a spot of tea make me happy, too," she explained with a wink.

Whereas yesterday Morgana couldn't get out of there fast enough, today felt completely opposite. "Yes, ma'am. I would really like that."

"Oh, goodie! I was hoping you would join me. I have the water all set." Ms. Lane walked into her deluxe kitchen and started placing her delicate pink floral China tea set on a silver tray. She poured the steaming water from the kettle into the matching pink floral tea pot and asked Morgana if she would please open the lofty sliding glass doors to the back yard, as she masterfully carried the tray. Morgana glided open the soaring glass doors. They were much easier to open than she expected them to be and they almost seemed to open automatically when she barely touched them. "Walk down the path to the gazebo at the end and we'll have our tea in there," Ms. Lane guided.

Morgana gasped with awe as she stepped outside into a lush, tranquil garden protected by walls of roses and bushes full of peonies in shades of whites, pinks, cranberries, and reds. Fresh gardens of fruits, vegetables and herbs were tended by endearing little fairy figurines, some with little ornate houses and delightful miniature gardens of their own. Everything looked so green and lush and precious. Tiny bells chimed with the breeze and the weather seemed soft and perfect, even though it was a hot May afternoon. Morgana couldn't see any other houses or hear any of the passing cars on the road just on the other side of the eight-foot tall fence. She felt like she was in a secret, enchanted garden. She imagined the fairy figurines came alive at night and tended to the flowers, and the flowers sang while the fairies danced in the moonlight.

At the end of the path, she saw a white, wicker garden table set in the center of white wooden gazebo with rose vines entwining its exterior columns in a loving embrace. The inside rounded dome ceiling of the gazebo was hand-painted like the ceiling of the Sistine Chapel or some other fancy church Morgana had found on the internet one time while researching a paper for her English Lit class. Sweet little cherubs and mythical creatures looked on as if they were participating in the conversations of those who sat with Ms. Lane in this sacred gazebo enjoying their afternoon tea. Morgana felt so special to be invited into this charmed garden as Ms. Lane poured her special blend of tea into the pink floral China teacups rimmed with gold.

Morgana noticed something floating in her tea cup. "When the filter on my mom's coffee pot goes out it spills the coffee grounds in her cup, too. This tea set looks antique. Do they make filters for it still?"

Ms. Lane just smiled and explained that this was called loose leaf tea. "It will settle to the bottom of your cup and that's when you know it's ready."

While they waited for their tea, Morgana consumed a piece of the succulent zucchini bread. It was warm with melted butter and was sweeter than she expected, so moist and delicious. *The best thing I've ever tasted,* she thought. "Oh, my, Ms. Lane! This is so good!" she exclaimed with a mouth full of warm buttery goodness.

"Well, I have a good recipe but I think the real secret is to use farm fresh and organic ingredients. And, of course, I bless it with love. I grow what I can here in my own garden, but that's why I also go to the farmers' market. You can taste the benefit of the freshness. Thank you, again, for helping me with those heavy sacks yesterday," Ms. Lane said graciously. Morgana nodded as she reached for another piece of the delectable bread. She noticed her tea leaves had settled and asked if it was time. "Yes, the leaves sink to the bottom after they've perfectly infused their flavor with the water, and when they settle to the bottom the water is the perfect temperature." Ms. Lane picked up her cup and saucer and Morgana enthusiastically followed the example.

Morgana had drunk her fair share of frozen cappuccinos and mocha lattes, and was never really interested in tea. But, as she sipped the delicate flavor and felt it warm its way down the back of her throat, and her eyes feasted on the beautiful surroundings, she felt so peaceful and calm. Ms. Lane's sweet soft voice described her favorite flowers, fruits, vegetables, and herbs in this sacred garden.

"How can you grow all these different things? And in this climate?" Morgana was thoroughly engaged in everything Ms. Lane was explaining.

"Well, I take time and care for my treasured plants. I nurture them and feed them. I'll visit and tend to each one of them like they are my dear friends. Have you ever grown anything?"

"Well, I think mushrooms are growing on my soggy bathroom mat, but I don't really think that counts."

Ms. Lane let out a hoot to Morgana's quip. "Oh, dear, you are a clever one."

Morgana felt good that she made the wonderfully wise women laugh. "Oh, I hate to leave Ms. Lane, but I really have to go study. I'm totally freaking out over my biology final, and math final, and English final, and, and, and…" Morgana trailed off thinking about each subject. She got up to leave, "Oh, please don't get up. I can let myself out."

"Well, it was lovely having you for tea, my dear," Ms. Lane said gently. Morgana leaned down to grasp the sweet old lady's hands and said good-bye and thought to herself, *It was lovely. Pure paradise.*

"Remember the basket of bread for your mother on the counter," Ms. Lane called out. She glanced over at the tea leaves in the bottom of Morgana's cup and knowingly smiled to herself. "Come back any time, dear."

"Oh, thank you, Ms. Lane. I would love to!" Morgana felt like she was skipping as she went into the house, happy and lighthearted after such a tranquil afternoon. She picked up the pink basket full of individually wrapped mini bread loaves, each adorned with a little pink bow. "So cute!" Morgana said to herself as she walked past the white bookcase with the beautiful, delicate antiques, by the wall of the precious smiling faces of angels, fairies, and cherub figurines, around the pony wall and out the front door. When the heavy wooden door clicked shut behind her she felt almost a sadness encroach about leaving such a precious space and sharing time with the sweet, gentle, old lady. Then she felt the dread set in, thinking about the pile of books that awaited her when she got home.

$\mathcal{C}$hapter Three

Tapping Through Finals

AS MORGANA CAME skidding into her inclined Y–shaped driveway, she noticed Ms. Lane waving to her from her recessed alcove doorway. Morgana waved back and remembered two weeks ago when she shared that serene afternoon tea in Ms. Lane's enchanted secret garden gazebo. Ms. Lane had transformed her whole backyard into a greenhouse so she could grow all her favorite flowers, fruits, vegetables, and herbs. She explained how Josef had helped her create it during the summers he spent with her after his parents died in a tragic car accident. Morgana hadn't known that part and felt so sorry for him. Ms. Lane helped him through those summers by keeping him busy with yard work to help channel his sadness, anger, and frustration into constructive projects. It was during one such summer that he mowed Morgana's lawns. It was the first time she saw him up close and there was something about his eyes when he looked at her. She felt like they connected on another level. She had tried so hard to impress him but was mortified after she did a lip skid across the grass and dumped the icy lemonade down the front of her dress. His boisterous laughter still burned in her ears.

Morgana shook off the memory and sighed at the reality of the mound of books glaring at her from the back seat as she reached for her purse from the passenger's seat. She was so stressed about her finals. She just wanted to get them over with, so she could get college over with, and then finally start her life. Morgana pushed open her car door and was startled by Ms. Lane, who was now standing in Morgana's driveway.

"Morgana, dear."

"Oh! Wow! Hi, Ms. Lane," Morgana replied, perplexed at how Ms. Lane got from her front door to Morgana's driveway so fast. *Was I lost in thought that long?* she wondered. "How are you?"

"I'm blissful. Thank you for asking. I would like to show you something. Perhaps you could join me for some tea?"

"I don't know, Ms. Lane. I truly would love to, but I'm totally freaking out about my finals this week. I really need every minute to study. I just can't grasp biology and the numbers get all mixed up in math. I feel like I can't focus and it's driving me crazy. I just want it to be over with!" Morgana was visibly stressed.

"I want to share something with you that I know will help, dear. It will only take a little bit and it will help you in the long run. I promise," the sweet elderly lady assured her.

Morgana remembered how relaxed and wonderful she felt that day in Ms. Lane's enchanted garden and couldn't refuse the sweet offer. "Okay, yes, ma'am. I would love to join you for tea but I can't stay long."

"Of course, dear." Ms. Lane smiled.

They crossed the street together and made their way to the recessed alcove, adorned with fresh potted flowers and a newly added sign: "Blessed are those who enter here." *Yes, they are.* Morgana smiled to herself.

Ms. Lane swung open the heavy wooden door and Morgana delighted in the bright and cheerful light, and the sweet aroma of orange blossoms filled her soul. They rounded the pony wall and stepped down into the sunken living room with its plush pink carpet and antique deep cherry wood furniture. Ms. Lane sat down on her Victorian-era, silky cream rayon upholstered couch with a tufted back which had intricately hand carved deep cherry wood along the top of the back, down the rolled arms, and across the front base.

Morgana sat in the matching armchair adjacent to her. She watched as Ms. Lane poured the tea into the Royal Antoinette teacups with pink and cranberry flowers and gold trim. She smiled to herself and pondered, *Who does she remind me of? Ah! Mary Poppins! Or maybe Mary Poppins' grandmother? How old is Mary Poppins anyway?* Ms. Lane was impeccably dressed, with cream colored Victorian style lace up boots, a long light blue pencil skirt, and matching fitted waistcoat. *Practically perfect in every way.* Morgana giggled to herself. *Although, Ms. Lane always wears soft pastels whereas Mary Poppins wore black.*

Ms. Lane handed Morgana her cup and saucer. "No loose tea leaves this time?" Morgana asked politely.

"Well, I know you're short on time so I went with a different type of tea. This is my special blend of chamomile and mint. It will help relax you, as well as help you focus. I also wanted to show you a little energy trick that can help you in most anything that you're trying to work through. This is called E.F.T. or emotional freedom tapping technique, or tapping for short. Dr. Roger Callahan first discovered the benefits of tapping, and then Mr. Gary Craig simplified the technique. However, it's based on energy meridians in the body that have been the basis of acupuncture and acupressure for thousands of years."

Ms. Lane set down her cup and saucer on the dark cherry wood coffee table with hand-painted cherry blossoms and gold leaf trim etched in its top. Everything in Ms. Lane's home was cheerful and elegant. The dark cherry wood furniture matched the cabinets in the open concept kitchen which adjoined the sunken living room. The white open book case with all Ms. Lane's antiques and treasures separated the living room from the dining room where the huge round marble table was situated which the wall of adorable figurines gleefully watched over. The soft microfiber floral fabric on the thirteen high-back chairs that surrounded the enormous white marble pedestal table had the same cranberry color as the heavy velvet damask curtains, the same cream color as the living room furniture, and the same pink color as the plush carpet. Everything coordinated and was sweet and delightful. Sprinkles of gold trim peeked out and glimmering crystals made everything sparkle. The fresh bouquets of flowers made everything feel so alive. She felt like she was in a living confection. Ms. Lane once said this home was filled with everything that made her happy and Morgana totally agreed.

Ms. Lane continued, "You start by tapping this point on the outside of your hand between your pinky and wrist. It's called the karate chop point. If you can imagine someone in the martial arts breaking wood with their hand, it's right below the first knuckle of the pinky where it attaches to your hand and your wrist bone. I know you have been stressed out over your finals. Describe to me how you are feeling."

Morgana had been quite frustrated and frazzled for weeks and kept herself locked in her room to study every day after school. She had organized a tutor, but it almost seemed like she knew less than Morgana and was only adding to Morgana's confusion and frustration. "Well, I'm just done with high school. It feels like a waste of time. I hate it there. I don't fit in. I have worked really hard so I can graduate early but I ended up alienating myself from all my friends. I'm just trying to get out of here so I can get on with my real life!" she ranted.

"Your real life?" Ms. Lane inquired.

"You know, I feel like I'm in this holding pattern. I can't stay but I can't move forward either. I'm just trying to get through with school, so I can get a job, and get on with my life."

"Do you plan on going to college?"

"Yes. I figured I'd go to the local j.c. to get my associates degree. I plan on completing that in a year and a half, and then I can transfer to a four-year college. I want to get that done as soon as possible, too. I'm thinking I'll get a juris doctorate because I think I want to become a corporate lawyer."

"Corporate law? That seems like a lot of work to get through."

"Well, yes, but it also means a lot of money, too. Right?"

"And what would you do with all that money?"

"I'm tired of struggling with money and always feeling like I don't have enough. And, I don't like it here in this one-horse town. I want to live in a penthouse on top of a skyscraper with 360 degree views of the city. I want to have plenty of money to take care of my mom and make sure she has everything she needs. I'll probably have to work long, hard hours, but that suits me just fine. But, first I just have to figure out stupid high school calculus! And I feel like I have all this pressure on me, like, if I don't do well on my finals I'll be stuck here forever! And I just want out. I just want to be free!" Morgana was all tense just thinking about her finals again. Her chest felt tight and her stomach was in knots. *I just want out*, she exasperatedly repeated quietly to herself as she took a big drink of tea.

"Well, E.F.T. won't get you out of here, necessarily," Ms. Lane explicated with a soft smiled, "but it will help with all the tension and frustration you are feeling. Let's start by gauging how you feel. On a scale between one and ten, with one being completely relaxed and ten being completely frantic, would you say you were about an eight, maybe, a nine?"

"More like a twelve!" Morgana laughed tensely.

"Okay, twelve," Ms. Lane sincerely obliged. "Now we say the set up statement as we tap the karate chop point. A statement that pinpoints how you feel. Like this, even though I feel frantic about my finals, I still love and accept myself."

Morgana scoffed at the sweet little old lady. "Not really feeling this whole thing, Ms. Lane."

"Just give it a try with me, dear," Ms. Lane encouraged.

With a deep relenting sigh, Morgana set down her tea cup and saucer and followed Ms. Lane's instructions. Using two fingers from her right hand, she started tapping the karate chop point on her left hand while stating how she felt. "Alright, even though I can't stand calculus, I love and accept myself," Morgana joked.

"That's perfect," Ms. Lane responded. "Speak from the heart. Keep tapping."

"Okay, even though I'm totally freaked out about my finals, I love and accept myself."

"Very good," Ms. Lane encouraged.

"Even though I feel kinda silly right now, and probably should be studying for my stupid finals that if I don't ace I will be stuck here forever, I still love and accept myself." Morgana couldn't help but laugh a little.

"Beautiful!" Ms. Lane expressed. "Now, we tap through the points. Start here, on your inner eye brow, right where it meets at the top your nose. Just lightly tap, anywhere from seven to twelve times, as you repeat a word or phrase that summarizes your feelings. Like, 'I hate math.' Then move to the next point, which is on the outside corner of your eye, either eye, it doesn't matter, and keep repeating the phrase or word. Or you can add to it, like 'stressing over finals.' And just keep moving through points. The next point is below your eye, right in the center on the bone. Next is under your nose on top of your lip, then below your bottom lip in the chin crease. Now we move down to your chest, feel your collarbone and move about two inches down from that to the side. If you push in a little bit, it might be sore. It's actually called the sore spot. The seventh point is under your arm, either side, in about the middle of your ribs. And, finally you can tap the top of your head, all while repeating your words or phrases."

Morgana tapped through the first round while repeating "I hate math" as she watched Ms. Lane demonstrate the points.

"What would you like to say for the second round?" Ms. Lane asked.

"Ummm. I dunno."

"Just say how you feel about what's bothering you. You mentioned feeling stuck. You can use that."

"Well, okay. I just repeat, what? I feel stuck?"

"Sure. And really focus on how you feel."

Morgana went through the second round, tapping the points while watching Ms. Lane. Inner brow, outer eye, below the eye, under the nose, on the chin, sore spot, under the arm, and back to the top of the head. She thought about feeling stuck, not being able to get on with life, and just trying to get out. She just wanted freedom. By the time she got to the top of her head, she focused on freedom and let out a deep sigh. The sigh was the cue Ms. Lane was waiting for.

"You are doing great, Morgana. What were you thinking just then?"

"Um, I think, I was thinking about getting out of here. Oh, I guess I was thinking I wanted freedom. But I don't even really know freedom from what."

"That's okay, dear. You don't have to be able to explain it just because you feel it. It's the feeling that is the key. The feeling is what we need to focus on. So, for the next round, I want you to close your eyes, you know the points now, so just close your eyes and think about what freedom feels like to you."

Morgana closed her eyes, thinking to herself, *Freedom. Okaaay, freedom. I don't know what that even feels like. Umm. Hmm.* She started tapping her inner brow and remembered how she felt that day sitting in Ms. Lane's enchanted garden. (Outer eye) She remembered how the sun gently kissed her face with its soft, warmth. (Under eye) And the delightful aroma of the roses and the leaves wafting in on the mild breeze. (Lip) She remembered thinking about the fairies dancing in the moonlight to the songs sung by the flowers. (Chin) She remembered how delicious the zucchini bread was. As she tapped the sore spot she thought about how good she felt when Ms. Lane laughed at her joke. She thought about how relaxed and tranquil she felt that day as she tapped her rib point.

When she started tapping the top of her head, Ms. Lane suggested she repeat a soothing word or phrase. "You can say it out loud or to yourself. In fact, all this can be done in silence, because the real power comes from how you feel and tapping into your truth."

Morgana opened her eyes and looked at the gentle, smiling face of Ms. Lane. While tapping on her head, she spoke straight from her heart and said, "I feel so grateful and blessed to be here with you."

Ms. Lane put her hand to her heart feeling honored. "Awe, that is wonderful. Take a deep breath." Morgana did as instructed. Ms. Lane handed her a glass of water that was on the tray with the delicate pink Royal Antoinette tea set. "Take a big drink and just sit for a moment," Ms. Lane said.

Morgana sat there drinking the cold sweet water. She felt the cool liquid running down the back of her throat. It was good and refreshing as she just sat there in a peaceful silence. Ms. Lane also sat quietly sipping her tea. Morgana just felt calm. No pressure. Not frantic. Ms. Lane gave her a couple minutes before she asked, "How do you feel when you think about your finals?"

Morgana thought about it and softly smiled. "Well, okay, I guess. It's weird. Like, I know I still have to take them, but the panic and pressure are gone. I feel like, I'll be fine. I'm going to still study tonight but I've been studying this stuff all year. I already know it."

Ms. Lane just smiled.

"Whoa! Wait! What!" Morgana cried out. "Did I just say that? I have been freaking out over finals for weeks. And in a matter of what, twenty minutes, you fixed it?"

"You did it, dear. I just showed you the points."

"That's crazy!" Morgana exclaimed. "How long will it last?"

"It will last forever, if you got down to your truth."

"My truth?"

"How you really felt. Remember, I said the feeling was the key. When you lock in on how you really feel, speak your truth, and can discover how you want to feel, then you open the energetic pathways to allow it to happen. You first focused on being stuck, which led you to the feeling of freedom, and then finally you were able to get to feeling grateful and blessed, which are two very optimal feelings," Ms. Lane explained.

"It worked so fast. Is it always like that?"

"Some things can take more rounds. It just depends on how many times you need to pinpoint the root feelings and get to your truth."

"That's amazing! I feel so good. Thank you, Ms. Lane."

"Do you have time for a cookie? I know I promised I wouldn't keep you long."

"I definitely have time for a cookie!"

While Ms. Lane went into the kitchen to fetch a plate full of pastel pink frosted sugar cookies, Morgana started singing to herself *Supercalifragilisticexpialidocious.*

Morgana aced her calculus final and got the highest grade in her biology class. She was singing Supercalifragilisticexpialidocious in her head the whole time she was testing.

Um diddle diddle, diddle um, diddle ay. Um diddle diddle, diddle um, diddle ay.

Chapter Four

The Enchanted Birthday

AFTER SHE GRADUATED from high school, Morgana got a part-time job as a perfume spritzer in a department store at the local mall. One morning before work, she was grabbing some orange juice when her mom walked into the kitchen and hugged her from behind.

"Oh, Mom," she groaned.

"I never see you anymore. What's happening in your life?"

"You want me to tell you my life in five minutes before I have to leave for work?"

"No, I want to spend the whole day with you listening to you fill me in on your life, goals, and dreams, but you only give me five minutes of time before you leave for work and exclude me from your life," her mother dramatically joked.

"Alright, what would you like to know?" Morgana laughed.

"Well. What do you want for your eighteenth birthday?" her mother asked surreptitiously.

"Oh, Mom," Morgana said shaking her head. "I'm fine. You don't need to get me anything and waste your money on me." She kissed her mom good-bye and grabbed her purse as she walked out the door.

Morgana had taken extra classes so she could graduate high school early and even though she was still only seventeen she had this nagging feeling like she was so behind. She graduated early and planned to get college over with as quickly as possible so she could get on with her life. She dreamed of life in the big city and her penthouse apartment with 360 degree skyline views. She secretly looked forward to throwing herself into long hours of corporate law work so she wouldn't have to deal with friends or family. *I don't need anyone*, she would tell herself. *I'll be busy with my work and have lots of money so I can buy whatever I want. I'll have my own beautiful apartment in the sky. It'll be great!*

Working at the mall handing out samples of perfume was boring, but Morgana really did like people watching. She would stand there for hours offering her perfume cards to the shoppers. She was shocked to find that some people would snap at her, "I don't want your stinky perfume!"

Whatever, you don't have to be so rude! she thought to herself. Other people would ask her for directions, or "Where was the bathroom," or "Did she have their favorite color lipstick?"

"I'm just the perfume girl. You'll have to ask the lady behind the counter."

"Oh, but those ones behind the counter can be so pushy!" the customer commented.

Morgana had to laugh to herself about that. She had witnessed some of the unscrupulous behavior of those makeup counter girls, and wondered why they behaved like that. But her mom loved the free samples of makeup Morgana had benefits to and it was just a summer job until school started in the fall.

What she really looked forward to were her afternoons with Ms. Lane, where Ms. Lane would indulge Morgana with tales over tea, like the time she was a model in her early twenties.

"It was very different then. We weren't the supermodels or social media stars like you have today. We were walking hangers that weren't allowed to have personalities. Of course, I guess depending on which rag-mag you read, not much has changed," she chortled. "But what I really loved to do was dance. I was a ballerina from the time I could walk, practically born with ballet slippers on my feet," she said with a twinkle in her eye. She still wore her silver hair pulled up in a perfect ballerina bun. "I danced and modeled until I fell in love. We were married, but then he was killed in the war. When my sister, Lynetta's husband was injured and needed her full time assistance, I moved in with them and their children, Jackson and Delilah. Delilah was Josef's mother and she was the sweetest little girl. But with all the death and injuries in those young children's lives it was hard trying to change their energies. Delilah married that poor boy Jayson, who couldn't let go of his own negativity, and then, sadly, they died in the car accident. I took in Josef during those summers after their crash, so I could teach him what I could about changing his energy and we cultivated this sacred garden. I taught him E.F.T. and muscle testing, and meditation. He's still got some low vibrations in there, but he is understanding himself more and more every day. That's all any of us can do, really."

Morgana didn't quite understand what Ms. Lane was talking about, but she had tried the E.F.T. for her finals and it worked wonderfully. She was excited to learn and hear more about everything, especially more about Josef, despite herself.

"So, my dear," Ms. Lane said, "a little birdie tells me you have a very important birthday coming up in less than two weeks."

Oh, Mom, Morgana thought to herself. "Yes, I'm just ready to get it over with…"

"So, you can get on with your real life?" Ms. Lane interrupted.

"Yes, ma'am." Morgana looked bashful.

"Oh, my dear, every moment is what we make it. You'll never get 'there' because you are where you are. You'll always just be 'here.' It's important to enjoy 'here' because that's where you will always be."

Morgana nodded at the sweet ol' optimistic Ms. Lane. *If Mary Poppins and the bubble gum pink Glinda the Good Witch had a baby, it would be Ms. Lane,* Morgana laughed to herself as she reached for her pink floral tea cup to see that the leaves had settled to the bottom.

Once she was finished enjoying the light flavor of another of Ms. Lane's special loose leaf tea blends, Ms. Lane asked, "May I see your cup?" Morgana was fully expecting Ms. Lane to add more hot water for a refill. "Let me show you show to read the tea leaves."

"You can do that for real?" Morgana was totally excited and surprised. "I thought that was just something they did in the movies!"

"Of course, dear. Reading tea leaves has been around for ages. You look for shapes or symbols the leaves make. They can include people, animals, and inanimate objects such as letters or numbers."

Morgana studied the blob of leaves at the bottom of the cup and guessed, "An ink blot? I'm going to get a pen for my birthday." She laughed at her own joke.

Ms. Lane looked for the deeper meaning, turning the cup and deciphering the hidden messages in the leaves. "Oh, interesting. My, my, my," she uttered with intrigue.

"What? You're just teasing me!" Morgana laughed.

"Okay, but don't be surprised tomorrow if you get asked on a date," Ms. Lane stated matter-of-factly.

"What?" Morgana grabbed the cup back. "It does not say that!" she said eyeing the wet mass. "Okay, then, should I say yes to this mysterious man in the leaves?"

"It depends."

"On what?"

"On what your true heart's desire is."

"Oh, Ms. Lane. You're so funny."

The next morning Morgana took a few extra minutes to try to straighten and style her long brown hair that she could never seem to tame. She wished she had smooth straight hair, and not this unruly not-curly-not-straight mess. She also didn't feel she was much good with her makeup and so she just added some mascara to her lashes and a dab of gloss to her lips. She analyzed herself in the mirror and sighed. When she was in elementary school she was always the tallest in her class, but then seemed to just stop growing once she got to junior high. Now, she felt her hips were too curvy, her thighs were thicker than she wanted them to be, and she was paranoid about her arms. She didn't necessarily think she was fat but it seemed like people told her she was. She remembered back when she was sixteen and got her driver's license. She proudly showed it off in class one day to her ex-boyfriend. But he read it out loud and announced her weight in class, "5'3" and 129 pounds! God, you're fat!" She snatched it back from him, completely humiliated. At this point, she was glad she was no longer dating the jerk, but she had been totally in love with him two years earlier when he broke up with her for someone else, making her feel really bad about herself. All this just reiterated her low self-esteem. She gave up on trying to style her hair and left for work completely deflated. "No one would ask me out," she said to herself.

"Well?" Ms. Lane inquired as she poured the tea later that day.

"Oh, Ms. Lane," Morgana scoffed. "A kind old man said to me, if he were younger he would ask to court me. I gave him your number." She winked and Ms. Lane let out a hoot.

"You're so silly. I told you it depended on your true heart's desire. Let me explain. How were you feeling when you went to work this morning?"

"Well, I was a little excited until I was trying to get ready. Then I noticed my thunder thighs, my confusing flat wavy hair, and how I had nothing to wear."

"Oh, dear. So, needless to say, you were in lower vibrations?"

"Lower vibrations?"

"Our emotions really are just energy in motion. Each emotion emits a frequency. Some emotions are high, fast moving vibrations. Some emotions are slow, heavy, low vibrations. Remember when we did E.F.T. and you started out feeling pressure and frantic? Those emotions are in the lower vibrational frequencies of energy. Then, after you went through a couple of tapping rounds you felt relief, good, blessed, and grateful. Those are higher vibrational frequencies. You moved yourself up the vibrational scale of emotions."

"Are you saying I can do tapping to get a date?" Morgana was skeptical.

"Well, sort of. What I am saying is you can change your vibrational frequencies to get higher responses. If you are on lower vibrations, you'll attract lower responses. The higher the vibrations, the higher the responses. The world is just a mirror and it reflects back to you what you are putting out. For instance, if you are in a bad, cranky mood, you will be surrounded by cranky people. Like moths to the flame, they are attracted to you by your frequency. But the same goes if you are emitting love, gratitude, and joy. Those are the frequencies that will be reciprocated."

Morgana wasn't entirely convinced, but she did remember how good she felt after she did the tapping and how she breezed through her finals. Plus, she loved this sweet old bubble gum pink Mary Poppins/ Glinda the Good Witch lady, who had become her dear friend. "Alright, so is it too late to try again tomorrow?" Morgana asked.

"No, my dear, that's why we get tomorrows. We always have another chance to try again," Ms. Lane replied whimsically.

While Morgana was getting ready the next morning, she started tapping on her karate chop point and said out loud, "Even though I hate my thighs, I love and accept myself. Even though I'm a hideous monster that no one will ever love.....Alright, umm, maybe that is a bit harsh. But she did say to find my truth, so let's go with it. Even though I sometimes feel like a hideous monster, I still love and accept myself. Even though I'm not my perfect size, I love and accept myself.

Brow: Thunder thighs! Outer eye: Thunder thighs! Under eye: Huge massive thunder thighs. Lip: Why can't I have nice lean shapely thighs? Chin: Thunder thighs. Sore spot on the chest: Look out below-its huge thunder thigh woman! Ribs: Thunder thighs. Top of the head: I really hate my thunder thighs.

Round Two

Brow: Hideous monster! Outer eye: I am a hideous monster! Under eye: Sometimes I feel like a hideous monster! Lip: How come he told me I was fat? Cuz I'm a hideous monster! Chin: But I only weigh 129 pounds, that's not a hideous monster. Sore spot on the chest: In sixth grade one of the other girl's moms came to weigh and measure us. I was the tallest in my class and she told her daughter I was 'one of the bigger ones.' I'm the same height now as I was then and I weighed 100 pounds then. Ribs: Why does everyone tell me I'm fat? Top of head: I guess because I'm a hideous monster!

Okay, well, I think I definitely need to do another round. Ms. Lane said the world is a reflection of my vibrational frequency. So, I'm emitting lower vibrations and people are just responding to that frequency. Okay, so fine. What's my truth? What is the root of this lower vibration?

Ummm, well, let's see. People are mean. But if they're just reflecting me, does that mean that I'm the mean one? Great, now I feel worse.

Okay, what's my truth? I'm trying to pin point the root feeling.

Okay. Shake it off. How do I feel? How do I feel? Oh, how about rejected! Ouch. Ya, that feels like it could be a root feeling.

Brow: Rejected. Outer eye: Rejected. Under eye: Rejected. Lip: They all rejected me. Chin: So if they are just a reflection of my emotions, that means I reject myself.

Well duh!

Sore spot on the chest: But Ms. Lane says we are who we are. If we don't accept ourselves as we are and where we are, we can never change. Ribs: So I guess I can accept myself. Oh hey, that's the set up statement. Oh, I get it. Even though I have thunder thighs, I can still love and accept myself. Top of head: Oh wow. Okay. I can accept myself as I am because I understand that I can't change until I accept who I am now. And now I may have thicker thighs than I want, but who really cares? If I focus on how I feel and make sure I'm in higher vibrations then I'll get high vibrational responses from people.

Hey! Relief! Tah-dah! I did it! So now, I close my eyes and remember what I was thinking. Ummm – what did I say? Oh, yah. I can accept myself. So, umm, okay. I guess I want to feel accepted. Close your eyes and feel what you think acceptance feels like. Hmmm. Acceptance? What does that feel like?

Think, Morgana. Think. No wait! Feel, Morgana, feeeel."

She took a deep breath and relaxed. A picture of herself diving into the ocean came to her mind. She imagined the refreshing water cool her face and body as she swam in the revitalizing salty water. She pictured herself emerging from the depths of the sea, coming to the surface for air, and seeing a beautiful white sandy beach in the distance. She felt so good swimming in the water towards the beach. Her body felt good. She felt relaxed and invigorated, proud of her strong legs that easily moved her through the waves.

"Hey," she shouted, "I can think of my thighs as strong legs! Wow, this is pretty cool!"

She stayed with the vision as she swam to the beach. She sat down on the warm sand, enjoying the beautiful, picturesque view of the white sandy beaches and the calming tranquil aqua blue water. Deep aqua blue, just like Josef's amazing eyes.

Morgana snapped open her eyes and yelled at herself, "Oh, no! Not him!"

She did feel better about herself as she finished getting ready, but tried not to think about his exquisite deep aqua blue eyes.

"Well, dear, how was your day?" Ms. Lane delightfully sipped her tea.

Morgana blushed with a laugh. "Well, you'll never guess. Okay, you probably already knew. But Cole asked me out tomorrow night!" She let out a little squeal.

Ms. Lane laughed, too. "Tell me about this Cole," she said as she settled back into her white wicker chair in the rose entwined gazebo. The hand painted cherubs and mythical creatures on the rounded ceiling all gathered closely to listen.

Morgana took a sip of her tea, and with a big, joyful smile said, "He's tall, dark, and sooo handsome! He works in a men's suit store in the mall. He's twenty-one and has deep dark brown eyes that you could just drink up," she said dreamily.

"Brown eyes?" Ms. Lane was inquisitive.

"Yes," Morgana replied, maybe a little more defiantly than she meant to. "Big beautiful brown eyes."

"Oh, I see." The corners of Ms. Lane's mouth turned up in a quirky little smile, then she added with whimsy, "I remember one of my dance partners had the most beautiful big round brown eyes. He could lift and twirl me with such ease and grace. I loved dancing with him. So, how did you and Mr. Cole meet?"

"I was on my fifteen minute break and ran to the food court for a frozen coffee. He was in front of me and we both were waiting for the lady in front of us to place her order. I kept looking at my clock cuz she was taking forever! He noticed me and let me go before him. I thanked him and explained I only had fifteen and had to go all the way to the other end. He said he was on his fifteen too, but his store was right there. Then he asked if I wanted to meet for lunch. I said I got off early today and had plans." She tipped her tea cup towards Ms. Lane to indicate that she was the intended plans for the day. "So, he asked if I wanted to go to dinner tomorrow night!"

"Ah, young love," Ms. Lane reminisced.

"Well, I don't know if it's love, but I haven't had a date in forever, so at least it's something."

"Cheers to that!" Ms. Lane lifted her Royal Antoinette pink floral tea cup with the golden rim. Morgana smiled and raised hers, too.

The next day over tea, Morgana was excited about her date. "But, you know what's funny. All day today, people were totally responding to me. My supervisor even said I sold more perfume today than I had the past two days combined. Do you think it has anything to do with my vibrations?"

"Of course it does, dear. Everything has to do with our vibrations."

"Is it because I'm excited?"

"It's because you're excited and optimistic. You're on a higher vibrational frequency and people can feel that. Well, the ones who are also on the optimistic wave. The ones on the optimistic vibrations are attracted to you and the energy exchange is a pleasant one. They felt your optimism and were drawn to you, and therefore, your product," Ms. Lane explained.

"That's pretty fun!" Morgana pronounced. "Oh, I gotta go get ready for my date! All the juicy details to come tomorrow over breakfast." Morgana winked.

"Have fun, dear. Don't do anything I wouldn't do." Ms. Lane waved good-bye.

At 7:30 p.m., Cole arrived in a new model BMW. Morgana wore a pair of dark jeans, a black lace top, and black platform sandals, with her long brown hair pulled back into a top knot pony tail. It was the end of June and still plenty hot that evening. She hoped they were going somewhere with good air conditioning.

Morgana had the day off after her date. While she put on her favorite black leggings and a t-shirt, she reminded herself how she good felt in her vision of swimming with her long, strong, lean legs, and how they were easily able to push through the ocean waves. She understood when Ms. Lane told her that whatever we think about grows in proportion to our vibrational frequencies, so she kept practicing feeling good about herself. It was a lot of work, but she kept trying.

"If you keep thinking about something you don't like about yourself, you're just going to get more not to like," Ms. Lane had explained.

She was now practicing the feeling of appreciation and acceptance. She slipped on her flip flops and headed out of the house, down her inclined driveway, and across the street to her wonderful neighbor's delightful house. She walked by the old, deep maroon Cadillac Deville parked in the driveway. *How that thing manages to still be in pristine shape is beyond me,* she thought.

> "You realize your car is more than twice as old as me? Why don't you get a new one?" she had asked Ms. Lane one time.
>
> "Oh, I don't know. It still runs great and gets me where I want to go. I don't need anything too flashy. I just love the memories I have in it. But maybe one day I'll get a little sports car."

Morgana reached the recessed alcove with the heavy wooden door. Fresh potted flowers bloomed with the sweet sign: "Blessed are those who enter here." She heard the footsteps of the lace up Victorian style boots with the kitten heels clicking on the hardwood on the other side.

"Good morning, dear!" Ms. Lane's bright smile greeted her as she opened the heavy door.

"Good morning! Do I smell coffee?" Morgana asked surprised.

"I love my coffee in the morning. I also made fresh muffins."

"For some reason I didn't think you drank coffee. I don't know why."

"You are usually here for tea time," Ms. Lane explained. "Would you like anything else for breakfast?"

"Nope, just one of your delicious muffins. Well, maybe two or three of your delicious muffins."

Morgana sat down at the giant marble countertop in the open kitchen. The beautiful heavy cranberry velvet damask curtains were tied open with a gold braided rope revealing the tranquil enchanted garden outside. Ms. Lane was busy on the other side pouring the coffee into the coordinating pink floral Royal Antoinette coffee cups with gold trim.

"I have the whole set," she explained. "Coffee cups, coffee decanters, tea cups and saucers, tea pots, plates and bowls. It's my favorite pattern."

"And it matches your whole décor," Morgana said with a smile. "I love how everything is so sweet and precious in your house. I feel like

I'm in a fairy tale. Oh, my God, Ms. Lane! These muffins are to die for!" Morgana gushed with her mouth full of delicious blueberry muffin. "I love the sugar crystals on the top like that. Oh, and the melted butter! Oh, my God!"

"I have a good recipe, and it's the whole, organic ingredients that make a big difference. Then of course, I bless them with love. Do you put cream in your coffee?"

"Yes, please. What's with the organic ingredients? Aren't they really the same thing?" Morgana asked before taking another huge bite.

"Fruits and vegetable are living things. And like all living things, they too have vibrational frequencies. Organic ingredients vibrate at a higher frequency than non-organic ones. They also have more vitamins and nutrients then their counter-parts. And while I'm cooking or baking, I bless my ingredients with love, infusing that energy into every last bite." Ms. Lane handed Morgana her coffee cup, then lifted her own cup to her nose and paused. She took a deep smell of the rich coffee aroma before she took her first sip. "Flavor is part smell and part taste. The senses of smell and taste are often referred to together as the chemosensory system, because they both give the brain information about the chemical composition of objects through a process called transduction. Breathe in your flavors to prepare your palate before you take in your food and it will enhance your enjoyment."

"It's like when you walk into a coffee house and it smells so good!" Morgana noted, as she picked up her coffee cup and followed Ms. Lane's instructions. She took a long slow smell of her hot steamy brew.

"Exactly. They are enticing you as soon as you step foot in the door. Our olfactory system is one of the strongest memory senses we have."

Morgana took a drink and her eyes widened. "This is so good. It's almost like it rolls on your tongue. What is it?"

"I get the coffee beans from Scotland. I make it with purified water. And the cream is fresh and organic."

"Plus, I'm sure you brew it with love, too." Morgana smiled.

"Of course."

"What does that mean, you bless it with love?"

"Well, first I thank it for coming to me. I thank it for sharing its essence. I thank it for its high frequency and I thank it for elevating my frequency so they are a vibrational match. When your energies match your food, it's much easier for the body to receive the vitamins and nutrients to process and digest. When you are in alignment, your body functions as it is meant to, keeping you thriving. How old do you think I am, Morgana?"

"Um, sixty-two?" Morgana figured she was probably closer to seventy, but wanted to be polite.

Ms. Lane laughed. "You're such a sweet girl. I am eighty-two years old," she stated proudly.

Morgana practically choked on her blueberry muffin. "What?" She took a swig of the rich delicious coffee to clear her throat. "You're joking?"

"No joke."

"But, you're amazing! I mean, you're so, so..."

"In alignment," Ms. Lane answered. "I love and accept myself. I focus on how I feel and I always reach for the best feeling I can. I make that easier to do by surrounding myself with things and people that make me happy."

"But you're always eating cookies and muffins. How do you keep so slim? I mean, your body is banging!"

Ms. Lane let out a hoot. "Thank you! I eat what I love and I love what I eat. I usually make those goodies myself and as I explained I use organic and blessed ingredients."

"And you never have to diet?" Morgana took another big bite of muffin.

"A lot of people eat when they are out of alignment, and therefore the body isn't able to do its job properly. If people could focus more on how they feel, as in, reach for the highest frequency they could to get into alignment before they ate, it would help their bodies digest, assimilate, and eliminate appropriately, and ultimately function better."

"Do you only eat organic?"

"I do it as much as I can, which is pretty easy since I make most of my meals. But there are times when I go out and eat whatever is available. And still other times when a big greasy cheeseburger is the only thing that will suffice," she said with a wink. "I will say, no matter what I eat, I say 'thank you' to all my food before I eat it to sync energies, organic or not."

"And then you can eat anything?"

"Well, I usually eat vegan on Mondays, vegetarian on Tuesdays. I tried macrobiotic Wednesdays for a while but didn't keep it up after that restaurant closed down. I like fish on Fridays, because I like how it sounds. And Saturdays and Sundays are fair game for whatever. I do it like this so I can relate to others. We all get to choose our experiences and I like being aware of all my options," she said whimsically.

"So, then you never have to watch what you eat?"

"I watch that I eat all my favorite foods and I feel grateful and blessed with every delicious bite."

"That is so cool. But I still don't know if I quite believe you're eighty-two."

"Well, enough about all this. Tell me how your date with Mr. Cole went!" Ms. Lane amusingly exclaimed.

"Let's just say – we were not in alignment!"

They both laughed!

Morgana detailed how he picked her up and instead of going to dinner, they went to a dank pool hall. It was seedy and dirty and all they served to eat was greasy fried food, which she technically wouldn't have minded, but it took forever to come out and by the time they served it to her it was cold and slimy. He shot pool and got into a shouting match with the guy at the next table over. She thought they were going to get into a fight so she went to the bar to get away from it. He came over to her asking what her problem was. She said she'd just call for a ride to come get her, but he insisted on taking her home. On the way home, he did apologize for almost fighting with that guy and said he was just trying to show off, "Cuz some girls like that." When he pulled into her inclined driveway he scraped his rear bumper on his nice fancy new car, and then was pissed when she wouldn't kiss him. He scraped his bumper again as he backed out of the driveway and she heard him cursing as he drove down the street.

Ms. Lane and Morgana were laughing hysterically.

"Well, dear, I guess the moral of the story is – you've still got some vibrations to clean up."

Morgana laughingly agreed.

July 9th, the day of Morgana's eighteenth birthday, finally arrived. Ms. Lane said instead of their usual afternoon tea, she would like to surprise Morgana "with something special."

"Don't go to any trouble Ms. Lane. It's just a stupid birthday. I'm a year older. Big whoop," she said dryly.

"Oh, my dear girl, birthdays aren't about how old we are. Our bodies renew themselves every eight years, so theoretically none of us should be any older than eight. But with age, comes wisdom. And in my wisdom, I feel birthdays are a celebration of you, as a person, being born, being alive, and being here in this time space. Birthdays are the time everyone gets to thank you for being in their lives. Don't take that away from me," she asserted with a smile.

"Well, I guess can't really argue with that, now can I?" Morgana begrudgingly agreed.

That night when Morgana got home from work, she wistfully looked through her closet for something nice to wear. She wasn't sure what Ms. Lane had in store, but she had said to wear something formal. Morgana had the blue taffeta tea length gown she wore two years ago to a homecoming dance, and a short black velvet dress she wore to her senior prom four months ago. What a disaster that was, she recalled. First of all, the venue was two hours away and everyone had to go on the bus that the school provided otherwise you wouldn't be allowed in. After sitting on a rickety smelly school bus for two exhausting hours, they shoved the girls into one big conference room to get ready and the boys in another. There were no mirrors and they just had to change their clothes in the middle of the room. Luckily, all she had to do was take her shirt off to pull the dress over her head. Then once she had the dress on, she removed her pants. The black velvet dress was one an ex-boyfriend had bought her years earlier. She didn't think her mom had enough money for prom dresses or frivolous stuff like that, so she didn't even ask. The dress was pretty enough and she had never worn it. She shoved her bus clothes into the bag she brought and tucked it into the corner. Had she known how the rest of the evening would go, she may have spent more time chatting with the girls in the make-shift changing room. But as it was, she hurried to meet up with her date, who was her boyfriend at the time. During the whole rest of the night he wouldn't let her talk to anyone. They sat at the table the entire time. All she was allowed to do was look and talk to him. They danced a couple of times but he was doing these weird obtrusive dance moves. Anytime she would try to look around and see who was there and who else was dancing, he would get up in her face, "Who are you looking at?" "No one. I'm just looking." After four miserable hours, they were loaded back on the bus for the longest two hour bus ride home. She broke up with him the next day as he accused her of using him just to take her to prom. *Way low vibrations,* she mused to herself. She chose the longer blue taffeta homecoming dress.

When she came out of her room, her mother was waiting for her in the kitchen. She, too, was formally dressed. "Happy birthday! Oh, you look so beautiful!" her mother gushed.

"Oh, Mom. What are you doing?"

"Ms. Lane invited me to tonight's festivities. Shall we?" Her mom held out her elbow as to be her escort.

"Oh, Mom," Morgana groaned and linked their arms.

As they waited in the recessed alcove, Morgana tried to imagine what they would be doing tonight. Usually, it was just her and Ms. Lane sharing stories over tea, talking about energy, vibrations, boys and school, but tonight with her mom there, she wondered how things would go.

The heavy wooden door swung open and there he was, with sun-kissed blond hair, golden tan skin, that smile, and those gorgeous deep aqua blue eyes. He was dressed in a black suit and tie with a button up aqua blue shirt in a color that matched his eyes perfectly, making them even more prominent.

"Welcome, ladies," he greeted in his silky smooth voice.

He held out his hand to offer assistance which Morgana's mother readily grabbed and he helped her through the doorway. Then he held out his hand for Morgana, which she politely accepted. Instead of leading her in, however, he bowed and kissed her hand.

"Happy Birthday, Lady Morgana," he cooed.

She felt her knees buckle and was really glad she had worn the longer dress so he couldn't see. She played it off as a curtsey and glued on a smile trying to mask the flurry of butterflies that were going off in her stomach, as he guided her into the house.

When she made her way past the pony wall and into the dining room, she realized that the house was decorated with candles, twinkling white lights, balloons, and fresh bouquets of flowers filled the room. The heavy cranberry velvet damask drapes were drawn back and the huge floor to ceiling glass doors were open to the garden. It, too, was decorated with candles and twinkling lights.

Ms. Lane ushered Morgana in and sat her down at the large marble island where pink sweet pea scented candles flickered. While secretly, Morgana wished Ms. Lane would be wearing the full bubble gum pink Glinda the Good Witch ball gown including the silver bejeweled crown and scepter, Ms. Lane did not disappoint. She was wearing a mint green full taffeta skirt with a shapely button up bodice which showed off her trim figure for a lady of her age. Her silver hair was pulled up in its signature ballerina bun and from behind you would swear she was half her age, if not more.

Morgana was elated. Everything was so beautiful. Besides Ms. Lane, Morgana's mother, and Josef, there were four other people. Two girls, who were about Morgana's age, that she had never seen before. Ms. Lane brought them over for introductions.

"Morgana, this is Brook and her sister, Blake. They are my great-nieces and Josef's cousins. They've been coming to my house for years, but somehow I never managed to get you three together," Ms. Lane said.

Brook was twenty-three, the same age as Josef. Blake had just turned twenty in May. The girls handed Morgana a beautifully wrapped present and they all gathered around to watch her open it. Morgana never really liked being the center of attention and especially now with Josef watching her, she feared how big of an idiot she would make out of herself. *I love and accept myself. I love and accept myself,* she chanted in her head to try to keep herself from doing anything too embarrassing.

Morgana pulled open the ribbon and removed the top, exposing a delicate fairy figurine. She carefully separated it from its Styrofoam home. It was the 'Queen of Summer Solstice' fairy figurine, quite fragile and intricate. It was similar to the ones in Ms. Lane's collection. Morgana was thrilled and grateful.

Next, Josef introduced the two guys, "his best mates." Morgana recognized them from that first fateful day she had helped Ms. Lane with the groceries from the farmers' market. The day Morgana was freaked out by Ms. Lane's house. *What was that smell?* she thought to herself. *I'll have to remember to ask the next time we have tea.* It was also the day she tripped in front of Josef, again, causing him to laugh at her, again, and causing her to be mortified beyond existence, again.

Tristan, a huge mass of a guy with a thick Scottish accent, held out his enormous hand for a handshake. Morgana would learn that he was also Brook's boyfriend. Mitchell, a suave type guy, next greeted Morgana and handed her a gift box that both the guys had put their names to. She opened the gift to find a set of stones, similar to the ones nestled in the cream velvet casing that Ms. Lane had on her white bookcase. Morgana's case was rich black with black velvet lining, which set off the brilliant color of each stone.

"They're chakra stones," Ms. Lane explained. A booklet was also included in the gift set that illustrated the color and purpose of each stone. Morgana didn't know what they were for, but to have something that Ms. Lane had was very exciting for her.

Next up was Josef. His present to her was in a thin square box. She opened it to find an amazingly exquisite amulet necklace. Three heart shaped aqua-blue gemstones, in practically the same color as his majestic deep aqua blue eyes, were encased in a delicate Celtic woven metal design.

She was stunned. "It's so beautiful," she managed to say. Josef took the necklace from the box and offered to help her put it on. She accepted and pulled up her hair as he walked around to clasp it from behind. She felt his breath on the nape of her neck and goosebumps rose on her entire body. If it weren't for everyone looking at her, she probably would have just melted off her bar stool into a puddle of goo on the floor. Such as it was, Brook, Blake, Tristan, Mitchell, her mother, and Ms. Lane all stared at her in awe, so she kept her eyes on the amulet and forced herself to remember to not liquefy.

Ms. Lane came up next with a big pink box with a big pink bow.

It was pink perfection. Morgana smiled with wide eyes expecting something pink inside. Instead was the most glamorous reversible hooded cape Morgana had ever seen. It was black soft plush on one side and cream silk on the alternate side.

With a huge proud smile, Ms. Lane helped drape it around Morgana's shoulders as she stood up and carefully fastened it about her neck. Morgana felt like a princess as she whipped the long cloak behind her like a flamenco dancer's skirt.

"It's so beautiful. Everything is just so beautiful. I'm sorry I've said that for every gift, but I really mean it. Thank you all for these magnificent presents. Honestly, I don't know what to say. I'm speechless. Thank you all." Morgana was astounded by all the marvelous gifts.

Just then, Josef came out from the walk-in pantry, vigilantly carrying a three-tiered candle engulfed pink birthday cake, handmade with organic ingredients, baked, and decorated by Ms. Lane, with love, of course. They all sang happy birthday and Morgana blew out her candles. She didn't even make a wish because this was more than she could ever wish for.

As Morgana savored each bite of her blessed handmade mouthwatering delicious chocolate and strawberry cake, she looked around at the friendly smiling faces, twinkling white lights, and flickering pink sweet pea candles. A little later, Brook and Tristan, her mother and Josef, were laughing and dancing to music on the patio as Mitchell played DJ from playlists on his phone, while Blake and Ms. Lane were watching from the dining table and having a cheerful conversation. Morgana was overflowing with feelings of blessings and gratitude. Her mom called her out to the patio dance floor and Mitchell joined in, too.

They laughed and danced the night away, under a bright smiling moon in Ms. Lane's secret enchanted garden, just like Morgana always pictured the fairies doing.

hapter Five

Being Fully Present

MORGANA TRIED NOT to race too much on her way home from work. Her birthday party last night was the most special night she had ever experienced. Ms. Lane really made it remarkable. Plus Josef was there! And Morgana didn't trip, fall, or make a fool out of herself at all! *Woohoo!* She was super proud of herself. When he had opened the door to welcome her and her mother, she practically gasped and wanted to run away. Luckily she was wearing high heels and knew if she tried to run she would surely trip. When he held out his hand, her legs couldn't move. Thankfully, her mom had graciously accepted the young man's hand. "Oh my, how chivalrous," her mother had acknowledged. He turned around and reached for Morgana, and when he touched her hand lightning bolts shot through her. His voice speaking her name, "Lady Morgana," was smooth and soft, like silk enveloping her soul and sent sweet shivers up her spine. When he put that gorgeous necklace around her he touched her shoulder and she felt his breath on the nape of her neck, the butterflies in her stomach stampeded so much she thought she was going to fly away.

Her tires screeched as she pulled into the inclined Y-shaped driveway and parked her car on the right. She ran into the house to her room, threw on her favorite leggings and T-shirt, and grabbed all the exceptionally beautiful gifts she received from her guests last night, then ran down the inclined driveway, across the street, past the old, deep maroon Cadillac Deville, into the recessed alcove, and breathlessly knocked on the heavy wooden door. A new white ornate wrought iron table was there with fresh potted flowers and the sweet sign that could not be more true in Morgana's mind: "Blessed are those who enter here." As Morgana was catching her breath, she heard the clicking of the Victorian style lace up boots with the kitten heels growing louder as her dear sweet old friend made her way to the door from the other side. The heavy door was opened by Ms. Lane, the sweetest aging Mary Poppins with her silver hair pinned up in the perfect ballerina bun. Today her long classic skirt was in a soft buttery yellow with matching waist coat and an ivory silk shirt collar peeked out the top of the buttoned up jacket. Morgana was holding the big pink box that she had placed all her presents in so she could go over each of them with Ms. Lane.

"You got a new table," Morgana commented as Ms. Lane welcomed her in with a big hug and kiss on the cheek.

"I went to the farmers' market this morning. It was just too cute and it made me happy. It weighs about 500 pounds but Josef and his friends were with me so I was able to get it. Sweet synchronicity," she said in her whimsical way.

Morgana stopped in her tracks as her heart started racing. "Oh, are they still here?" she inquired trying not to sound too eager.

"No, dear, they all headed back about an hour ago. But Brook asked me to give you her number if you wanted to give her a call some time."

"How nice. I really enjoyed meeting her and Blake, and the boys, too. It was so nice of them to come to a stranger's birthday party."

"They feel like they know you from how much I talk about you," Ms. Lane happily explained. Morgana blushed.

"My girl, Blake, can be a bit of a wild child, but she just likes to have fun. Brook and Tristan have been dating for five years now and she sounds like it's getting very serious. Those are my great-nieces from Jackson's side. He and his lovely wife, Cindy, took Josef in as one of their own when Delilah and Jayson passed away. During the summers the girls took dance, ballet, and other classes, but Josef was a little introverted, as to be expected, so I asked if he could stay and help me. We would spend hours in the gazebo as I told him stories of his parents so he would still feel connected to them. He painted the rounded ceiling of the gazebo, did I ever tell you that? He spent a whole summer on it. If you look closely two of the cherubs are snuggled together and he painted his parents faces on them. He's so talented. He painted my oven range hood, too, carrying the secret garden feeling from the outside and brought it inside. I'll always treasure those summers. He's such a good boy."

"You didn't have any children?" Morgana asked prudently.

"Well, I was a model and a dancer when we first got married. He wanted children right away, but I thought it would be smarter to wait a few years and build up a nest egg. Then he died and I felt like I had lost everything. My mother always tried to teach me about energies when I was younger, but I was too stubborn to listen. I don't know if it would have changed anything if I knew then what I know now," she slightly paused, then continued, "but at least I was open enough when my sister invited me to live with her and her two children when her husband was injured. She spent a lot of time nursing him back to health. And I got the glorious gift of helping to raise my niece and nephew and they filled my heart with love. Sweet synchronicity."

"What do you mean by synchronicity?" Morgana tried to understand.

"Well, I believe that the coincidences that come our way are opportunities for miracles. There is a philosophy that states, 'There are only two ways to live your life. One is as though nothing is a miracle, and the other is as though everything is a miracle.' I choose to believe in the latter. Life is a miracle. Existence is a miracle. We live on a planet that is suspended in space and rotates at about 1000 miles per hour, miracle. The weather, the seasons, the sun rises and sets, and are all perfectly tuned to maintaining life, all miracles. Then you bring it down to each and every living thing and all our energies are interconnected. Just like we all breathe the same air, we all are connected through the grace of energy. It's a miracle. People think of miracles as uncommon events, when really everything is a miracle. And when you are in alignment with your energies, you sync up with everything and everyone you need. I felt like I had lost everything, but my sister shared her family with me as if they were my own and I never felt that I had missed anything. And with me being there for her, she was able to spend extra time nursing her husband and he made a complete recovery. Another miracle. The day you pulled into your driveway right when I needed some help, I didn't know when you would be home. You could have stayed late at school or any number of events. But there you were, right on time to help out little old me. Coincidence? Yes. Miracle? Yes. That's synchronicity."

Morgana remembered she was late getting home that day. She was supposed to meet with a tutor, who ended up getting sick and forgot to call to cancel. Morgana had waited in the library for twenty-five minutes before she finally received a text. Irritated, Morgana got into her car and some jerk nearly ran her off the road. All of those things caused her to be almost an hour late. When she finally did make it home, she had to collect all the contents of her purse that spilled out everywhere and she was so frustrated when her phone was just beyond her reach and she smacked her ribs on the emergency parking brake. Had she been on time, she would have just run into the house as usual and never have seen Ms. Lane, or if she had stayed and studied she also would have missed the timing.

"Okay, I remember that day. I was having a terrible day. You want to call that a miracle?" she sassed.

"You were on a different vibrational wave than me, that's for sure! But I needed help and the universe delivered you. You were the hero from my perspective," Ms. Lane uttered with a smile.

Morgana laughed when she remembered something else about that day. "And Ms. Lane, I have to ask. What was that God awful smell when I came in that day? Everything was so dark and dank and really pretty creepy."

Ms. Lane hooted in laughter. "See, you were on a different vibration. Things even looked different to you."

Morgana definitely agreed. How could the precious little faces of the fairies, angels, and cherubs that she adored so much, have given her the creeps. She laughed at herself. "And that smell? I didn't imagine that horrific scent. It burned my lungs!" Morgana teased.

"I was making one of my special blends of essential oils. It can only be made during a certain time of year when the specific ingredients are at their peak. I have to slowly simmer it for twelve hours, while of course blessing it with love, and then it needs to cool and set. It's sensitive to the light for its potency until I can bottle it in brown bottles. I went to the farmers' market that morning while it cooled and had to keep the house dark until it was ready to dispense," Ms. Lane explained.

"Essential oils? What do those do?"

"Each one has its unique properties and results. You can add them to humidifiers, or atomizers to cleanse the air. You can add them to an oil carrier and use on the skin to help treat different things. Here, let me get you a bottle." Ms. Lane got up from her high-back chair at the huge round marble table and her heels clicked on the hardwood floor as she disappeared down the hallway. From the dining table Morgana looked at the wall of sweet figurines and laughed again at herself for being so freaked out that day. Ms. Lane returned from the back bedroom with a little brown bottle in her hand. The label on it read: Moon Meadow Lane Essential Oils by Beloved Grace Organics – Special Frankincense Blend.

"What does it do?" Morgana asked.

"This one is frankincense. It is a common type of essential oil used in aromatherapy that can offer a variety of health benefits, including helping relieve chronic stress and anxiety, reducing pain and inflammation, boosting immunity and even potentially helping to fight cancer. It's really good stuff."

"Do all essential oils take time like that?"

"No, and actually this is the only one that I still make from home. Jackson runs the family plant where we make all our organic natural products, like teas and oils. Josef is just finishing up business school and he is possibly planning to be by Jackson's side until Jackson decides to retire. Brook is creating a line of candles and wax scents infused with the essential oils. I usually have some of her aroma flavors filling the house."

"That's why it always smells so good in here." Morgana smiled. Then she cautiously asked, "Ms. Lane, you never wanted to remarry?"

"Well, dear, it wouldn't be truthful if I said I pictured myself growing old without my husband. But my life has been so full of love and adventure that I feel so blessed. I figure synchronicity would have brought me someone if I was ready, so I guess I didn't need that this time around. But I'm not dead yet, maybe I can get myself in alignment with some hunky young dancer." Ms. Lane let out her hoot of a laugh that Morgana just cherished and they giggled together as they sipped on their tea.

"Okay, Ms. Lane. What are these beautiful gifts I received last night? Oh, and before I forget," Morgana handed her a thank you card, "how do I get these thank yous to the others?"

"I'll text you their addresses, if you would like."

The eighty-two year old whipped out her smart phone and shared the contacts with Morgana, who was simply amazed by the tenacity of her beloved old friend. *She may hook up with a hunky young dancer yet,* Morgana thought to herself with a giggle.

First, Morgana retrieved the box from Brook and Blake, with the fairy figurine named, "Queen of Summer Solstice". Ms. Lane explained, "There are many different figurines, many different fairies, and many different origin stories. But this particular fairy is the queen fairy of summer. Her job is on the summer solstice, which is June 21st, and she is charged with notifying all the flowers, animals, trees, and season to start their summer tasks. The summer solstice is the longest day of the year, and with her wings made of sunlight she turns the wheel of time for summer, after the solstice the days start getting shorter."

Morgana watched as Ms. Lane pointed at each nuance that was carefully hand-painted in dazzling hues to reflect the sun, from the vibrant shading in the folds of her golden gown to her warm expression and flowing auburn hair. Sparkling faux gems were on her lovely tiara and hand-applied kisses of glitter were on her delicate gold spun wings.

"She almost looks alive, like she is ready to start flying," Morgana commented.

"You can always tell when something is made with love." Ms. Lane smiled.

Next, Morgana brought out the black box, lined with black velvet, cradling seven different colors of crystal stones. Ms. Lane described, "These are chakra stones. We have seven energy store houses, if you will, in our bodies. According to ancient medicine, these are where all the meridians of energy meet. Like the tapping I showed you where you tapped on specific energy points on the face, the chakras are the main power stations of the entire body. This set also includes engraved reiki symbols. Each spiritual healing stone has a specific color and therapeutic vibration, emitting positive energy to attune and cleanse your frequencies. Each of these stones has been specifically programmed with information to help balance, align and attune each chakra, with over two hundred unique tunings programmed into each."

Ms. Lane detailed all the stones. "Your first chakra, the base or root chakra is located at the base of your body and it's usually represented by the color red. It connects to the physical body, survival, and past impressions. The African shamans have used the stone tourmaline to promote the awakening from the 'dream of illusion' and to promote the experience of the self as part of the universal spirit. It acts to stimulate the reflex points associated with the lower back.

The second chakra is the sacral, represented by orange and it connects to physical vitality, sexual desire, and earthly emotions. Carnelian is a stone of creativity, individuality and courage. It protects against envy, fear and anger, and helps to banish sorrow from the emotional structure.

The third chakra is the solar plexus, represented by yellow and it connects to will, personal power, perseverance, emotional energy. The stone citrine activates, opens, and energizes the naval and solar plexus chakras, directing, via personal power, creativity, and intelligent decisiveness, the energy necessary to enhance the physical body. It stimulates both mental focus and endurance.

The fourth chakra is the heart, represented by green and it connects to love, surrender, balance, acceptance, devotion. The stone jade emits a calming, cooling energy which can work on all the chakras to gently remove negativity and to reinstate the loving, gentle forces of self-love.

The fifth chakra is the throat, represented by light blue and it connects to communication, expression, and higher self-will. The blue lace agate stone is most useful at the locations of the throat chakra, heart chakra, third-eye chakra and crown chakra. Activating these chakras helps one to enter into high-frequency states of awareness.

The sixth chakra is the third eye, its color is indigo, dark blue or purple, and it connects to the mind, seeing, inner vision, intuition, and comprehension. The azurite stone can act to stimulate intuition and to enhance awareness. It is effective in dispelling unwanted energy from one's etheric fields. It also provides a protective energy to the user.

The seventh chakra is the crown, its color is white or violet and it connects to intelligence, God consciousness, and spiritual intelligence. Amethyst is a stone of meditation. It opens and activates the crown chakra."

"Do they really work?" Morgana was trying not to be skeptical.

"We control our energies by choosing what we want to focus on. Everything comes from within you, but these are infused to give assistance. If you tune your energies, you can feel the connection of all the essence of life. Just like you can see when something is crafted with care and love, or taste when something is homemade verses production. It's the Beloved Grace of life that you're feeling, tasting, and connecting to."

"Beloved Grace?"

"Love is a term that has so many meanings. Some people only know conditional love. When I say 'love' I mean, gratitude, blessing, bliss, heartfelt, light hearted, and joy. These are the higher vibrations on the energy scale and they really do lift the spirit. Whereas, heavy emotions like anger, sadness, and depression literally can weigh you down. The Chinese call energy 'Chi.' In Hindu philosophy they call all the cosmic energy that permeates through the Universe 'Prana.' I like to call it 'Beloved Grace' because when I tune into it, I feel so beloved and I like to send that frequency back out to all that I can. There is great love in this world and universe and it is always there for us, all we have to do is allow it to flow through us."

Morgana loved hearing Ms. Lane talk about energy, Chi, Prana, and Beloved Grace. It was so different than anything she had heard about life. She had only heard sayings like, "It's a dog eat dog world." "Welcome to the jungle." "Life's a bitch and then you die." And "The world is going to hell in a hand basket." Morgana felt so good and different in the few months she had been coming over for afternoon tea, sipping from the Royal Antoinette pink floral China tea set with gold trim, sitting in this house filled with items that Ms. Lane carefully selected to bring into her home that brought her joy and made her happy, or being in the sacred garden that she and her great-nephew lovingly created, and sitting under the rounded dome gazebo where he hand painted his parents likeness into cherubs, so they could still share in all the conversations.

She noticed changes in herself, too. She used to be so much more tense, angry and demoralizing to herself, just trying to get each day over with. Now she relished the few hours she spent with her very own fairy godmother. Ms. Lane had lived across the street Morgana's entire life and if it weren't for that one fateful day, she never would have known about any of this. *Sweet synchronicity*, she thought to herself. Morgana felt so grateful for that fortuitous day.

Morgana reached into the big pink box and carefully brought out the delicate platinum chain with the hand crafted Celtic woven white gold metal holding onto the three heart shaped aqua blue stones. Ms. Lane just smiled. "I will let Josef tell you about that piece." And that's all she would say. Morgana would have pushed a little harder but she could tell Ms. Lane wasn't going to give.

"Fine." Morgana gave up. "Then, please regale me with what this is." Morgana reached into the big pink box, and lifted out the black plush velvet hooded cloak with the cream silk on the reversible side.

"This, my dear, is a ceremonial cloak. Ceremonies are an important punctuation to a new beginning or transition. Every tradition has many celebrations. You just graduated from high school and wore a cap and gown, did you not?" Morgana nodded. "Certain religions have a rite of passage from child to adult, like a quinceañera, bar mitzvah or bat mitzvah. Proms can be a rite of passage. They used to be the first formal occasion and date for a young couple. Baptisms, christenings, debutant balls are all ceremonial traditions for coming of age. Then you have weddings, holidays, birthdays, and funerals, all traditional ceremonies, each to distinguish a passage in time. Over the years the meanings of things may have shifted, people may have forgotten the original reason why we do the things we do, but the important thing to remember is everything is what you make of it. You get to choose to make everything you do special and give it meaning to you. When you graduated and got that piece of paper, I know you probably were relieved you 'got it over with.' Am I right?" Morgana laughed sheepishly in agreement. "But can you think of a single moment while you sat in your gown and felt proud that you accomplished something? You did it. You graduated high school. You set the intention and followed it through to completion, and did it earlier than most, right?"

"Well, yah, but that's just because I was miserable there," Morgana defended.

"Give yourself some credit. Regardless of the so-called reason," Ms. Lane winked, "you completed a rite of passage. Take a moment to soak that in. And this cloak is for you any time you feel like you have accomplished something, or completed something. Like when you feel you have reached a goal or took a big step, or even for when you've taken a bunch of little steps. Celebrate and honor momentous occasions. You are the only one who can give value to your dreams. Think about someone who climbs Mount Everest. Don't you think they are proud of accomplishing that goal? Does it have any effect on humanity? Did they find the cure for cancer up there? No, but it's a huge undertaking and they did it. Not every one can say they've climbed Mount Everest and not everyone can say they've graduated from high school. A ceremony can be a private event, or it can be the event of the decade. The important thing is it will be what you make it in your heart."

"Okay, I think I kinda get what you're saying. I didn't make a big deal out of my prom, and I hated every minute of it. But some of those girls spent hundreds of dollars, if not more, on their dresses and outfits, and hair and makeup. They were stuck on the same bus I was, but to them it was great fun, part of the night; whereas to me it was a waste of time. Same with graduation, I just wanted to get it over with and didn't want to bother with it. But some of those kids were the first in their family to graduate. And what really makes sense to me now, is how you made last night so special." Ms. Lane cleared her throat correctively. "Okay, so, I mean, I really felt special last night. And even though I didn't know half the guests," she laughed, "it still meant more to me than my own prom and graduation combined, because I was fully present in the moment."

Ms. Lane smiled a huge smile, and lovingly grabbed Morgana's hand. "That's my girl. You got it."

$\mathcal{C}$hapter Six

Deep Sorrows and Magnificent Inspirations

BE FULLY PRESENT. Live in the moment, Morgana would chant to herself day after day, standing in the midst of a sea of shoppers. Some days she did better than others. Some days she just couldn't deal with the barrage of pushy, rude, ridiculous creatures that stalked the racks like carnivorous vultures ripping and tearing shards of fabric off the boney hangers.

"Uhggg, Ms. Lane. I can't do it! I can't keep standing there smiling and offering sweet perfume samples that they snatch from my hands in disgust. Sometimes they look at me like I'm the anti-Christ! It's perfume, people! It's just supposed to make you smell nice!" A completely exasperated Morgana held her head in her hands until it slipped through as it if were too heavy for her to hold and landed on the marble island like a lump. She rolled it to one side as if her neck wasn't able to carry the hefty load and with her cheek pressed against the cool countertop she anguishly fed herself one of Ms. Lane's delicious cookies out of the side of her mouth. "Why can't everybody just be happy?" she said with a mouthful of sweet warm chocolate chip cookie.

"Oh, my dear child." Ms. Lane laughed as she witnessed Morgana, with chocolate chip residue on her lips, pathetically contemplate and attempt to drink from her tea cup without lifting her weighty head off of the countertop. "Aren't you a sad sack?" Defeated, Morgana lifted her head, but stayed hunched over, with her chin barely off the table and sipped her tea. "Why do you think it's your responsibility to make everyone happy? That's quite a fantastic obligation."

"Well, I don't think I need to make everyone happy, but is it too much to ask for them to be a little bit nicer to me? They ignore me, or they shove me, or they bombard me with the same inane questions. Where's the bathroom? What time do you close? Is there a Starbucks in this mall?" Morgana pretended to be a flight attendant pointing two-fingered hands at imaginary exits.

Ms. Lane couldn't help but chuckle at her poor pitiful young friend. "You only have two weeks left until the fall semester starts back up, right?"

"Oh, yah, great. More mindless classes that have nothing to do with anything. When do I get to start doing what I want to do?"

"What do you want to do?"

"I don't know!" Morgana whined and dropped her head back on the counter into her folded up arms. "I just want to live my own life and not have to deal with stupid grumpy people and their stinky attitudes," she mumbled from within her buried state.

"Well, that seems like a good place to start. You know what you don't want. Come now, let's go sit in the garden. It always helps ground me when I feel like I don't know what to do."

Morgana sluggishly lugged herself off her barstool, quickly snatched up another cookie, and then slowly shuffled her feet out the glass doorway and down the stone walk as if her flip flops were cross country skies drudging their way through deep sloshy wet snow. She plopped down in the white wicker arm chair in the rose vine entwined gazebo and laid her heavy head back and stared listlessly at the hand painted sweet smiling cherubs and mythical creatures looking on from above. She remembered Ms. Lane said Josef spent an entire summer painting this picturesque scene and two of the cherubs were painted with the faces of his dearly departed parents. She started focusing on the details in the little smiling faces, leaning in as if to hear and be a part of every word spoken under their sacred roof. Her eyes searched the scene and saw so many nuances and facets she never noticed before. Josef had painted this during his grief and anger over the loss of his parents, and she could see how he poured every ounce of love and emotion that he had within himself into creating this perfect safe haven for them to live on in spirit. Tears filled her eyes as she realized that it wasn't just two cherubs that had his parents likeness carefully painted into the relief, but each grouping of characters depicted different scenes of parts of his life or possible life with his parents. One grouping showcased three sweet little angels playing in a wooded area feeding a miniature unicorn pony. Ms. Lane once told Morgana when Josef was little, every year on his birthday his parents would take him to a petting zoo. He ignored all the other animals except the miniature ponies that he would spend all day feeding and petting. Eventually they found him a horse ranch with miniatures and he loved spending all day there.

Another area in the painting looked as if one of the cherubs was driving a cloud. His parents never got to witness him getting his driver's license, they died shortly after he received his learner's permit. There were waterfalls and water pools in another section of the scene that looked like the waterfalls just outside of town. Morgana only knew it as the place the high school kids would go on weekend nights for bonfires and parties, but families would also have picnics there. Morgana guessed his parents probably took him there or maybe he just wished they had. By now tears were streaming down her face, "Oh my God, Ms. Lane. Josef painted these as family scenarios. I mean, it looks like... It's heartbreaking, yet so beautiful and sweet at the same time. I can even see the two of you in there planting this garden!"

"Yes," Ms. Lane spoke softly. "We don't always have to be happy. Sometimes deep sorrows can inspire magnificent and beautiful things."

They sat in silence for a while, Morgana imagining the images alive and living out the childhood memories of an orphaned young boy. "Is there anything I can do for him?" Morgana gently asked with a tight throat as she wiped the tears from her wet cheeks.

"Just follow your heart, dear."

A few days later, Morgana meandered through the mall during her lunch break. She was drawn into a western store that she would normally never have noticed. As she sipped on her venti mocha blended coffee walking through the fields of denim shirts, jeans, and racks of boots, humming the tune of "Happy Trails" that her grandmother used to sing to her when she was little, she saw a table up by the registers with a display of colored handkerchiefs and various belt buckles. A lone little porcelain miniature pony stood in the midst. She picked it up and there was a 50% off sticker on the bottom. "Is this for sale?" she asked a sales associate who was passing by.

"Um, yah. I think it's the last one," the disinterested associate replied. She immediately bought it before they changed their minds and kept it for display purposes only. As she scurried down the mall back to her department store with her treasured prize carefully wrapped in her purse, she noticed a new perfume kiosk opening in the middle of the mall. *How much more fun would it be to be in the center of the action?* she thought. With school starting back up next week, she had already given her notice to the department store. She wondered if this would work better for her schedule. She snapped a picture of the phone number to call and tried not to run as she hurried back to her post, positioned between the brand specialists in their white lab coats and the snobby counter where they charged "$90 for a lipstick dah-ling," that she imagined only wealthy dowagers could buy.

With her new school schedule starting at the local junior college, she had a few days off and happened to be home one day when Ms. Lane and Josef returned from the farmers' market. Morgana stalked her prey and waited, peeking out the blinds for him to walk outside to get ready to leave. She didn't want to interrupt their time together, but she also knew he had to get back early, so he wasn't going to stay for dinner, as Ms. Lane had explained to Morgana the day before. She peered between the small gap of the plastic blinds, staring at the recessed alcove, squinting to see if she could see the heavy wooden door latch wiggle. She strained her ears as if she could hear Ms. Lane's lace up Victorian boots with the kitten heels clicking on the hard wood floors walking to the door. Then finally it opened. She quickly grabbed the polished black gift bag with navy blue tissue paper that she had carefully chosen because she thought the combination looked 'manly' yet still 'pretty'.

She tried not to look like a creeper as she pretended to casually walk down her inclined driveway. "Don't trip. Don't trip. Don't trip," she commanded herself out loud. "Hi, Josef," she waved as he walked towards his car.

"Oh, hey, Morgana." Oh, how she loved his velvety voice say her name.

She thought to herself, *You can do this. Nice and confident.* "Hi, there," she said as they both reached his black Mustang that was parked on the street in front of Ms. Lane's house. It was a couple of years old, but she could tell he took really good care of it. "Did you drive Ms. Lane to the farmers' market in this?" Morgana joked.

"No, we take her ride. Have you seen the size of her trunk? You can fit a small army in there! It's almost big enough for all the groceries she buys," he jested. She laughed but she really just loved watching him smile.

"Um, I saw this and it made me think of you." *Oh, no!* She should have practiced what she was going to say. "Anyway, it's nothing really. I mean, it's just a little something. I thought you might like, is all." *Oh, God*, she groaned at herself. She handed him the glossy black gift bag with the clashing navy blue tissue paper that she was now second guessing. "Have a safe drive home. See you around," she blurted out.

"Don't you want to see me open it?" he asked in his smooth voice that stirred up the butterflies in her stomach.

Why did I do this to myself? she thought. "Oh, yah. Um, I mean you can open it later if you want. I know you have to get home today." *Oh God!* She shouldn't have said that. How would she know that if she hadn't talked about him with Ms. Lane. She felt like a total creeper.

He laughed as he removed the tissue paper and carefully unwrapped the little porcelain miniature pony figurine. He didn't say anything as he held the little creature in his hand.

Say something, she commanded herself. "Well umm, if you don't like it, I can take it back or something."

"Thank you, Morgana," he said gently and leaned over to give her a hug. He smelled so good, she breathed him in.

"Um, well, anyway. I hope to see you around some time." *Idiot!* she scolded herself. "Talk to you later." She waved and turned to briskly walk up her inclined driveway without looking back until right before she walked into her house where he couldn't see her. He was still standing in the street and just about to open his car door. *Stupid! Stupid! Stupid! He hated it. What was I thinking? Oh, man!* she blasted herself.

"Bye, Josef!" she called out to him as he started his engine and drove off. "Well, either he didn't hear me or he thinks I'm an idiot and he's trying to ignore me. Stupid! Stupid! Stupid!" she berated herself as she walked in and slammed the door behind her.

New classes started and it had been two weeks since Morgana had been over to see Ms. Lane. It was 4:30 p.m. and Morgana was really missing her friend and their afternoon tea time. She clandestinely pulled out her phone and sent Ms. Lane a text.

M – How's your tea? (teacup emoji)

ML – Not the same without you. (sad face)

M – In art history watching a slide show. Have you ever been to the Louvre? (Eiffel tower)

ML – Yes. Its breath taking. (smiley face)

M – We should go one day. (airplane)

ML – I would love that (heart)

M – Me tooooo! (laughing smiley)(thumbs up)(heart) Miss you (tear face)

ML – Come over any time dear (pink unicorn)

A couple weeks later, Morgana walked down her inclined driveway, across the street, past the well-kept but so old, deep maroon Cadillac Deville and its small army sized trunk. She reached the recessed alcove with the heavy wooden door. The usual pink flowers were replaced with freshly planted orange and crimson ones, and the sweet sign: "Blessed are those who enter here," sat prominently amongst the new fresh florals on the white wrought iron table tucked in the corner. A new thick natural coir welcome mat featured fall leaves, harvest vegetables, and said "Thanks" in curvy font. The clicking heels of her lace up Victorian boots grew louder and then the heavy wooden door swung open.

"Hello, my dear!" Ms. Lane hugged Morgana and then she walked in, around the pony wall, past the sweet angelic faces, into the dining room with the huge round marble table. Fall may not have yet arrived outside, but it definitely made its full bloom impact on the inside. Glittered garlands of fall foliage accented the white bookcase and the tops of all the kitchen cabinets. Fresh floral bouquets of orange, yellow, and crimson flowers were placed around Ms. Lane's loving and cherished home. The delicious scent was of heartwarming sweet pumpkin spice rather than the light fresh citrus she used for the summer.

"It's so pretty in here. I love all the fall-ness," Morgana complimented as she breathed it all in.

"Next to winter, spring, and summer, fall is my favorite."

"Wait," Morgana laughed, "you listed all the seasons."

"I guess I do love them all," Ms. Lane chortled. "But September is an important month. The fall equinox is the 22nd and it's also Mabon, a three day blessing harvest festival we have to celebrate and give thanks for the fruits of the earth. You should come. I'm on the board committee so I'll be there. I'll be busy with the committee and planning, so why don't you snappy Brook to see if she'll be able to show you around. I know Tristan will be competing in the games," Ms. Lane suggested.

Morgana had to laugh, "Do you mean snap chat? Well, I did text her a few weeks ago. She said she was headed out of town and would let me know when she got back. I haven't heard from her, so I'm assuming I got the brush off."

Ms. Lane scoffed gently and shook her head. "Nonsense, dear. Brook has been with my sister at the farm in Italy for the past couple of weeks. I think she just got back yesterday. I know she loves going to Mabon and would be happy to take you."

"Your sister lives in Italy and you're just telling me this now?" Morgana exclaimed.

"Oh, yes. She and her husband manage the family's organic farms for the ingredients of our products. Well, they're mostly retired now, but they still oversee production there. Jackson manages the plant and Josef and Brook are working their way through, finding their niche in the family business."

"I remember you saying Jackson ran the plant, but somehow I didn't realize what you were saying. And I think you left out the part about, oh, I don't know – your sister lives in Italy!" Morgana teased. "Do you ever go visit?"

"I do. I was there for two weeks back in March."

Morgana remembered her mother did tell her the nice lady across the street would be gone for a few weeks and she was supposed to keep an eye on her house. Morgana was getting ready for spring break at the time and didn't pay much attention.

"Do you go often?"

"Not as much as I used to, but I love Italy in the spring. It's my favorite season at the farm," she said whimsically. "Let's text Brook to see if she can take you to the festival."

Chapter Seven

The Magical Lot

MORGANA'S TIRES SCREECHED as she pulled into her inclined Y-shaped driveway. Brook and Blake would be there in thirty minutes to take her to Mabon, a three-day harvest festival that had started that morning. Ms. Lane had described it as sort of a Renaissance fair meets the Olympics. She tried telling Morgana it was like the Highland games but Morgana was confused about that. Although, she did look at Highland game pictures on her phone and it looked like fun. There would be sporting events, dancing, kiosks, and food all in celebration of thanking the earth for its bountiful harvests. She didn't know what to expect but she loved the way Ms. Lane's eyes lit up as she described it. Ms. Lane said she was on the high council. Morgana assumed she meant like the decorating committee or something.

At Ms. Lane's suggestion, Morgana packed her black and cream birthday cloak and the beautiful amulet necklace with the aqua colored gemstones that matched Josef's amazing eyes. Morgana never asked Ms. Lane if he was going to be there. She hadn't heard or seen him since that day in the street when she gave him the miniature pony figurine. He just held it in his hand and stared blankly at it, Morgana thought. She was so embarrassed. She always felt like that stupid, clumsy, thirteen-year-old girl with the sticky icy lemonade running down her sundress every time she was around him. His boisterous laughter still hauntingly rang in her ears.

She gently packed the long silky cloak and carefully laid the amulet box in her suitcase. It was perhaps the most beautiful thing she had ever seen. She didn't know what one wears to harvest festival so she packed some jeans, comfortable yoga pants, a hoodie, and a sweater. The days were still sunny but it cooled off at night. She heard Brook honk from the driveway, grabbed her overnight bag, and ran out the door.

Brook was driving her new white A5 Audi convertible, a present from her family for graduating college. Blake welcomed Morgana with a hug and held open the car door so she could climb into the backseat.

"This is so cute!" Morgana complimented the sporty car.

"Oh, thank you. I love it!" Brook agreed as she loaded Morgana's bag into the back. With the thunk of the trunk closing by Brook, and Blake pushing the seat back, they both hopped in and were off.

"Careful to back out on an angle. The driveway is pretty steep and it might scratch your bumper," Morgana warned.

"Thanks." Brook slowly angled out the driveway. They all waved and blew kisses at Ms. Lane's empty house. She had left for the event yesterday. They zipped down the road with the top down and gleefully sang to the blasting radio.

With the wind and the music there wasn't much conversation, but there was plenty of laughing, seat dancing, and car karaoke during the two hour drive. Morgana didn't know where they were going. She had tried to look it up on her GPS, but Ms. Lane explained that it was just a remote empty location under the vast starry sky surrounded by distant mountains.

> "But it's not the location that matters," Ms. Lane softly noted. "It's the feeling you get that's important. It's hard to explain, you'll just have to experience it for yourself."

Nestled in the soft leather backseat, enjoying the open air, and the welcoming feeling of her new friends, Morgana felt like she was already experiencing some of that magical essence Ms. Lane was always talking about. After about an hour and a half they exited the freeway and turned down a small two lane road. Morgana leaned forward so she could listen as Brook explained the location changed periodically as the cities developed.

"There are different festivals everywhere held during this weekend of the fall equinox, but of course, since Aunt Katherine is the beloved

Grand High Chairman, this is the best one! Our Mabon is held in an open area in nature. People come from all over the world and it's quite big. We'll check into the girls' tent and then we'll go watch Tristan practice." Brook said excitedly as they turned off the road onto the dirt drive. Morgana looked out to see dozens of tents with colorful flags and she smelled delicious food aromas that were carried in the fresh air. There was music and chatter of hundreds of people. Brook found a parking spot and Morgana and Blake exited the car as Brook closed up the convertible top. Blake was talking about how excited she was to check out the cute guys in their uniforms, kilts, and dress robes. Morgana was flabbergasted at the thought of uniforms, kilts and dress robes. She couldn't wait to see what this was all about.

They walked into the entrance and were welcomed by the greeting attendants. "Welcome, Miss Brook and Miss Blake," the attendant greeted them by name with a smile.

"Hi, Jamie!" Brook greeted back. "How is everything going?"

"We are anticipating one of the biggest turnouts yet. I think there's almost two-hundred people expected. The games are over there." Jamie pointed to the left, "And the girls' tent is over there." He pointed off to the right.

"Are you going to be able to see Tristan compete?" Brook asked.

"Here's the events schedule." Jamie handed them a tri-folded paper brochure. "I should be able to see the finals on Saturday. Tell Tristan good luck! And Josef, too. His matches are on the Level III fields."

Morgana's ears pricked up as she pretended she wasn't interested in knowing where Josef was or what he was doing on the Level III fields.

"I believe archery is at 4 p.m." Jamie pointed out on the brochure.

"Great! Thank you, Jamie. See you later." Brook said good-bye to the young man and the three girls walked to the right where he had pointed out the girls' tent.

Morgana was trying to soak in everything that she was just a witness to: Josef is here, he does archery, he's competing in the tournaments, and Ms. Lane is the beloved Grand High Chairman.

They were in a dirt field in the middle of nowhere, yet it had been transformed to look like a small medieval village, with tents, and kiosks selling clothes and jewelry, and a farmers' market selling fresh foods. There were barbecues puffing delicious smoke into the air. People had trucked in trailers and kitchens and decorated them to look like thatched roofed cottages. There were pubs and shoppes, selling handmade trinkets and gifts. Some people were in Scottish kilts and plaid dresses. Some people were in belly dancing outfits. There were samurais, warriors, princesses, knights, and pirates.

Morgana thought about her jeans and hoodie and felt a little out of place. Brook and Blake were in jeans too, so she figured it was okay. As they walked to the girls' tent, Blake explained that they set up a guys' tent, a girls' tent and family tents. There were hotels about forty-five minutes up the freeway for those who didn't want to sleep on cots in huge tents with hundreds of strangers. But Blake really was just excited about getting to the game fields so she could check out the "man scene." They entered the tent and Blake was right, rows and rows of standard cots. *I should have brought my pillow*, Morgana thought.

"Brook! Over here!" A slim, tall, pretty blonde girl waved at them from across the room.

"Tiffany!" Brook cried out and hurried over to her best friend who had scouted out cots for them.

"You finally made it! What took so long?" Tiffany gave Brook a hug like they hadn't seen each other in years.

"Hi, Blake!" Tiffany reached out and hugged Blake. "You look so pretty!" Tiffany smiled but Morgana sensed Blake wasn't as excited to see Tiffany as Brook perhaps was.

"We stopped to pick up Morgana," Brook explained as she introduced Tiffany to Morgana.

Tiffany's bright demeanor dimmed a little as she reached her hand out to shake Morgana's. "Hello, I'm Tiffany, Brook's best friend, since forever. We all grew up together. I'm practically family." Morgana reached her hand out but Tiffany barely touched it and quickly lost interest, turning back to Brook. "Quick, unpack your bags into the foot lockers so we can go see our boys. I made us matching shirts! And you'll have to tell me all about Italy."

Morgana picked a cot on the other side of Blake, who was next to Brook, with Tiffany on the far end. She watched as Blake opened the foot locker, took out the bed linens, and put in her suitcase. Morgana quickly did the same.

Tiffany and Brook were laughing as Tiffany gave her a black shirt that said, "Team Tristan" in white glittery lettering. "I had these made for when we watch Tristan and then we can put on these for Josef!" She pulled out two aqua blue shirts with black crystal lettering that read "Josef's Targets." Tiffany giggled a little harder than necessary.

"Can we go now?" Blake's impatience was the perfect icebreaker.

"Why don't you and Morgana head to the fields while we change," Brook suggested.

"Works for me." Blake exasperatedly turned and started walking out. Morgana quickly closed and locked her foot locker and raced to catch up with her.

"Tiffany is obsessed with Josef, always has been," Blake started saying to Morgana, "She's a bit of a creeper if you ask me. He's too nice to tell her to get lost. Who knows he might like her, but she's been chasing him for years so you think if he liked her, they'd be together by now. All I know is we need an iced coffee and to get to the games!" Blake was determined and focused. Morgana thought Blake looked like her game was man hunting.

As they trekked across to get to the gaming fields, iced coffee in hand from one of the makeshift kitchen vendors, Blake explained that there were all different types of competitions happening as she looked at the brochure Jamie handed out when they first arrived.

"We've got all kinds of sporting events, dancing, music, cook-offs, beer and wine tasting. Tristan does the caber toss on the Level II fields, and I do want to see Josef's archery competition on the Level III fields. But what I really want to see this year are the samurais. They are skilled masters, not just thickheaded brutes." Morgana threw Blake an inquisitive look. "My ex is a hammer thrower. I'm sure he's here somewhere. That's why I want to stay as far away from the Celtic Level II fields as I can. We'll go see Tristan, for sure, though. But if you want to hang out with me, I'll be with the samurais."

This was all new to Morgana, so she didn't really care: samurais, cabers, hammers, arrows, whatever. She just knew she didn't want to spend too much time with Tiffany, and Blake seemed to share in that notion. "Samurais sound great!" Morgana stated. And so they headed to find themselves some skilled warriors.

"Today is Friday, so these are just the qualifying rounds. Tomorrow are the finals. Tomorrow night will be the awards ceremony and then dinner," Blake detailed the weekend's events to Morgana as they crossed the fields. Men and women athletes were competing in various games out in the dirt fields marked off with ropes and streamers. Blake spotted the Level I fields and there were about fifteen men dressed in different color samurai uniforms. One by one they went into the circle and performed various tasks like sword handling, martial arts steps, and a set of attack moves. Morgana watched as each warrior went out, and though she couldn't see their faces, she could see how they grounded themselves and felt each movement. Indeed, they were skilled like dancers, deadly dancers, she surmised. After an hour or so, Morgana was getting hungry. The delicious aroma of kettle popcorn, barbecue, and sweets was getting too much to resist. "I'm getting hungry are you?" she asked Blake. Blake's attention was focused on something more to her liking.

"You go ahead. I'm going to stay a little longer," she said as she playfully tossed her hair to the side, not taking her eyes off her newest prey.

She's the real deadly dancer, Morgana thought to herself. "Okay, I'm going to go check out the food. Will you be here for a while?"

"Probably, but Tristan's caber toss starts in an hour. So I'll meet you there for sure."

"Okay, perfect." Morgana followed her nose back to the makeshift medieval village to check out the food scene. She wandered through the cute wannabe cottages, each decorated in its ancient roots. There were areas set up for all kinds of wine tasting, ale tasting, sake tasting, and tea tastings. "Where's the pie tasting?" she joked out loud to herself. She watched the villagers in their costumes and felt transported to a different time. Everyone was friendly and happy. They were all there to celebrate and give thanks to the earth for its bountiful harvest. Morgana sampled teriyaki chicken, corn on the cob, and kettle corn as she meandered through the sweet temporary shops. There were many artistic shops with handmade trinkets and beautiful jewelry. There were chocolate shops, tea shops, lots of holistic shops with chakra stones like the ones she got for her birthday. There were even shops with porcelain figurines like the ones Ms. Lane had on her wall and in her garden. There were clothing stores with everything from gorgeous kimonos, Renaissance gowns, to cloaks in silks and wool. She was enamored with this mystic world market to which she was transported. She walked into one of the cottages with essential oils, teas, and handmade soaps. "Beloved Grace Organics."

Hey, Ms. Lane's stuff, she thought to herself. The lady at the counter asked if she needed any assistance.

"Do you know Ms. Lane?" she asked the helpful sales clerk.

"Yes, of course. She is one of the founders of Beloved Grace Organics," the proud salesclerk boasted.

"Hi, I'm Morgana. Ms. Lane is my neighbor." Morgana introduced herself.

"Oh, Morgana! It's so nice to finally meet you. Aunt Katherine speaks so highly of you. I'm Cindy Meadow, Brook and Blake's mom."

"Oh, my gosh! It's so nice to meet you!" Ms. Lane loved her nephew Jackson and his family so much, Morgana felt like she knew them. She gave Cindy Meadow a big hug.

"Did you have a nice ride up with the girls? Are they watching Tristan?" she asked motheringly.

"Brook and Tiffany are watching Tristan. Blake and I were watching the samurais, but I got hungry. I'm meeting back up with them at 3 p.m. when Tristan's match starts."

"That's wonderful. Are you enjoying your first Mabon festival out here at the lot?"

"Oh, I love it. It's so cute and quaint. I feel like I've been transported back in time. Everyone is so friendly and helpful. Did all these people get transported here? It's so nice, not like at the mall where I work," Morgana laughingly joked.

"You are feeling the connection. Everyone is here to give thanks and celebrate the earth. We are all here with that single purpose and on a similar vibration and you can feel it," Cindy explained.

"You sound like Ms. Lane!" Morgana laughed.

"Oh, I take that as a huge compliment." Cindy smiled. "Aunt

Katherine is one of my favorites. She is so wise, kind, and smart as a tack. All this was her idea, from Beloved Grace Organics to this very gathering for Mabon. She's a very special lady to so many people."

Morgana leaned in close to Cindy Meadow and secretly whispered, "Is she the real Mary Poppins?"

Mrs. Meadows whispered back, "She is Mary Poppins and so much more!"

"I thought so!" Morgana agreed. "I better get going if I'm gonna make it to watch Tristan. Are you coming?"

"I won't be able to see qualifiers today, but I know he's a shoe in. I'll be able to watch all the finals tomorrow. I can't believe those cabers. Have you ever seen it?"

Morgana said no and waved good-bye. "I'm looking forward to it!" On her way back she bought some caramel popcorn, fruit, and some waters for the other girls and made her way to Level II fields.

The levels referred to the different terrain and sections. Level I fields were smooth flatter grounds for games where athletes needed to walk or run around depending on the sport. Level II fields were more rocky, but had been cleared a bit, making them fit for games like caber tossing and hammer throwing. The level III fields were for athletes that didn't need too much clearing, so it was perfect for the archery competitions. This whole festival was set up by volunteers and committee members.

Morgana crossed over into the caber tossing area. Huge wooden poles as long as nineteen feet were lying on the ground. She watched as a trunk of a man wearing a kilt lifted a huge limbless tree and tossed it. It flipped end over end and the several dozen onlookers cheered.

Oh, my God! That's what this is? Holy crap! Morgana thought to herself, amazed. She saw Blake, who waved at her, so she hurried over there while the judges calculated their scores. "What is that?" Morgana cried out. "They're throwing frickin' trees!" Blake laughed out loud at her.

It was then Morgana noticed Brook and Tiffany both wearing their matching "Team Tristan" black shirts and short yellow and black kilts, with thigh-high black stockings. "You guys look so cute," Morgana said, kind of caught off guard. Blake groaned.

"Oh, quiet Blake. You wore this exact outfit last year to Tim's hammer toss," Tiffany quipped.

Blake looked like she was about to snap back at Tiffany, but Brook stepped between them. "Oh, Morgana, what did you buy?"

"Oh, umm, I didn't know if you guys would be hungry, so I got some snacks and waters. I also met your mom. She's so nice." Morgana felt the tension between the two girls.

"Snacks and waters. That was so thoughtful. Thank you. Look, Tiffany, Blake, would you like a water?" Brook offered the girls each a water which they took, finally breaking away from each other's stare down.

Tristan was called up to take his turn. His huge chest muscles rippled under his shirt, his arm muscles flexed and bulged as he lifted the tall wooden pole. Morgana met Tristan that first day at Ms. Lane's house and thought he looked like the Hulk. Now with this nineteen foot caber in his hands, she thought he probably was the Hulk. He tossed it with such force it flipped and flopped, landing in front of him at the 12 o'clock position. The crowd let out a huge cheer. Brook and Tiffany squealed and hollered. Blake and Morgana clapped and shouted. Morgana wasn't sure what it all meant, but it seemed like he did what he was supposed to do and he easily qualified for the finals. He wiped off his hands as his coaches congratulated him. He looked to the crowd, scanning for his girl. She waved and clapped in her "Team Tristan" outfit that matched the kilt he was wearing. He smiled back and gave her a wink. She gushed and turned to Tiffany giggling about how "awesome her boyfriend is."

They sat through the rest of the qualifiers, sharing the caramel corn Morgana had brought for everyone. When the match ended, Brook and Tiffany ran down to the field to talk to Tristan. Morgana quickly asked Blake, "What's with you and Tiffany?"

"My ex is her brother, Tim. He cheated on me, so I dumped his ass. She doesn't think he cheated and thinks I'm a bitch for breaking his heart. When I wore that outfit last year, she told me 'it was a bit much.' Now, she stole the idea. I don't know what's going on with her. She's been Brook's best friend since they were sixteen. But I think now that Brook and Tristan are together she's becoming jealous, even more so since she can't get Josef. I think her plan was best friends marrying best friends, but Brook spends all her time with Tristan and Tiffany is getting left out. Come on. Let's head over to the Level III fields."

As the caber tossers were moving out, the hammer throwers were coming in. Tiffany, Brook, and Tristan stopped to talk to Tim. Blake and Morgana were already walking away. "Hi, little Timmy!" They heard Tiffany's voice call out from behind. Blake walked a little faster.

Blake and Morgana found the archery field. Tiffany, Brook and Tristan showed up a few minutes later. "Oh, God," Blake moaned, "here they come."

"Tristan, you remember Morgana," Brook said making small talk as she saw her little sister roll her eyes.

"Of courrrse. Hellllo, Lassie!" Tristan rolled with his thick Scottish brogue and held out his huge hand.

"That was incredible. How on earth can you lift that heavy thing, let alone huck it like that? It was amazing!" Morgana shook Tristan's big hand, hello.

He laughed. "Good trrrraininggg, Lassie!"

A voice announced, "Archery qualifiers to the lineup." Five at a time came to the line and aimed their arrows at the targets down the course. On cue, they shot in unison. Some hit, and some missed their targets. The ones who missed were disqualified. The next group stepped up to the line, Josef was included. Tiffany cheered louder than anyone. "Arrows ready!" said the announcer and they all shot in unison.

"Bull's-eye!" Josef's arrow hit the middle of its target. He was in all three of the archery competitions and easily qualified for the finals. He joined the group who were all cheering and clapping for him when it was over. Tiffany ran up and hugged him. Tristan congratulated him with a friendly smack on the back. Brook, Blake, and Morgana each congratulated him.

"Hey, Morgana. How's it going?" Josef asked, flashing those deep aqua blue eyes.

"Hi. Nice job hitting those targets," Morgana said bashfully.

Tiffany was still clinging to Josef and took over the conversation. "Yes, you were amazing. I can't believe they don't just give you the trophy now," she said.

"Oh, well," Josef said as he tried to remove himself from her entangling limbs, "it's all just good fun for the festival. Has anyone seen Mitchell yet?" he asked, trying to change the subject.

"We'rre surpposed ta meet him at tha dancerrs. Trrina is in tha show," Tristan explained.

So they all headed towards the dance area in the middle of the makeshift village. That's where the grand celebration dinner would be tomorrow night. Brook and Tristan walked hand-in-hand, while Tristan and Josef discussed their tournaments today. Tiffany walked next to Josef, trying to stay close to him. Blake and Morgana walked behind, Blake pointing and laughing at Tiffany making a fool of herself, and Morgana swearing to herself that she will never fawn over Josef, or any guy, like that.

Tables were set up around the dance floor area, and Mitchell waved them all over to join him. He greeted everyone with hugs for the girls and back smacks for the guys. He, of course, remembered Morgana and said it was good to see her again. "Well, gentleman, I'm sure I don't even need to ask. Everyone qualified for tomorrow, no doubt?"

Tristan's Scottish accent hailed his mate, "No need to be askin 'bout Joosef. Bullseeys acrross tha bord."

Josef joined in, "And Tristan's caber flipped its way to its perfect mark, like a trained seal." The group all laughed.

A waitress came over and took their drink order. "Guinness, lassie," Tristan requested, "and a chocolate heatherr crrream for me sweet bonnie." He lovingly squeezed Brook. Mitchell and Josef ordered the house ale and Tiffany tried to ask Josef for his opinion on what she should have, finally just ordering the same drink as Brook. Blake and Morgana didn't have on the "Over 21" wrist bands so they ordered ginger ales.

"At least you're with me this year," Blake whispered to Morgana. "Last year I was the only one under age. You'd think it wouldn't matter out here in the middle of nowhere, but they say it's for the best to follow the law. Whatever, is what I say. Who would even notice out here?"

The music started up and Trina and her belly dancing troupe came out first. They were so elegant and beautiful in their colorful bedlahs. Their chains and beads glimmered as their hips rolled and dipped, with yards of flowing fabric wrapping behind and around them. Morgana thought it was remarkable. Mitchell obviously loved it. Tristan and Brook snuggled together. Josef was enjoying it, but Tiffany was trying to engage him in conversation asking if she should become a dancer. Blake's eyes were roaming the area, scanning for her samurai warrior from earlier.

"Looking for someone?" Tiffany called Blake out.

"No, I'm wondering whose watching Tim in his heat since his sister is here disrupting the show for all of us," Blake snapped back.

Tiffany backed off a bit. "He said he'd be okay today. But I'm definitely going to watch him tomorrow." She sat back quietly in her chair.

Blake finally saw who she was looking for and excused herself from the table. Morgana tried to ignore their tension and went back to enjoying the beautiful dancing. However, she couldn't help herself from sneaking peeks at Josef, who seemed to get more good looking every time she saw him, if that was even possible. She really couldn't fault Tiffany for trying so hard to be with him. As for her, she was trying so hard to not even look at him. Luckily, she was really enjoying the dancers.

After Trina's belly dancers were finished, Scottish highland dancers came out. Then Irish step dancers. The finale was a Geisha troupe. There were three of them that first came out in traditional kimonos, their hair pulled up, white makeup with red lips and wooden okobos shoes. One played a sha miser, a guitar looking instrument, while the other two did a traditional Geisha dance routine. Then drums started pounding. Torches were lit around the edge of the dance area and three fully dressed samurais came to the floor. They did a sword dance that was dangerous and amazing. Morgana was thrilled with the talent and techniques. The original three Geisha dancers returned, but this time they had let their hair down and instead of kimonos, they were wearing body suits as they did flips and maneuvers usually only seen in a Cirque Du Solei show. The six dancers entwined, the body suit girls flipped over the samurai swords to the sounds of the drums. It was intricate, beautiful, and masterful.

Morgana had never seen anything like it and was completely

engrossed. She didn't realize that Josef was laughing at her. He had offered to buy everyone dinner and he was trying to ask her what she wanted.

"What? Oh. Are you seeing this? They're amazing!" Morgana defended, and quickly and graciously ordered steak and mashed potatoes off the menu, then went to back to being captivated by the dance.

When the performance was complete the six dancers came out into the middle of the floor. One by one the body suit girls took the traditional Japanese bow, and then the three samurais each took off their helmet, reveling that they too, were female dancers. The crowd went crazy! Morgana was flabbergasted. The swords were heavy and long and sharp, and those ladies were flipping and throwing them. It was so spectacular! Morgana jumped up from her chair to give a standing ovation. Mitchell, who was joined by Trina during the performance also stood up, clapping and cheering. Josef tried to stand up but Tiffany was partly leaning on him trying to talk. Tristan and Brook were snuggled up clapping together, looking so in love and happy. Blake had moved to a different table so she could talk to her new friend.

Attendants started serving dinner while a live band was setting up their instruments. The dinner table conversations were about the festival, games, and the dancing. Morgana really liked Trina and they spent the better part of the evening talking about all the different dancing styles. When Morgana began eating her dinner, her food was so succulent and delicious. She hadn't really paid much attention to the menu, she had just kind of pointed. There weren't many choices, just chicken, beef, or salad, with baked or mashed potatoes, and green beans or broccoli. Being out in the middle of nowhere in this little medieval makeshift village, Morgana was amazed at how wonderful everything tasted. The broccoli was so green, perfectly cooked. The mashed potatoes were creamy and buttery, perfectly seasoned. The steak cut like butter. Its flavor burst in her mouth and was delectable. There was a basket of fresh baked bread that she helped herself to, as well. She immensely enjoyed herself and her new friends. She loved talking to Trina about dancing, while Tristan, Josef, and Mitchell were having their own conversation and laughing, and Brook was enjoying listening to their stories. Poor Tiffany fluctuated between feeling left out and trying to get attention from Josef. She had only ordered the salad, and kept trying to offer Josef a bite. He thanked her, but declined.

Around midnight the music stopped and it was time to head back to their tents. Tiffany gave Josef a huge hug and a kiss on the cheek. Morgana just said good night and waited for Trina who had not been dating Mitchell that long, "just a few months," she told Morgana later that night. Trina gave Mitchell a nice good-bye kiss and then she and Morgana started back to the girls' tent. Mitchell and Josef said good-bye to everyone and they headed to the guys' tent.

Morgana and Trina were able to get Trina a cot next to hers, and they stayed up whispering for about an hour. Tiffany and Brook came in about twenty minutes after they did, as Brook and Tristan had a hard time saying goodnight. Blake finally came in about 1:30 a.m. and plopped in her cot fully dressed. Morgana rolled over to see Blake quickly drift off to sleep with a huge smile on her face.

The next morning Morgana was awakened by Tiffany and Brook grilling Blake about her new friend and what time she came in. Morgana opened her footlocker and picked out her clothes for the day.

Trina was waking up with a big stretching yawn. "Where's the coffee?" she said sleepily. Just then her name was being called from the front entrance. "Yes?" she called back, confused.

"There's someone at the door for you," they yelled back. Trina and her little dancer's body swiftly and gracefully jumped off the cot and hurried to where they were calling out her name. A few minutes later she returned carrying five hot cups of coffee and a bag of creamers and sweeteners.

"Courtesy of my man, Mitchell," she announced proudly. All the girls shrieked and giggled as they each grabbed a cup and doctored them up.

"Oh, heaven!" Blake called out as she took her first sip. Morgana, too, agreed as the liquid warmed her body. The blankets were good during the night, but the cot left little room for comfort. However, she was surprised at how well she actually did sleep and how excited she was today. The girls kept talking about the grand ceremony that night, and the dinner, and the dance. Morgana was excited to see more dancing so she asked Trina if her troupe was performing again.

"Oh, no, tonight's dance is the traditional Mabon dance. Everyone gets to be involved." She grabbed Morgana's hands and started waltzing her around. "La la la," she sang. "Grab your clothes and let's go get ready."

"Come on, Blake, let's go," Morgana called out. Blake readily grabbed her makeup bag and coffee and followed along, happy to get away from the interrogation of her well-meaning sister and her possibly not-so-well-meaning friend.

After Morgana, Blake, and Trina got ready, they met up with the boys for breakfast. Tristan and Josef had a few hours before they had to go to their fields for their tournaments. Brook and Tiffany showed up shortly after everyone ordered breakfast. Tristan had ordered Brook something, but no one ordered Tiffany anything and so she had to wait for her food to come out when everyone else was almost done. Morgana could definitely see why Tiffany was so jealous of Brook and Tristan. They were so affectionate and kind to each other. He always took care of her and knew what she liked and didn't like. He was very caring and gentlemanly, holding her chair and giving her his coat, which was several sizes too big and wrapped around her like a blanket. It was just precious watching them. Mitchell and Trina were a beautiful couple. Trina had long supple dancer's legs, and a lean, toned body. Mitchell was tall, lean, and solid. He was a little smaller in build than Josef, and had more of a runner's body, whereas Josef's build was big, muscular, and cut. To Morgana, Josef was the most beautiful creature she had ever seen, with those dreamy deep aqua blue eyes, the color of tranquil seas that Morgana could just get lost in. *Oh crap! Was I just staring at him?* she asked herself and quickly looked down at her breakfast plate like she was a paleontologist unearthing new dinosaur bones.

The breakfast conversation progressed to the night's formal dinner and the awards ceremony. Morgana perked up at the word "formal" as she looked down at her jeans and hoodie.

"Oh, tonight is a formal? Does that mean, dress up formal?" she asked. Trina and Blake gasped. Brook looked almost apologetic, she didn't realize Morgana didn't know. And Tiffany looked smug.

"Oh yes, tonight is the festival. Everyone gets dressed up. The High Council is here for the game awards ceremony. We have a great feast and then the ritual dance, which is just like a grand royal ball they have in Vienna. Only it's the most sacred and wonderful feeling you've ever had," Trina gushed. "It's the most beautiful thing, a dance beneath the stars. I can't wait!"

"I can't wait to see you in your dress. I think that will be the most beautiful thing," Mitchell announced.

"Oh, you'll just have to wait and see," she said flirtatiously as they cooed and kissed each other.

"We have time right now to find a dress, Morgana," Blake suggested. "I think I might see if I can find something else in honor of my new friend, who is schooling me in the ways of the samurai," she said slyly as she placed her hands together in prayer pose and bowed her head.

"Yes, who is this mysterious man?" Brook wanted to know.

"Oh, sorry, no time to talk now. Let's go Morgana!" Blake quickly got up from the table and Morgana followed.

"Oh, who do I pay for this?" she tried to ask as Blake pulled her away.

"I'll get it," Josef offered with a smile.

"Thank you!" Morgana called back as she was being dragged by Blake through the tables and chairs.

"Oh! She's so nosey!" Blake jokingly complained to Morgana about her older sister as they made their way through the makeshift medieval village. They first stopped at the "Beloved Grace Organics" store.

"Hey, Mom. How's everything going?" Blake gave her mom a big hug.

"Oh, good morning, girls! Everything is great! People are loving the festival. Did you all have a nice night? Are you enjoying yourself, Morgana?" Mrs. Meadow gave Morgana a welcoming hug.

"Yes, ma'am. I so enjoyed the dancing last night and the music. It was all so fun! I'm really loving everything!" Morgana excitedly replied.

"How are the cots?" Mrs. Meadow inquired.

Blake jokingly answered, "Puffy as a cloud." And then added, "Or maybe I just didn't notice because I was floating on my own cloud."

"What's his name?" Blake's mom knew her daughter so well.

"Jai! He's competing with the samurais. He's a martial arts instructor. He's twenty-two and so hot!" Blake was bursting with smiles. "What essential oil can I use to smell like cherry blossoms?" Blake went picking through the various brown oil bottles, smelling them each, trying to decide which one would be the perfect temptation for her new warrior conquest.

"Is there anything I can help you find, Morgana?" Mrs. Meadow offered assistance, after laughing at her daughter.

"Um, well. I just found out tonight's dinner is a formal. So, Blake and I are on our way to look for dresses. I don't know what else I need," Morgana said bashfully.

"Oh, fun!" Mrs. Meadow cried out. "I heard Mary Thompson has a wonderful selection of dresses this year. Each are hand embroidered and carefully crafted. I'm sure you'll find a gorgeous dress! Blake, let Mary know to put Morgana's dress on my tab. You get whatever dress you want. My treat, sweetheart." Mrs. Meadow gave Morgana a big hug.

"Oh, my gosh. Thank you. But I… I really couldn't," Morgana declined the generous offer.

"Nonsense. Those dresses can be pretty expensive. I want you to enjoy yourself and feel like the belle of the ball. Your first Mabon festival is a very special occasion. Don't you worry about it. I get a great discount." Cindy insisted.

"Thank you. That's so kind and wonderful of you. I really appreciate it!" Morgana gave Mrs. Meadow a big hug back.

"I think I'll take this one, Mom. Can you mix it for me?" Blake handed her mother the fragrance of her choice and Mrs. Meadow walked behind the counter.

"Essential oils are concentrated, so if you mix them with a carrier you can make organic perfumes," Blake explained. "Do you want to pick one out?"

Morgana wandered over to the oil display and wondered what scent Josef would like. She found one that smelled like sweet almond cookies and decided that was perfect for the fall evening festival. "Can I use this one?" She handed over the bottle and Mrs. Meadow happily created Morgana her very own organic perfume.

"This is so delicate compared to the perfumes I spray at the mall," Morgana noted, smelling the delicious custom perfume Mrs. Meadow handed back to her.

"These are organic and free from harsh chemicals. The scents warm with your body temperature and last twice as long as some of the commercial brands," Mrs. Meadow explained. "I still enjoy a few of my favorites, don't get me wrong, but these are meant to lift your mood and enhance your spirit. But I guess that's what they all say too, right?" Mrs. Meadow laughed at herself and winked at Morgana.

"Bye, Mom. Thank you." Blake gave her mom a hug and waved good-bye.

"See you at the games," Cindy Meadow called out to the girls and they headed towards Mary Thompson's Renaissance Dress Shoppe.

"Hi, Mrs. Thompson."

"Hello, Blake. How are you?" Mary Thompson, a good friend of the family greeted Blake with a warm smile.

"Good. How's business this weekend?"

"We've been quite busy. Everyone is excited for the dinner tonight. Is Tim winning an award this year?"

"Oh, we broke up. I haven't really seen too much of him this weekend," Blake explained.

"Well, that's too bad. How's your sister? I heard Tristan threw quite the toss yesterday," Mary inquired, knowing all about the girls' lives.

"Brook is good. Tristan is awesome at tossing. They are completely in love, even more head over heels for each other than one of Tristan's cabers!" Blake laughed at her own joke. "Mrs. Thompson, this is my friend, Morgana. Mom said she wanted to get her a dress for tonight. It's her first Mabon. Actually, this is your first festival all together, right?" Blake asked. Morgana readily shook her head, yes, as she didn't even know there were other festivals.

"Well, your first festival! That's a very special occasion. What kind of dress were you thinking?" Mary inquired. Morgana shrugged her shoulders and looked completely confused. Blake had found her way to the silk kimonos and wasn't paying attention to Morgana and Mary's conversation.

"Um, well, Ms. Lane gave me a black and cream cloak that I planned on wearing. And I also brought an amulet necklace with aqua heart-shaped stones in it. So, maybe something that goes with those?" Morgana said innocently.

Mary Thompson stood back a bit and glanced at Blake, who also looked over at her. Their eyes seemed to lock, but neither spoke.

"I think I know what will be perfect for you." Mary put her gentle hand on Morgana's shoulder with a special look in her eye. "Let me go get it." She came back with a black velvet Victorian style, lace up corseted dress, with long bell sleeves, and a sweetheart neckline. It was embroidered with a Celtic weave design along the trim in the same aqua blue color as Morgana's necklace.

"Oh, my God!" Morgana was stunned. "This is the most beautiful dress I have ever seen."

"Try it on, honey. I want to make sure it fits perfectly." Mrs. Thompson showed her to the temporary dressing room with the curtain door. Morgana pulled it on over her head, but wasn't quite sure how it all worked.

"Come out when you're ready and I'll tie up the corset for you," Mary called out.

"I'm not sure what I'm doing in here," Morgana sheepishly responded.

"Just come out and we'll get you situated." Morgana came out and Mary Thompson's eyes widened. "Oh, it's perfect! Come over here." She walked Morgana over to the mirror and showed her how to lace up the corset and adjust the waist. Morgana felt very beautiful in the dress.

Blake walked over and cried out, "That's awesome! You look so pretty!"

Morgana stared at herself in the small mirror and was overwhelmed. She was so excited for tonight! Blake picked out a silky kimono style dress for herself and the girls decided they needed some shoes too. Mary showed Morgana some black Victorian style lace up boots with a small kitten heel, perfect for the dress and even more perfect because they looked like the ones Ms. Lane wore. Morgana loved the dress and the shoes, and was filled with gratitude for Blake, Blake's mom Cindy, Mary Thompson, and Ms. Lane.

"Come on, we gotta get to the games. Can we leave these here until later?" Blake asked.

"Yes, of course. I'll steam them for you so they'll be ready for tonight."

"Awesome. Thanks, Mrs. Thompson." Blake gave her a quick hug and they were on their way to the game fields.

"Let's get an iced coffee, then go see Jai! We have plenty of time before Tristan's match. Then we'll head to see Josef." Blake laid out their time line as they made their way across the dirt fields. They got to Jai's samurai trials just as they were starting. She saw Jai and waved. He waved back and then put on his helmet. He definitely pulled out all the stops and performed his best in his heats. He got the highest score in two of the three matches giving him the best score overall, winning his game.

"Oh, good! He is going to get an award tonight!" Blake proudly gushed.

"How many games are there?" Morgana pulled out the game schedule to count fifteen different games in seven categories.

"This is just a small game. It's not a real competition like the nationals or anything for these games. It's just a sampling of different sports and fun events to do at this festival," Blake explained to Morgana. "The awards they hand out are more about the ceremony and being called up by the High Council, which is an honor," Blake continued. The judges turned in their scorecards and Jai was formally announced as the winner. Blake cheered and shouted, "Woohoo! Go Jai!" Morgana clapped along. Blake waited until Jai could come over and talk to her. She introduced him to Morgana and explained they would be watching the caber toss next. He had to put away all his gear and they decided to meet up at the archery field later. He gave her a quick kiss on the cheek and headed back to his coach and gear. "Isn't he so hot?" Blake raved.

"Yes, he is!" Morgana encouragingly agreed.

"He's so sweet, too. Last night, we talked under the stars. He told me about his DoJo and how he's excited about all the classes he's instructing. Plus, he has several private students and he's doing really well. He's also obviously serious about the tradition of the samurai and he incorporates the ancient traditions in all his lessons. Plus, he's a really good kisser!" Blake giggled.

They arrived at the Level II fields and Brook waved them over. Brook was wearing her "Team Tristan" glitter shirt outfit with the kilt that matched Tristan's. She was wearing black thigh-hi stockings and black tennis shoes.

"Oh, where's Tiffany?" Blake sarcastically questioned Brook with a smirky smile.

"She's with Tim. She'll meet us later at Josef's match," Brook sassed back.

"Of course she will!" Blake laughed.

"You know you're not funny," Brook ribbed her little sister. "You know she has to take her brother's side, and you really don't know for sure. Do you?"

"I clearly saw the writing on the wall and that's all the proof I needed," Blake stated her case.

"I wish you two could get along," Brook jokingly pleaded.

"In all seriousness, doesn't she seem different to you though?" Blake asked of her sister with some concern.

"Well," Brook explained, "she's definitely feeling a little left out of my life. I spend most of my free time with Tristan. And since we graduated college I've been busy with the business. She still manages the clothing store and I don't know if she got the promotion they promised her. I try to talk to her about her vibrations and focus, but she says she's fine and knows how to get what she wants. I'm not sure she's focused on the right feeling but she says her focus is on what she really wants."

"You mean, 'who' she really wants," Blake corrected.

"Ya, that too. She's focusing on a 'who' instead of how she wants to feel," Brook agreed.

Just then, the announcer called out to begin the games. The girls turned their attention to the field, as Mitchell and Trina showed just in time. Morgana stood, astonished, at the men lifting those huge, heavy, long caber poles and tossing them. Tristan walked up and balanced the caber upright, with the tapered end downwards, against his shoulder and neck. Then he crouched, sliding his interlocked hands down the caber and under the rounded base, and lifted it in his cupped hands. On standing he balanced the caber upright then took a few paces forward to gain momentum. He flipped the tapered end upward so that the large end hit the ground first and the caber fell directly away from him. He did it the most times within the time limit. Brook was so proud of her man. She squealed and shouted. Blake, Trina, and Morgana clapped and cheered as loud as they could. Mitchell whooped and hollered. They waited for the final scores to be announced, then Tristan was congratulated by everyone. Afterwards they all headed the Level III fields to watch Josef. Jai saw them coming and met them at the area roped off for archery. Blake introduced Brook to Jai and Brook was very courteous and happy to meet him. Tristan shook his hand and was impressed with his grip, as they bonded over their handshake.

"Ah, lassie. He's a strrrrong one therrrre," Tristan teased Blake in his Scottish brogue accent.

They all gathered around and waited for the archery tournament to start, when they saw Tiffany crossing the field. She was wearing her glittered 'Josef's Target' aqua shirt that exposed her tan stomach. Instead of the short kilt she wore yesterday, she was wearing even shorter tight black short shorts and tall stiletto ankle boots. As she came over to the group she called out, "Hiiii, Josef!" But his coach was talking to him so he didn't acknowledge her.

Blake was laughing hysterically. "A bit much, don't you think?" she said between bouts of laughter.

"Lassie, be surrrre to watch yerrr step in t'ose boots," Tristan warned.

Brook agreed. "Tiffany, I'm not sure those shoes are appropriate. Especially out here on the Level III field. It's awfully rocky."

"Oh, no worries. I'm a professional at walking in shoes like this. I'm a natural," Tiffany boasted. "If there was a sport for walking in heels, I would definitely win the award."

"Archers Ready!" the announcer called, interrupting the discussion. Morgana watched as Josef stepped up to his mark. She was surprised to see that he was wearing a black kilt. She had spent so much effort trying not to look at him yesterday, she didn't notice. She just noticed how good he looked. Today, since there were a lot less archers in the finals, she closely watched him. He was so controlled and masterful with his long bow. He was graceful and strong as he pulled the arrow back and held it until the bell rang announcing they could release. His arrows forcefully flew through the air and nailed their bullseye mark, dead center. He was truly an artist with his bow. She watched as he controlled his breath and synced his exhale with the launch of the arrow, almost like his breath carried it straight to the target. It was beautiful to behold. He was beautiful to behold. She quickly looked around to see if anyone noticed her intense gaze. Luckily Tiffany was in front, cheering and bouncing, trying to get attention. Brook and Tristan were holding each other. Mitchell had his arms wrapped around Trina holding her from behind and was more interested in the back of her neck as he softly blew his breath and played with her hair. Blake was talking with Jai. Morgana was relieved, and clear to stare. For each of the heats, Josef stepped up to his mark and with precision and proficiency he commanded his arrows dead center into their targets. Final scores were calculated and Josef's name was announced. Tiffany squealed and the crowd cheered.

"Ah, me mate's got t'easy," said Tristan, "T'ose arrrrrows don't weigh anyt'ing. Am I rrrright tharr Jai?" Tristan gave Jai a jolly smack on the back.

Josef came over to join them and Tiffany ran up and gave him a hug. "I knew you could do it. I wrote you a cheer!" She stood in cheerleader formation.

"Ready? OKAY!
Here's to the one with the great aim.
Here's to the one who's got the game.
Here's to the one; we all know his name.
Josef! Josef! Josef!
Gooooooo Josef!"

She pumped her arms and kicked her legs as she cheered. Blake was practically on the ground rolling in hysterics. Brook clapped and elbowed Tristan so he started clapping too. Mitchell was attached to Trina, who was smiling and trying to clap with Mitchell wrapped around her arms.

At the end of her routine, Tiffany did a high jump split, and just as everyone feared, when she came down one of her spiked heels tipped on a rock, breaking the shoe and possibly Tiffany's ankle. She let out a blood curdling scream and she crumpled to the ground, landing her butt on the same offending pointed rock. She screamed even louder.

Tristan and Josef lifted her up. She of course, glommed onto Josef and held onto his neck for dear life. Her tight short shorts exposing the huge bruise that was starting to form on her butt check.

"I gotta grab my gear," Josef hollered back as Tiffany wailed on his shoulder.

"I'll get it," Blake called out, still barely able to catch her breath from laughing so hard. "Jai, can you (gasp) help me? You too (gasp) Morgana?" Tristan helped carry a blubbering Tiffany and Brook picked up the broken heel, and then tried to keep up with the long strides of the two large guys.

Blake, Jai, and Morgana went to grab Josef's bows and arrows and bag. Blake knew his coach, who had seen and heard, like everyone else within a mile, all the commotion. Still trying to catch her breath, Blake gave Coach the whole story, he tried not to laugh too, and handed over Josef's gear.

As the trio made their way through the fields towards the medical tent, Tim came up to them. "Your sister probably just broke her ankle," Blake blurted out. "We're headed to the medical tent right now."

Who knows what Tim was going to say, but after Blake said that, all he could do was laugh. "What'd she do now?"

"Cheer squad, in stilettos, on Level III," Blake bluntly explained.

"Josef?"

"Yep."

"Ah, man!" Tim just shook his head. "I'll check on her later. You're going there now?"

"Yes."

"Alright. Thanks for the info." Tim headed off.

When they got to the medical tent, they could hear Tiffany's wails before they even entered. Tristan was standing outside by the entrance. "You'd t'ink they'd be sawin' herrr leg off, the way she's carrrrin' on," he shuddered.

"Jai, you're being so great. Let me just give this stuff to Josef and we'll go get a drink, Okay?" Blake said to her new friend.

"No problem," Jai kindly replied.

Morgana couldn't help it, she had to follow Blake inside to witness the scene for herself. The wails were as loud as sirens. Tiffany's foot was bandaged and elevated on pillows, as she lay on a flat cot just like the ones in the sleeping tent. The attending nurse was adjusting Tiffany's pillows and Brook was sitting next to her rubbing her hand.

Every time Josef tried to excuse himself, Tiffany's wails grew even louder. "Don't leave me!" she cried. "I'm in so much pain!" He looked so hopeful as Blake and Morgana approached that this could be his chance to escape.

"Josef, your coach really needs you to go back. He's got some issues with the entry form or something and they're saying it may disqualify you! He really needs you now," Blake lied.

"Oh God, Tif. I'm sorry. I gotta go. You're in good hands. It's not broken, so just get some rest and you'll be okay. I've got to go take care of this." Josef understood Blake's help and went right along. A quick exchange and Josef grabbed his gear from Blake and Morgana, and got out of there as fast as he could.

"Tiffany, we let Tim know you were here. He said he'll come by in a little bit to check on you," Blake cut Tiffany off before she could object to Josef's departure.

The nurse came over with some hot tea. "Drink it up, dear. It's belladonna tea and it'll help with the pain."

"It'll also put her ass to sleep," Blake whispered to Morgana.

"So, it's not broken?" Blake feigned concern.

"No, not broken, but swollen and bruised really badly. It's up her entire leg, from her twisted ankle to where she landed on the hard ground on her left thigh and rear." Tiffany tried to let out another wail but the nurse caught her arm and told her to finish her tea.

"So, Brook. You look like you've got this handled. Jai's waiting for us outside, so if you don't need anything else, we're gonna go," Blake excused them as Brook nodded. "What shall I tell Tristan if he's still outside?" Blake inquired.

"Oh, just let him know I'll meet him before dinner on the dance floor," Brook said

Tiffany let out a whooping cry. "The dance! I'm going to miss the dance! OH myyyyy gaawwdddd!"

"Drink your tea, sweetie," the nurse insisted.

"Got it. Let's go!" Blake turned on her heel and headed out with Morgana right behind her.

Tristan was still standing guard outside. "Did t'ey amputate't?" he joked.

"It's not even broken," Blake said exasperated. "Frickin' drama queen! Anyway, Brook said to meet her before dinner at the dance floor and you are free to go." Blake patted Tristan's large chest.

Tristan looked relieved. "Yup, that worrrrks fer me."

"I'm also gonna go," Morgana excused herself. "I'll let you explain all this to Jai and I'll see you later." She knew Blake wanted some time with Jai, who was hanging out silently witnessing all the interactions.

Morgana meandered from the medical tent back through the center of the village. Tables and chairs were being rearranged and a stage area was being set up. Banners and flags in reds, oranges, yellows, and crimsons were adding fall coloring the grounds. Some of the smaller shops and kiosks were being taken down to make room so everyone could sit together at the great feast and dance all night under the stars. People were excited and happy. Crews were bustling about, laying down carpets and setting up torches to illuminate the space once the sun set. Musicians were tuning their instruments and the weather was cooling from the warm autumn day as the sun dipped behind the mountains. Morgana decided she better head back to the girls' tent and get ready before the sinks filled up. She passed by the dress shop and peeked her head in. "Hi, Mrs. Thompson."

"Hello, Morgana. I have your dress all ready to go for you. I know those tents don't give you much room, so if you want to come back I can help you get dressed."

"Oh, that would be fantastic. I was wondering how I would do it. Thank you! I'll just go freshen up and be back here as soon as I can."

Morgana quickly hurried back to the tent. She was happy to see Trina and her dance troupe there. "Oh, you are all so beautiful!" Morgana said with admiration when Trina invited her to meet her dancers. "I was just going to grab my stuff and try to wash up before the stampede," Morgana joked to Trina.

"How's Tiffany? Was it broken?" Trina asked to get the update.

"No, but I guess it's twisted pretty badly and she's bruised up the left side from where she landed," Morgana explained.

"Oh no, is she going to miss the dinner?"

"I think so."

"That's really too bad," Trina expressed. "I'm sure she was really looking forward to it. Anyway, I'm sure you're looking forward to it too. This is my second Mabon. There's just no explaining it. You gotta let yourself feel it, and when you do, you feel this overall sense of peace and connection. Everyone together, unified in joy. It's breathtaking. You'll see. What are you wearing?"

"My dress is at Mrs. Thompson's shoppe, but it goes perfectly with these." Morgana pulled out her black cloak with the cream silk side, and carefully unwrapped the amulet necklace with the Celtic woven metal holding the heart shaped aqua blue stones.

"Oh, that's stunning!" Trina analyzed it with the eye of a professional jeweler. "You can tell someone hand crafted this with great care. The intricacies are immaculate. Where did you get it?"

"Um, actually, Josef gave it to me for my birthday," Morgana admitted.

"Wow!" Trina said stunned.

"I know. Right!" Morgana agreed. And then said bashfully, "Um, Trina, I didn't know tonight was a formal. I didn't really bring any makeup or anything," Morgana sheepishly confessed.

"Oh girl! I got you!" Trina grabbed Morgana's hand and led her over to the dance troupe's makeup station. Within twenty minutes, Trina's dancers had Morgana's hair partly braided and pin curled with long waves down the back, embellished with rosettes and curling wisps to frame her face. She was shocked when they all told her they were jealous of her hair's luscious natural beach waves. Trina did Morgana's makeup to bring out the blue in her eyes and soft rose lips. Morgana had the girls at the makeup counters do her makeup a couple times before but she always felt like a clown when they were done. But Trina lightly blended and softened the products to enhance Morgana's natural features, leaving her feeling fresh and lovely.

"Oh, thank you. Thank you so much, Trina. All of you! I feel so... so, lucky," Morgana shared with tearful eyes.

"You better believe that's waterproof makeup too. You're gonna want that on a night like this," Trina said as she gave Morgana a big squeeze.

"I have to go get my dress. I'll see you there. We're all meeting on the dance floor before dinner."

"Sounds good. I'll meet you there," Trina agreed.

Morgana loved how good she felt as she glided to Mrs. Thompson's renaissance dress shoppe with the makeshift thatched roof in the mystical makeshift medieval village.

"Oh, you're hair and makeup look lovely Morgana. Princess perfect!" Mrs. Thompson greeted her as she came in.

"Thank you so much. Trina and her belly dancing troupe really hooked me up!"

"Well, let's complete the look." Mrs. Thompson motioned to the curtained dressing room. "We have to do this in layers," she explained and they laced her up from Victorian boots to corseted top. Mrs. Thompson helped her carefully put on the amulet necklace, and although she didn't say anything, Mrs. Thompson seemed to know this piece. Lastly, they placed the cloak around Morgana's shoulders, deciding to put the black side out and the cream side in to showcase the black velvet dress.

"You are a vision, my girl," Mrs. Thompson said proudly.

"Everyone has been so nice to me, Mrs. Thompson. I just feel so..." Morgana had said lucky earlier, but now she felt deeper, more profound. "I feel so blessed. Thank you for being so kind to me. This has been the best weekend ever!"

"I'm so glad you feel it. It's wonderful to feel alignment," Mrs. Thompson smiled and then she expounded, "Alignment is when you are in the natural flow of life. Your gut, heart, and head are all in sync. Everything feels right as rain. It doesn't necessarily mean everything is perfect, but it means that you can easily navigate through life. It's like, even though you may get stuck in traffic, all your favorite songs are playing on the radio. You may not get all the green lights, but you notice a butterfly on your windshield while you're waiting at the red light. It's like being guided to the right places at the right times. It's being in a state of allowing and witnessing the beauty of life unfold for you."

Morgana felt like she was floating out of Mrs. Thompson's dress shoppe. "Is this what alignment feels like?" she asked herself. She felt blessed, lucky, excited, connected, beautiful, and peaceful, as she walked towards the meeting spot she was listing all the marvelous emotions she was feeling. She walked onto the empty dance floor area where she was the first of the group to arrive. It was softly lit by torches, as to not compete with the starry night sky. She looked up at all the stars.

They looked like they were all smiling little faces sharing this moment with her. She could see far into the vast night and she felt so big and connected, like she could just reach out and scoop up those glistening bright night diamonds and hold them in her hand by the dozens. She closed her eyes and deeply breathed in the brisk night air. It cooled her lungs with fresh delicious oxygen. She could almost taste the cool weather on her tongue. She exhaled and slowly drew in another breath to savor.

She felt like she was breathing with the timing of the sky, with the earth, and with the universe. Was she breathing or was she being breathed? There were drums in the distance, or was it her heart beat, or was she feeling the pulse of the night? She felt deep and united with the world around her. "This is what alignment feels like," she said to herself. She opened her eyes when she heard footsteps approaching.

There he was. Those exquisite deep aqua blue eyes, lit by the distant torches, were locked onto hers. His sun-kissed blond hair and golden tan skin were illuminated by the flickering firelight. He wore a long black wool jacket that had an embroidered black leather collar, and underneath he had on a black shirt, black leather pants, and black boots. He looked regal and forceful, like a dark prince, and even more gorgeous than ever. He was quite close. Held by his gaze, her heart skipped a beat, as she felt like they were transcendent in time.

He approached with his irresistible smile. "This look really suits you, Lady Morgana." He bowed as her name rolled off his tongue like silk.

"Thank you, kind sir." She played the part and curtsied back.

"I'm so glad you wore your necklace." He paused and his eyes softened as he gazed at the bejeweled amulet. "It belonged to my mother," he confessed with a light sigh and then he looked at Morgana and smiled. "You look beautiful."

A stunned Morgana ran her fingers over the delicate jewelry around her neck. She now understood the look on Mrs. Thompson's face. She had recognized the necklace, as it once belonged to her dear friend, Delilah. Morgana didn't know what to say. "Oh, I shouldn't, I shouldn't be wearing this. I didn't know," she paused. "I didn't know it belonged to your mother." Morgana was starting to panic a little.

"It's alright." He reached for her nervously shaking hand that was holding the amulet to her chest and took it in his hand. He looked her in the eyes and gently said, "You deserve to have it. I know you will take good care of it."

Morgana nodded and he tenderly kissed her hand before letting it go. Morgana didn't know what to say, she had tears coming to her eyes thinking about the enormous gift of his deceased mother's necklace bestowed upon her. She held back the tears and changed the subject. "Congratulations on your win today. It almost seemed like you commanded those arrows with your breath into their bullseye." He gave her a little knowing smirk. Then, thinking she was being clever, she added, "I'm sure Robin Hood himself couldn't have done better." Josef let out that boisterous laugh and Morgana assumed she had made an ass out of herself and ruined the moment. Luckily Mitchell and Tristan walked up and Tristan gave Josef a playful smack on the back.

"Looking good, gentlemen," Josef commented on his mates' attires.

Tristan was in his formal Scottish suit jacket and yellow tartan kilt. Mitchell posed and smoothed his jacket. "My girl and I are channeling the Arabian Knights tonight. Hello, Morgana, you are looking mighty stunning this evening," Mitchell greeted her, as did Tristan.

"The other lassies should be herrre any minute," Tristan's Scottish accent rolled. "Brrrook texted they werrre on thar way."

After a few minutes of the guys chatting about the award ceremony and how hungry they were for dinner, Trina, Brook, and Blake came across and joined them on the dance floor area. Brook was matching her man in a lovely corseted dress in the same tartan as Tristan's kilt, and had a long cloak fastened at her shoulders. Trina was beautiful in a flowing belly-baring saree and a short matching wrap jacket. Blake choose a Geisha style wrap dress that had a wide belt with pink cherry blossom flowers on it that matched the trim on her long wide sleeves and the bottom rim of her long gown with slits all the way up the sides. Jai walked up in his formal Japanese suit and was introduced to everyone again. They all headed over to find a table and got ready for the evening's festivities to begin.

There was live music playing as they found some seats. The circular tables were covered with table cloths in the colors of fall leaves, and silver chargers and goblets that reflected the flickering flames of tea light candles. The raised stage area held a long decorated table and thirteen chairs and dinner settings. Fresh fall foliage and flowers accentuated all the tables.

Despite feeling like she embarrassed herself earlier in front of Josef, Morgana was back to feeling excited and connected. She didn't know what was about to take place, but the venue was surreal, people were formally dressed in beautiful gala attire, and she felt glamorous and lucky to be there. She remembered how Josef's beautiful eyes looked at her when they were talking about his mother's necklace. He looked so dashing in his stately black suit that really showcased his sculpted facial features and, of course, his amazing deep aqua blue eyes.

"How is Tiffany?" Trina asked Brook.

"She's fine. Sleeping soundly now. They did some acupuncture and gave her some belladonna tea. She should be set till morning. She's going to be devastated that she missed tonight."

"And dancing with, or should I say dry humping, Josef all night!" Blake exploded with laughter.

Josef just shook his head at Blake. "I'm glad she'll be alright."

There was more chatter at the table until someone walked in front of the stage. The tables were situated so everyone could see, as he announced that the members of the High Council were arriving. Morgana eagerly watched as twelve members arrived, dressed exquisitely with matching long leather cloaks draped on their shoulders. Six men and six women all took their seats.

"Please rise for our beloved Grand High Chairman, Ms. Katherine Lane."

Everyone stood and cheered and clapped as Morgana's sweet little fairy godmother came out with such a commanding and dominating presence. She wore a crimson red corset gown with buttons from waist to neck, her silver hair pinned in the perfect ballerina bun. She had on an amazing black silk cloak with leather trim and cream lining wrapped around her shoulders. Morgana looked down at her own cloak, her birthday present from Ms. Lane, and while it wasn't identical to the magnificent one Ms. Lane was wearing, it was quite similar. The Grand High Chairman walked on the stage in front of the long dining table.

The crowd was still cheering and clapping even though now she was smiling and waving her hands to quiet the group.

"My beloved friends!" the beloved Grand High Chairman began to speak, which silenced the masses. "Please be seated." Everyone took to their chairs. "Tonight we are here to honor and give thanks for life, for our mother Earth, our universal friends, and our connection with All that Is." There were sporadic cheers from some tables. Ms. Lane continued, "We are all here on the leading edge of existence to learn and to grow. We are all here to evolve and to share and to align. We are all in this together. Blessed are all those who share in this time space. Let us give thanks for the earth and ground that we walk on, that grows our food, our trees, grasses, and flowers. Let us give thanks for the air that we breathe, that gives us life. Let us give thanks for the sun, stars, and moon that shine down on us, sending us love from that which is beyond." Ms. Lane held her hands towards the sky. "The hours of daylight and darkness are equal at the fall equinox. The sun will begin to decline in its power and the darkest of nights will gradually become longer-lasting. Thanks are given for this waning sunlight and the resulting final harvest. Respect is paid to the approaching dark of winter. The completed crops are celebrated along with all the efforts put forth. A farewell to the end of summer is declared. This autumn equinox, also known as Mabon, who was a Welsh God, is particularly a celebration of harvesting vineyards and wine. It is also associated with the Apple Harvest, as apples are viewed as symbols of life renewed. It was also considered by the Druids as a time to honor aging deities and the spirit world. They would give offerings of drinks to the trees as a way to honor the God of the Forest. My friends, we join today, as a way to honor All that Is and all who are here in this time space. Today we also reflect on the fruits of our personal harvest, such as accomplishment on our jobs, our families, and just dealing with every day stresses and strains. Let us raise our glass and give thanks and feel gratitude." Everyone lifted their silver goblets and toasted to the words of the beloved Grand High Chairman.

Morgana looked around. Some people had tears in their eyes. Some were holding tight to their loved ones. Some were looking to the sky. Some were looking down. But all of them were softly smiling and feeling the rapturous joy of the evening. It was so peaceful and calm. Tristan had his big arms wrapped around Brook and she was snuggled up in his chest. They both had their eyes closed, but seemed to be breathing in unison. Mitchell and Trina were holding hands and looking at the sky. Blake held Jai's hand, and then reached for Morgana's, who delightedly reached back. Josef also reached for Morgana's other hand and then Trina's. Soon the circle of good friends at the table were all holding hands and just basking in the night air, enjoying the company, the starry night sky, and All that Is that enveloped them. Morgana felt amazing. Everyone at all the tables had their hands linked.

"May we all be blessed with an abundance of joy and happiness. Thank you all for coming tonight." Ms. Lane, the beloved Grand High Chairman, walked to her chair in the center of the long table, six members on her left, six on her right, and took her seat. The crowd cheered.

The announcer returned in front of the stage and unrolled the scroll and began to read:

"It is said that our ancestors would join together on this night to give thanks to heaven and earth, the sun in the sky, and all the glory in the kingdom on earth. We carry on the tradition of connection and unity as we gather together in love and friendship from all parts of the world. We share our skills, our wares, and our foods. We celebrate each other. We celebrate life. We celebrate joy. And we are filled with gratitude. Thank you all for being here tonight.

In the tradition of skills, we hold tournaments to showcase those who have honored their talents and tonight we award our champions. In the caber toss exposition of might, strength, and control, let us call forth Tristan MacLeod."

Tristan got up from the table with hoots and hollers from his friends. He walked to the stage and stood next to the announcer.

"In the samurai demonstration of warrior nobility, let us call forth Jai Watanabe." Jai stealthily got up and joined Tristan at the stage. Blake squealed and the others cheered.

"In the archery exhibition of skill and mastery, let us call forth Josef McClellan." The girls at the table all squealed and cheered, making him blush. Mitchell, the only guy left at the table, squealed the loudest, making Josef laugh as he made his way to the stage.

The other champion names of the tournaments were all called forth to the stage. Ms. Lane, the Grand High Chairman, came down from her seat and put a medal around each of the champion's necks and shook their hands. As the awarded champions made their way back to the tables, the Grand High Chairman announced, "Let the feast begin!"

The music started up and silver food trays, filled with meats, potatoes, and tons of fresh vegetables, bread and cheeses were served to the center of the tables. Silver goblets were filled with wine or water. Large steins were filled with meade and ale. It was all so regal, fun, and fantasy. Morgana was lost in the thrill of it all. Her table mates were talking and laughing. The food was divine. The air was fresh, and the stars were smiling down. When the meal was done and being cleared away the band started playing a sweet melodious tune.

"They're playing our song, love." Mitchell was the first to get up and take Trina's hand and led her to the dance floor. Tristan and Brook, and then Jai and Blake, followed.

"Well, I guess you're stuck with me. May I have this dance, Lady Morgana?" Josef presented his hand.

"I don't know how to dance like this," she squeaked out, her heart beating in her throat at the thought of trying to make her feet move correctly while being held by Josef.

"It's easy. Everyone does the same steps. I will show you the way." He was gentle and caring, and his smile was irresistible.

Please work for me! Morgana silently prayed to her nervously shaking knees and her jelly legs, as Josef led her to the dance area idealistically lit with torches around the perimeter. The other dancers were already lining up in two rows, with men on the left, and the ladies on the right. Josef found a spot between Tristan and Mitchell, setting Morgana in between Brook and Trina.

Morgana leaned over to Brook and whispered, "What do I do?"

Brook whispered back, "It's real easy. A couple steps forward and a couple steps back, then they twirl us. But it's not about the steps, they are easy, repetitive, and fun. The point is about losing yourself in the rhythm."

And it was! Morgana picked it up quickly. Brook was right, repetitive and rhythmic with the drums beating in time. And Morgana was lost in the feeling. Josef was strong. She loved being in his arms. There were probably a hundred couples in sync with their footsteps and the drums. It was sensational! Everyone was having a great time, laughing, dancing, and soaking up the feeling of the universe.

"Hey, where's Blake?" Morgana asked.

"She and Jai are probably off somewhere around," Brook replied.

I can't believe they are missing this, Morgana thought to herself. They all danced for hours. It was almost meditative with the steps, and the drumming, and everyone in unison. Morgana felt like she was dancing with the night sky, lost in the tranquil blue of Josef's eyes. It was magical!

At midnight the band signaled the end of the night's festivities. Tristan and Brook walked away together to say good night, as did Mitchell and Trina.

"Thank you for dancing with me," Josef said to Morgana. "I love that you smell like almond cookies." He took in a deep breath of her. Morgana remembered the organic scent she had picked out earlier.

"Thank you for being a good teacher," Morgana replied. Then asked, "This really is a magical place, isn't it?"

"The magic is the feeling from within you. And when we let it flow through us, nights like this are definitely the enchanted effect," Josef explained with a soft smile.

Morgana closed her eyes and took a long deep breath to engage all of her senses with the feeling of the night. She opened her eyes and stared at the sky, basking in its twinkling light. She thought Josef was looking up too, but she was surprised to find him looking at her. She looked at him and smiled. For the first time, she didn't feel so nervous standing next to him.

"You are beautiful. That look really does suit you." He reached over, lifting her chin gently with his fingertips and leaned in to softly and delicately kiss her lips. "Till the 'morrow, my sweet Lady Morgana." He backed away and bowed slightly. She smiled and did a small curtsy.

She felt like she floated back to the girls' tent and fell asleep with a big smile on her face.

The next morning the girls all packed up their stuff and made their way back to Brook's car. All the makeshift thatched cottages were already being taken down and returned to their normal metal trailers. Tristan and the guys had left already. "Tristan had to work today so they left pretty early," Brook explained as they loaded their suitcases in the trunk of her white Audi convertible. Morgana climbed into the soft leathery backseat.

Blake was regaling Brook of her evening with Jai. "Learning the ways of the warrior," she said dramatically as she put her hands together in prayer position and bowed her head. Morgana was only half listening to their conversation as she reminisced about her own magical evening under the stars.

"Thanks for the ride!" Morgana waved good-bye as Brook carefully backed out of the inclined driveway. She stood there waving long after they had gone, as she looked at the house across the street. Ms. Lane didn't seem to be home yet, so she grabbed her suitcase and made her way back to her room still floating on a cloud from the enchanted weekend and dancing all night with Prince Charming.

hapter Eight

Connecting with Loved Ones

IT HAD BEEN two weeks since Mabon before Morgana could make it over to Ms. Lane's. She was dying to talk to her about the magical feeling she had experienced. She raced home, skidding her tires on the inclined driveway. She barely unbuckled her seatbelt before ejecting herself from the car, leaving everything behind, save for her car keys. She practically ran down the driveway, across the street, next to the old, deep maroon Cadillac Deville, down the walkway to the recessed alcove with fresh fall flowers and the sweetest sign: "Blessed are those who enter here." A happy little ghost was peeking out from behind the flowers and there was a "Happy Halloween" doormat positioned in front of the partly opened door. Morgana knocked as she entered the delicious smelling home.

"Come in, dear!" Ms. Lane's voice called from the kitchen where happy instrumental music was playing.

Morgana made her way to the large marble kitchen island and ran to give her sweet little old fairy godmother a big hug. "Hi! I've missed you so much!"

"Hi, dear. It's good to see you, too." Ms. Lane gave her a big squeeze back.

"It smells yummy in here. What are you baking?" Morgana sniffed her way around.

Ms. Lane set out a batch of green sugar cookies. "They're witches fingers." A laughing Ms. Lane handed Morgana an oblong cookie with knife slits representing knuckles and slivered almonds for fingernails.

"I'll get you my pretty!" Morgana wagged the severed cookie finger at Ms. Lane in her best wicked witch voice. They both laughed while Ms. Lane poured some hot tea and they settled into the sunken living room decorated with happy little Halloween ghosts and small bouquets of black flowers.

"How's everything going, my dear? I haven't seen you in a while."

"School sucks. My job is pointless. I'm just trying to get through."

"Well, that's a nice positive attitude." Ms. Lane laughed at her dramatic young friend.

"Alright, I don't technically mean all that, but I kinda do," Morgana confessed with a mouth full of a delectable witch knuckle. "Ms. Lane, I felt sooo amazing at Mabon. I felt the breathing of the universe. I felt so alive and loved. And then I go back to school and I feel completely depleted again. And by the way, Ms. Grand High Chairman – you didn't tell me you were like some fancy grand master! You're a badass!"

Ms. Lane chortled as she sipped her tea. "I am honored by the position they blessed me with. I love being a part of the action. So you enjoyed yourself at the festival?"

"Oh!" Morgana dramatically threw herself back in her chair. "It was magical! I felt so blessed. Everyone was so nice to me. Hey, why didn't you tell me it was a formal affair?" Morgana sat back up straight.

"If I had told you, would you have been excited or apprehensive?" Ms. Lane inquired.

Morgana remembered her experiences with formal dances. "Um, okay, maybe that makes sense."

"And if I had told you it was a formal, you probably would have packed a dress you already owned, right?" Morgana shoved another piece of knuckle in her mouth, nodding sheepishly. "I thought if you didn't know, you would be more open to asking and receiving help. I hoped you would be able to share in the whole experience of the evening and not be closed off. I knew my friends would take good care of you." Ms. Lane smiled.

"Well, okay. I'll let you off the hook because you were so right, on all accounts. I definitely was open to help and I got better than I could ever hope for. Did you see my dress?" Morgana drifted into the memory of dancing the night away with Josef and the sweet kiss at the end, which sent her reeling even though it was just a small kiss. Brook had mentioned on the ride home that day that it was Josef's turn to visit the farms in Italy, as they both were learning the ins and outs of the family business and he would be gone for several weeks after Mabon. She knew he still wasn't back in town yet. "I truly felt connected there. It was peaceful yet exciting. Everything was delicious and amazing. I can't wait 'til next year!" Morgana said blissfully.

"We celebrate Samhain at the end of the month," Ms. Lane informed her.

"What?" What is that?" Morgana got excited. "Is it like Mabon?"

"We are hosting it at the same place, but it's not a formal festival like Mabon. Samhain is more of a celebration of those who transitioned to the other side. We take the time when the veil between dimensions is believed to be lifted the most, and connect with our ancestors and dearly departed. It's still a fun night with bonfires and connection," Ms. Lane detailed.

"Can I go?" Morgana begged.

"Of course, my dear. You are always welcome to all the events."

"All? How many are there?"

"There are eight throughout the year. After Samhain at the end of October, we have the Winter Solstice in December. That one is another formal. The Winter Wonderland Ball, we call it. Everyone wears white and when we all dance we look like flittering snowflakes. It's one the of oldest winter celebrations, celebrating the rebirth of the sun and the beginning of winter."

Morgana was filled with excitement at the thought of two more events like the one she experienced at Mabon. "And you are sure I can go?" Morgana pleaded.

"Well, I'll have to check with the High Council. Oh wait, that's me," Ms. Lane teased. "Of course you can go," she said with a wink and ate her crooked witch's finger cookie.

On a Saturday afternoon, Morgana jumped in her car and headed out towards the secluded magical lot beneath the stars protected by the surrounding mountains. This time Ms. Lane swore to her it wasn't a formal, but did suggest she bring her black and cream cloak, and possibly the amulet necklace.

"He told me it was his mother's," Morgana had shared with Ms. Lane.

"I wanted him to be the one who told you."

Morgana decided to wear her Victorian style lace up boots with some jeans, and an oversized cowl neck sweater to showcase the ornate aqua blue stone amulet around her neck.

As she got out of her car, parked at the base of the majestic mountains, she took in the new scene. Last time she was here it was a thatched roof medieval village with pubs, dress shoppes, perfumeries, and café kiosks. This time there were thirteen small bonfires illuminating the area. A couple small kiosks were set up that sold beverages, like coffee and hot chocolate, and snacks, but nothing like the huge festival of Mabon. The air was cooling quickly as the sun set behind the mountains, but as she walked through the bonfires she felt their warmth. Blankets were spread out on the ground with groups of two or more people stretched out on them. Some blankets had solitary people on them who seemed to be mediating or praying. Morgana knew that Brook and Tristan weren't going to make it tonight. Blake was going to see if Jai wanted to come, but his martial arts studio had tournaments all weekend, so Blake went with him instead. Morgana wasn't too concerned if anyone would show, she liked getting to know her new friends, but she was fine being alone and just wanted to come back and feel this sacred place again. She stopped by one of the kiosks to see what they had. They were handing out little mini cauldrons hanging from a trio of sticks, only about twelve inches high.

"What are they?" she asked the helper.

"They're message senders. You put a tea light inside the cauldron and write down a wish, a prayer, or any message you want to send to the other side and out into the universe." The helper pointed to a stack of parchment paper cut into the size of post-it-notes. "And then you burn it in the cauldron to release it out to the cosmos," the helper explained.

"How sweet," Morgana said. "Are you selling them? I don't see prices."

"We loan these out for tonight. I do have ones for sale. Some people bring their own."

"Oh, can I use one?"

"Of course." The friendly helper showed her the ones to pick from and afterwards she made her way to a nice secluded blanket that overlooked all the bonfires. She wrapped her cloak around her and set to watch the last of the sun light fade out.

"May I join you?" his silky voice spoke from behind. She turned to find Josef holding two cups of hot chocolate his hands.

"Hi!" she replied surprised. "Please, of course, sit down."

"Would you mind?" He handed her the drinks and removed a strapped satchel from his shoulder and then proceeded to pull out two cushions. "You're going to want this." He handed her one of the square foam cushions, then sat down on the other. He also pulled out a small notebook and pen and set it next to the mini cauldron. "May I?" He offered to light the candle with a lighter from his satchel.

"Please." Morgana was quite surprised that he was there, she thought he was in Italy, and that he found her out here on a blanket.

"I saw you at the cauldron kiosk, so I thought I would get us some hot chocolate since you already got the cauldron."

"Good thinking. Thank you. Ms. Lane said this was different than Mabon, and she wasn't kidding." Morgana made conversation as she sipped on her hot chocolate after handing Josef back his cup.

"Tonight is about connecting to our ancestors or family members that have transitioned. It's a personal experience, but we gather together to join like vibrations. Some years they host bigger soirées, but this year we all voted for a smaller Samhain and a bigger winter solstice celebration," Josef explained.

"Ms. Lane told me about the Winter Wonderland Ball and everyone dresses in white like dancing snowflakes." Morgana giggled at the sweet image in her mind.

"It's definitely a sight to behold," Josef agreed with a smile. "I'm really glad that you are here tonight," he said as he looked over the bonfires. "I usually come alone with my notebook to talk and connect with my parents."

Oh, God, Morgana thought, *tonight is about connecting with loved ones who have transitioned – as in those who have died.* Josef's parents were both dead, or on the other side. She had come here to connect with the stars, like she did during Mabon. He was here to connect with his departed parents.

"Oh, Josef. I. I'm so sorry." Morgana didn't know what to say.

"They died eight years ago when I was just fifteen. I was so mad and devastated and guilty all at the same time. I didn't know what to do. Luckily, Uncle Jackson and Aunt Cindy took me in. But I was a mess. I was rude and disruptive for several years. I got in a lot trouble, almost got kicked out of school. I felt like I had lost it all and like I had nothing left to live for. Uncle Jackson is a very patient man, but he was at his wits end with me. I spent the summers with Aunt Katherine, the Grand High Chairman of the Council. They all hoped she would have better luck with me. She saw I had all this rage and she made me," he laughed, "garden and mow yards. It did get me out of my head and it definitely got me out of her hair. The summer after I barely finished high school and didn't have any plans for my future, Aunt Katherine sent me out to mow the neighbors' yards. I mowed my way down one side of the street and worked my way back up the other side. It was terribly hot that day and I was feeling extra angry. I was mad at my parents for dying. Mad at Uncle Jackson for sending me off. Mad at Aunt Katherine for making me mow people's yards. But mostly mad at myself for being mad at the world. I was on the last house of the day and almost done with the backyard, when the most adorable young lady came out of the sliding glass door carrying a tall glass of lemonade on a silver tray." Morgana felt her cheeks starting to burn with embarrassment. Josef continued, "I saw her spill a little lemonade as she came out the door, but I pretended not to notice. She made her way to the lawn and caught her heel in the soft ground and fell, drenching herself in sticky, icy, lemonade. I could tell she wasn't hurt when she sat up and inventoried herself. I literally couldn't stop myself and I laughed. I laughed the hardest I had laughed in the three years since my parents' death. I laughed from the depths of my soul. Morgana, you brought me back to life that day. It was the first time I had any sense of relief since they had died. I felt so guilty that they had died. I was lost and didn't think there was any point to life. Then I saw the most adorable, kind of pitiful, yes, but precious look on your face and I felt the anger melting away. As I laughed I felt relief from the guilt and anger and sadness. I'm still working on some issues, even to this day, but it's because of you Morgana, that I'm here at all."

Morgana couldn't believe what she was hearing. The day that she had always felt was the most humiliating day of her life, was the day that brought life back to this most wonderful human being.

"I never thought I would laugh again. You helped bring me back to the land of the living. I said, you deserve my mother's necklace and that's why." Morgana touched the amulet at her neck. "My father made it for her. He was a very talented artist. The three stones represented the three of us. And the aquamarine diamonds matched her eyes. I guess they match mine, too. We were so happy. My parents were so in love and I was the apple of their eye. We did everything together. One of my favorite things to do was see the miniature ponies." Josef reached into his bag and pulled out the little figurine pony that Morgana had given him. "I was caught off guard when you gave it to me. But it's perfect and I love it. I brought it here tonight to show it off." He smiled with a little laugh.

Again, Morgana thought she had totally blown it that day she gave him the figurine. Her mind was soaking it all in. His laughter at her brought him back to life, so much so that he gave her his mother's necklace that his father made for her to represent their perfect family. She couldn't help herself, she started crying. "I didn't know," was all she could say.

He wrapped his big strong arm around her shoulder "It's alright. It's all right little one," he soothed. He reached into his bag with his free hand and brought out some tissues.

She started laughing through the tears. "What all do you have in that magic carpet bag?"

He laughed. "I try to come here prepared. It's a very powerful evening." He paused, then added, "Are you okay?"

"Yes, I was just overwhelmed with emotions." She took a sip of her hot chocolate. "I have relived that day when I spilled the lemonade down my dress over and over as the worst day of my life. But now, in a way, it was the best day of my life because I helped someone. I didn't know that I helped you, until now, but it's funny how things work."

"Synchronicity!" they both said together and laughed.

"Is there anything you would like to say to the ancestors, or anyone?" Josef offered a page from his notebook.

Morgana showed him the small square piece of parchment she got from the cauldron kiosk. "I'm not sure what I would say. Are you really suggesting that we can, umm, talk to the dead?" Morgana stumbled over her words.

"Energy can neither be created nor destroyed, but rather, it transforms from one form to another. Science has proven that at our very core we are energy, and we're made up from the same material and atoms as everything in the universe. Everything is all just energy in different forms. We are energy. These mountains are energy. The stars are energy. When you focus energy you can change it from a lightning bolt to a desk lamp. We harness energy from wind and water to power our cities. The candle burns energy into the atmosphere. What is the energy at our core? Some would call that our soul, our spirit, our energetic body. Some traditions call energy Chi or Prana. So if energy can never die and can only change form, then when we leave these physical bodies our energy must transition, it moves on, but the essence of that person still remains. When you focus on the energy of souls or spirits, you can connect with them and harness their energy. Some people are better at focusing on transitioned energy than others. Samhain nights make it easier for those of us who are still practicing," Josef explained.

"Why tonight? I always thought it was just about trick or treating and Halloween candy," Morgana joked.

"Many traditions celebrate a day of remembrance to pay their respects and receive guidance and inspiration around this time. All Saints' Day, or All Hallows, on November 1st commemorated Christian saints and martyrs. All Souls' Day on November 2nd was a remembrance for all souls of the dead. In Mexico, the indigenous customs of honoring the dead at this time of year, *Dia de los Muertos*, in early November, is a multi-day holiday that focuses on gatherings of family and friends to pray for and remember friends and family members who have died and help support their spiritual journey. The ancient pagans celebrated this holiday as New Year's. Samhain means 'summers end' and marks the end of summer, the end of harvest, and the onset of winter. Samhain shares the ancient spiritual practice of remembering and paying respects to the dead with these related religious holidays. Samhain's long association with death and the dead reflects Nature's rhythms. In many places, Samhain coincides with the end of the growing season. Vegetation dies back with killing frosts, and therefore, literally, death is in the air. This contributes to the ancient notion that at Samhain, the veil is thin between the world of the living and the realm of the dead and this facilitates contact and communication. For those who have lost loved ones in the past year, Samhain rituals can be an opportunity to bring closure to the grieving and to further adjust to their loved ones being in the Otherworld by spiritually communing with them. They would have huge feasts with enormous bonfires. It was also during this festival that they viewed a time as 'no time.' Everyone had to be so chore oriented in those days, so 'no time' was a time that they could screw around and play. Probably the precursor to today's trick-or-treating," Josef commented. "So, out here, our tradition is to write your message on the parchment, and as you write you are infusing your energy to the question or whatever you put down. Then when you burn it in the candle, its energy is released to where it needs to go. 'Cuz even though they are always available to us, they do have their own lives, ya know." Josef smiled.

"I'm sure there are many social functions that they are attending. Lots of cloud parties and such," Morgana quipped.

"Exactly!" Josef agreed with good humor. "But I will say, I bring my notebook out here on this night, and I feel like I can hear them speak to me. I write it down so I can read it over again later. I do this other times too, but I know that sometimes I'm not as focused as I am on Samhain."

"I know I felt connected to something during Mabon. Maybe it was those who have crossed over. It's nice to think that they are still with us," Morgana said as she looked out over the small bonfires. She could hear whispers and voices from the others around them. *Or was it voices from the other side*, she thought to herself. She stared into the flames of the bonfires and watched their glowing hot dance. The smoke rose from the fires and connected to the night sky, almost like a rope, or a beanstalk linking the two worlds. Morgana wondered what it would be like to climb up and how far she could go, and who would greet her as she traveled to the other side? She was lost in thought and her eyes softened their gaze. She was transfixed on the fire and she could almost see spirits dancing around it. The spirits of our ancestors and those who came out tonight to play in the 'no-time' of the earthly realm. She reached for her pen and scribbled a note on her piece of parchment: "Blessed are we sharing in this time space. Thank you all for coming." She set it in the mini cauldron and watched its essence go up in flame.

Josef wrote something down in his notebook and tore half the page out and lit it in the cauldron. Morgana moved the cushion she was sitting on and laid down using it as a pillow, and looked up into the sky. Josef did the same. They lay there basking in the energy of the night, in the energy of the majestic mountains, and in the energy of the love from the spiritual ancestors dancing all around them.

*C*hapter Nine

Focusing On the Feeling

MORGANA WAS NOW working at the perfume kiosk in the middle of the mall. She had been there a few weeks and she liked it better being out in the open, plus she no longer had to deal with the makeup counter girls. She also liked that during the slow hours, they said it would be okay if she did her homework, as long as she was friendly and helpful to customers. Her schedule was pretty full, classes from 8 a.m. to 5 p.m. and then work from 6 p.m. to 11 p.m. Plus she worked some hours on the weekends. She was exhausted but kept pushing herself so she could "just get out of there." The worst part was it left no time to see Ms. Lane, who usually had her committee meetings on the weekends.

Morgana really wanted to talk to her about her experience at Samhain and how she and Josef spent the evening talking about his parents and ancestors and other ones who transitioned. Josef had told her how Ms. Lane showed him to focus his attention to connect with his parents and that's when he was able to paint the gazebo roof with the little vignettes of things he did with them and of things he wished he could have done with them. Morgana was feeling more comfortable around Josef. He still made her heart skip a beat and the butterflies in her stomach flurry, and she could get lost in his eyes, but at least she didn't slobber all over herself. And now she knew that his laugh, that boisterous laugh that haunted her, was actually his first laugh in the years since his parents had transitioned. He said it was Morgana who brought him back to life. She was glad she tripped that day, now that she knew what a profound effect it had had on him.

Morgana's phone beeped, a text from Ms. Lane:

ML: The kids are all coming over for Thanksgiving. Can you make it too? (Turkey emoji)

M: Would love to!! (Heart)(heart)(heart)

ML: Great! Dinner is at 5.

M: Can I bring anything?

ML: Just your wonderful self (smiley)

M: You got it!

ML: See you next week!

Morgana was so excited. She couldn't wait. She had Thursday and Friday off school and didn't have to work until 6 p.m. Friday evening. *I will definitely bring something for my hostess*, Morgana thought to herself, *but what?*

"Am I interrupting?" Morgana was startled. It was Cole, the jerk date that almost got into a fight at the pool hall and was mad at her for not kissing him at the end of the night. He was standing there with two blended ice coffees and a pitiful look on his face. "Forgiveness?" He offered her one of the frozen beverages. "I am sorry I was such an ass. I guess I was having a bad day and I really took it out on our date."

"You were pretty crazy," Morgana stated, eyeing him up and down.

"I know. I have no excuse. But now you're working in direct line between me and my coffee, so I figured I better make amends before I go into withdrawals from my frozen caffeine addiction."

Morgana had to laugh. He was polite and funny, and asking for forgiveness. "Okay, truce. But only because I understand your addiction." She greedily took the sweet frozen chocolatey heaven and took a huge sip.

"You work here now? Moving up in the world!" Cole joked.

"I know! I get my own director's chair and everything," Morgana jested. He was nice and friendly. Clearly he was having an awful day on their date because this guy was smiling and happy and talkative, not at all like he was that night. Morgana decided she would let him off the hook. *Because, who knows*, she thought to herself, *my vibrations may have had something to do with it, too.*

It was nice having Cole there at night, they would park next to each other so they could walk together to their cars. Plus, whenever he got a break or lunch he would always ask if she wanted anything. Morgana didn't really get to take breaks, so he kept feeding her frozen chocolate caffeine addiction.

On Thanksgiving Day, Morgana was trying to figure out what to bring to Ms. Lane's house as a hostess gift. She knew Cole had to work that day so she headed to the mall to see him and this time she was able to feed his addiction. He was happy to see her and gratefully accepted the beverage.

"Do you have any ideas what I can get the sweetest old lady, who has absolutely everything, as a hostess gift?" She asked his opinion.

"Flowers?" he suggested at first.

"She grows her own," Morgana replied.

"Hmmm. What does she like?" Cole asked.

"Lots of stuff. She's very worldly, you know."

"Well, there's that world market store. Maybe you can find something unique for her in there."

"Cole, you're a genius. Thank you! Are you working tomorrow?" Morgana asked.

"Not till Saturday," Cole responded.

"Okay, see you then. Happy Thanksgiving!" Morgana gave her friend a quick hug and headed to the world market store. As she walked down the mall looking at the different stores, one caught her eye. It had beautiful porcelain figurines in it. There was one of a dancing Fall Fairy with exquisite details, and a delightfully cheerful smile. She looked at the price, *$100! Oh, geez! Oh, well, Ms. Lane is totally worth it.* Luckily, there was a sale and Morgana got 30% off. She was happy about that, but really happy about her gift. Ms. Lane didn't have that one. Morgana had it gift wrapped and headed home to get ready for Thanksgiving dinner.

In her Victorian lace up boots, jeans, and a black silk top with a sweetheart neckline to proudly display her treasured amulet necklace, Morgana wrapped her black and cream cloak around her shoulders, grabbed Ms. Lane's hostess gift, and made her way down the incline driveway, across the street to the sweetest house on the block. Josef's Mustang was parked on the street, as well as a silver BMW X5M, a big black lifted Chevy truck, and a white Toyota 4Runner. She rounded the bushes to the sidewalk into the recessed alcove and knocked on the heavy wooden door. It was Mrs. Meadow, Brook and Blake's mom, who answered the door. Cindy Meadow gave Morgana a big welcoming hug as she stepped inside.

"Hi, Mrs. Meadow. Happy Thanksgiving!" Morgana surmised that one of the cars must belong to the Meadows, probably the new silver BMW X5M. Morgana made her way around the pony wall and passed the smiling faces of the cute figurines. She looked closely to make sure Ms. Lane didn't already have the fall fairy that she carried in the giftwrapping. Then Morgana's heart sank. Sitting at the huge, marble table, beautifully decorated with harvests cornucopias, was Tiffany, leaning on Josef as he was trying to talk to Mitchell and Tristan.

"Hi, everyone," Morgana said.

Trina got up from the table and gave her a big hug. "Happy Thanksgiving!"

Mitchell and Josef were on the other side of the table backed against the wall, and even if Josef wanted to get up, he was blocked in. "Hi, Morgana." All he could do was smile, almost apologetically.

Mr. Meadow came over to greet Morgana and take her cloak. As he helped her remove it, Morgana was directly facing Tiffany and Josef. Morgana heard Tiffany gasp, but just then Brook was at Morgana's side giving her a big hug. "Happy Thanksgiving. So glad you could make it!"

"Hi, Brook!" Morgana hugged her back.

The heavy cranberry damask velvet curtains were tied back, exposing the wall of windows that looked out on the enchanted secret garden lit with twinkling white and orange lights and mini lanterns hanging from small shepherd hooks. Blake and Jai waved from outside as Morgana walked into the kitchen where Ms. Lane was putting the final touches of love on her dinner.

"Hi, Ms. Lane. Happy Thanksgiving!" Morgana's sweet fairy godmother was wearing cream Victorian lace up boots with a matching long cream skirt and a soft orange high button silk blouse with an antique diamond and pearl pendant broach pinned at the collar. Her silver hair was pinned up in its signature ballerina bun.

"Hello, my dear. You look stunning."

Morgana gave her a huge hug. "I love your broach! It's magnificent!"

"Thank you, dear. I've had it forever," she said with a wink.

"I got you a little something." Morgana handed her the appealing gift bag.

Ms. Lane carefully removed the happy fall fairy from her Styrofoam bed and held the delicate creature in her hands. "Oh Morgana, I love it. She's a beauty!" Ms. Lane's eyes shined. Morgana was so pleased she was able to get something Ms. Lane liked.

"I know right where to put her." Ms. Lane moved a couple things around on the white bookcase and put Morgana's fall fairy in a prominent spot in the center. "I love it! Thank you, dear. You didn't have to do that." Ms. Lane gave her young friend another big hug.

Then Ms. Lane made the announcement, "Let's gather round everyone. Soup's on!" They gathered around the huge marble kitchen island full of mouthwatering foods: mashed potatoes, candied yams, stuffing, broccoli and cheese casserole, fresh baked rolls, cranberry sauce, three bean salad, green salad, and a gravy boat, all displayed in ivory dishes with a gold leaf design, and surrounding a huge twenty-pound turkey. It was a beautiful display. They all held hands and Ms. Lane spoke, "We join together to give thanks to All that Is, to everyone here tonight, and for this bountiful meal."

Mr. Meadow added, "We give thanks to our beloved hostess, Aunt Katherine. Thank you for having us all here and cooking this fantastic feast." Everyone agreed.

Morgana piped up, surprising herself, "Blessed are we who have the privilege to be in your life, Ms. Lane." Everyone agreed, except Tiffany, who agreed with the words, but not necessarily with the speaker.

"Enough of all that," Ms. Lane said graciously. "Let's eat!" Everyone definitely agreed on that! They all dished out their plates then sat at the huge marble dining table. Morgana sat next to Trina and was very happy when Ms. Lane sat down on her other side.

"Oh, my gosh! Ms. Lane this is so good!" Morgana cried out.

"You definitely still got it, Aunt Katherine," Jackson complimented. "You should have seen Mom and Aunt Katherine cooking up a storm back in the day. It was a flurry of flavors and aromas. You couldn't tell where one sister ended and the other began. Jai, you would almost swear they were samurais with steak knives and wooden spoons." Everyone laughed.

The dinner conversation was happy and light. Tristan, who thoughtfully sat closest to the food, was on thirds as the others finished up firsts and seconds. "Oh, don't forget dessert," Ms. Lane announced.

"Forrrget desserrrt? I would neverrrr do such an atrrrrocity," Tristan rolled in his Scottish accent making everyone laugh.

"I invited your mother, Morgana, but she said she had to work tonight. I promised her a plate," Ms. Lane shared.

"Okay, I will be sure to fix her one. And maybe some extra for me," Morgana joked.

"You better hurry before Tristan finishes it off!" Brook teased her man.

"Hey, I'm a grrrowin' lad!" Tristan rolled.

"There's tea and coffee, too, if any one desires," the thoughtful hostess offered.

"I think I would like a brandy," Jackson announced. "Anyone else?" He went to the china buffet table under the wall of smiling porcelain figurines and pulled out a crystal decanter with matching highball glasses, pouring several for the takers around the table. Mitchell and Josef took theirs and held them up to toast Ms. Lane for a fantastic dinner. Everyone held up their cups or glasses and cheered.

After a bit, Mrs. Meadow went into the kitchen and started cleaning up with Ms. Lane. The guys were sipping their brandy and talking football. Morgana got up to clear her plate and walked by the big sliding glass door as Jai opened it from outside for him and Blake to come in. Morgana heard Tiffany's shrill voice say, "Who does she think she is wearing his mother's…." Blake shut the door, rolling her eyes.

"We're going to go, Mom. Aunt Katherine, thank you so much! Everything was amazing. Good to see you Morgana. Bye, Dad!" Blake and Jai said their good-byes and went out the front door.

Morgana helped clean up while making some left over plates for her mom and took some pie for herself. "I really can taste the love, Ms. Lane. Thank you for inviting me." She gave her a soft hug.

"Are you leaving?" Ms. Lane was sort of surprised.

"Yes, I'm totally exhausted. This was my first day off in weeks. I think I'm just going to take my pie and watch a movie at home."

"Okay, dear."

"I don't have to work until tomorrow night. Any chance I can come over some time tomorrow?"

"Would you prefer breakfast or lunch?"

"Umm, better make it noon for lunch?"

"Sounds good, dear. See you tomorrow."

Morgana took her plates and stuck her head out through the sliding glass door to say good night to Brook and Tiffany. "Oh, you're leaving?" Brook asked.

"Ya, I'm beat. Too much turkey." Morgana hugged Brook good-bye with her free hand and then waved to Tiffany, who seemed to sarcastically pretend to wave back.

Tristan and Mitchell flanked Josef around the large marble table. He tried to get up but Morgana just waved good-bye. Jackson did get up and helped her with her cloak. He said good night and closed the heavy wooden door behind her as she made her way out.

Her house clock said 9:30 p.m. when she got home and curled up in bed with her piece of pumpkin pie in front of her favorite Thanksgiving movie. About an hour later she heard car doors closing and sneaked a peek out her window. Josef drove off in his Mustang. Mr. and Mrs. Meadow got into their BMW X5M. The big Chevy truck was Tristan's. He held the doors open for Brook and Tiffany, who was in the rear passenger's seat. The Toyota 4Runner was Jai's. Morgana tried not to care, but secretly was glad Tiffany didn't leave with Josef. She fell asleep after her movie ended and slept in the next day.

At 11:55 a.m. she walked down her inclined driveway, across the street, to the recessed alcove with the heavy wooden door. The clicking of the Victorian lace up kitten heels grew louder and then the door swung open.

"Good afternoon, dear!" It had been quite a while since Morgana got to see her beloved fairy godmother, except for the previous night, but it was different with a crowd of people. They walked into the kitchen, Morgana noticing the fall fairy prominently displayed on the white bookcase in the center of the room. "I made turkey sandwiches and leftover mashed potatoes and stuffing." Ms. Lane handed Morgana a plate.

"I'm surprised you have leftovers."

"I know my crowd. It'll be a cold day when Tristan MacLeod can out eat my cooking," she said with a wink. "I love my leftovers. That completes the holiday for me," she added.

"I totally agree." Morgana toasted Ms. Lane with her sandwich. They enjoyed their leftovers and fresh iced tea.

"Umm, Ms. Lane," Morgana hesitated. "Can I ask about Josef?"

"What about him, dear?" The little corners of Ms. Lane lips turned up.

"Well, it's just that, we danced all night at Mabon, and talked all night at Samhain. I know he was in Italy in between the two. But then I don't hear from him, and then he's here with Tiffany draped all over him." Morgana kind of wished she hadn't said that last part out loud.

"Josef has a lot on his plate right now. He's finishing up grad school and trying to learn all the aspects of the family business," Ms. Lane explained.

"Why would he need school if it's a family business? I mean, umm." Morgana felt like she put her foot in her mouth again.

The wonderful Ms. Lane just smiled at her. "Josef went through a tough time after his parents transitioned. He almost flunked out of high school and made some tough choices. Now he feels like he needs to prove himself and redeem himself to his uncle and the family, before he can take over. He's a bright boy, but he still carries a lot of guilt and shame over his parents' passing. Guilt and shame are the lowest of frequencies. The poor boy just can't forgive himself."

"Forgive himself for what?" Morgana pried, slightly, trying not to overstep her boundaries.

"The day his parents died, they were on their way to pick him up. He was a popular boy, but just barely fifteen. Some older kids were having a party out by the falls. There was underage drinking and he didn't have a ride home, so he ended up calling his parents to come get him. They were killed by one of the kids who was driving drunk. He feels like if he hadn't been where he wasn't supposed to be in the first place, they wouldn't have died. He also wishes if he had just ridden home with one of the drunks, maybe he would have died, but at least they wouldn't have. It's a lot for a young man to handle," Ms. Lane sighed.

Morgana's eyes were filling with tears. She remembered the gazebo painting of the family of cherubs at the falls. "What do you say to someone who's going through something like that?" Morgana pleaded for answers from the beloved Grand High Chairman, who was also her self-proclaimed fairy godmother.

"You just have to love them. You help them channel their feelings towards constructive things. You give them time and you encourage them to focus on positive aspects. Tragedies happen all the time, but the ones who leave us really are in a better place. They're still here, just with no boundaries. The ones left behind are the ones who suffer the most because what they are feeling is the separation of energy. They feel disconnected, but they're not, really. We are still all connected. You have to believe everyone is on their own path. We make a plan before we come forth to this existence and we do our best to follow that plan. Sometimes journeys seem like they get cut short because on this side we can't see the whole picture. But those on the other side are still here, we just have to hone our focus and practice feeling for them. They definitely don't want us dwelling in the lower frequencies of sadness, guilt, or shame. They want us to live and experience this world as joyfully as we can. They're still here with us, every step of the way."

The tears were streaming down Morgana's face, she would brush them aside with her napkin, but they kept leaking out. "He told me how in love his parents were, and he was the apple of their eye," Morgana said weepily.

"Yes, they were so in love. Jayson doted on Delilah. They were happy together. But, Jayson didn't have a very good childhood. His parents divorced when he was twelve and it broke his mother's heart. She died shortly after. Jayson was only twenty when she passed and he hated and blamed his father. Rage like that takes its toll on a person. Delilah tried to help as much as she could, but he always shut her down when it came to his father. You can't force, or make, anyone change or deal with their issues. It's a personal journey. We all have to find our own happiness and then emanate it outwards. That's all you can do to help others, just be the example of alignment. And when they are ready, they'll feel your love, and hopefully find their own peace within."

"Josef told me that he laughed for the first time since they transitioned the day I her tripped over myself dumping icy lemonade down my dress." Morgana started to smile still wiping away the tears.

"Yes, that was a very good day," Ms. Lane said with impassioned gratefulness. "He returned with a big smile on his face and laughed as he told me all about how preciously pitiful you looked trying to be so grown up bringing him a cold drink. It was so great to hear him laugh again. He has a great boisterous laugh, don't you agree?" Ms. Lane asked.

Morgana had to think about that. This whole time, she only thought of him boisterously laughing at her stupidity, but really he was just fully laughing – because of her. "Yes, he does have great laugh." Morgana sighed deeply with the relief of her own realization. "Umm, can I ask something about Tiffany?" Morgana paused.

"Go on, dear."

"Well, Brook and Blake were talking at Mabon, and they said something like Tiffany was focusing on who she wants and not how she wants to feel. What does that mean?"

Ms. Lane started to explain, "It's the difference between trying to dominate your life and going with the natural flow of life. When we are in alignment with the flow of life, you are effortlessly in the right place at the right time. You are living the life of your dreams and you feel blissful. Synchronicity is at its highest. It starts from within. You find the alignment from within yourself and then it emanate outwards from you and syncs up with the matching vibrations of the universe. The universe is always trying to give us the best, but it's up to us to be open and receptive. Just like you and the formal at Mabon. You were open and alive and in the flow. You manifested the dress, the makeup and hair, and the dance that matched how you felt. But you didn't try to contrive it, you just allowed it."

"And it was better than anything I could have imagined," Morgana interjected happily.

"Exactly. You didn't have any agenda except to feel connected. And therefore your night was..."

"Oh, so magical!" Morgana finished Ms. Lane sentence with a romantic whimsical sigh.

"Precisely. The synchronicity of events played out beautifully and to your liking. But, poor Tiffany. She tried to control the events. Her focus was on a particular person and trying to control that person, and not how she wanted the evening to feel. A lot of people think, 'if I could just get the job or the boy or the house,' they would feel complete. Their focus is on the object and not on the emotion, which is why a lot of the time they get the job and they hate it. Or they get the boy and the relationship doesn't work out. Or they move into the house and it causes even more problems. If they were to focus more on how they want to feel at the job, then the universe could match up to the feeling of a job that is fulfilling and lucrative. If they could feel what a happy, healthy romantic relationship felt like to them, the universe could bring them the perfect mate where they would be in love, happy, and in tune with one another. If they could focus on what really makes a house feel like a home for them, then the universe could line up a home full of love and laughter, family and friends, great times and wonderful memories. Nowadays we want instant results. We don't put in the time and effort, so we are disappointed by the results. Tiffany's dominating energies are overpowering to Josef's lower energies, so that is why she can be the way she is. If he were to shift his frequencies to a higher resonance or if she softened her energy, they might make it more comfortable for each other. Josef has his work cut out with that one."

"Um, so if he were to lift his frequencies, and she didn't, what would happen?" Morgana tried to be nonchalant.

Ms. Lane smiled. "Well, then I guess he would just vibrate out of her reach, and into the arms of someone on the same frequency,"

"Oh, I see." Morgana acted like she was disinterested.

Ms. Lane sipped her tea with a smirk on her lips. Then she blurted out, "Oh, before I forget, here is the website for Mrs. Thompson's dress shoppe if you want to peruse it for a winter solstice dress. Let me know the one that you want and Mrs. Thompson said she would give us a good deal. Text me the one you want this week so we can get it delivered in time."

"That's right! It's only three weeks from now. I'll be out of school by then. Is there anything I can do to help you or the festival?" Morgana offered.

"I think we have it covered, but I will let you know if something comes up."

At work that night Morgana searched for a dress on Mrs. Thompson's website. *Geez, they're so expensive!* Morgana thought to herself. *$200. $350. $529! Dang! Where's the clearance?* She was still searching Saturday night when Cole stopped by with her frozen coffee.

"What are you looking at?" he inquired.

"Oh, hi. Umm, well, my neighbor is hosting a party for the winter solstice," she said timidly.

"Winter solstice. That sounds fancy." Cole wriggled his fingers in a playful teasing manner.

"Shut up! It is fancy. And fun. And magical!" Morgana defended with a light smack on his hands. "I'm trying to pick out a dress."

"Let me see." Cole snatched her phone away and looked at the pictures. "Wow. This is a fancy occasion." Cole was surprised. "These are really pretty. What is that style, sort of old world?"

"You're not interested," she sassed.

"No, really. You promised not to hold the pool hall guy over my head. I do work in fashion," Cole pointed out.

"Alright. You're right. I guess they are kind of modern medieval renaissance." They laughed. "My neighbor said it was a winter wonderland gala and everyone wears white. This is her friend's site and she said she would give me a discount, but I don't know how much I can spend on a dress."

"Oh, this one is pretty." Cole's attention was on scrolling through the dresses.

"That one is three hundred dollars!" Morgana objected.

"Ya, but it comes with a matching cloak," Cole observed.

"I already have a cloak," Morgana admitted.

He gave her a look and then said, "Okay, but does it have fur trim?"

"No, it doesn't!" Morgana grabbed her phone back and looked at the beautiful white dress with the coordinating fur trimmed cloak. It was gorgeous with crystal accent details. Morgana pictured herself showing up wearing it with her amulet.

"Can I go?" Cole asked, interrupting Morgana's thought process.

"Huh? You would want to go? Umm, I don't know." What she really didn't know was how to dance all night with Josef while Cole sat at the table. But worse, what if Josef danced the night away with Tiffany and she was stuck watching from the table. "Um, look Cole, I gotta be honest. Are we coffee buddies or are you looking for something more?" Morgana was prudently blunt.

"Hey, I realize that I really blew it on our date and I don't blame you for keeping your distance. For now we are coffee buddies but I'm available for more down the road if we get to that point," Cole stated.

"Wow, that was honest. Thank you." Morgana was a little surprised. "So, since you were so honest, can I tell you something without you hating me?" she grimaced.

"Shoot," he said.

"Well. I kind of have had a crush on this guy since I was thirteen. He's my neighbor's nephew, well, great-nephew, and he's probably going to be there," Morgana said carefully.

"Ahhh crushes." Cole shook his head. "I had a crush once. My baby sitter, Pa-tri-cia. She was French and beautiful." Cole stared off dramatically.

"What happened?" Morgana engaged.

"She's now my step-mom," he said frankly.

"She married your father?" Morgana laughed in shock.

"No, my mother." Cole nodded his head.

"Ohhh."

"Yah. That happened," he laughed.

"So, you understand." She continued, "So, the best friend of my crush's cousin is OBSESSED with him and she's probably going to be there, too. I don't really know what to do. I don't want to lead you on and I really enjoy our coffee talks." Morgana waited to see how her new buddy would respond.

"Hmmm. That's a tough call. Do you risk being the loser sitting alone all night watching Mr. Wonderful dancing with Ms. Obsessive? Or do you let a friend take you and risk Mr. Wonderful being so jealous he declares his love for you in front of everyone?" Cole got down on one knee in a theatrical fashion.

"Get up, you dork!" Morgana was blushing. "Another thing," Morgana added slyly, "it's about two hours from here....in the middle of nowhere."

"Ooh, sounds intriguing." Cole drummed his fingers together

devilishly. "Well, I must confess if there is to be a virgin sacrifice, I'm disqualified."

"Shut up!" Morgana was laughing hysterically.

Monday, during her class, Morgana texted Ms. Lane a picture of a simple white dress on clearance for $39.99.

M: What about this one?

ML: Kinda too simple. I like this one.

Ms. Lane texted back the dress Morgana and Cole were looking at.

M: Umm, but I don't need the cloak.

Morgana tried to lead away from the expensive dress.

ML: Your cloak is more of a spring/fall. This one is for winter.

M: I love that one too. How much do you think Mrs. T. will charge me?

ML: I'll ask her. BRB

Morgana laughed at her little old friend texting in code. Ms. Lane texted a short while later.

ML: $39.99

M: Whaaaaat? No way!

ML: Yes, as a favor to me (winkey face)

M: Really? R U sure?

ML: Yes ma'am (big smile)

M: U R so awesome! (heart)(heart)(heart)

ML: I have ordered it and you can pay me when you pick it up. (smiley with money tongue)

M: Yes ma'am! (smiley)(smiley)(smiley)

M: Umm – Cole wants to come too...

ML: Cole??? (confused face)

M: We've been talking. We're coffee buddies. I told him about Josef....and Tiffany. He's offered to be my dance partner if I'm stuck on the bench. What do you think? (confused face)

ML: I think you shouldn't worry about the drama twins and you should have a fun night with your friend. (winkey face)

M: I think you are brilliant! And HILARIOUS! Thank you. (smiley)

That night Cole came over with their frozen chocolate addictions. "I got the dress!" Morgana said excitedly.

"Oh-ho! Ms. Fancy Pants! You get yourself a sugar daddy?" Cole teased.

"Nope – better. I have a fairy godmother!"

"Well, Cinderella. May I escort you to the ball?" Cole asked in a princely manner.

"If it pleases you, kind sir," Morgana replied.

Over the next couple weeks during his breaks, Morgana told Cole about Mabon, Brook and Tristan, Blake and Jai, Mitchell and Trina, and of course, Josef and Tiffany. She told him about the boys' tent and the girls' tent but she wasn't sure what to expect for the winter solstice. Her schedule kept her from seeing Ms. Lane so they texted again.

M: Are they going to set up tents like Mabon?

ML: Yes, but it's only Saturday night.

M: So we can get ready there?

ML: Yes

M: Will Mrs. T have her dress shoppe set up?

ML: No, we don't have the vendors like Mabon since it's pretty much just dinner and dancing.

M: Is the dance the same?

ML: A couple extra steps, but pretty much.

M: I'm excited! (smiley)

ML: Me too!

M: Will you be up on stage again?

ML: Yes

M: Am I allowed to talk to you when you're up there?

ML: Of course! But it is an official post, so I stay there.

M: You don't get to dance?

ML: Ahh, I did years and years of dancing. Now it's nice to watch.

M: UR awesome!

ML: LOL(blush face) I dropped your dress off at your house.

M: Oh cool!

ML: It's gorgeous!

M: Can't wait. Oh your money.

ML: I know where you live. I'll get it another time (winkey)

Morgana felt like she had thoroughly prepared Cole for where they were going. He was coming to pick her up and she reminded him ten times about the driveway. "I remember," he said shaking his head at the memory of his behavior the last time when he scraped his bumper.

When she got into his new model 7 series BMW, but before he backed out, she pulled out the amulet necklace and held it in her palm to show him. "Josef's father made it for his mother before they died. Josef gave it to me for my eighteenth birthday." Morgana didn't go into Josef's personal story. She just wanted Cole to know that her necklace had a history.

"Holy cow! Those are diamonds! And that's astonishing craft work." He ran his finger over the intricate metal design. "And he just gave it to you?"

"He told me he knew I would take good care of it," she stated.

"And why are you worried about his crazy obsessive chick? Looks to me like he's made his choice," Cole said.

"Well, you'd think, right? But he doesn't call or talk to me besides at festivals like this or when he's at his aunt's house. My birthday was six months ago and I've talked to him, like," she counted on one hand, "like maybe five or six times total. But look, I want you to know, tonight I am so thankful that you are going with me. And, at the advice of my fairy godmother, we are not going to worry about the drama twins and you and I are going to have a blast. Deal?" Morgana held out her fist.

"Deal." Cole bumped her fist with his and they both did the explosion sound.

"Now careful as you back down the driveway."

"Roger!" Cole took care and only barely scraped the bumper on the way out.

# Chapter Ten

Whimsical Winter Wonderland

"YOU HAVE NO idea where you are going, do you?" Cole joked.

"I'm telling you, it's just up the way," Morgana laughed. "I said it was in the middle of nowhere."

"I didn't think there still was a 'no where.' How come all our houses are built on top of each other when there's all this available land?" Cole commented.

"You got me. But there's our turn."

"Oh, even further off the beaten path. Where no one can hear you scream," he teased in a fake haunting voice.

"Shut up," she laughed. "It's magical out here. You'll see." Morgana was so excited for the night. She tried to explain it a little to Cole, but she wanted him to feel it- the love and connection with the earth and the sky, for himself. There were no words to describe it. She hoped he would be able to experience it for himself. "Here." They turned down the dirt entrance and drove through the provisional parking lot to find an available space to park.

"Oh, I can't wait to see it!" Morgana jumped out of Cole's luxury car. He handed her the zipped garment bag with her beautiful winter wonderland dress and then he grabbed her small overnight bag and his suit case. They walked up to the entrance and Morgana couldn't believe how cute it was. "Last time it looked like a medieval renaissance village and now it looks like a Swiss chalet! OH! It's a quaint little Christmas village!" she gushed. There were a dozen or so trailers linked together and decorated to look like tiny snowcapped houses with little twinkling lights that looked like snowflakes. There were lit gas lanterns flanking a walking path and soft blue lights illuminating the background. "Isn't it precious? I love it," Morgana said whimsically.

Cole was impressed. "I gotta say, I feel like we're in a northern country. And strangely back in time. How long were we driving?" He laughed and looked at his watch, shaking it like it wasn't working. "But, I really like it. It's pretty cool."

"Okay, so I'm guessing that's the guys' tent, and the girls' tent must be over there. So, you'll be okay? We'll meet back here in thirty minutes." Morgana gauged the time.

"Yup, I'll be fine and meet you back here." Cole handed her bag over and watched as she walked off towards the girls' tent. He was pretty impressed with the little impromptu village and was starting to get what Morgana was talking about. There was something about the way the mountains touched the sky, being out here in the middle of nowhere, and finding a tiny Christmas village covered with "snow" in a place where it never snowed.

Morgana made her way to the girls' tent and looked around for Trina, Brook, or Blake. She didn't see anyone so she found a row of cots to save for everyone and started getting ready. She had been practicing how to do her hair and makeup the way Trina had shown her. She carefully drew on the eyeliner, brushed on the blush and bronzer, and finished off with some lip gloss. She bought a headband that looked like braided hair and had embellished it with crystals to match her dress. She put on her gorgeous white ball gown and then wrapped the cloak around her shoulders with the faux fur trim that would keep her warm on the frosty winter night. The sweetheart neckline perfectly showcased the aqua heart stone amulet necklace that enhanced the color of the crystals on her white dress. She laced up her new pair of white Victorian boots and was happy with her end result. The dress was exquisite and fit her perfectly. Mrs. Thompson really did a nice job once again. She put on some long white gloves and locked all her stuff in the foot locker. Still no sign of other girls and so she left to go meet Cole.

As she walked through the makeshift Christmas village, she took in deep breaths. There wasn't any real snow but the cold winter air smelled like it. The sun was just about out of light with its last rays reaching as far as they could, holding on to the last seconds of daylight. Morgana came around the corner and Cole was standing there looking her way. He looked so handsome in his all white suit and tie. He even had an overcoat with a faux fur trim collar that coordinated with her cloak.

"Wow!" she said, slightly stunned. Cole always looked great, very GQ, but out here at the enchanted lot, she really noticed him. "You look great!" She smiled and touched his coat.

"You look stunning," Cole said with sincerity. "I don't know if this is appropriate, but I got this for you." He handed her a clear plastic box with a wrist corsage of a blend of white frosted flowers.

"Cole, that is so sweet. Thank you." Morgana was really touched at the sweet gesture.

"May I?" he offered, taking the flowered elastic band for her to slip onto her wrist. He was so kind and thoughtful, and he looked fantastic. She flashed to their disastrous date and couldn't believe this was the same guy. "Shall we?" He wrapped her hand up in his arm and they slowly headed towards the dinner tables, enjoying the sights as they walked. Morgana deeply breathed in the night air and Cole followed her lead. "I can feel the night. It's amazing," Cole whispered. Morgana smiled and leaned her head on his arm as they strolled through the twinkling little whimsical village.

The dining area was a confection of soft blue and white table cloths and linens accented with silver chargers and goblets, reflecting the flickering flames of tea lights in white frosted candle holders. Back lit with more soft blue lights to give the winter wonderland hue, the stage was set with the long table, covered in winter white floral arrangements with glittered snowflakes for the thirteen council members. It was so peaceful and soft. Morgana saw Mitchell and Tristan holding one of the lovely holiday tables and steered their way over. *Here we go.* "Tristan! Mitchell! Hi guys!" she called out.

"Lassie!" Tristan waved them over.

She gave them each a hug and then introduced Cole. "This is my friend Cole." Cole and Mitchell shook hands. Then Cole looked up at six foot five, 350 pound Tristan as he reached out to shake his hand. "You must be the one who pulls sequoia trees out by their roots to use as tooth picks." Tristan gave him a hearty laugh and a jolly smack on the back. "Good God, man," Cole exclaimed. "Eat a sandwich. You're practically wasting away to nothing," he joked. They all laughed and Cole shook his hand as if Tristan had crushed it.

"Where are the others?" Morgana asked trying not to feel awkward awaiting Josef's arrival.

"Jai an' Josef are fetchin' some drrrrrinks," Tristan rolled, "and the lassies arrrree gussin' up and should be har any minute."

He didn't mention if Tiffany was here or not. *Oh, God, what if she didn't even come?* Morgana thought to herself. She scanned around and then she locked onto his beautiful deep aqua blue eyes. He looked so gallant in his white double breasted wool coat. He smiled at her and she felt her whole soul light up. She was second guessing her decision to bring Cole. *Josef would be too polite to ask me to dance in front of him. He's so kind and thoughtful. Did I mess things up?* But just then, Tiffany came out from behind him, nipping at his heels. Morgana was, in a sense, relieved to see her.

"Hi, Morgana," Josef greeted her as he arrived back at the table with his hands full of drinks. Jai came up and set down several glasses, too. Morgana put on her "big girl smile," and tapped Cole on the arm discreetly.

"Hi, Josef. Hi, Tiffany. Hi, Jai. This is my friend Cole."

Tiffany was trying to get Josef's attention to help her set down the glasses she was holding, but with the announcement of Cole's name, she finally acknowledged Morgana's presence.

"Cole, you say? Who's he?" Tiffany quizzed.

Cole didn't miss a beat and he grabbed Tiffany's hand and leaned down to kiss it. "I am Cole Williams. Miss Morgana's coffee buddy and personal chauffer for this wonderful evening's festivities. Charmed to meet you," he said with thick charisma.

Tiffany, surprisingly, was flattered by Cole's manners. "Well, well. Welcome, Mr. Williams. It's a pleasure." Cole then shook hands with Jai and Josef. Morgana gave Jai a hug and when she tried to hug Josef, Tiffany dramatically announced she had something land in her eye and shouted that she couldn't get it out.

"Shall we get something from the bar?" Morgana looked at Cole, who caught on.

As they walked away out of earshot, Cole exclaimed, "Boy howdie!" He laughingly cried out, "You weren't kidding about those two."

Morgana just shook her head. "Right!"

"I kinda feel bad for the guy. She's got her talons hooked in pretty deep," Cole said.

"I can't tell if he's too nice or too stupid," Morgana confessed.

"I think you and Tiffany need to fight it out for Mr. Wonderful in a good mud wrestling match," Cole optimistically joked.

"Shut up!" Morgana flashed him a dirty look as she laughed.

"It could be hot oil, if you prefer," he teased.

When they returned from the bar, Brook, Blake and Trina had arrived. Morgana gave them each a hug and introduced them to Cole.

Tiffany chimed in, "You say you're coffee buddies?"

Cole took the lead, and explained, "Well, we met while waiting in line to get our fix of frozen chocolate coffee addictions. Morgana was jonesing in a bad way. She had to get back to her post but the lady in front of us couldn't figure out if she was moving in or just placing an order. I could feel Morgana's plight as she glanced at her phone's clock every two seconds and I could see the sweat beading on her brow. I offered my place in line in hopes to get the number that was attached to the phone, her now shaky, clammy hands clung to for dear life. She was weak in her desperation and I knew that was the prime moment to pounce on my prey. She agreed to go on a date and I wanted to really impress her, so I took her to a shady pool hall thinking I could show off my mad skills with a cue stick. Unfortunately, the only skill I showcased was mad asshole. She kicked me to the curb. But," Cole dramatically drummed his fingers together under his chin in a villainous way, "I knew her one weakness, her Achilles heel, if you will. And you know I exploited the crap out of that until she had no choice but to forgive me!" Cole completed his regaling story with a dramatic effect. Morgana and the whole gang were laughing, except for Tiffany, who just smiled humorouslessly. "So, now I'm pretty much just her coffee dealer trapped in the friend zone," Cole said laughing and hung his head like a sad puppy. They all laughed.

"And, what do you do for a living?" Tiffany interrogated.

"Dang, easy Tiffany!" Blake snapped.

"Oh, well, I just meant, he's not really Morgana's personal attendant," Tiffany retorted.

"I am the manager of a men's designer suit store until I finish my last semester at college. Then I will be transferring to Paris to continue my apprenticeship as a fashion merchandiser," Cole answered.

"Paris!" Tiffany exclaimed. "Will you go with him?" Tiffany turned her interrogation onto Morgana, who was completely caught off guard by Cole's Paris announcement.

"Umm. Well. I." Morgana was at a loss.

"Everything with my transfer is still in the works, so I don't even have exact dates. But Paris has delicious coffee so maybe I'll be able to get my buddy to visit me some times," Cole answered.

Just then, the announcer said that the High Council was to be seated. The twelve members all came out and took their place. Everyone stood as the thirteenth member, the beloved Grand High Chairman, Ms. Katherine Lane, came out to take her seat and proclaim the commencement of the Winter Wonderland Grand Ball. Waiters came out setting up large silver chaffing dishes in the center of each table perfectly fitting inside the winter themed floral centerpieces, lighting the fuel cans beneath to keep the delicious roasted chicken, potatoes, and vegetables warm from the cold. Dinner was absolutely amazing with the flavors bursting with every bite. Cole kept looking at Morgana in disbelief at how good everything was and she nodded back in total agreement and they even toasted their forks together on the down low. Eventually the chaffing dishes of food were cleared away and replaced with silver coffee carafes and warm bread pudding.

A short while later, while most were finishing their desserts, an announcer came up to the front of the stage. "Attention. Your attention, please everyone," he called out. "We need to see Tristan MacLeod, please. Is Tristan MacLeod here tonight?" Tristan gave an inquisitive look, and Brook was perplexed as Tristan's huge body got up from the table and headed towards the stage area. He was almost there, when the announcer called out for Brook. "Brook Meadow. Are you here tonight? Brook Meadow." Brook got up and started to walk, giving Blake a confused look, who was also baffled and shrugged her shoulders.

Tiffany said with excitement, "I wonder if they're going to call me and Josef up next. Do you think this about King and Queen of the Ball or something?" Blake let out a groan. "What?" Tiffany snapped back.

Brook reached the stage area and stood next to her big man, Tristan. They were wearing matching white and cream tartan patterns and looked every bit the King and Queen of the Winter Ball. "Mr. McLeod," the announcer stated in his official voice, "It is said that on this night, you have something you would like to say." A stunned Brook looked over as Tristan kneeled down on one knee and pulled a ring box out of his coat pocket. Even on one knee he was almost the same height as Brook, who was covering her mouth with her hand and tears of joy welled up in her eyes. Trina, Blake, and Morgana all squealed from their table.

"Me bonnie," Tristan's Scottish accented voice cracked as he spoke. "I love yuu. Wud yuu be doin' me the honorrrr of being me brrride?"

"Yes! Yes! Yes!" she cried. He put the gorgeous diamond ring on her finger, then stood up. She jumped into his mighty arms and they twirled around and kissed. The whole crowd cheered and applauded. Mr. and Mrs. Meadow ran up to the stage area and congratulated and hugged their daughter and her new fiancé. Blake went running up there, too. Tiffany saw Blake get up and she looked like she didn't know what to do. Finally she did get up and tried to get Josef up, too. He declined, so she played it off and went up to the stage shrieking in excitement when she got to Brook.

Cole quickly turned to Morgana, "I'm going to get a drink from the bar. Can I get you anything?" he urged.

Morgana was caught off guard. "Um, no. I'm good," she said glancing at his full glass.

"Okay. I'll be back." Cole quickly headed off.

Morgana, realizing he was giving her this moment with Josef, shifted chairs and said to him, "How exciting for those two!"

"Yes, Tristan's been a nervous wreck for days," Josef said with laugh.

"Oh, you knew?" Morgana smiled.

"I helped him plan the whole thing." Josef look at her with a slight smile. "Cole seems nice."

"He's a really good friend," Morgana said, accentuating the friend part. "I figured your dance card was probably full tonight. Cole agreed to make sure I didn't miss out on the dance of the snowflakes."

Josef looked at her sincerely. "I definitely wouldn't want you to miss out on that. You look really beautiful tonight, Lady Morgana." Josef kissed her hand and with that got up from the table to welcome back the newly engaged couple making their way through the throngs of congratulating guests. Trina and Morgana finally got a chance to hug their friends and see the princess cut diamond ring set in a platinum Celtic weave band.

The music from the dance area started up and they all made their way over. Brook wrapped up in Tristan's huge arms, staring at her bejeweled hand and kissing his arm at the level she reached on his massive frame. Josef was next to Tristan and Tiffany was next to Brook talking about wedding dates. Brook was laughing at her pushy friend at the thought of picking out a date already. "Gosh, I haven't even got that far yet!" Mitchell and Trina, Blake and Jai were right behind them, and Morgana and Cole hanging back bringing up the rear.

"Wow. That's cool right?" Cole said.

"You're really cool," Morgana said, complimenting her friend and giving him a quick peck on the cheek. "Thank you."

"So, you talked to him then?" Cole asked.

"I guess. He told me I looked beautiful and kissed my hand, then got up and walked away. I don't get it. And to be honest, I'm about done with it. But, Cole, are you really moving to Paris?" Morgana stopped in her tracks suddenly remembering Cole's surprise announcement.

"It's been the plan I had worked out with my bosses. I'm going to business school and fashion is big business. They're from Paris and have a huge set-up over there that I'll run. It's not until after I graduate this summer," Cole tried to assure her.

"When were you going to tell me?" Morgana asked.

"I actually had a fancy dinner date all planned out. But, it kinda fell out tonight," he confessed.

Morgana thought about the predicament she put Cole in tonight, with Tiffany's insufferable inquiries and Josef's presence, and realized she couldn't be mad at Cole one bit. "Alright then, it sounds like you owe me a dinner date."

Cole was relieved at her response. "You're on!" he agreed.

"Are you ready to dance like a snowflake?" Morgana asked as she held out her hand.

"Let's do this." Cole grabbed on and they walked to the dance area and lined up with the others.

Josef actually moved next to Cole and said something to him. Tiffany followed Josef and lined up across from him. "Cole seems really nice," Tiffany said curtly.

"Yes, he really is," Morgana replied genuinely.

The motion was given and the men, in their white attire, all bowed to their partners. The ladies, in their white full skirted gowns curtsied back. It was really beautiful to see everyone dressed in their whites. The dance floor area was lit by gas lamps around the perimeter, and soft blue lights in the back drop. The bright shining stars seemed so close, like you could touch them.

The dance was quite similar to the one Morgana already knew, the only difference was the girls did a double twirl to really let their skirts flare out like spiraling snowflakes. Cole was a natural and they danced and twirled. Morgana breathed in the night and smiled at the stars looking down enjoying the show. Cole was right in tune and in step. "It's almost hypnotic," he whispered to her as they danced.

She felt so alive. She forgot about the drama twins, Paris, and engagements, and just relished in her blissful night of feeling like a snowflake flittering its way down from a cloud. The music ended around midnight. Morgana and Cole had laughed and danced and joined in a world of their own. "I feel amazing!" Cole cheered. "It was like a trance more than a dance. I felt the energy moving with us. I felt the music in my blood. I couldn't tell where my hand ended and yours began."

"I know, right! Isn't it magical? I didn't know about the extra twirl. How did you know what to do?"

"Your boy, Mr. Wonderful, told me before we got started. He also said to let my feet follow the music, and let my soul guide my body. What a total rush! A total peaceful, tranquil rush! Oh wait – does that even make sense?" He laughed at himself. "I'm too pumped to sleep!"

"Do you want to just head home then, or do you want to sleep on a cot?" Morgana remembered last time on those cots and it's not really sleeping, more like "just getting through" the night.

"Sure, I'm game if you are," Cole responded with his amped attitude.

"If you're okay to drive, let's go change and meet back here in twenty minutes." Morgana liked the idea of continuing the night and driving home under the stars.

As she was walking away, "Hey, Morgana," Cole called out. She turned to look at him smiling at her. "You really do look beautiful tonight." Cole was standing there, lit by the starlight in his white suit that coordinated with her dress and she stopped.

"Cole, you look very handsome. I am really glad you came with me tonight. Thank you." She blew him a kiss and turned away to head back to get her clothes from the girls' tent. Cole stood there and watched her walk away. He took a deep breath and looked at the stars smiling down on him. He felt great. He turned to head towards the guys' tent and that's when he saw Josef standing in the distance. Cole gave him a wave of his hand, and Josef tipped his head in return.

Morgana walked into the girls' tent. A crowd was gathered around Brook as she delighted in showing off her new diamond engagement ring. Morgana quickly changed and zipped up her dress in the garment bag and grabbed her night bag. Blake saw her approaching with all her stuff in tow. "You're leaving?" she asked.

"Ya, we decided we'd rather just head home instead of trying to sleep on cots," Morgana said with a chuckle.

"Ya, that makes sense. Cole is great. What's going on with you two?" Blake gave her a glance.

Morgana really laughed. "Nothing really. I just couldn't deal with it tonight." She shot a look towards Tiffany, who was fawning all over the newly engaged Brook. "Cole came with me to keep this night magical and not get caught up in drama. He did a marvelous job at it too," Morgana stated.

"Well, he's a hottie, that's for sure!" Blake quipped. "And he seems to know how to handle dramadies pretty well. Is he really moving to Paris?"

"I don't know, we haven't really talked much about it," Morgana said.

"Well, that'd be a bummer. Unless you get to go with him!" Blake suggested light heartedly.

"We'll see. That's too far to think about. When the dust settles around here, let Brook know I'm happy to help if I can with any wedding plans," Morgana offered.

Blake groaned and pointed at Tiffany. "I'm sure everything will be taken care of," she said sarcastically.

"Have a good night. Enjoy your cots." Morgana gave Blake a hug.

"You know, I wonder if Jai would want to leave, too. Mind if I text him? Then we could caravan to the turn off." Blake whipped out her phone after Morgana nodded, and started texting in a mad fury.

B: Wanna go now or stay til am?

J: Huh? R U ready 2 go?

B: Morg and Cole R leaving now. Sounded like an excellent idea.

J: Sure!

B: Meet in 10 min at dance area. Find Cole."

J: Will do

Blake gathered up her stuff and made her way through the crowd to her sister. "Hey sis, I'm gonna head home tonight."

"What? Is everything okay?" Brook looked concerned.

"Oh, no, it's all good. Morgana and Cole are leaving too, and I would rather not sleep on a cot tonight. We're gonna convoy to the turn. We'll be fine."

"Well, okay." Brook seemed confused but didn't have much say in the matter.

"Love you, sis. Congrats! We'll talk tomorrow." Blake gave her big sister a hug.

"Good night, Brook. Congratulations!" Morgana hugged Brook good-bye and they headed off to meet the guys. Cole and Jai were already at the meeting spot talking about martial arts, chi, the dance, and the night when the girls arrived.

"Hey, you guys have another hour down the hill. If you want to you can all stay at my house then continue in the morning? I have couches way more comfortable than cots. Just follow us at the turn off if you decide to, okay?" Morgana offered.

"Thanks. We'll definitely let you know!" Blake said and they walked to their cars. Cole followed Jai's Toyota 4Runner out of the dirt parking lot, onto the two lane road, to the freeway.

"Wasn't it amazing?" Morgana said whimsically.

"So amazing. I can't describe it," Cole agreed. Then added, "Mr. Wonderful seems like a cool guy."

"Ya, I don't know. He's all great and stuff but then nothing. Whatever, enough about him. You were fantastic. Thank you again for coming. And I'm so glad you felt it. I kind of thought maybe I was just imagining it, ya know? Didn't you just want to grab the stars in your hands?"

"Totally!" Cole agreed, and was happy that she didn't care to talk about Josef. "It's like they were so close. What is it about that place?"

"Well," Morgana pretended like she was reading from a notebook, "It's not the place, per se. It's all about the energies of everyone out there. We were all there unified, as one, with one thought, with one goal- to connect. And when like-minded people get together in unison, the energy permeates through us all- past, present, and future. That's how Ms. Lane explained it to me once," Morgana shared.

"Oh, speaking of your 'little fairy godmother,' as you like to call the baddest chick on the stage!" Cole teased.

"I told you she was the Grand High Chairman. Oh, wait, maybe I didn't mention that part. You were freaked out about virgin sacrifices so I didn't think I should tell you about the council." Morgana was laughing hysterically.

"You're probably right. You gotta see it to understand it." Cole laughed too.

Morgana's phone beeped about twenty minutes before the turn off with a text from Blake:

B: We R good 2 go home. But totes starved. Wanna stop at the diner at the top?

Morgana read to Cole, and they agreed.

M: We're down.

At 1:45 a.m. the two cars pulled off the freeway and pulled into the mostly vacant parking lot of an all-night diner. The foursome laughed and talked, and had a great time over eggs and pancakes, and lots of coffee. About an hour later, Jai and Blake headed down the freeway as Cole made the turn towards their town.

"They're a lot of fun," Cole commented.

"Ya, I never just hung out with the two of them. They're great," Morgana agreed.

Thirty minutes later they were almost to Morgana's inclined driveway, when she looked at Cole as he was driving. "I really had a good time with you tonight. I guess it was your evil twin who took me to the pool hall," Morgana joked.

"I take full responsibility for being a complete ass that night. I had a really bad day and I just didn't handle things right. I found out my ex was dating my ex-best friend. The whole time we dated, she kept telling me what an asshole he was. He was always getting into fights and was a real womanizer. She actually made me choose between them. I was working and going to school. I didn't have much time anyway, so I just kind of lost touch with him. She and I had broken up six months earlier and then all of sudden they were together. I didn't care, mostly, but just kinda figured I'd try to impress you by being an ass. I'm sorry," Cole explained.

"Okay, you have officially apologized enough. You are now hereby absolved of your bad date title." Morgana motioned the rap of a gavel.

Cole laughed. "Thank you, your honor."

He parked the car and gathered her things out of his trunk and then walked her to the door. "Are you going to be okay getting home?" Morgana asked.

"I've only got twenty minutes to my house and I think I've got just enough caffeine in me to make it," he said.

Morgana opened her front door and set down her things inside. "Good night Cole. Thank you for sharing this magical evening with me."

"I really want to kiss you, Morgana, but I'm not going to. Tonight was awesome and a kiss would finish it off perfectly. But then, what would it mean tomorrow? I don't want to convolute our friendship," Cole said as he stood there looking at her.

Morgana didn't move either. She completely agreed with everything he just said. She wanted him to kiss her but she didn't know what it would mean.

They both stood there.

"Fuck it! I'm sorry." Cole quickly grabbed up Morgana into his arms and locked onto her lips with an amazing, delicious kiss. She melted into his embrace and kissed him back.

It was the perfect finishing touch to their awesome day.

Chapter Eleven

Changing Thoughts

MORGANA'S PHONE BEEPED with a text message, waking her from a deep sleep. She opened one eye and fumbled around to find the offending buzzer. She tried to focus her sleepy eye and read a text from Cole:

C: Just woke up and I'm starving. Interested in some grub?

M: Ya, me hungry.

C: I'll pick you up in 45 min?

Morgana almost fell back to sleep in the thirty seconds between texts.

M: Still in bed, moving slow. I'll be ready, I think.

C: Cool – see you soon.

Morgana closed her eyes again but then shot straight up as she remembered last night when Cole wrapped her up in his arms and kissed her so deeply and passionately her knees went weak.

"Oh shit! What did we do?"

She quickly jumped into the shower. She still had crystals in her hair from the snowflake dance. It was such a magical evening. She and Cole had so much fun dancing, she almost didn't notice Josef and Tiffany. She did notice they didn't dance all night like she and Cole did, and she definitely noticed they were not nearly having as much fun as she and Cole were. Cole was such a good dancer. He was strong and smooth and coordinated. He easily twirled her and they both loved watching her skirt as it floated. "You look just like a glistening crystal prism," Cole had said. They laughed and danced all night. And then that kiss! Morgana had a head full of sudsy shampoo running down her face, and the memory of his strong, sweet kiss made her knees dip. She finished rinsing off and wrapped her wet hair up in a towel as she exited the shower. She looked at herself in the foggy mirror as she brushed her teeth thinking about Cole. There was no drama and there was no Tiffany in the way. He was sweet, attentive, funny, and gorgeous. And even though she really enjoyed his company, when she thought of Josef she felt her soul came alive. "Damn you, Josef!" she shouted to herself as she spat out her discarded toothpaste. She put on an oversized sweatshirt and some leggings, and wrapped her damp hair in a loose bun. She was smoothing on some tinted moisturizer and smiling at the beautiful floral wrist corsage Cole had given her, when her doorbell rang. She opened the door to Cole, standing there in a knit sweater and dark denim jeans. She was used to seeing him dressed in his suits that he wore to work and last night he looked dashing in his white suit that coordinated with her winter wonderland dress, but she was surprised to see him in his casual attire and he still looked like he belonged on the cover of GQ.

"Hey, come in. I'm almost ready." She showed him to the living room and scurried back down the hall to her room, frantically trying to figure out what to wear. She put on a sweater dress and some boots over her leggings. She added some mascara, bronzer to her dewy fresh face, and topped it off with lip gloss. She slapped in some product to her damp hair to give it that "messy, wavy, I woke up this perfect" look. She wasn't much of a makeup girl but, *Hopefully, this is enough to at least make me look awake,* she laughed to herself. She grabbed her purse and walked out to the living room where Cole was looking at her baby pictures that her mother had displayed all over the house.

"Is this you?" he laughed.

"Shut up!"

"Could you even see past those cheeks?" he teased some more as they exited the house.

"Yah, yah. Laugh it up." Morgana took it in good humor as he walked her to her side of the car and opened her door for her. She just realized that he did that a lot for her that she never noticed. She sat in his new luxury 7 Series BMW and noticed how clean and nice he kept it. She didn't really pay much attention to cars, "Cuz everyone's car was better than hers," but she was noticing all these nuances about Cole that never occurred to her before. He got into the driver's side and the scent of his cologne delighted her senses as she watched him, now expertly, navigate down her inclined driveway.

"So, I was thinking big juicy cheeseburgers," Cole said.

"Sounds good to me!" Morgana agreed.

They talked on the way to the restaurant. The mood was easy and light hearted. Neither of them mentioned the kiss, but the relaxed feeling they shared the day after meant the kiss didn't need to change their great friendship. Although, Morgana was starting to wonder if she wanted their relationship to change.

They were seated in a big comfy booth eating their burgers. "Okay, so this is pretty good," Cole said, "but the food last night was incredible." They relived their favorite moments of last night's event: the perfectly chilled weather, the sweet little snowy Christmas village, the twinkling lights, and the majestic mountains.

"And that feeling of, of, peace? Or magic? Or something," Cole tried to describe the sense of ethereal power of the evening.

"Right!" Morgana exclaimed. "I don't know what you would call it either, but that's really close."

"And I want know how they made each bite of food dance on my tongue like that!" Cole exclaimed.

"I don't know how they make the food that good out in the middle of nowhere in those trailers," Morgana said, then added, "Ms. Lane explains that not only is the meal all organic, but it's blessed and made with love."

Just then the pushy waitress interrupted their conversation to ask if they were done with their half-eaten meals. Morgana had just taken a big bite. "No, we're still working on them," Cole politely clarified. She turned in a huff.

"Not sure how much love is here," Morgana commented after she finished chewing. They both laughed.

"After this, do you feel like watching a movie?" Cole suggested.

"Sure, what's playing?" Morgana felt in the flow. Everything was so easy with Cole. He got out his phone to check movie times and they found one that sounded like fun. Cole paid the bill, after denying Morgana's attempt to split it, and they drove over to the movie theater.

"I like this theater because they sell our frappes!" Cole was giddy like a child. "They're not the best, but hey, can't complain when I can have my fix with Dolby Digital Surround sound!" Morgana laughed at his excitement. He bought their tickets, by playfully pushing her out of the way, and their frozen chocolate concoctions, because "it was his job as the supplier." So, she insisted on paying for the popcorn. They found the perfect seats and practically had the theater to themselves.

"Movies come and go so fast," Cole noted. "I'm surprised we could still catch this one."

The lights dimmed and the movie started. Morgana felt good being there with Cole. At the end, they both really liked the movie. "So, I think I need some ice cream or something to wash down all that popcorn you forced me to eat," Cole joked.

"I forced you?" Morgana laughed.

"Well, you had to buy the jumbo, and then ate like, what, two handfuls?" Cole teased. "So, are you up for some ice cream?"

"Sure, I guess I owe you since I FORCED you to eat all the popcorn," Morgana teased back.

"Damn straight, you do!" he said with a laugh.

For the third time that night, Cole opened her car door. He always opened the business doors for her, too. He was really considerate and she was really having a nice time. He took them to an ice creamery and they each created their designer flavors. She tried to push him out of the way so she could pay, but ended up just bouncing off him. He paid.

"So, I'm leaving Christmas day to go visit the fam' for a week. I was wondering if you were available Christmas Eve to grab a coffee or something. I'm not working that night, are you?" he asked as he stole some of her ice cream.

"I think I work that morning from 10 to 2. I'm available for coffee or something," she smiled.

"Do you have any big family plans?"

"Well, my mom is the 911 operator manager and works all the time. We really never see each other. Christmas is not only the busy season for emergencies, but it's also the flu season. So, she covers for a lot of people who call in sick," Morgana explained.

"And your dad?" Cole asked politely.

"He left us when I was just a baby, and I don't hear from him much," Morgana stated dryly. "I don't have many memories of him, and now it's just a random card every decade or so. I think he remarried and had a couple of kids, but I really don't know."

"You don't know if you have siblings?" he was comforting in his questioning.

"It's not that," Morgana said. "It just doesn't seem like he has room in his new life for me, and since I never really met him, I don't see any point. What about you?" She shifted the conversation onto him.

"Well, Mom's now married to Pa-tri-cia," Cole said her name wistfully.

"Ah, yes, your babysitter." Morgana remembered the story about his crush on her.

"Yes, my babysitter." Cole chuckled. "So, I'm going to go see them for a couple of days, then I'm going to check on my pops. He was quite sad when mom left him. I keep trying to tell him there was nothing he could do. He didn't have what she needed – a vagina!" Cole stated humorously.

Morgana rolled with laughter, "Yes, that's true! There was nothing he could do. Well, I guess if he wanted..." They both laughed.

"Well, listen. Since your mom is working Christmas Eve, instead of coffee let's go out for dinner and celebrate the season," Cole suggested.

"Well, I was planning on eating a whole apple pie under the tree and watching Christmas Classic cartoons," she joked and then added, "alright, I would like that very much."

He dropped her off after their ice cream and walked her to the door. He gave her a hug and there was no awkwardness. She sort of wanted him to kiss her again but still wasn't sure how she felt about their relationship. He made no effort to kiss her and ended the night with a nice good night hug. She waved as he drove down the inclined driveway and down the street. It was nearly 11:30 p.m. They had spent the whole day together and it was really fun. Ms. Lane's old, deep maroon Cadillac

Deville was parked in her driveway. *Oh, she's home!* Morgana was hoping she could see her tomorrow after work for tea.

The next day Morgana sent her sweet fairy godmother a text during work.

M: Are you home?

ML: Yes

M: Can I invite myself to tea today?

ML: You are always welcome (smiley)

M: Thank you! (heart)(heart) See you at 4?

ML: Perfect!

At 3:45 p.m. Morgana skidded up the inclined driveway and changed out of her work clothes. She put on her favorite leggings and a long sweater with her black Victorian lace up boots to match Ms. Lane's. She walked down her inclined driveway, across the street, passed the old, deep maroon Cadillac Deville, and down the walkway to the recessed alcove with the heavy wooden front door. White poinsettias adorned the white wrought iron table with the sweet "Blessed are those who enter here" sign, cheerfully lit with the white Christmas lights that hung in the alcove. Morgana heard the clicking heels grow louder and then the heavy wooden door swung open. "Hello, dear!" Ms. Lane was wearing a light green button up silk shirt with a holly leaf print cardigan sweater and long solid green skirt.

Morgana gave her a big hug. "I feel like I haven't seen you forever!"

"It's nice to see you too!" Ms. Lane squeezed her in return. They stepped down into the sunken living room, which was now completely decorated in pink and white Christmas decorations. Next to the crackling fireplace was a tree with pink glass ornaments and white snowflakes and twinkling with lights. Morgana breathed in the sweet holiday confectionary spirit.

"It's so cute in here!" Morgana smiled at her little pink fairy godmother.

"Thank you. I love this holiday. It's my favorite."

Morgana laughed, "You say that that about every holiday."

Ms. Lane chortled, "I guess they're all my favorite."

On the tray next to a white teapot with pink snowflakes, lay some pink iced sugar cookies with white snowflake designs.

"Even your cookies match your décor!" Morgana thought everything was so precious, just like Ms. Lane herself.

"I love snowflakes. I love pink. I love filling my life with everything I love." Ms. Lane was always so light hearted and blissful. "So, what's been happening with you, dear?" Ms. Lane settled into her soft high back Victorian-era silky cream rayon tufted couch and listened as her young friend regaled her with stories about Cole and dancing all night at the winter solstice dance, about the drama twins, and the late night at the diner with Blake and Jai.

"He kissed me!" Morgana blurted out. "Cole kissed me and, Ms. Lane, it was soo amazing!" Morgana told her about Cole's ex-girlfriend and his reaction on their first date. "He's just so polite and wonderful, and sweet."

Ms. Lane listened intently to Morgana's lengthy story, but felt something amiss. "Why do I feel a 'but' coming?" Ms. Lane inquired.

"But, but…he's not," Morgana sighed and slumped in her chair. "He's not him," she said so softly Ms. Lane barely heard. "Plus, he's moving to Paris this summer." Morgana remembered his career plans.

"You've always wanted to go to Paris." Ms. Lane offered solace.

"Well, ya, but I don't know if I could move there," Morgana said with confusion.

"Well, I'm sure it'll all work out." Ms. Lane handed Morgana another perfectly pink frosted sugar cookie.

"These are so delicious," Morgana said with a mouth full of crumbly butter cookie.

"I spoke with your mother and it sounds like she has to work Christmas night. So why don't you come over here for dinner?" Ms. Lane invited.

"I would love that," Morgana accepted. She was happy to have plans with her favorite fairy god-mother. "Is everyone coming too?" Morgana thought of Thanksgiving with everyone. It was really nice, with the exception of the drama twins.

"No, they're all in Italy with my sister. Brook and Tristan are scouting out wedding venues while they're there. That was so lovely the way he proposed, didn't you think?"

"Well, since I'm sure a lot of those people know Brook and watched her grow up, that it was probably the best way to do it." Morgana laughed. "It was very sweet and touching. She looked so happy and surprised! I don't know how I would want to be proposed to. How did Mr. Lane propose to you?"

"I was dancing on Broadway and doing some modeling. Richard was an up and coming business man doing really well in the real estate market. He brought some clients to see our show one night and we met backstage. He was so handsome and charismatic, quite the charmer. I could feel his energy and he was vibing high. I was excited when he asked for my number but, of course, I didn't let him know that." Ms. Lane blushed at her memory of her love. "He was so fun and exciting. We went out dancing and to the hottest parties. It was an amazing time. One New Year's Eve, we were on our way to a formal party. He had rented us a limousine, when all of a sudden the car stopped and the driver informed us the car had died. I was a little scared but Richard comforted me. He was always so fun and spontaneous. So he grabbed a bottle of champagne and suggested we walk to the beach while the driver waited for the tow truck. The beach was just on the other side of the road behind the brush. He held my hand and helped me through the bushes. When we got to the other side there were tea lights on the sand in the shape of a heart, and he stepped into the middle, got down on one knee and proposed." Ms. Lane beamed.

"AWE! So the car didn't actually break down?"

"No, he had the whole thing planned."

"That's so romantic!" Morgana gushed.

"He told me how much he loved me and how I had showed him the true meaning of life. Back then, I only knew to follow your heart and feel for high vibrations. My mom had tried to teach me more but I just wanted to dance and have fun, which was good enough for me at the time. When I met Mr. Lane and we got wrapped up in the social scene, I forgot about true happiness and spent a lot of time with materialistic things. The only problem with that is, you want to focus on feeling the higher emotions and not just on the goods. When you focus on the goods only, life can get shallow. When you focus on the emotions and the connection, then your life is fulfilled and joyous, and the goods become just a bonus. A lot of the people we were hanging out with weren't that nice, but somehow you lose yourself in the lower frequencies and it starts feeling normal. I was mostly modeling by then because it paid more, and had given up my true passion of dancing, which had always filled me with joy. Sometimes there are dark energies in the modeling field. I was established enough, more or less, but still champagne for breakfast, lunch, and dinner became my routine. I lost my connection... Well, you actually can't lose it. But I definitely wasn't focusing on my connection. In the beginning of our relationship, Richard had told me that I had helped him find the true meaning of life, how to follow bliss, to live with abandon, and to love the world, but as we got wrapped up in the fast-paced lifestyle, we got distracted from those higher focuses. In addition to that, he was coming from a different place than me and he hadn't ever really let go of his negative energy. And I only say that because, he enlisted in the army, which I completely admired him for, but he enlisted after he had spent so much time reading the news reports, which were drowning in negative energies. He felt it was his calling, but he ran over there with the intention to 'kill the bad guys' rather than to 'save the good guys.' With such a heavy heart and focus on killing, it's no surprise that he was killed. I didn't realize this about his energy at the time. My mother tried to tell me but I said I was too fabulous and nothing could go wrong. I was thirty-three and he was only thirty-five when he died. Afterwards, my mother was so loving and consoling to me. It was then, I was open to learning. She taught me and my sister how to shift our energies. And then Lynetta used those principles to heal her husband, Henry, who had been terribly wounded." Ms. Lane softly smiled at Morgana, who had tears in her eyes and sadness on her face.

"Do you miss him?" Morgana carefully asked.

"Well, the thing about energy, dear, is when you learn to focus it, you have access to anything and everything. I still talk to him every day. He teases me about all my pink décor, but he helps me find more." She winked. "Here." Ms. Lane pointed at a crystal pink ballerina dancer ornament hanging from her tree. "I was visiting my sister in Italy in March, you remember, and I had wandered into a little shop off the beaten path. I smelled Mr. Lane's favorite cologne wafting in the air, when I walked into the shop and saw this precious dancer. He had guided me there so I would get it as a gift from him." Ms. Lane smiled with love at her new treasure from her departed husband.

"You mean, nine months ago?" Morgana was surprised.

"Yes, he's always with me." Ms. Lane touched her heart.

"That's so awesome!" Morgana cried out.

Ms. Lane nodded. "Totally!" the little old lady agreed with enthusiasm.

Ms. Lane invited Morgana to stay for dinner. "I'm just having some soup and a sandwich, but I'd be delighted if you wanted to join me."

Morgana happily accepted and they spent the next several hours sharing stories over delicious broccoli cheese soup and club sandwiches. "Even your soup and sandwiches taste amazing. Will you show me how to cook like you one day?" Morgana implored.

"I would love to, dear."

Christmas Eve, Morgana got a text from Cole while she was still at work:

C: What time shall I pick you up?

M: I can be ready any time after 4.

C: Perfect. I'll see you at 4.

M: Ok

That seemed kind of early for dinner, but considering the last time they started lunch at 2 p.m. then didn't get home until after 11 p.m., she figured they would end up doing something fun. She squealed her tires pulling up into the Y-shaped driveway and went inside to get ready for Cole to pick her up. She chose a red knit sweater that had an attached neck choker and a deep v-neckline, and dark jeans with boots. While she was deciding if she should try to wear some red lipstick, the doorbell rang. She opened it to Cole, who once again, looked striking, this time in dark jeans, a deep red button up shirt and a black sports coat.

"Merry Christmas Eve!" Morgana greeted her friend with a big hug and welcomed him in. "Here, I got you a little something. It's nothing big." Morgana handed Cole a green gift bag with red tissue paper. Cole opened it to find a personalized coffee mug with a picture of the two of them and a caption that read: "Coffee Buddies Forever."

"Now, when you're in Paris you'll always have something to remember me back here," Morgana explained.

Cole laughed and gave her a hug. "I love it." Then he said, "Hang on, I have to get something from the car." Cole walked out the front door and Morgana grabbed her purse and jacket. He came back in carrying a white gift bag with sparkling white snowflakes and glittery white tissue paper. "I got you a little something too." Cole handed her the gift.

"Oh, it's beautiful," Morgana said at the packaging. She opened it to find a boxed glass ornament. She took it out of its box and "floating" inside was a sparkling white crystal snowflake. "Oh, my gosh, Cole. It's breathtaking." Morgana was stunned.

"Now you'll have something to always remember our first Winter Wonderland dance of the snowflakes," Cole said, sort of quietly. Morgana held it carefully by the top and inside the glistening, sparkling snowflake looked like it was dancing.

"Oh. Cole. I really love it. Thank you!" Morgana was touched. It was very beautiful. She carefully hung it on her tree.

They walked outside and there was a Range Rover parked in Morgana's driveway instead of Cole's BMW. "I borrowed this from my boss," Cole covertly explained.

"I see." Morgana was intrigued. "Why do we need this, may I inquire?"

"No, you may not," he replied curtly.

He opened her car door and when she got in there were two Christmas themed frozen coffees in the cup holders. Morgana was amazed. She had never been treated like this before. In the back seat were a couple of parka jackets, which made Morgana even more curious. Cole jumped in and backed down the inclined driveway.

"Ha-ha!" he exclaimed. "No dragging ass in this machine!" Morgana laughed and they were off. They drove through town and kept heading eastward. Morgana guessed they were headed up the local mountains to the small village that had just been dusted with fresh snow.

"If we're going where I think we're going, I haven't been there in years," Morgana said. Sure enough they made the turn and started up the long road to the little mountain top village. "Oh, my mom and I used to come up here when I was really little," Morgana said wistfully. "We would come up here for picnics and spend the day at the lake." She continued, "I don't remember the last time. She works so much, especially ever since she got promoted to manager. Then I started over working at school, and once I got my driver's license, I was never home anymore anyway. It's funny how time flies, I guess."

"My family would come up here for the holidays," Cole shared. "We would rent a cabin from Christmas to New Year's. Just me, mom, and dad…and Pa-tri-cia."

"Pa-tri-cia? I thought she was just the babysitter?"

"Well, she started out that way, then became my nanny, then became mom's personal assistant, then…" Cole laughed. They reached the mountain top and drove through the little village. It was all decorated with twinkling lights and holiday cheer. The fresh powdered snow really put them in the holiday spirit.

"It's a lot bigger than I remember," Morgana stated.

"Well, it's a big ski resort town now. Do you ski?"

"I think I tried it once, when I was really young, but nothing since. We're not skiing tonight, are we?" Morgana asked in slight panic.

"No-no," Cole insisted. "I was just thinking ahead."

"I see," Morgana said, now even more slightly suspicious of what was in store for their evening.

Cole pulled the SUV into a parking lot that was lit with lights and trimmed with big red bows. It was an ice skating rink in the middle of town with a huge Christmas tree in the middle. "Do you skate?"

"I guess we'll find out!" Morgana eagerly jumped out of the car.

Cole grabbed the parkas out of the backseat. "It can get a little cold on the ice." He helped her put hers on.

"Where did you get these?" Morgana was slightly impressed.

"You will discover I like to be prepared," Cole replied. They rented some skates and laced up. Morgana used to roller stake all the time when she was young, but hadn't done much of anything in years. She was shaky when they started out. Cole was very helpful and caught her whenever she was about to fall. She was having a blast and soon got her legs back. After a short while they were zipping around the ice laughing and racing with Cole skating backwards teasing her to keep up. A couple of times she tried to pass him and pushed him into the wall in good fun. They skated for a couple of hours when Cole asked, "Are you sufficiently dizzy from going in circles?"

"Yes, I think I'm good." Morgana pretended to go cross eyed. They returned the skates and Cole held her door as she got back into the borrowed luxury SUV. He drove them towards the lake and pulled into a restaurant that had sweeping views over the water.

"Reservations for Cole Williams," he said to the maître d' once they were inside.

"Yes sir, Mr. Williams. Right this way." They were seated at a table right next to a large window so they could see out over the water and the town's point. Cole looked at his watch and the maître d' said, "Three minutes, sir."

"Thank you, François."

"You know him?"

"We come here a lot for business parties," Cole explained. "My bosses throw a lot of parties."

"Interesting. So, this is all just a typical night for Mr. Big Shot?" Morgana was now completely skeptical.

"No, ma'am. I'll explain later. Now, shut your mouth and look over there," Cole said with a charming laugh and pointed to the point. Morgana kept looking at him with slanted eyes, but he reached out and turned her head just in time to see the huge Christmas tree on the point light up as the last sign of sunlight faded out.

"Aaahhhh! So pretty!" Morgana exclaimed.

"See and you almost missed it," Cole ribbed her.

"Well, I was almost impressed with all this, but it turns out this is, what, your typical Tuesday night date?" Morgana taunted him.

"First of all, this is only available on Christmas Eve. Secondly, no, I haven't skated in over three years. And third, this is definitely not a typical date. It's Christmas Eve and I wanted to share something magical with you," Cole stated his case in a matter-of-fact manner.

Morgana laughed. "Alright, counselor, you've made your case."

"I am pre-law," Cole touted, as he straightened his sport coat.

"No, you're not. Are you?"

"I actually am. I may continue into business law depending on how things go once I get to Paris."

"I didn't know that. I'm trying to get through junior college so I can transfer outta this dump and go into business law. I plan on getting a corporate job somewhere in a high rise and practicing corporate law."

"Hey, great! Mr. and Mrs. Big Shot! I mean, not, Mr. and Mrs. Well, you know." It was the first time Cole stumbled over his words.

Morgana pretended not to notice so much and changed the subject back to the big lit Christmas tree reflecting on the water. "Oh, look at its pretty reflection." She pointed out.

The waiter came over to take their order and the rest of the meal was fantastic.

"Anything for dessert, sir?" the waiter asked afterwards.

"If it's alright with the lady," Cole responded, "we would just like to have two hot chocolates to go, please."

Morgana smiled. "Sure."

François returned. "Sir, your ride is here."

"Thank you, François."

"Ride?" Morgana asked, but was teasingly ignored as Cole helped her from her chair and they walked to the front door. A one horse open sleigh was waiting outside. "Oh, my gosh," Morgana whispered with delightful surprise. "Is that for us?"

"Your chariot awaits." Cole held out his arm to escort her to the white sleigh carriage. He helped her climb in and there was a nice heavy Sherpa blanket inside that they snuggled under. François handed Cole their hot chocolate in paper cups after they were all situated.

"I can't believe this!" Morgana said as she settled in next to Cole and sipped hot chocolate as they were carted around to see all the Christmas and holiday lights in the quaint little mountain town. "This is pretty magical. Thank you, Cole." Morgana rested her head on his shoulder. He was their tour guide and pointed out the points of interest. There were huge homes completely decorated to the hilt. Whole blocks of homes were connected by strings of lights. Morgana love seeing them all. "We don't really decorate much compared to these people," Morgana said as she thought of her little tree that she and her mom put up a couple weeks ago. They had Christmas music playing and baked some cookies. It was probably the most time they had spent together since the previous year's Christmas tree trimming.

After an hour-long sleigh ride, they returned to the restaurant parking lot and back into their SUV. Cole helped her descend from the carriage and opened her car door. He had pre-started it, so the heater was warm and toasty when they got in. She held her frosty fingertips up to the vents to warm up. Cole got in on the driver side and did the same. "Luckily, the steering wheel is heated too!" he cheered. It started snowing as they drove through the little Christmas village on their way out of town. "I wanted to drive the four-wheel just in case of black ice or snow," he explained.

"I appreciate that," Morgana replied. "It's funny that this is just a little over an hour away from home, yet the whole world away. I never think about coming here. Thank you. This was wonderful." Morgana patted Cole on his shoulder, and he carefully navigated down the mountain through the falling snow. "Good night dancing snowflakes," Morgana said as she dreamily looked out her window when they reached the midpoint down and left the snow line. They cruised home sharing previous Christmas Eve stories and their favorite presents.

"Mine was probably my first bike," Cole reminisced.

"I guess mine has to be my Barbie Dream House!" Morgana giggled.

It was nearly midnight when they rolled up the inclined driveway. Cole walked her to the front door to say good night. "Merry Christmas, Morgana." He leaned in for a hug but this time it was she who initiated a deep, passionate kiss. He immediately responded and wrapped her up in his arms.

Oh, he is such a great kisser! Morgana thought as she savored his sweet lips. "Thank you, Cole. This evening was magical and that was the perfect ending to a fantastic day," Morgana said using his own words from the other night.

"I'll be back New Year's Eve. Do you have any plans?"

"Only if you want to make some!" Morgana laughed.

"Alright. Will do." Cole smiled and double raised his eyebrows mischievously.

"No skiing!" Morgana joked.

"Okay. Back to the drawing board, I guess." He pretended to be disappointed. He leaned in for another quick kiss and said good night. Morgana felt so happy and excited. She was looking forward to what he would plan for New Year's.

Christmas morning she and her mom exchanged presents over a French toast casserole, a staple tradition of theirs. She told her mom about her date with Cole and how wonderful it was to visit the mountain town again.

"Oh, gosh, we haven't been there since you were at least seven years old. That was before I got the job as the 911 operator. Your father used to take me up there when we were dating, but he never did anything like that!" They laughed and talked for a couple hours before her mom had to get ready for work. "It's really good spending time with you, sweetie." Her mom gave her a big hug.

"Oh, Mom," Morgana groaned, but gave her an extra hard squeeze. "I love you, too. Merry Christmas."

"Sorry I have to work tonight. Are you sure you'll be alright at Ms. Lane's?"

"Oh, totally. It'll just be the two of us and I love hearing all her stories. She's pretty cool."

"You have definitely taken a liking to her. I'm glad. She shouldn't be alone on Christmas either. It's good you two will have each other." Morgana waved goodbye as her mom drove down the inclined driveway. She grabbed the Christmas present she got for Ms. Lane and headed over to the sweet confectionery holiday house.

"Merry Christmas!" Morgana said as the heavy wooden door opened. "Am I too early?"

"Nonsense, dear. Come on in." Ms. Lane gave her a hug and she entered the delightful holiday home of her self-proclaimed fairy godmother.

"Oh, dinner smells delicious. Can I help with anything?"

"No, I have it all under control," Ms. Lane replied.

"I hope you didn't go to too much trouble. I would be happy with TV dinners or something."

"Oh, now you tell me." Ms. Lane feigned exhaustion and they both laughed. "That's total nonsense. We can't have that on a night like tonight. Although, this is just His honorary birthday. His real birthday is in August. It was moved to December 25th in hopes to convert those who still followed the Olde Ways," she said with a wink. "Anyway, the point is peace, love and goodwill to all," she said in her whimsical way. "Dinner isn't quite ready. Shall we have some tea in the living room?"

"Sure, I have to tell you about my date with Cole last night." Morgana described how romantic and magical it was, how caring and sweet Cole is, and what a good kisser. "I had to. I couldn't help myself!" Morgana squealed. "It was all so perfect." Then she paused. "How do you know when someone is the right one, Ms. Lane?"

"Well, dear, everyone is the right one when you're vibrating in harmony. We are all united and connected by Beloved Grace. We are all soulmates here to share our journey with one another."

"Aghh!" Morgana groaned.

"But," Ms. Lane continued, ignoring her young friend's sass, "there are certain someones who light up our souls, who make our hearts sing, and who change our lives for the better. When you sync up with someone like that, there are no limits to how deep your love and connection can go."

"How do you know when you've met someone like that?" Morgana buried her face in a pink Christmas snowflake pillow because she already knew the answer that she didn't want to hear.

"You feel electric. Every one of your senses heightens. You see clearer, you feel better, your heart lifts. It's a lot like what people feel when they are first falling in love, but when two people are completely in sync, that feeling can last a lifetime. They have to focus on it. It is energy after all, and if they don't give it much attention it can fade. That's what they call falling out of love, but really it's neglected energetic pathways between two bodies."

"How old were you when you met Mr. Lane?"

"I was almost twenty-two and we were married when I was twenty-four."

"I really like Cole. I think I could fall in love with him. But," she buried her face in the pillow again, "he doesn't light up my soul like…" she trailed off, not wanting to finish the sentence. "No! You know what? You say it's all about energy and Cole and I have great energy together. I will just focus my energy on him, and not on people who have drama issues, and don't call me, and have other girls on their heels. I'm done with all that!" Morgana declared proudly.

Just then the doorbell rang and it startled Morgana a little. Ms. Lane looked a little confused herself, and went to see who was at her front door. Morgana stood in the sunken living room and watched while Ms. Lane walked around the pony wall to the heavy wooden door. As she swung it open, Morgana saw him first and her jaw about hit the floor.

"Merry Christmas, Aunt Katherine!" His silky voice sent shockwaves up Morgana's spine. In his hands he held a big pink box with a sparkly white bow.

"Josef!" Ms. Lane cried out. "What a surprise! I thought you were in Italy."

"I couldn't leave my favorite great-aunt alone on Christmas," he said as he entered the home and gave her a big hug. It was then that he noticed Morgana standing in the living room. "Hey, Morgana. Merry Christmas." He flashed his gorgeous smile at her and it about knocked her over.

"Merry Christmas," she said politely. He came around the pony wall into the sunken living room and gave her a big hug. Her heart sang. *Shut up!* she commanded it mentally.

"Dinner is almost ready. You're just in time." Ms. Lane winked at Morgana. "I guess it's good we didn't have TV dinners after all."

"You were in Italy?" Morgana interrogated Josef.

"Yes, I just flew back and drove straight here," Josef replied.

"How's my sister doing?" Ms. Lane and Josef chatted about Italy, Brook and Tristan, wedding plans, Christmas in Europe, and Jai's first visit.

"It was all well and good, but I had to get home to make sure you weren't all by yourself feeling neglected," Josef teased, and hugged his great-aunt.

"I was lucky enough to have the lovely Miss Morgana join me tonight. I was in wonderful hands."

Ms. Lane smiled at her dear friend, who nodded affirmatively.

"I am grateful you are here," Josef said directly to Morgana, making her heart want to leap out of her chest and jump into his big strong hands. She stopped it in her throat by gritting her teeth and just smiled at him. Then she went and hugged Ms. Lane. "I'm grateful to be here, too."

"Me, too!" agreed Ms. Lane. "Dinner is ready." They gathered in the kitchen. Ms. Lane held onto Morgana's hand and then she reached for Josef's. He came around the island and the three of them held hands in a circle. Ms. Lane spoke, "Dearly beloveds, we are so thankful for this day. It is the season of the heart and we are grateful to share it with us that are here in body and with those that are here in spirit. We welcome in all good things, and may all those who share this time space be blessed with an abundance of those good things. Wherever you share love, it is Christmas, and we are surrounded by love."

Morgana felt so good in their presence. She felt safe, loved, and protected. She felt supported and connected to All that Is. She felt the season of the heart. She felt so grateful to share it. She couldn't help it and tears of love spilled down her checks. With a small crackly voice she said to the others in her beloved circle, "Thank you for letting me be here with you guys tonight. I feel so connected and loved."

"You are, dear. You definitely are." Ms. Lane gave her hug and Josef wrapped his arms around both of them.

"Group hug!" he announced.

"Alright. Alright. Let's eat," Morgana said, "before I drown us all in tears." They all laughed and grabbed their plates. Ms. Lane had made a pot roast with potatoes and carrots, and fresh baked biscuits. Morgana surveyed the feast with hungry eyes, and then wondered why was there so much food if it was just going to be the two girls. *That little sneak. Did she know he was coming?* Morgana eyed Ms. Lane suspiciously. "It's a nice coincidence that there's so much food, Ms. Lane."

"Sweet synchronicity, dear," Ms. Lane responded whimsically. Morgana was still suspicious.

"This is fantastic Aunt Katherine," Josef said when they all sat down to eat.

"Oh, my gosh! Ms. Lane, this is so delicious!" Morgana agreed.

They all enjoyed the scrumptious dinner and Josef talked about Italy and the farm, and how all Brook talks about now is the wedding.

"I'm Tristan's best man, so I guess I've got my work cut out for me," he said with a laugh.

"Have they set a date?" Morgana asked.

"They're pretty sure June, if they can find a venue."

"Oh, wow, this June? That'll be here before you know it," Morgana stated.

Josef nodded. "Brook keeps saying she wishes your garden could hold two hundred people, Aunt Katherine."

"Oh, dear." Ms. Lane let out a hoot. "That's a lot of people for my little backyard."

"I'm sure it'll be the wedding of the century," Josef joked.

"Who's in the wedding party?" Morgana wished she hadn't asked that as soon as the words left her lips.

"Well, me and Mitchell, Blake, and Tiffany, as the maid of honor. I don't think Brook had a choice on that one," Josef explained with a little uncomfortable laugh. "And, of course, the beloved Grand High Chairman, Ms. Katherine Lane, will be officiating."

Ms. Lane bowed her head in acknowledgement.

"You will? You can do that?" Morgana was surprised.

"Yes, for sure. I am honored to do so."

"That's so cool! You're so awesome!" Morgana said to her sweet little fairy godmother, who amazed her more and more every day.

They finished up their delicious Christmas dinner and helped clean up. Ms. Lane invited them into the living room next to the Christmas tree and crackling fire. They each had some decaf coffee with their apple pie à la mode and opened presents.

Morgana found Ms. Lane a snow globe with a pink ballerina inside. Ms. Lane gushed about how much she loved it and it was a perfect fit to her collection. She immediately added it to the white bookcase in a perfect spot with her others.

Ms. Lane handed Morgana a big box wrapped in pink and white Christmas tree wrapping paper. Morgana loved how sweet everything looked that Ms. Lane did. She opened it to find a gorgeous soft aqua blue velvet dress with a sweetheart neckline. "Oh, Ms. Lane. It's so beautiful!" Morgana gasped.

"Another one of Mrs. Thompson's creations," Ms. Lane explained. "I'm hoping you'll wear it to my birthday party in January."

"Yes! Definitely!" Morgana readily accepted the invitation. "I would love to! Thank you!"

Josef's big present for Aunt Katherine, included her favorite white pillar candles from Italy, some organic olive oil from her sister, and an Italian napkin ring set with silken napkins and from Brook and Blake. Ms. Lane was very happy with all her gifts.

About 8:30 p.m. Ms. Lane announced, "I hope you kids don't mind if this tired lady toddles off to bed. I have had a wonderfully long day." She gave them both a hug and told Josef the guest room was all his if he wanted to stay. She walked down the hall to her bedroom. Morgana and Josef were left sitting in awkward silence in the pink living room.

"She doesn't even have a TV," Josef commented.

"Well, um, if you want to, we could go to my house and watch a movie." Morgana didn't know who said those words that were coming out of her mouth.

"That would be nice," Josef accepted.

"Um, okay." Morgana was still shocked with herself. They cleaned up the pie dishes and Morgana gathered her new beautiful dress and headed out the heavy wooden door. Josef stopped at his car as Morgana started up the inclined driveway to her front door. He caught up by the time she unlocked it and they went inside. Her house had a long tiled entry way, with a spindled half wall open to the living room, which she pointed to for him. "Let me just go set this in my room. I'll be right back. Make yourself comfortable." She walked into her room and hung up her velvet Christmas present. The butterflies in her stomach were fluttering like crazy at the thought of Josef sitting in her living room. She gave herself a little pep talk in her mirrored closet door. "We can do this. Everything is fine," she soothed. "It's just Christmas and he's in my house." She crescendoed. "Oh! My! God! Why did I invite him here? Who said that? Did I say that? I can't believe I said that." Her pep talk wasn't working. She took a deep breath and grabbed the present she bought for him, not even knowing if or when she would have the chance to give it to him. She had to concentrate on walking and made her way down the hall to the living room. He had started a fire in the angled fireplace on the left side of the room and turned on the lights on the Christmas tree on the right side. He stood in front of the tree, his deep aqua blue eyes and gorgeous chiseled face lit by the golden fire light. If he had a bow on his head, she would have sworn Santa had answered her letters. He was holding a small gift bag in his hands. She felt having him there was the best gift of all.

"I hope it's okay I made a fire. It looked like there was a fresh one in there, already."

"Yes, mom and I had one this morning. Thank you for starting it." Morgana handed him her gift box that she wrapped in silver wrapping paper with green and silver ribbons. "I got this for you."

"I got this for you," Josef said with a sweet smile and handed her a little red wrapped gift bag with red and white candy cane tissue paper. They sat down on the couch and Josef insisted, "Ladies first."

Morgana removed the tissue paper and exposed a small black velvet jewelry box. She opened the case and inside was a set of earrings in the same Celtic style with the aqua blue heart diamonds as the amulet necklace. Morgana was astounded. "They're beautiful," she almost whispered.

"I had them made to match your necklace. Do you like them?" he asked.

"OH, they're so amazing. They're a perfect match." Morgana was really touched and shocked. They were gorgeous and he had them made for her.

He started opening his gift as she stared at her exquisite new jewelry.

"Oh, awesome!" he exclaimed and Morgana looked at him.

"Do you like it?" It was a brown leather binder with leather ties. "A very old world looking journal," Morgana explained.

"Yes, it's fantastic. Thank you."

Morgana stood up, as did he. She leaned into hug him, to thank him for her extravagant gift and he leaned into hug her. He smelled so good and he felt so good in her arms. Her heart and soul were electrified and she wished they could just be frozen like this forever. She looked up at his chiseled face and got lost in those deep aqua blue eyes. He slowly bent his neck down and his soft lips so very lightly and delicately touched her lips. It only lasted a split second, but in her mind time stopped and it seemed like an atomic bomb of light when off inside her. He carefully but quickly pulled back away from her. She almost fell forward a little, eager for more. He held her one hand to help steady her, but let go as soon as she was stable.

"Um, do you have something to drink? Water or something?" he said quickly.

She was confused and only thirsty for him, but then started feeling a little rejected. "I'm sorry. Is everything all right?" she asked, her heart was sinking and the old mortified feeling began to rise.

"Oh, yes, yes, of course it is, Morgana. Please don't be mad at me. I shouldn't have kissed you. I'm the one who is sorry. Look, if you want me to go, I totally understand." He started gathering up his jacket.

"No! No! Don't go! We were going to watch a movie." Morgana didn't know what just happened or what changed, she just knew that she didn't want him to leave.

"Are you sure?" Josef looked so apologetic, almost hurt or wounded.

"Yes, please stay. I don't know what happened, but I don't want you to go. I have caramel popcorn, and I don't think we have any kind of alcohol, but I probably have hot chocolate or something." Morgana looked concerned, but Josef laughed, clearing the air for both of them.

"How can I refuse caramel popcorn and hot chocolate?" he said with a gentle smile.

"Okay." She was relieved. "Pick out a movie and I'll make the hot chocolate."

Morgana had to walk past him to exit the living room. When she did he gently caught her hand and softly spoke into her ear, "It's complicated, but I promise I will explain one day."

She looked up at him, bringing her free hand to his cheek. "I'll hold you to that."

He took both of her hands in his and kissed them, before letting her walk away into the kitchen. As she waited for the milk to heat up, she closed her eyes and tenderly touched her lips with her fingertips remembering the feel of his sweet lips on hers. She opened her eyes and reached way back into the cupboard to pull out the silver serving tray. She hadn't used this since the day she was thirteen and tried to impress him as he mowed her yard. She poured the hot chocolate into the cups and set the popcorn all on the tray, then carried it into the living room. Josef was sitting on the couch and watched her walked in.

"Hey, you've been practicing I see," he said with his boisterous laugh.

"Don't make me laugh or I'll spill!" They laughed together.

Morgana nestled under the blanket from the back of the couch that Josef had laid out for them. They each took a sip from their cups as the movie started to play. They sat close together and shared the caramel popcorn as they watched the train make its way through the snow to the North Pole.

The sound of the garage door opening woke up Morgana. She must have fallen asleep during the movie. She was lying with Josef's arms wrapped around her. He had fallen asleep, too. She didn't want to move. She just wanted to stay in his arms forever. But when the door into the house closed, she quickly sat up, which woke Josef. During those first couple seconds of sleepy confusion of trying to remember where he was, he saw Morgana tenderly smiling at him, which caused him to take in a deep happy breath.

"My mom is home," Morgana said. That woke him right up and they stood up as her mom rounded the corner.

She was startled and said, "What is going on here?"

"Mom, you remember Josef, Ms. Lane's great-nephew. We were just watching a movie," Morgana explained.

"Josef? Yes, I remember." Her mother sounded perplexed as she surveyed the scene before her.

"Hi, Mrs. Anderson. It's nice to see you again. I'll be going now, Morgana. Thank you for the movie and the popcorn." Josef gathered his jacket and new leather journal binder, and made his way to the front door. Morgana walked him out.

"Sorry, I fell asleep on you," Morgana said. "I didn't even see them reach the North Pole."

"Ya, I'm pretty sure the caramel popcorn and hot chocolate combo put us into a sugar coma," he jested. "Thank you for a nice time."

"Merry Christmas, Josef."

"Merry Christmas, Lady Morgana." He kissed her hand and walked down the inclined driveway. She watched him get into his Mustang and listened to its engine fade out as he drove away. She came back inside to find her mom still standing in the living room.

"Why was he here?" her mother asked sternly.

"What? We were watching a movie. Ms. Lane doesn't have a TV." Morgana was completely surprised at her mother's reaction.

"I thought you said it was just going to be you and Ms. Lane," her mother continued her interrogation.

"He was in Italy and surprised her so she wouldn't be alone on Christmas," Morgana defended. "What's with the third degree?"

"How old is he, Morgana?"

"What? I guess like twenty-two or twenty-three. What's that got to do with anything?" Now Morgana was starting to get upset, matching her mother's already upset vibrations.

"You're only eighteen! He's too old for you!" her mother declared.

"Are you kidding me, right now?" Morgana snapped.

"NO, I'm not kidding! I don't think you should be hanging out with him. I don't approve," her mother ordered.

"What are you even talking about? I'm eighteen and you're hardly even around," Morgana shouted.

"I don't appreciate coming home and finding my daughter in a compromising position."

"Oh my God! Are you joking? Nothing happened. We were watching a movie, drinking hot chocolate, and eating caramel popcorn. Ooo scandalous!" Morgana popped off.

"Weren't you with Cole last night and now Josef tonight?" her mother yelled.

"What? So. What is your problem?" Morgana was getting pretty heated.

"My problem is that I feel like I was being set up and lied to. Maybe Ms. Lane isn't the good influence on you like I thought."

"What?" Now Morgana was furious. "You have no idea what you are even talking about. Look, I don't know if you had a bad day at work or what, but you're completely out of line. I'm going to bed. Good night!" Morgana tried to walk away.

"Morgana, wait," her mother said sadly with a deep sigh. She paused, and then with a heavy voice, "I saw the way you looked at him,

Morgana. I saw you look at him…the way I looked at your father. I was barely eighteen when I had you. I love you and wouldn't change my life with you for anything, but I don't want you to make the same mistakes I did. You have your whole life ahead of you."

Morgana's temper cooled and her defenses came down at her mother's honesty. "You got all that in the thirty seconds you met him?"

"I got all that in the first three seconds. The last twenty-seven seconds just confirmed it. Come here." Mrs. Anderson wrapped her arms around her daughter. "I'm sorry. I did the best I could for you, but I still wish I could have done better. I know you have big dreams and big goals, and I just want you to have the opportunity to make them happen. Dreamy guys like that have a way of making our own dreams set sail off into the sunset without us, leaving us high and dry. Guys like that somehow manage to make ship wrecks out of our lives," her mother said with deep sorrow in her voice.

"But that doesn't always have to be the case," Morgana said, pulling away from her mother's embrace.

"I wish it didn't, but it does. Boys like that are nothing but heartbreakers," her mother assured her. "It's best just to stay away."

Morgana hugged her mother good night and went to sleep thinking about what she had said. *Boys like that are nothing but heartbreakers.*

"That's not true. Right?" Morgana asked Ms. Lane the next day while having tea. "Why would she say something like that?"

"Because, it might feel true to her. But that does not mean it has to be your truth. The universe is a loving, nonjudgmental universe, and it will give you everything you ask for and more. You know the old saying 'careful what you wish for?' What that means is, whenever you have a thought, that thought is an energy wave. That energy wave emanates out from you like a beacon and matches up with other thoughts on the same wavelength. It goes out into the ethers and gathers more and more energy. If you keep thinking the same thought, or more accurately emitting the same emotional vibration of that thought for at least sixty-eight seconds, then you have now created a tsunami of an energy wave. It washes out to the universe as your frequency. The universe responds back and matches that frequency with more and more. So, if you think boys like that are heartbreakers and you hold onto that thought making it a belief, then the universe resonates that belief. And it will bring back to you example after example of that being your truth," Ms. Lane explained.

"But, what if I don't want that to be my truth?" Morgana asked.

"Here's the tricky part. Because, you can't un-think a thought, and the more you think about it, the more you emit that thought wave. Whether you say 'I want that' or 'I don't want that' either way, you are saying 'that.' So the way to handle it is: A – don't give it a second thought. Literally. We process ideas and thoughts thousands of times a day. Some things stick, but most of them don't. If you have a thought that doesn't feel 'right' for you, don't think about it, and just think of something else instead. But if a thought that you don't want happens to get its hooks into you, you have to change your thoughts. You can't say, 'I'm not gonna think about that thought,' because by default, you are thinking about it. So you have to change your thoughts. Or change your mind. In this case, the thought is 'boys like that are heartbreakers.' So change the thought. Talk yourself through it. Give it a try," Ms. Lane suggested.

"Okay, so I don't want 'boys like that to be heartbreakers.' I don't want boys to be able to break my heart. So, I change my mind to think it's better to be the heartbreaker? Well, no. I don't want that. Ummm. Help?" Morgana struggled.

"Well, how do you want to feel?" Ms. Lane guided.

"Ummm, I want to feel loved and connected and treasured and respected and taken care of and safe, but independent and strong," Morgana listed.

"Perfect, there you go," Ms. Lane commended.

"But I didn't talk about heartbreaking boys." Morgana was confused.

"Exactly, dear. You didn't let that thought in at all. You emanated strong high vibrations, so the universe will match those thoughts and it will bring back to you boys and relationships that match those frequencies. You can control your thoughts just like that, and therefore you can control your life experiences. If you focus on what you want, more importantly on how you want to feel, you will be in the driver's seat of your life," Ms. Lane described.

"So, what about mom? Is she stuck with that thought?" Morgana inquired.

"No, no one is stuck with a thought. But some of us can be stubborn with our thinking. We need to pay attention to the vibrational waves that are returning to us regarding the thoughts that no longer serve us that we may be holding onto. In this instance, your mom may keep attracting 'boys that are heartbreakers' and that should be her signal to decide if she wants to keep putting that vibration out there. If we don't pay attention to what we are attracting, then our bodies will try to signal us. Starting with an ache here, a sore there. When we manifest a physical aliment that just means we are really holding onto a thought that no longer serves us, and is doing us no good. Some people think their bodies are betraying them when they get sick, but the truth is their bodies are just showing them proof of a negative emotional block they have. It's up to the person to learn to listen to their bodies and find out what the message is. Or better yet, change their thoughts altogether. If you spend all your time and energy trying to figure out 'what's wrong' with you, then you're just adding energy to that thought. If you can just focus on feeling the best you can at every moment, then feeling good becomes your focus, and then your life just starts feeling good."

"So, you feel good all the time?" Morgana asked, a bit sarcastically.

"Well, I said 'the best' you can. That could mean sad instead of depressed. That could mean angry instead of sad, frustrated instead of angry, complacent instead of frustrated, or happy instead of complacent. Try to work your way up the emotional scale. But, when you feel anything besides joy or happy, it's usually the sign that you're focusing on the lack of what you want."

"Oh, man! You lost me," Morgana cried out.

Ms. Lane chuckled. "Okay, so you're eighteen years old. What do you want from life?" Ms. Lane posed the question.

"Well, I don't want to have to worry about money. I don't want my mom to have to work so much. I want to her to have a happy relationship or get married even. I guess, I want to travel. I want to get school over with. I want to start my real life. I want to stop feeling like I'm behind."

"So, you listed a bunch of things you don't want. First, you said you 'don't want to worry about money.' What's the focus of that sentence?" Ms. Lane asked.

"Money," Morgana replied.

"And what emotions do you feel when you say that sentence?"

"I don't want to have to worry about money." Morgana repeated it slowly. "Well, I guess, sad. I'm worried about money."

"And is that how you want to feel?"

"No!" Morgana expressed. "So, when I say I don't want to worry about money, and what I'm feeling is sadness or maybe even anger that I don't have enough, then that's what the universe is matching up with?"

"Yes."

"Well, crap! That's not good."

"No," Ms. Lane responded with a wise laugh.

"So, how do I fix it?" Morgana asked earnestly.

"Well, I'm sure you picked up that vibration growing up. Maybe money was tight?"

"Oh, geez. Money has always been tight. My mom is always worried about money."

"So, you have to change your belief about money. It might be a bit ingrained in your system because it's not just your belief but your mother's as well."

"What do you mean?"

"Just like her belief was 'boys are heartbreakers,' that was her belief that you chose not to accept. It was easy for you to let it go and change your thoughts. But with money, you believed her belief and have now made it your own. Plus, money scarcity is a common thought amongst many in the world. So being worried about money has a huge energy wave and it washes over you again and again. So, try to change your thoughts. Tell me how you want to feel about money."

"Um, well, okay. Let's see. I want to feel like there's enough, no, more than enough to go around for everyone," Morgana said.

"Okay, that's a good thought. Let's think about that. Do you think there's enough money in the world?"

"Well, ya. Some people have billions and trillions, but some have none," Morgana stated.

"Okay, so let's try to narrow it down to you. It's nice to think globally, but if you get too far too fast it can feel overwhelming," Ms. Lane explained.

"Okay. Fine. I want a million dollars," Morgana said defiantly.

"Great! To do what with?"

"Umm. To travel and to buy mom a house and to get a new car and maybe some new clothes, I guess," Morgana said much less confidently.

"You don't sound so sure about that," Ms. Lane pointed out. "Let's talk about travel. You keep bringing that up. Where do you want to go?"

"Umm, Paris, maybe. Cole might be moving there. Did I tell you that?"

"Yes, but let's not get sidetracked. Where else?"

"Oh, okay. Umm. Paris, I already said. So, Europe. I would like to see castles and stuff. And Australia looks fun. And, I guess there's a bunch here stateside that would be cool to see. I've never even been on an airplane before," Morgana rattled off.

"Wonderful, dear. But you can see how you're kind of all over the place, right?" Ms. Lane inquired.

"Ya, I guess I am, huh?" Morgana agreed.

"Can you see how it's hard for the universe to lock in on your signal and bring you what you want when you only kind of know what it is you want? Close your eyes for me." Morgana did. "Take a deep breath in and tell me how you want to feel."

Morgana peeked out one eye. "Feel about what about?"

Ms. Lane smiled. "Close your eyes and just tell me how you want your life to feel right now."

"Right now, right now?" Morgana asked.

"Yes, right now."

"Well, that's hard, because right now I feel great. I love being here talking to you. I feel safe here. I have fun here. I have everything I need. I love how I feel here. This chair is really comfortable. I love all your holiday decorations. I love your delicious cookies and tea. It feels warm and cozy here. I love how much I learn from you. I love just being here with you and not having to think about stupid boys, dumb school, and my crappy job while I'm here." Morgana opened one eye to see the response she knew was coming.

"Bring it back to want you want, not what you don't want," Ms. Lane said to her one eye.

"I know. I know. I love how you listen to me," Morgana giggled. She opened her eyes and added, "I feel like I'm in alignment when I'm here."

"Being in alignment is within you no matter where you are. Focus on those feelings you just listed that made you feel aligned and search for them everywhere you go. And try to go more places where you find them. Not everyone is looking for the same feelings. That's why we have options. So, go where it feels good to you," Ms. Lane explained.

"That's why I come here as much as I can!" Morgana took another pink iced cookie off the pink snowflake holiday tray and took a big bite.

"And it makes me happy to have you here, dear," Ms. Lane said with a big smile.

"Will you show me how to bake like you one day?" Morgana said with her mouth full of sweet cookie.

"I would love to!" Ms. Lane agreed.

hapter Twelve

Anam Cara

MORGANA WAS REALLY enjoying her winter break from school. She worked the day shift from 10 a.m. to 3 p.m., and got home in time for afternoon tea with Ms. Lane. She loved hearing all her stories and then she would go home to binge watch television shows or movies. Cole called a couple of times from his parents' house and they ended up talking for hours. She tried getting info about their New Year's plans, but he wasn't telling.

"You'll just have to wait," he said. "How many days do I have left, four or five?" he teased.

"We're down to two, so this better be good," Morgana replied.

"Two? Oh, crap. I guess I better come up with something quick!" he joked.

"Whatever! And you know I'm not impressed with your date-by-the-number dates, either," Morgana taunted.

"Date-by-numbers! Oh, I see how you are." He laughed at her taunts.

"That's right. I'm not one of your gold-digger girlfriends." Did she just say girlfriend? *Uh-oh*, she thought.

Cole played it off, "That's right. You're my special coffee buddy. I've never had one of those before."

"Ya, and you need to get back, quick. I need my fix!" Morgana said. "My Cole fix, not my coffee fix," she added sincerely.

"Me too. Good night, Morgana."

"Good night." They hung up. She lay in bed thinking. She really did miss him. He was so fun and a joy to be around. She hadn't heard a peep from Josef since Christmas, four days ago.

The next day, Morgana skidded up into her inclined driveway and changed into her favorite leggings and sweatshirt before heading over to Ms. Lane's house. She was surprised when the heavy door swung open and she hadn't heard the signature Victorian lace up boots clicking on the hardwood floors. "Welcome dear!" Ms. Lane welcomed her.

"Hi – What are you wearing?" Morgana was caught off guard to find Ms. Lane in flat ballet slipper shoes, pants and a sweater.

"It's baking day!" Ms. Lane announced with a big smile. "Come in! Come in."

"Baking day? You're going to teach me how to bake like you? Yay! I'm so excited!" Morgana rounded the pony wall, passed the angel faced shelves, and went around the huge round marble dining table into the kitchen. The velvet cranberry damask curtains were tied open, showing off the beautiful secret garden brightly lit by the winter sun.

"I figured we would start with a classic, chocolate and butterscotch chip cookies," Ms. Lane said excitedly.

"Oh, yes!" Morgana pretended to wipe her mouth.

"Wonderful! I went ahead and set out all the ingredients we'll need." Morgana surveyed the large marble kitchen island with all the familiar ingredients: flour, sugars, eggs, vanilla, baking soda, salt, butter, a bag of chocolate chips and a bag of butterscotch chips. Ms. Lane also had a nice Kitchen Aid mixer and silicon heart-shaped measuring cups and spoons, all pink of course.

"You'll notice all the ingredients are organic." Ms. Lane pointed out. Morgana nodded. "Now, here's my favorite part." With a box of matches in her hand, Ms. Lane was giddy as she walked up to a white candle in the middle of all the ingredients splayed on the marble island. "In the olden days," she said with a wink, "you had to light your fire before you could start cooking and that's where we get the saying- cooking from scratch." Ms. Lane dragged the match head against the scratchy surface igniting the sulfite and lighting the fire. She held the lit match for a moment. "I love that sound and smell," she said while breathing in and with a happy little smile. In front of her was a white pillar candle, one of the ones Josef brought her from Italy. Ms. Lane lit it and said, "Bless these hands with love and light." She lit another candle to the right of the stove, "Bless these ingredients with love and light." And a third candle to the left of the stove, "Bless this oven and heat with love and light." Then she explained, "You see, I have my three candles in a triangle around my ingredients and cooking space. The white candle represents purity, purity of love, purity of the ingredients, purity of the air."

"Of the air?" Morgana wondered.

"There's lot of negativity floating in the air around us. Not so much in my house," she smiled, "but it's there. I like to feel like I've created a safe space for my baking. So, first we have set the mood by blessing it. Which is to say, we have set the intention of the whole experience and all ingredients to be blessed with love and light. Blessing, love, and light are all very high vibrations. And, now, for the pièce de résistance, we set the tone. She picked up a remote control and aimed it towards the bottom shelf of the white bookcase. Horns started blowing, the ivory keys of a piano starting tapping, drums started banging, and wonderful, cheerfully fun music filled Ms. Lane's delightfully decorated home. "Bah! Bah! Bah!" Ms. Lane horned along with the song and she started dancing around the kitchen to the happy instrumental music. She had two aprons for Morgana to choose from, "Bless this mess" or "Hot stuff in the kitchen." Morgana chose "Bless this mess." They both put on their aprons to the music and Ms. Lane took Morgana by the hands and they danced and laughed around the island.

"So, you're just rockin' out?" Morgana laughed.

"Well, yes. You set the intention of blessings and love, you infuse your feelings in the ingredients and fire of the oven, and then you have fun! Life is what you make of it. So make it fun!" They spent the next hour mixing the dough, baking the cookies, and laughing and dancing around the kitchen. When the first batch was cooled just right, Morgana took a sample bite.

"Woo Hoo! They're delicious. I love this. Do you do this every time?"

"You don't have to every time. I will light a candle and bless the ingredients. If you do it regularly it keeps the vibrations happy and your food yummy."

"You're so awesome!" Morgana said to her sweet Mary Poppins fairy godmother.

"Vibrations are awesome. I'm just on the awesome vibe!" Ms. Lane winked and laughed at her young friend.

Morgana boxed up her lovingly blessed baked cookies to share with Cole when he picked her up the next day at 6 p.m.

"Ohmygod!" he cried with a mouth full of deliciously blessed chocolate and butterscotch goodness. "You made these?" he asked.

"Sang to them myself, I did," Morgana shared with a laugh.

"I mean, you can't beat a chocolate chip cookie, but I think I really can taste that they were baked with care," he said, downing another one. "That sounds crazy, right?"

"I know! You can taste the difference. I agree. It's probably the organic ingredients, but I think it's the infusion. I can't explain it, but I'll take it!" Morgana took a cookie from the box.

"Hey! Hey!" Cole grabbed the box away jokingly. "Those are mine!" Morgana smiled and shoved the whole cookie in her mouth. "Well played," said Cole. "Too bad you have chocolate all over your face now." He laughed at her with her mouth so full of cookie she could barely chew it. "What's the matter, cookie got your tongue?" he teased. She struggled to chew and swallow the huge bite and laugh and breathe. "Death by chocolate. Too bad, I had a pretty nice night planned," Cole joked.

"You jerk!" Morgana finally freed her mouth. "Do I really have chocolate on my face?"

"Yes, all over." Cole continued to laugh as she pulled down the car visor and flipped open the mirror. There was no chocolate on her face or lips. Cole just laughed as he expertly backed his luxury BMW down the inclined driveway. He drove to the wealthy side of town. They passed mansion after mansion.

Morgana wondered what vibrations the people in these homes were on. "Do you think they're happy living in those huge houses?" she pondered out loud.

"That's kind of the catch, isn't it? There are always bigger houses and more extravagant things to buy, but if you're not happy with yourself, it doesn't matter how much stuff you have," Cole expressed.

Morgana was impressed, yet again, by Cole's deep mentality.

He pulled into the driveway of one of the huge mansion homes. Morgana tensed. "Cole?"

There was clearly a party being set up as they drove on the long driveway past the main house. He pulled up to the guest house and parked in the attached garage. "Do you live here?" Morgana was confused and started feeling nervous and very self-conscious.

"My bosses live in the main house, and yes, I live in the guest house," Cole replied.

"Who are these guys?" Morgana asked starting to hyperventilate a little.

"I mentioned clothing was big business, right?" Cole laughed as he got out.

Morgana wasn't laughing, for some reason she was starting to panic. "Well, I guess I just didn't realize." She was stunned and still sitting with her seat belt on in the car.

Cole came around and opened her passenger door. "Are you okay?"

"I don't know....I've never...I mean...I'm in shock...I guess," Morgana stumbled over her words as she was trying to breathe and still not getting out of the car. Her eyes were the only thing she could move, as she scrutinized her casual attire feeling embarrassed at her dark wash jeans and silver lame tank top that only hours earlier seemed fun and festive, but now just looked cheap and stupid.

"It's okay. Get out of the car," Cole slightly commanded. "Look," he bent down next to her car seat to get on the same level with the paralyzed looking Morgana. "I'm not taking you to the party, unless you want to go." Morgana's face flashed with fear. "Which clearly you don't. I was hoping I could cook for you and you could show me some of that kitchen magic you told me about," he said with charm.

Morgana's neck finally broke free of its frozen state and she was able to turn her head and look into Cole's soft deep brown eyes. He smiled at her and held out his hand to help her exit the car. She almost had tears in her eyes and barely could whisper, "I'm a little out of my element apparently."

"I see that. Come on. Let me show you around my house." Cole stood up and held out his nice strong hands and took Morgana's shaky hand in them. She finally stood up and he helped steady her with a soft kiss on the forehead. "Come on. That a girl. One foot in front of the other. Yes, we're walking. That's it. You can do it." Cole egged her on until she cracked a smile.

"Oh, I see," Morgana said still a little bit winded. "You're the cabana boy."

"And she's back, ladies and gentleman!" Cole laughed heartily. They went inside Cole's two-thousand square foot, two bedroom guest house with lofty twelve-foot high ceilings and wide planked hardwood floors. Cole led her to the couch and then brought her a glass of water.

"My God," she said after a long drink. "It was like my life flashed in front of my eyes and all I could see was my broken home and my ragged clothes and it felt really awful," Morgana explained. "What do you think that was all about?"

"Some people just have more, but that doesn't make them any more of a person. Utilizing what you have to help those you can is what makes the difference."

"Says the sexy cabana boy," Morgana joked.

"Pierre is Pa-tri-cia's brother. He and his partner, Da-veed, live here and own many designer suit stores. I am their apprentice. And did you just call me sexy?" Cole called her out.

Morgana choked a little at Cole's inquest and almost spit out the sip of water she just drank. She gulped it down. "No, no! I don't think that's what I said," she retracted with a laugh. "I said something about you having a nice house."

"That's strange, cuz I could have sworn you called me sexy. Hmm. I'll have to review the security tapes later," Cole taunted.

"Shut up! There's not a security camera in here. Is there?" Morgana inspected the room suspiciously.

"Maybe there is, maybe there isn't," Cole taunted. He walked over to the stack-stone linear fireplace and turned on the warming flame with a button on his touch pad. Morgana watched her sexy cabana boy while still sipping on her water. He was so caring and polite. From her seat on the deluxe double stuffed tufted couch, she looked around his immaculate home. With another button on his touch screen, Cole opened the eleven-foot tall vertical blinds exposing his view overlooking an infinity edge pool that flowed directly into the city lights of the town below. It was a beautiful view.

Morgana almost gasped at the stunning view, but noticed Cole looking at her. "Nice pool, boy," she smirked.

Cole just shook his head laughingly. "Anyway! Are you hungry? Shall we make some magic?" He reached out his hand to help her off the couch.

"Do you have any white candles from Italy?" she sassed sarcastically.

"Italy? No. How about France?" Cole snarked, matching her sarcasm.

"Well, I guess, if that's all you have. But don't blame me if the food sours!" They both laughed.

"They're actually from Pottery Barn so who knows what's going to happen," Cole confessed. They set out all the food onto Cole's white quartz countertop. Morgana set the white candles in the triangle shape like Ms. Lane showed her and Cole handed over a box of matches.

"Do you have the music ready?" Morgana asked as she took out a match. Cole held up his electronic touch pad and she raked the match head against the rough box surface. "Bless these hands with love and light," she said as she lit the first candle. She lit the second one to the right of the stove, "Bless these ingredients with love and light." And a third candle to the left of the stove, "Bless this oven and heat with love and light." She pointed to Cole. "Cue the music."

"You said you didn't know what Ms. Lane was listening to, so I found inspiring uplifting instrumentals." Cole pressed play and delightful horns, guitars, and flutes started their tune.

Morgana closed her eyes and felt the beat. "Oh, I like it." She started moving to the music. "Alright. What are we making?"

"One of my favorite recipes, roasted shrimp with feta," Cole replied as he pre-heated the oven and turned on the flame under a large pan. He starting dicing the fennel and Morgana watched him shake his hips while he sliced and diced. While the fennel was sautéing, they danced together to the fun happy music, laughing and talking. Morgana zested the lemons as Cole stirred in the tomatoes. The view from the kitchen looked out over the pool and the twinkling city lights below. Morgana let herself get lost in the music and in the moment. She was dancing and laughing and felt so happy and alive. They added the shrimp and crumbled the breadcrumbs and feta on top, then put the pan in the oven. For the next twenty minutes while they waited, they danced the steps they knew from the winter ball. They were both having a great time lost in the trance of each other and the dance. The buzzer went off and startled them both, causing them to laugh hysterically. "That was fast!" Cole said and removed their dinner from the oven. He served up their plates and they sat down at his pre-set dining table.

Cole took the first bite. "No way! Holy cow!" he shouted.

"What?" Morgana asked and took a bite. The flavors burst in her mouth. "Oh, my God!" she cried out. "This is delicious!"

"It's one of my favorites, as I said, so I knew it would be good. But I really can tell the difference. It's so much more flavorful and so tender. Oh, man! I guess you'll just have to make it with me every time now!" Cole said. They toasted their forks and enjoyed their delicious blessed meal, still rocking to the uplifting music.

They were finishing up when they heard the party at the main house get loud. "I guess it started," Cole said looking at his watch. Morgana took a deep breath and smiled uncomfortably. "We're not going unless you want to," Cole assured her with a smile.

"Okay, thank you. You don't have to make an appearance or anything? You know, like serve jumbo shrimp shirtless or something like that?" Morgana teased, as she tried not to panic.

"Nope. Lucky for you, I took the night off." Cole took her taunts.

"Seriously though, do you usually have to go to their parties?" Morgana asked trying to get more information about Cole's job.

"Yes, they keep me busy. But it's pretty fun and I am so grateful for all the opportunities they've given me." Cole started cleaning up and Morgana walked over to the window to peek at the huge extravagant party going on just outside.

"Do you like parties like that?" she questioned.

"I guess. It's just part of the job. I mingle with the designers and the models, and just try to tout my bosses."

"Models?" Morgana couldn't help but feel even more self-conscious. She had been practicing her positive thoughts and was doing pretty well, but hearing Cole say he hung out with models made her stomach turn. "Why would your bosses live here?" She changed the subject.

"This is just one of their weekend houses. They're not here a lot of the time. They put me here so I could learn all the ins and outs of my own store before I go to Paris and run the stores there. It's a small mall, but every store counts."

Morgana's heart sank a little at the thought of Cole moving away. "Oh, ya. I tried to forget the fact that you were abandoning me this summer. Now I know it's to run off and live with models." She tried to be funny, but she was actually really sad at the thought of Cole leaving.

"Well, since you don't want to go to the party, my other option was to watch a movie. We can slip into the main house and use the theater room." Morgana shook her head no. "Okay, well, we can watch it out here, but it's kind of loud, or we can watch it in my room."

"Those are my only options?" Morgana asked suspiciously.

"We can do anything you want, but that was my plan for the evening," Cole charmingly explained.

"What movie did you have in mind?"

"I thought we would pick one out together."

"No popcorn?" Morgana joked.

"We'd have to go to the main house if you want theater style, or I have the microwave kind here. But I was actually thinking..." He opened his freezer exposing chocolate chip mocha flavored ice cream. "Ice cream."

"Oh! You've been holding out!" Morgana yelled.

"Hey, I know what my job is. I'm the supplier. Look through the movie selection and I'll dish us up," Cole said. From his touch pad, he pulled up the list of movies. Morgana scanned through and narrowed it down to a couple, then Cole picked from those. "Shall we adjourn to the bedroom?" Cole joked suggestively.

"I'm only going in there to watch a movie and eat ice cream. And maybe build a fort!" she joked back.

"Hey, that'd be sweet!" Cole said as he led the way to his bedroom. They curled up on the bed. "Oh, geez! What is this bed made from, a cloud?" Morgana sank into the soft foam mattress and ultra-plush bedding. They started watching the movie and indulged in the sweet chocolate chip mocha ice cream. The movie ended at 11:30 p.m.

"Can I make you a latte or anything?"

"Ya, sure. That'd be good." They went into the kitchen and Morgana watched Cole work his fancy built-in cappuccino maker. "You're kidding?" she said, shaking her head.

"You mean everyone doesn't have cappuccino at a push of a button?" Cole snarked. "Would you like a mocha or vanilla?"

"Ah, mocha please. Duh," she stated.

"That's what I figured. Here you go. Follow me." He handed her the hot cup of mocha latte, grabbed the imitation snow white mink blanket off of the back of the couch and headed outside.

"Where are you going?" she called out.

"Just follow me," he demanded. She followed him outside and up a staircase to a roof top patio. The view was amazing. He wrapped the blanket around her as she sat in an espresso colored woven resin wicker gliding loveseat.

"May I?" He asked if he could sit next to her. She patted the cushion and he plopped down, snuggling under the blanket. They sat there gliding, taking in the view, and sipping on their mocha lattes.

"Are you really moving to Paris?" she asked sadly.

"Yes, June 5th, right after I graduate. I have to go start a new store and get it up and running," Cole said, still staring off at the city lights below.

"How long will you be there?"

"At least five years. The plan is to open up three new stores, and possibly even go to law school while I'm there.

"That's a lot of work. Will you ever have time to come back here?" Cole turned and looked at her. "I hope so."

Just then, they heard the partygoers counting down to midnight. "Ten, nine, eight, seven, six." Cole held onto Morgana's hand. "Five, four, three, two, one! Happy New Year!" the crowd all cheered. Fireworks started going off. Cole and Morgana had front row seats from his exclusive elevated rooftop patio.

"Happy New Year, Morgana."

"Happy New Year."

He leaned over and gave her sweet soft kiss and they sat back and watched the firework display. Morgana felt completely confused. She was really starting to fall for Cole, but with him moving out of the country and her conflicting feelings for Josef, she could hardly stand it. Her head started swimming. She looked over at the ostentatious main house and all the loud, drunk, glamorously dressed up partygoers. She couldn't see herself in that world, and Cole was being pulled there by his benefactors. She understood his position. They were paying for his school, room and board, and basically handing him his dream job. But here he was with her on the rooftop patio away from everyone. She felt guilty as though she was keeping him from where he was supposed to be.

"This was a perfect night for me. Thank you. But I can't help but feel like that's your world over there," Morgana said quietly after the fireworks finished, with tears forming in her eyes.

Cole turned to her and said, "I'll admit, it's been my primary focus for a long time. But there's something about being with you that just feels like home." He leaned in to kiss her and she met his lips with hers and a passionate, delicious kiss. He was such a good kisser. She tried hard not to think about the thoughts that flurried in her mind- Paris, extravagant parties, models, and Josef. She just wanted to enjoy his sweet taste. There was something about him that felt like home to her, too.

She suddenly pulled away. "I'm so confused. I feel like I'm falling for you, but what happens when you leave. I don't know if I can do this. I'm sorry!" She got up and raced down the staircase and went inside Cole's beautiful two-thousand square foot guest home, professionally decorated with rich, high-end designer furnishings. She felt she didn't belong here and started to hyperventilate again. Now the tears were streaming down her face and she was feeling dizzy. "I'm sorry, I have to go!" she confessed with much panic, as he came in the door behind her.

"Hey, what's wrong? You look like you're about to faint." Cole was concerned and ran to her side.

Morgana struggled to keep her eyes open and the room started to spin. "I have to…" Cole caught her as her body collapsed. He picked her up and carried her to the guest room. After placing her on the bed he got her some water to drink and a cold compress for her head. "I'm so embarrassed," she whispered, barely able to keep her eyes open.

"Don't be. You're fine. Just go to sleep. You're safe." She barely heard his words as she passed out.

She woke up a few hours later and went into the kitchen to find her phone: 3:30 a.m. She tiptoed down to Cole's room and saw him sleeping. Even asleep he looked like he belonged on the cover of GQ. She had her phone and was about to set up a ride to come get her, but Cole woke up.

"Hey, are you okay?" he said sleepily.

"Ya, don't wake up. I think I'm just going to go."

Cole opened his eyes. "No, I'll take you home." He pulled back the covers, exposing his shirtless body only wearing pajama bottoms.

Morgana took a deep breath and walked over to him. "Where's your pajama top?" He pointed to the drawer on the dresser. "Can I sleep in here with you?" He pulled open the covers on the other side of the bed. She quickly changed in the attached bathroom and snuggled next to him in the soft cloud bed.

"Good night," he said.

"Good night."

Hours later, she woke up to the sound of the fancy built-in coffee maker. She lay there in Cole's perfect cloud-like bed, and then remembering her behavior the night before, jumped up. She went into the kitchen and smiled when she came out to find Cole, still shirtless, standing in the kitchen preparing a tray of coffee and juice. "Ah, I was going to bring this to you."

"I don't deserve it. I'm so embarrassed," Morgana said with her hands over her face.

"Don't even worry about it. I have that effect on people," Cole said with his charming smile.

"Oh, brother," Morgana groaned, rolling her eyes.

"Feeling better, I see." He laughed. "Coffee? Juice?"

"Yes!" Morgana picked up each one and took a drink from both. "What time is it?"

"10 a.m. Do you want to play some tennis?" Cole teased.

"You play tennis?"

"Yes. Usually Da-veed and I have a morning game when he's here. But I doubt he's awake yet this morning."

"You don't seriously expect me to play tennis, do you?" Morgana inquired.

"No, ma'am, I was just offering." Cole laughed. "Are you hungry? I have bacon and eggs or I can call up to the house and get you whatever you want."

"You're killing me! Are you trying to make me faint again?" Morgana gasped. "Bacon and eggs are fine."

"No, ma'am, just messing with you."

Morgana opened the French doors to the pool deck and sipped on the freshly squeezed gourmet orange juice. She turned to look at Cole cooking away in the kitchen. "You're really going to cook bacon without a shirt on?" Morgana asked.

"Someone is wearing my shirt, so I guess I have to," Cole said smugly. "Besides, there is such a thing as a lid."

"Can I help?" Morgana asked.

"No, I think I got everything under control. But you can turn on some music, if you want."

Morgana looked at his complicated, fancy touchpad and couldn't figure out how worked. "Umm, what do I press?"

Cole took the controller and some nice ambient music started to play. "There we go. How's that?"

"Nice." Morgana felt something off in Cole's behavior. Her heart hurt in her chest. She had made such a fool of herself and could tell he was over her immature behavior. She excused herself and ran back to Cole's bathroom and quickly changed back into her clothes. She looked at herself in the mirror and tried to convince herself not to cry. She felt humiliated and devastated. She had ruined everything. She splashed her face with some cold water and tried to smooth down her tangled bed hair. Her eyes were turning red as she fought back the tears and she kept rinsing her face with cold water.

Cole came and knocked on the door. "Breakfast is ready. Are you okay in there?"

"Fine. Be right out." Morgana dried her face and yelled at herself in the mirror. "Stop crying. Your friendship is over. Enjoy your breakfast. You'll catch a ride and you'll never have to see him again," she told herself, which only made the tears well back up again. "Stop!" She wiped them away with the towel. She finally came out to find Cole sitting outside at the table on the patio.

Apparently while she was holed up in his bathroom he changed into jeans and a designer sweatshirt. He had placed a zip up hoodie on her chair. "In case you're cold," he offered.

"Thank you," she said avoiding eye contact, and wrapped it around her shoulders. She picked at her bacon.

"Is everything okay? Do you like your eggs?" Cole asked.

Morgana nodded, afraid that if she spoke the tears would spill out from behind her eyes. She didn't look at Cole and just focused on her food. Cole was about to say something when his house phone rang. "Yes? (Pause) A car?" He looked at Morgana with her head hung low. "Oh, yes, I guess that is for me." He hung up the phone. "You called for a ride?" He was confused.

Morgana got up and took her plate to the kitchen, grabbed her purse, the tears were streaming down her face. "I'm so sorry. I'm sorry I ruined everything!" She went out the garage door and ran down the driveway to find her ride. She heard Cole calling her name but she just kept running.

"It was so awful!" Morgana was re-telling the whole story to Ms. Lane later that day. "He probably thinks I'm a psycho! What kind of idiot faints on a date? One minute I'm hyperventilating, next we're kissing, then I'm fainting. I ruined our friendship by taking it to the next level. Then I ruined the next level by being a freak. What's wrong with me? He just lives in this world that I don't belong in. Extravagant parties with models. Paris. Designer fashion. Look at me! I wear five dollar leggings and flip-flops. I don't even know how to do my makeup. I'm just not cut out for that glamorous lifestyle. But he's so sweet! And then, to top it all off, I'm thinking about jerk-face Josef, who doesn't call or communicate at all. He gives me custom earrings to match the necklace his dead father made for his dead mother and then disappears. What's with that?" Morgana cried to her fairy godmother.

"You are kind of all over the place there, dear," Ms. Lane said with a gentle smile.

"I just don't get it. What's wrong with me?" Morgana said with her head buried in Ms. Lane's pink pillow, on her pink chair, in her little pink home. "I'm sorry to talk about your niece and family like that," Morgana apologized sincerely after realizing what she said.

"Well, dear, they are dead. It's okay." The sweet old lady smiled at her young friend. "What do you want, dear? What's your focus?"

"I just want to not feel so awkward in my own skin. I want to feel like I belong somewhere and to someone. I want to feel safe like I did kissing Cole, but I want to feel my soul light up like when I'm with Josef. You know, if I didn't know Josef I would think Cole was my match. Except for the fact that he lives in this glamorous world that makes me hyperventilate and faint! Oh, man!" Morgana exasperatedly threw her hands up and buried her face in the pillow again.

Ms. Lane gently smiled. "Take a deep breath and try again. What do you want?"

Morgana took a deep breath, tears filled her eyes. "Dammit!" She wiped the tears away. "I want to stop crying!" She said it so forcefully that Ms. Lane set down her teacup and looked at her.

"Listen to me. Your tears and emotions are your guidance system. They are letting you know when your focus is off your true heart's desire. You don't want to shut off your guidance system. Alright, dear." Ms. Lane never spoke like that before to Morgana.

Morgana looked at her and nodded in agreement. "Yes, ma'am. What do you think they're telling me?" Morgana asked forlornly.

"Well, my guess is that they're letting you know you have a resistance to letting people in. You're strong willed, which is good, except for when you use it as a defense to keep people out. You're young but you're teetering on believing that boys are heartbreakers. You're afraid of being abandoned and you don't feel like you deserve love. But these are all easily adjustable if you're ready to let yourself be open," the wise elder women described.

"Open to what?" Morgana was a bit shocked at how blatantly accurate Ms. Lane's assessment was of her inner turmoil.

"Open to life, to love, to miracles," Ms. Lane said as she closed her eyes and felt each word. "You know how you felt at Mabon and the winter solstice, and even at Samhain?"

"Yes, open and connected." Morgana remembered how great she felt.

"You can feel like that all the time. When you let go of resistance, then you're in the flow with life. All your decisions feel right because you listen to your inner guidance. Your life feels joyous. You feel loved from within. You feel safe from within," Ms. Lane explained.

"How do I do that?" Morgana felt desperate for that connection again.

"With practice, my dear. Just practice feeling good. Practice feeling the connection," Ms. Lane said with a smile. "Close your eyes and remember how you felt. Let it wash over you. Let yourself go back. Remember how the connection felt."

Morgana took a deep breath and tried to remember the magical feeling. She struggled with it.

It was a week later, and Morgana hadn't heard from Cole. She worked the week before school started, and never saw him. Two more weeks went by, and still nothing.

She did, however, see Josef at Ms. Lane's birthday celebration the week after New Year's. Morgana wore the beautiful aqua colored velvet dress Ms. Lane had given her for Christmas. She wore Josef's mother's amulet necklace and the new earrings Josef gave her. The party for Ms. Lane was held out at the beautiful lot where the mountains meet the sky. The celebration for the beloved Grand High Chairman was amazing. A sunset ceremony with a four-foot-high cake loaded with candles. Ms. Lane had her entire family gather around her to help blow them all out. Her sister, Lynetta, and her husband, Henry Meadow, even flew in from Italy to be there. Morgana watched Ms. Lane and her sister, her sister's children, and grandchildren all gathered around their dear sweet aunt. She watched Josef hold on to his favorite great-aunt tightly. The two odd men out, Ms. Lane, with no husband or children of her own, and

Josef, the orphan with no parents, but there they all were, a tight family unit. Brook and Blake were there with their parents, Jackson and Cindy. Morgana could see how much they all loved each other. And with the grand celebration, how much Ms. Lane was loved by all.

The family sat together at a big table. There wasn't a High Council stage this night. Morgana chose a seat at a table in the back and observed it from afar. It had only been a week since she left Cole standing in his garage calling out her name as she ran down the driveway with tears flooding her eyes, and she was still in anguish. She was trying to stay open, like Ms. Lane showed her, but she couldn't help feeling sad and ashamed. Even on this night, Ms. Lane's special night, she kept trying to reach for the connection she usually got from this place but her heart hurt and she felt so disconnected from everyone and everything. She watched Josef, staying close to his favorite aunt, and Morgana just felt alone. She didn't belong in Cole's world, and now she felt like she didn't belong in Josef's world either. The cake was served and everyone sang to the birthday girl, but Morgana couldn't lift her spirits and she just wanted to go home. After a bit, she tried to slip out and headed back to her car.

"Hey, wait, Morgana!" She heard his silky voice calling her name, and her heart ached in her chest. She turned around to see Josef jogging to catch up to her. "Are you leaving?" he asked.

"Ya, I'm not feeling too well, I guess." She avoided looking at him.

"Are you okay to drive?" He was really concerned.

"Ya, I'll be fine. I just figured I better go now, you know." She tried to keep walking and fought back the tears that were rising.

"Hey, what's going on?" Josef was trying to reach out, but she didn't know how to say her heart was confused with whatever game he was playing with her, it was breaking over her lost friendship with Cole, and she was devastated that she couldn't feel the connection to this place.

"I'm just not feeling well. I'll be fine. See you around." She walked away and didn't turn around as the tears broke free and started streaming down her face. She knew he was still standing there watching for a while before he turned around and went back to the festivities.

Morgana got into her old car and started down the dirt path. She didn't feel any connection to the mountains, stars, or magic. Her heart pained in her chest and the hot tears burned down her checks as she made the turn onto the freeway.

January was almost over when she finally saw Cole one day while she was at work. He was with a group of business men in Armani suits all carrying Italian leather briefcases. She tried to make eye contact with him but the group kept walking. Cole looked very much in his element leading the pack of designer suits, as she looked on from her minimum wage job, in the middle of the small mall, in the middle of small nowhere town. *I've got to get out of here!* she reminded herself.

Two weeks later, Morgana had her nose buried in her school book one night while at work. The mall was practically empty and it was almost closing time.

"Hi."

Morgana looked up to see Cole holding two frozen chocolate blended coffees.

"Hi!" She jumped out of her tall director's chair but tried to stop herself half way through and sort of fell over. "Hey. Hi. How are you?" she said catching herself.

"Good. And you?"

"Good. I'm good. Good. How are you? Oh, you already answered that, didn't you? Sorry."

"Are you closing up?" he asked, standing off a bit.

"Um. Wow. Ya." Morgana looked at her clock. "Ya, I guess it's about that time. My, how time flies when you're having fun, right?" She tried a weak laugh. "Um, so what have you been up to?" she asked as she packed her school books up and locked the kiosk. Cole just stood there, watching her. "I get it. You're watching to see if I'm going to freak out on you." Morgana deeply sighed. "I'm so sorry. I totally suck. I don't know what else to say."

"Can I walk you to your car?" he asked.

"Really? Yes, please! That'd be great!" Morgana finished locking up and Cole handed her one of the coffees then grabbed her book bag for her. "Thank you for the coffee. Thank you for carrying my bag. And thank you for talking to me again," Morgana said nervously. Cole was still standoffish, but at least he was walking with her and that was great.

They got to her car and she noticed he was parked next to her. Her eyes filled with tears. "I've missed you," she broke down. "I've missed this. I've missed us. I'm so sorry I ruined everything."

"What do you want from me, Morgana?" Cole asked directly.

"What? What do you mean? I just want you in my life, however I can have you," she cried. "I'm sorry I don't know how to be in your world and you're moving away to live a life that I've only read about in fairy tales. But these last weeks without you have been miserable," she tearfully confessed.

"Why did you leave like that?" he demanded.

"I was embarrassed and ashamed. I don't feel like I fit into your life, but I feel like I fit in with you. It was very confusing and I didn't know what to do. You seemed mad at me and I couldn't bear it. I'm so sorry!"

"Mad at you? I was worried about you. I was trying to feed you. I didn't know if you had an allergic reaction or what happened. And then you left like that. I didn't know what to do, so I gave you some space."

"Space? Is that what you've been doing?" Morgana felt a little relieved. "You don't hate me?"

Cole sighed and finally relented. "No. Come here. I don't hate you." He wrapped his arms around her and gave her a hug.

She sank into him and cried. "I thought I lost you."

"I'm right here." He held her. "You know, most girls only like me because of that lifestyle. You're the first one who didn't like me because of it," Cole admitted with a laugh.

"You, I like. All that fancy schmancy stuff, not so much. Sorry," she said tearfully. "Although, I could get used to that coffee machine."

"Good to know!" he said in his villain voice.

She was still hugging him, not wanting to let go. He was still holding on, too.

"Look, my bosses are throwing me a birthday party next week," Cole said and he felt Morgana stop breathing. "But if you don't want to go, why don't you make it up to me and plan something for the night after," Cole suggested.

"You won't be too hung over?" Morgana joked.

"I'll be fine. But maybe don't make plans to go on any roller coasters or anything." He laughed. "Are you working tomorrow night?"

"Yes."

"Me, too. I will see you tomorrow, then?"

"Okay, but I'm not letting you go, yet." Morgana was still clinging to her friend, under the lights, in the empty mall parking lot. "Thank you," she said again with a deep sigh of relief.

"See you tomorrow." He kissed her on the forehead and she let go. He opened her car door for her and she waited until he got into his car. He followed her to the turn when she went right and he went left.

She was so happy they were speaking again, but now what did that mean? He was still moving in four months. He was still in the fancy life. She didn't even want to go to his birthday party. "Oh crap," she said to herself. "Now I'm all confused again. But at least we're talking and everything else will work out."

With her new school schedule she hadn't seen much of Ms. Lane. Morgana sent her a text during class the next day.

M: Cole talked to me! (smiley)(smiley)

ML: That's wonderful!

M: His birthday is next week and he asked me to plan something.

ML: What are you going to do?

M: I dunno

ML: Let me know if I can help.

M: I definitely will. My new schedule sucks. How are you?

ML: I'm good. Thank you for asking. And thank you for my new apron.

Morgana had given Ms. Lane a pink apron with white glittery lettering that said: "Fairy Godmothers do it with magic."

M: Sorry, I left your party early.

ML: Josef said you weren't feeling well. He was worried.

M: I wasn't feeling connected. I'm sorry (teary face) I know you warned me about that. You were right, of course.

ML: When we pinch ourselves off to one thing, we pinch ourselves off to everything.

M: It was really bad. Forgive me?

ML: There's nothing to forgive. We all just do the best we can. Sometimes we do better than other times. (winky)(hug)

M: U R awesome! (heart)(heart)

ML: Hope to see you soon.

M: Me too!!!!

That night at work Cole stopped by with their frozen coffee fixes. Morgana got up and gave him a big hug. "I'm so happy to see you!" She told him how she went to Ms. Lane's birthday and was so closed off she not only couldn't feel the magic or connection, but she left early because she felt like she didn't belong. "Kind of like at your house, I guess," she confessed.

"You left Ms. Lane's birthday celebration!" Cole was flabbergasted.

"I know. It's weird. I felt so bad about you." Her eyes teared up again.

"Hey, hey. No crying at work," Cole said to make her laugh.

"Thank you," she said wiping her eyes. "Ms. Lane once told me shame was the lowest vibration. I was definitely down there and I really could tell how different things felt. To not be able to feel the connection at her birthday was almost, like scary, you know? And um, I even walked away from Mr. Wonderful, who was chasing me down trying to get me to talk." Morgana waited to see Cole's reaction.

He got a smug smile on his face. "Really? He was there?" Cole asked, intrigued.

"Yup. And she wasn't," Morgana added.

"Well, now. Isn't that interesting?" Cole drummed his fingers together. "A fascinating change of events," he said in his villainous voice.

"Shut up!" Morgana laughed. "See how much you mean to me!" she said seriously.

"I do. Thanks." Cole was touched. "I gotta get back. See you at closing time?"

"I'll be here." Morgana felt relieved and she had an idea for his birthday, too.

The following Saturday, Cole picked her up at 4 p.m. for his birthday plans with her. "I hope you don't mind driving," she said.

"Not at all, but that means you'll have to tell me where we're going," he said trying to get out the information she'd been taunting him with all week.

"Ha, nope! You'll just have to listen to the navigation." Morgana held out her phone programmed with the destination.

"Please turn right," the phone voice instructed.

"Alright then." Cole obliged and backed down the inclined driveway.

"So, how was the big birthday blowout extravaganza?" Morgana asked about the previous night's festivities.

"They went all out, that's for sure. You would have absolutely hated it!" Cole chuckled. He went on to detail a night of topless waiters and waitresses in saranwrap-like shorts serving hors d'oeuvres on clear platters, a stripper jumping out of his birthday cake, and endlessly flowing champagne.

"Real classy," Morgana said sarcastically, pretending she was about to vomit.

"It was a bit extreme," Cole chortled.

"Strippers? Really?" Morgana tried not to be jealous and shook her head.

"Well, Da-veed and Pierre like to party," he mused.

Morgana groaned and said, "And nothing says 'party' like a house full of drunk, naked people, I guess."

"Apparently," he said and laughed, too.

"Well, I guess we should turn around now, because there aren't any strippers where we are going," Morgana joked.

"Nonsense. Strippers come where ever they're called," he teased.

"Shut up!" Morgana laughed and jokingly shoved his arm.

"Alright. We've been driving from almost two hours. I know where we are, but where are we going?" Cole tried to get info out of her but she still wasn't giving in.

"You'll see. Not much further."

"Your destination is on the left," the automated voice stated.

Cole pulled his luxury vehicle into a parking lot adjacent to the beach. They got out and Morgana let him help her with her bags. It was February and pretty chilly down by the ocean, hardly anyone was there. It felt like they had the whole beach to themselves. Morgana pulled out a queen size cotton sheet and laid it out on the sand. Then she pulled out several white votive candles and three small glass lanterns. The moon was bright and full, lighting the rolling waves. Morgana placed Cole in the middle of the sheet and handed him a blanket. Then she took out a stick from the bag to draw a circle in the sand around them and placed the three lanterns in a triangle with them in the middle. She lit the three candles, "Bless this night with love and light," she said as she lit all three. Cole observed her with a smile as she set everything up. She grabbed a small wrapped gift out of her bag and sat down next to him.

"This is a friendship circle," she said, pointing to the circle in the sand and handed him his present. He unwrapped a ring box with two silver rings inside that read: "Anam Cara." Morgana took out a ring and took Cole's right hand. "Anam Cara is Gaelic for Soul Friend. Cole, I don't know where our lives will take us. You'll probably end up marrying a model, have model children, and live in a model castle somewhere, but I want you to know I will always treasure this time we've spent together. Will you be my friend forever?"

"Wow, a friendship proposal. This is all so sudden," Cole joked.

She laughed. "Alright. I know it's kind of corny, but I don't know how I fit in with models and strippers and Paris and saranwrap fashion, but I know how I feel when we're alone like this. I'm not going to stop you from your life that you've worked so hard for. I can't compete with all that and clearly I can't handle being anywhere near it. But I was devastated when I thought I had lost you. So maybe if we commit to being soul friends, you'll know you always have a place to come when you need a break from all the glitz and glamour and endlessly flowing champagne," Morgana said hopefully.

"Well, when you put it that way, how can a guy refuse? Yes! Yes! I'll be your friend!" Cole laughed and Morgana put his ring on his right hand. He put the other ring on her right ring finger and they fist bumped the rings together then made the explosion sound.

"And so it is and so shall be, blessed by the light of the moon, may our friendship endure for as long as we both agree," she decreed.

Morgana pulled out two sandwiches, a couple of soda cans, and some chips from a soft cooler she had in one of her bags. "I made us sandwiches for dinner." Morgana reached into the bag after they finished their sandwiches and pulled out a plastic lidded bowl. "Oh, one more thing." She removed the top and placed a birthday candle in the middle of the small personal cake she had made. "Happy birthday," she said as she handed it to him. He blew out the candle and they shared the cake, eating straight from the plastic bowl with plastic forks. They talked, enjoyed the cool salty air, wrapped up in their blanket, and watched the moon float across the sky. They lay under the blanket talking and watching the stars until they were thoroughly cold.

"I think my nose is getting frost bite," Morgana said.

"What? I can't hear you. My ears are frozen," Cole joked.

"I guess it's time to go." Morgana laughed.

"What?" he joked again. They folded up the blanket and sheet and packed away the lanterns, then headed back to the car.

On the way home Morgana said, "Oh, hey, I never asked what you got for your birthday."

"Huh? Oh, umm, nothing really," Cole answered.

"Ya, I guess they figured all night lap dancing was gift enough, huh?" she guffawed.

"Ha ha. Ya. I guess so," Cole answered quietly.

"What is it?" She sensed something.

"Uh, nothing. I'm just trying to defrost." Cole tried to play it off but Morgana felt like there was more.

"Umm, okay," she said a little confused.

"Okay, actually," Cole started, "they got me and a guest a week in St. Barth's for spring break. I wanted to ask you but I didn't know how that would fit into your life," he jested. "It's the second week of March. Do you have a passport?"

Morgana mocked, "A passport? You're joking? No, I don't have a passport."

"Would you like to go with me?" Cole asked seriously. "It'll just be the two of us in a private villa on the beach for a week, all paid, all-inclusive."

"I couldn't...I can't afford...I don't have...." Morgana struggled to finish her thoughts. She was trying to figure out what would happen if they spent a week together and how much it would cost. "How do I get a passport?" she finally said.

"I'll take you down to the county courthouse," Cole offered. "We would need to go soon though. It takes a couple weeks to process."

"Are you sure you want to go with me?" Morgana asked.

He laughed. "Yes. I'm sure. Can you handle going away with me?" he asked.

"All-inclusive beach resort. I guess I'll just have to force myself," Morgana said with big eyes.

"I don't want you to have to force yourself, Morgana," Cole said seriously.

"Cole, I was only joking."

"I know. I'm just saying, you won't be able to bail if you faint, is all."

"Oh ya, you're right. Shut up!" She playfully shoved him. "If you can help me get my passport in time, I would really love to go with you. That's freaking awesome! Right?"

"Very!" he agreed.

"Cole?"

"Yes?"

"Um, where's St. Barth's?"

He just laughed.

"Mom is totally jealous and wants to go." Morgana later shared the details of the trip with Ms. Lane.

"A week in the Caribbean," Ms. Lane surmised. "Wow. That's a big step."

"Well, um, I think we're going as friends," Morgana said innocently, looking at her Anam Cara ring.

"Of course, dear." Ms. Lane smiled at her naive young friend. "Everyone goes to the most romantic place on earth as friends."

"Oh, God. Do you think it's romantic?" Morgana asked with fear.

"I went there many times. It was very romantic. Of course, I was there with my love and everywhere we went was romantic." Ms. Lane smiled at the memory of her love filled past. "When are you going again?" Ms. Lane asked.

"March 11th through the 17th."

"Oh, perfect. You'll be back just in time for the Ostara celebration. And, not that it matters, but Josef's birthday is March 18th."

Morgana gave her sweet old friend the stink eye. "Anyway! What, may I ask, is Ostara?"

"It's the celebration of the Spring Equinox. When the world

awakens from its winter slumber, when the buds open their petals, and the animals shake off their winter coats. We'll be having a Saturday night dinner and dance and Sunday brunch out at the lot. And this time, maybe, you won't be so pinched off and you'll be able to enjoy yourself." This time Ms. Lane gave her young friend the stink eye.

They both laughed.

Chapter Thirteen

An Emotional Week in Paradise

"IS THIS ALL you packed?" Cole questioned Morgana as he loaded her small suitcase in his trunk.

"Ya. I only have two bathing suits. I brought a couple pairs of shorts and shirts, and a sun dress. Oh, and an extra pair of flip flops. What else do I need?" Morgana asked.

"Nothing, I guess," Cole replied with a laugh as he closed the lid.

"I did bring sunscreen. I figured they'd have soap and shampoo there, though. Right?"

"I'm sure we can get some if we need to."

He backed down the inclined driveway and they headed to the airport.

"Oh. I'm so nervous. I've never been on a plane before," Morgana confessed.

"Ever?"

"Nope," she answered with an anxious smile.

Cole laughed at how excited and nervous she looked. He expertly navigated her through TSA and to their terminal. Morgana was wide eyed the whole time as they boarded the plane and sat in business class. She enjoyed the service and the movies. It was all very exciting. They made it through customs after they landed and a private car waited curbside to take them to their private villa.

"What!" Morgana gasped as she walked through the double door entry into a huge, sprawling, pristine villa with white granite floors that met white walls and white furnishings that all kept the view of the crystal blue ocean waters just outside unobstructed. Dark wood door frames were the only contrast and they perfectly outlined the white sandy beaches. "The water practically comes up to the door!" she cried out as she opened the wall of glass doors that led out to the deck. "No way! A pool too!" On the right side of the house layout was the gourmet all white kitchen accented with stainless steel appliances and also an eat-in table and full bar next to more glass doors that opened directly to an infinity edge pool. "You could sit on the edge of the kitchen and dangle your feet in the water, or you could swim in the pool and look out over the rolling ocean." Morgana said.

Cole was with the attendant who delivered the bags and laughed as Morgana explored the white villa in disbelief.

"Champagne, sir?" the attendant asked.

"Yes, please. With strawberries," Cole responded.

"Very good, sir."

"Shut up!" Morgana's voice came out of one of the five bedrooms she explored. Each room was also white on white, with the exception of the dark rich wood door frames on the French doors with wooden louver window shutters and white flowy sheer curtains. The headboards and nightstands were stained to match the espresso shade of the wood frames. Big, thick, fluffy, white goose down comforters covered the beds and begged to be laid on.

Cole went through a checklist of services for the next six days. In-room massages, parasailing, scuba diving, horseback riding, ATV'ing, and two sunset dinner cruises.

"Shut up!" Morgana exclaimed from the fully stocked kitchen and bar. "There is so much food here!" she said as she rounded the corner. "Who lives here?"

"It's just a vacation rental Da-veed and Pierre use frequently. They have a pre-set package list that is accommodated. Strawberry?" Cole offered her a perfectly chilled strawberry from a silver platter. "There's chocolate, too, if you would like to dip," he said with a smirk.

"Thank you." Morgana snatched the hand-sized fruit and dunked it in the chocolate sauce. "Oh, dear Lord!" she exclaimed at the succulent sweet flavors as its juice dripped down her chin.

Morgana awoke the next morning in a damp bathing suit and with a massive headache. There was a bottle of water and a bottle of aspirin on the nightstand next to her bed. She swallowed three pills and a huge drink of water. She wobbled out into the palatial white villa and found Cole outside on the veranda looking perfectly GQ in an open white shirt and black board shorts.

"Heeey, goooood morning sunshine," Cole greeted her as she stumbled from the kitchen with a glass of orange juice.

"Oohhh, what happened?" she groaned.

"Well, you decided to take advantage of the legal drinking age in the Caribbean and drank the whole bar!" he explained with an animated laugh.

"Really?" Morgana tried to think but it hurt too much. "I remember the champagne and strawberries," she struggled.

"Yes, you said you wanted to be like my model friends," he ribbed her.

"Oh, yah." She grimaced as the memories were coming back.

"Then after two bottles of champagne, you decided to hit the hard stuff." Cole was really enjoying rubbing it in. "Here have a Bloody Mary. It'll help. Did you find the aspirin?"

"Yes, thank you," she said slurping down the drink hoping anything would keep her head from exploding all over Cole's perfectly exposed chest and white shirt.

"I have us signed up for scuba diving in two hours. Think you'll be up for it?" he asked.

She looked up at his perfect fresh face through one blurry eye. "Ya. That sounds great," she said a little sarcastically, then sucked down another gulp of her Bloody Mary. "This is actually pretty good. I'm surprised." She slowly stood up with her drink and walked into the refreshing beach entry infinity edged pool. "Be a dear will you, and fetch my sunglasses," she called out to Cole in her best regal voice.

He laughed and obliged, then joined her in the pool. They stared out over the crystal blue water. Morgana flashed to a vision of blue water matching Josef's deep aqua blue eyes. *Oh, for real?* she berated herself, rolled her eyes which made her head pound. "Ahh!" she cried out.

"Are you okay?" Cole asked.

"Oh, yah, just the throbbing!" She laughed at herself and dunked her head under the water.

When she surfaced, Cole pointed out a buffet of food. "It's included."

"Of course it is." Morgana took in a mouth full of pool water and sprayed it at Cole. "So is this!"

"Hey!" He playfully splashed back. He got out and grabbed them a plate of fresh fruit and croissants, then brought it back to the pool. After Morgana ate a couple croissants, finished her Bloody Mary and some coffee, she was feeling better. "You up for swimming with the fishes?" he asked.

"I hope that's not a mafia reference," Morgana joked as she pulled on a pair of shorts and tank top over her still wet bathing suit. Cole laughed. "What?" she said. "Aren't we just going to get wet again? I'm sorry I don't have a different outfit for each activity," she snarked.

"It's not that. I was actually just thinking how great you are," Cole said sincerely.

"Oh." Morgana was caught off guard by that. "Thank you. You're pretty great yourself."

"Shall we scuba?" he asked.

"Let's!"

Cole escorted Morgana to the private dock at the end of their beach. "How many times have you been here?" she asked as they waited for the boat.

"I've been coming here with Pierre and Da-Veed since I was sixteen. This is the first time they let me come on my own," he explained.

"Wow. You really have been planning this for a while."

"Yup, six years. It's all I thought I wanted."

He helped her climb into the boat when it arrived and they sailed around the cove as the instructors gave Morgana a diving demonstration.

"We can just snorkel at our beach in front of the house, but we'll see more fish over at the reef," Cole explained.

Morgana was just enjoying the open salty air rushing on her face. This truly was paradise. They spent the day swimming in the clear blue water. Morgana loved every minute of it. Cole would point out different kinds of fish as they swam close together. They were served lunch on the boat, fresh fruit and tuna salad sandwiches.

"I've never had tuna that didn't come from a can," Morgana confessed.

"It's a little different, isn't it?"

"I like it. It's really fresh."

"Well, we can ride back with the boat or we can try to swim back," Cole announced.

"Is it far to swim?"

"It's not a leisurely swim, but we can do it if you want."

"Let's ride back in the boat, and keep swimming at our beach," Morgana suggested.

"Sounds good." Cole let the crew know to pull the anchor and they were off. Morgana loved the wind on her face as the boat glided through the waves. She closed her eyes and felt the warm rays of the sun on her cheeks. When they reached the dock Cole helped her out and she ran along the water's edge kicking and teasing the lapping sprays.

"Oh, I love it here! Can we just move here and live here forever?" she praised.

"If that's want you want, I'll see what I can do."

"Oh, my God! There's a hammock over the water!" she cried out with excitement. "Come lay on it with me." They climbed in the ultra-soft braided hammock in the warm shade and gently rocked with their feet dangling in the surf. "Oh. This is heaven," Morgana cooed and snuggled up in Cole's arms. "Let's just stay here for the rest of our lives."

"Okay." He kissed her on her forehead. She soon dozed off in his arms, listening to the breeze rustling the tree tops and the soft rolling waves tickling the sandy beach. Several glorious sleepy hours later, Cole whispered to her, "Hey, sleeping beauty."

"Mmmmm," she lazily replied.

"Do you want to go on a sunset cruise?"

"Mmmm. Okay. Do I have to move?"

"Ya, 'fraid so."

"But this is sooooo relaxinnnngg. I don't have a care in the world. All my worries are miles away," she murmured and drifted back to la-la land.

"Hey."

"Mmmm."

"We're going to miss the boat."

"You're going to make me move?"

"We can do this again later. And technically, I guess we don't have to go."

"No, no. I'm getting up." She didn't budge.

"Hey."

"Mmmmm. Oh, you mean now?"

"Yes."

"Mmmm. I'm sooooo comfy though."

"I know. I'm enjoying this too. Did you want to change?" he asked.

That got her to open one eye only to give him a "look." "No. I'm good." She snapped closed her eye again.

"Alright. I'm getting hungry. Upsie daisy little miss lazy." Cole moved his arm out from underneath her, dropping her head.

"Oh! You're mean!"

"I'm mean?" He laughed.

"Fine! Let's go have fun and enjoy our youth," she said satirically as she dragged her body like she was old and feeble and sat up in the hammock.

"Let's go, grandma. I'll fetch your walker," Cole taunted.

"Fetch me my whooping stick, too. I'll give you young whippersnapper a paddling!" she called out in her best elderly impersonation.

"You'd have to catch me first grandma!" Cole jumped out of the hammock, making it spin and dump her in the cresting wave.

"Oh! You really are gonna get it now!" she cried and kicked and splashed water at him, then chased him down the beach. They made it to the dock as the boat pulled up.

"Hey, perfect timing," Cole proudly announced. Morgana tried to get him with one more big splash but ended up losing her balance, and getting knocked over by a wave, completely falling in. Cole turned just in time to see the whole thing and laughed hysterically as she pulled herself up. She was completely soaked and took a runner's start at him, jumping up on him, knocking him down in the sand with her landing on top. The wave crashed over, soaking him completely, too.

"Ah, nice refreshing dip before dinner," she said triumphantly as she let another wave come up and over them with Cole getting the brunt of the salty surf. She tried to get up but he pulled her down and kissed her as another wave washed over them both.

"Should we tell them to leave?" Morgana teased in a seductive voice.

"No, let them watch!" Cole said with a smirk and double raised his brows.

"Shut up!" Morgana laughed and got up, helped Cole up, and they ran to the dock to board the trimaran boat.

"Sorry about my clumsy friend," Cole announced to the awaiting crew. "She can't help but fall for me," he said as he smoothed his hair like a "cool guy."

"Oh, brother!" Morgana rolled her eyes and shoved him out of her way as she walked to the bow of the boat for a better view. Cole came up with a couple of towels, handing her one to dry off. She wrapped it around her shoulders and turned to watch the vast blue view. Cole sat down next to her, and the server brought over some Mai Tai cocktails.

"With little umbrellas!" Morgana squealed and took a big sip. "I bet the guy who invented these fun umbrellas lives on an island just like this."

"Actually, he lived in San Francisco," Cole stated in a matter-of-fact tone.

Morgana gave him a serious look. "I'll have you know," she also stated in a matter-of-fact tone, "that if I didn't like this drink so much," she pointed the base of the tiny umbrella at him. "I may have had to throw it on you."

"Oh, really?" Cole imparted.

"Really, Mr. Smarty pants!" She laughed.

"Well, then, lucky for me that you like it. Can we get another round here, please?" he called out to the server. They watched the blue sky turn bright crimson and orange as the sun melted into the ocean below. They ate barbeque shrimp kabobs and drank Mai Tais as the trimaran sailed its course.

"Thank you for bringing me here." Morgana laid her head on Cole's shoulder. "I feel so peaceful here by the ocean. There's magic here, too," she said. "It's different than at the lot, but I can feel the connection."

"Thank you for coming," he replied and rested his head on hers. They docked the boat and Cole helped her step off. They walked along the wet sand back to their palatial villa.

"Wud you rather be a mermaid or a wudland fairry?" Morgana

randomly asked as the alcohol from the Mai Tais started to really take its effect on her.

Cole chuckled and replied, "Umm, I've never really thought about it."

"I feel sooo peaceful here by the ocean. I luv'd swimming with the fishes and feeling like I could breathe underwater today. It was majessstic. But wat if you could neverrr see the mountains, or a baby deer drinkin' from a babblin' brook from freshly melted snow?"

The waves were lapping at their calves, and Morgana was dreamily talking as the intoxication of the alcohol and serenity mixed, when Cole stopped and wrapped her up in a wonderful passionate kiss. Morgana tasted the salty water on his lips. He finished the kiss and slightly pulled away. She was a quite tipsy from the Mai Tais and his kiss made her head buzz even more.

"Mmm, that was nice. Were you tryyying to shud me up?" she slurred.

"Are you drunk?" he asked.

"Not liiike I waz last night," she wobbled.

"No, last night you were obliterated," he said with a laugh.

"Do you knnnow how to make thossse Mai Tais?" She laid her heavy head on his shoulder.

"Yes."

"Do you thinkkk we could have one while we swimm in our pool? I'dd like that."

"Sure. If that's what you want." They walked up to the house and Morgana staggered straight into the beach entry pool. Cole went into the house and made them some drinks, but he didn't put any alcohol in hers.

"MMMMM!" She took a huge gulp. "This is yummmmy!" she cried out.

"Glad you like it," he said as he joined her in the pool.

"Do you thinnnnkkk we could live herrre? Ms. Lane alllways says lllife is what we make it. So hooow come more people don't just lllive lllike this? It's alllll work work work. Stress stress stress." She flopped her head from side to side.

"Well, I guess because people lose sight of what's important. They think they have to work hard for the money and then that becomes the goal."

"Mmm, that sounds lllike something Ms. Llllane would say." Morgana tipped her heavy head back into the pool and tried to float. "SSSoo, I guess the secrettt is to do something you lllove and sharre it with someone you lllove." She dunked down and swam under the water to the edge of the pool where Cole was floating with their drinks. "Do you lllove what you dooo?" she asked as she surfaced, then grabbed her drink and took a long thirsty guzzle.

"Ya, I guess," he said hesitantly. "I do a lot of stuff that goes with the job, but I love the opportunities and the perks," he said waving towards the villa.

"You'rrre lllucky. You'rrre lllliving your llife. I feel lllike I'm stuck in a holllding pattern, ya know? Not able to lllland and not able to flyy away. I really wish I could just fllyyyyy away. Wud you fly awaaay wid me? OH! Nevermind! Don't answer that." She grabbed her mouth, splashing herself. "I promised youuu I wouldn't takkke you from your lllife." Morgana took another giant drink, finishing off what she thought was a Mai Tai but was really only orange juice, pineapple juice, and sweet and sour mix. "Wud you please mmmake me manother one?" she purred.

"Of course." Cole swam over to the pool side bar and mixed up another alcohol free Mai Tai.

"Mmmmm, thunk ya!" Morgana took another big swig.

"Well, what do you want to do with your life?" Cole asked.

"Cole, you don't understannnd. I ddidn't even know places like this esisted." She splashed her hands into the water. "I spent my whole lllife just trying to get outta that one horse town that I don't care wherrre I ggo. I've just got to finishhh schooool and then I can get on with my llllife. Lllike you'rrre doing. You getttto finish school and move to Parrrriss," she emphasized romantically. "And socialize with the richhe and famous while I'llll still be here, well therrre, mizzerable, trying to fight mmmy way out." She swung at the pool water like a boxer. "That's why I've decided I'mmmm gonna becommme a mmmermaid!" she shouted and dunked under the water again. She surfaced close to Cole. He reached for her arms and pulled her to him.

"But if you were a mermaid, you'd miss the mountains." He gave her a small kiss. "And the baby deers." Another small kiss. "And babbling brooks made from freshly melted snow." This time he locked onto her lips with a long sweet amazing kiss. They floated in the pool kissing until 2 a.m.

"Come on, little mermaid. Let's go to bed." Cole helped the still slightly buzzed Morgana into one of the guest rooms where she had put her suit case and then went to his room down the hall. Morgana tried to keep her balance as she ransacked her bag for her modest white nightgown with a square neckline and thick ruffled straps. She pulled on the dry gown over her wet hair and clumsily kicked off her stubborn wet bathing suit. Then she snuck down the hall to see what Cole was doing. She discovered him rinsing off in the shower in his en suite.

Holymother! she said to herself as she caught a glimpse of his amazing naked body, and then ran out of the room before he caught her creeping on him. She scurried back to her room and locked the door behind her. "OH!" She was breathless and dizzy. She went into her en suite and talked to herself in the mirror. "Did you see him? He's beeeeaautifulll. What amm I doinggg here? OH crap. How did I get here?" She jumped into the shower washing off the salt and chorine from the day. "Oh crap. Oh crap!" She repeated, her head felt fuzzy and the shampoo was running in her eyes. "What am I going to do? Don't hyperventilate! Oh crap! I can't breathe. Now I can't see, crap! I have soap in my eye. Ow!" She soaped herself up and rinsed off. "Holy hotness. Oh crap!" She toweled off and put her modest nightgown back on. She tiptoed to her bedroom door and tried to quietly unlock it. She cracked open the door to peek out to try to see his room. The house was dark and still. She quickly closed the door and turned off her light. She pressed her ear against it. Silence. She cracked it open again.

"Cole?" she quietly called out down the hall.

"Yes?" a sleepy voice came out of the darkness.

"What are you doing?"

"Sleeping."

She took a deep breath and gathered as much composure as she could in her intoxicated state, then fully opened her door and tiptoed down the hall. "Cole?" she whispered into his room.

"Yes?"

"Can I sleep in here with you?" A big wave of white goose down comforter flew back opening up for her to climb in. She tucked in next to him and he spooned up against her.

"Cole?" she barely whispered.

"Yes?"

"Do you want to have sex with me?" she squeaked.

"Very much so. But when you're sober," he said and kissed the back of her head.

"But I might be too nervous when I'm sober," she confessed in a slurred whisper.

He chuckled. "That's a risk I'm willing to take."

"Cole?"

"Yes?"

"I accidently saw you in the shower," she giggled.

"Go to sleep," he ordered.

"Good night, Cole."

"Good night, little pervert." He laughed and pulled her tightly against him. She giggled and dozed off still feeling like she was rocking in the ocean waves.

In the morning there was a knock at the door that woke them.

"Oh wow, it's 10 a.m. I ordered us some massages." Cole rolled out of bed and walked to open the door to let in the massage therapists. "Yes, on the veranda. Thank you." He instructed them where to set up their tables. He came back down the hall to find Morgana with the blankets pulled over her head. "Wake up sleeping beauty," he cooed.

"Ugghh, tell them to come back later," she muffled into the pillow.

Cole pulled back the blankets to completely uncover her. "Come on. You can do it," he teased.

"You're so demanding!"

He scooped her up and tossed her over his shoulder. "That's it! No more Mr. Nice Guy." She squealed as he carried her like a sack of potatoes down the hall. He brought her out to the veranda and set her down next to the massage table.

"What do I do?" she whispered.

"Lay down on the table," he whispered back.

"Do I take off my nightgown?"

"Yes."

"With everyone watching?" She blushed.

"No one is watching. See how they've turned away. Take off your gown and get under the sheet. Lay on your stomach first." He showed her the folded sheet.

"I'm nervous."

"It's a massage, not surgery," he joked.

"Okay. Look away." She made sure he turned his back, and quickly undressed then climbed under the sheet on her stomach. "Okay." Then she watched as Cole walked over to his table and untied his pajama bottoms.

"Hey, you don't get to look!" he teased. "Cover your eyes," he ordered. Morgana put her hand over her eyes but was clearly peeking through her fingers. "Hey!" Cole laughed as he expertly sat on the massage table, removed his pants, and climbed under the sheet, in one fell swoop, without exposing anything. He looked at her quite smugly and laughed at her still pretending to cover her eyes.

Nearly two hours fabulous later, the massage therapists had just left and Morgana felt like warm jelly. "Holy cow! That was amazing! I don't think I can move." She was back in her modest white nightgown, splayed out on the cushioned lounge chair.

"Are you hungry?" Cole called from the kitchen.

Morgana was lost in thought, transfixed on the aqua blue ocean view. Cole came over with a plate of fruits, cheeses, and croissants and sat on next to her on the edge of her lounge chair. "Are you there?" he asked.

She broke her gaze from the view and looked at Cole, her eyes taking a minute to adjust. She looked at his gorgeous GQ body, his big soft brown eyes, and his endearing look as he held up a plate of food for her. She sadly smiled at him and her eyes filled with big tears. He got concerned and set the plate down. "What is it?"

"You know I'm struggling to feel like I deserve to be here…in this palace…with you." She started crying. "No one has ever been this nice to me. Guys usually just use and abuse me. You're so amazing, and sweet, and attentive, and freaking gorgeous! And I'm just this!" she cried, looking at herself with disdain.

"What? Oh, Morgana. You're wonderful. I've never met anyone like you. This is what you deserve and more." He handed her a napkin to dry her eyes and stroked her leg that she tucked up next to her body to sit in the fetal position. "You're being too hard on yourself. You're beautiful. You're smart. You're honest. You're not superficial in any way. You're funny. And you're great mermaid." That got her to smile. "There's that beautiful smile. You're amazing. And I am lucky to be here with you," he said, genuinely.

Morgana stretched out her leg and climbed on top of Cole's lap to kiss him. He wrapped his arms around her and kissed her deeply and passionately. She pulled back and he removed her nightgown then kissed her breasts. He was able to stand up with her wrapped around him and he carried her in his strong defined arms as she kissed his neck down the hallway and into the bedroom where they made love. They lay in the fluffy white goose down bedding together afterwards, the warm ocean breeze blowing into the room from the open French doors. Cole nuzzled into her neck holding onto her as she stroked his right hand with hers, both of them wearing their matching Anam Cara rings.

"Are you hungry?" Cole asked a little while later.

"Yeah, I am. What did you have in mind?"

"Let's go to town and check out the local fare."

"Sounds like a plan," Morgana concurred. They got ready and drove into town on the golf cart that came with the villa. They spent the afternoon looking at shops, tasting the local vendors, and having a really fun, lovely day. Cole offered to buy her several different things, such as local jewelry and dresses, but she wouldn't let him. "I agreed to come because it was already paid for. That's not included," she would say.

"So proud. Aren't we?" he teased.

"Shut up! It's not that."

"Oh really? I'd love to hear your defense, counselor."

"Ummm. Well, I just don't think you need to waste your money on me, I mean, stuff like that," she said rather defiantly.

"Oh, I see." He laughed. "Interesting." He looked devilish.

"And what does that mean?" she demanded to know.

"Oh nothing. Nothing at all," he taunted. "Will you at least let me buy you an ice cream?" He walked up to a vendor pushing his small cart.

"Yes. Ice cream is never a waste of money," she declared, and happily accepted the frozen treat.

"Hey, we gotta get back. We have sunset parasailing tonight," he announced.

"What?" she exclaimed. They made their way back to the golf cart and returned to the villa. They walked down to the dock and waited for the parasailing boat to arrive.

"How much did this week cost?" she asked.

"Oh, hell no! I'm not telling you that!" he said with a laugh.

"Why not?"

"Ahh, because you'll freak out. No, thank you. I'm having a wonderful time. Aren't you?"

"Yes. Amazing."

"Let's just leave it at that then. Da-veed and Pierre come here three or four times a year, and to them this is nothing. So, I don't want you to concern yourself. Okay?" he demanded. "Just relax and enjoy it."

"Was it that much?" she replied, reaching up to grasp her tensing chest.

"Let me put it this way, the amount to them is probably equivalent to the amount you spend on frozen coffees in a month. Can you accept that?"

Morgana tried to figure out the math. "I drink three week, plus the ones you buy me."

"No, you can't include those cuz you don't buy them."

"Well, I would if you would take my money!"

"But I don't, so you can't count 'em," he chuckled.

"I'm worried," she confessed nervously.

"Worried? About what?"

"That I'm costing you too much money." She started to breathe quickly.

"Oh, no! Don't you go into panic mode. We're about to fly above the water attached to a boat by a string. Don't you get yourself upset about money right now," he lightly warned. "Babe, it's alright. I know it's a lot of money to you. It's a lot to me, too. But this is how they like to spend their money. This was a gift to me and I wanted to share with you." He hugged her.

"But what about all the starving kids in Africa?" she cried.

"What? Well, uh, I guess they can come with me for my birthday next year." That made her laugh and she was able to take a deep breath and relax a little. "It's a crazy world, I know. What would Ms. Lane say?"

"Well, I guess she would say, I can't worry because worry just blocks energy. And money is just energy. We even call it currency. And she always says, you can't be poor enough to make someone rich. You can't be sick enough to make someone well. All you can do is focus on feeling good and try to be a good example to help others find their own happiness."

"Make sense to me," Cole concurred. "You feel better?"

"Yes, thank you."

"Are you ready to be flown like a kite?"

"Yes. I mean, ummm, well. As ready as I'll ever be, I guess," she confessed with a laugh.

"That's good, because here they come." The boat pulled up to the dock and they loaded up. The crew helped them get all strapped in and handed them each a drink.

"Ooh! Mai Tais!" Morgana's eyes got big.

"Hold onto it until we get up," Cole suggested. When the time was right they were released into the sky.

"Oooh Gaawwwwd!" Morgana squealed. They reached the end of the line and floated in the sky, sipping their Mai Tais and watching the sun dive into its watery bed for the night. "That was so cool!" Morgana cheered when they were back in the boat on their way home. "It was so beautiful. I love that." She danced along the beach and up to the villa after they returned. "Hey, someone is in the house!" She was startled.

Cole laughed. "No, it's okay. They're making dinner for us."

"Shut up! How did they know when we'd be back?"

"It's a pretty smooth operation they got here," Cole commented.

"I'll say." Morgana smiled. "Thank you again for bringing me." She reached out to hold his hand.

"Thanks again for coming." He folded her arm up in his arm and kissed her hand. They walked arm in arm into the open villa where the dining room was set up for their succulent lobster dinner. They spent the rest of the night swimming in the pool, talking about swimming under the water yesterday and floating in the sky today. Morgana was so happy and content being there with Cole.

"I wish we could stay here forever," she said floating next to Cole in the pool. He kissed her and carried her out of the beach entry into the bedroom where they made love and fell asleep in each other's arms.

The next day they took an ATV ride along the trails taking in the sights and then went dancing that night at a local club. When they got home, Cole mixed them up some drinks and Morgana felt so free, she stripped off her sundress and jumped naked it into the pool. "It tickles!" she giggled.

Cole laughed. "Who is this swimming naked in my pool? Not the same girl yesterday who was afraid to take off her nightgown for a massage?" He followed her lead, neatly folding his clothes on the table before jumping in. She pretended to not peek between her fingers covering her eyes. After couple hours of laughing and talking about being the last two people in the world, they started kissing. Cole grabbed a condom from the bar by the pool and they made love on the veranda.

"Are there condoms everywhere?" she asked.

"Well, it's part of the preset package," Cole explained.

"Oh, God. I don't even want to know," Morgana said, shaking her head as reality struck. She got up from where they were laying and ran naked down to the beach jumping into the rolling salty waves. Cole wrapped a towel around his waist and went after her, bringing a towel for her.

"Morgana?" he called out into the dark night.

"I'm here," a quiet voice call back.

"Where are you?" He found her lying down in the sand while the waves washed over her naked body. He sat down next to her in the sand. "Are you okay?"

"Sorry," she apologized. "I just... I almost forgot that this wasn't real. For a split second I forgot about Paris, models, strippers, and millionaire benefactors who have thousands of condoms everywhere." She paused with a deep sigh. "You have quite the life, Mr. Williams," she said distantly as her silent salty tears blended in with the salty ocean waves and were carried out to sea with the tide. They sat in silence, listening to the waves crash under the moonless night sky. "I think I need a shower," Morgana broke the quiet and stood up. Cole wrapped a towel around her shoulders and they walked back to the fantasy palatial villa.

More tears streamed down her cheeks with the suds of the shampoo as Morgana rinsed her hair in the shower in her en suite. Cole didn't say anything and neither did she when they had entered the house. She wished she had turned into a mermaid and returned to the sea. She had been so happy the last few days here in paradise but it was rapidly coming to an end. Soon she would have to go back to her minimum-wage job, her boring classes, her desperate struggle to leave her small town and her suffocating life. She toweled dry and put on her modest white nightgown. She didn't know if she should find Cole or just sleep in this guest room, but she wasn't tired so she decided to go to the kitchen for a drink of water. She walked out onto the veranda with her bottled water and stared out into the dark watery view. The soft Caribbean breeze rippled her white nightgown and tousled her long wavy hair. She closed her eyes and took in a long deep breath to take in the night air. The next thing she knew Cole's arms were wrapping around her from behind, his warm breath was on her neck, his soft lips delicately touching her skin.

"I'm sorry," she started to say.

"Morgana, I love you," Cole interrupted softly.

Tears filled her eyes again and her heart swelled. "I love you, too," she said. He kissed her neck harder and stroked her body. She turned and they passionately kissed their way back to the bedroom to make love.

Morgana got up early the next morning to make them breakfast. Cole came out just as she had everything ready. "Good morning sleeping beauty," she teased tensely. "Would you like some coffee? Omelettes are almost ready."

"Omelettes, that's nice. Coffee sounds great."

"Here you go." She handed him a freshly brewed cup and pointed to the breakfast table. "Have a seat. Would you like some toast?" She tried to cover up the quiver in her voice and served him his breakfast, then got her own plate ready.

"So what's on the agenda for today?" she asked, avoiding eye contact.

"Is everything alright?" he asked suspiciously.

"We have two more days where I can pretend we are the last two people on the planet and this is our world. So I'm going make the most of it," she said, trying to be calm but fighting back the tears. "So, what are our plans for today, dah-ling?" She forced a smile.

"Horseback riding and a sunset cruise."

"Oh, lovely. That will be most wonderful."

"Morgana…" he started.

She cut him off. "How is your omelette? I didn't know what you liked, but I make pretty good omelettes. Do you like it? I can make something else if you want."

"It's delicious," Cole conceded.

"Fabulous. What time is horseback riding?"

"Not until 4 this afternoon," he answered.

"Fabulous. Umm, maybe we can go for a swim. I love our pool. It's right here, so close. Just at the tip of our fingers. Isn't that just so convenient?" she quickly rambled off and tried to eat her breakfast but was unable to. "That was delicious. You finish up while I go put on my swimsuit," she said as she got up, clearing her plate and throwing away the omelette she only managed to take half a bite of. She barely made it to the guest room and locked the door before she burst into tears. There was a soft knock at the door. "Umm, I'm indisposed at the moment, dah-ling. I just need a few minutes," she said tearfully.

"Morgana, let me in," he insisted. She unlocked the door and hid her tear streaked face, pretending to be looking for her bathing suit and avoiding looking at him as he entered the room.

"Umm, I'm just trying to find my suit, dah-ling. I'll be right out," she squeaked through her tight throat.

"Morgana," Cole said calmly, "you only packed five things." he tried to joke.

"Ha ha. Ya, they did have shampoo," she said still avoiding eye contact.

"Babe," Cole said softly. "Please, look at me."

Morgana stopped what she was doing and buried her head in her hands, sobbing. "This isn't how I wanted to spend our last days," she said through deep breaths of sobs. Cole went into the en suite and grabbed some tissue then maneuvered her to sit on the bed next to him. "I'm sorry I mess," she cried harder, burying her face in his chest.

"You're fine." He stroked her hair. "What's this all about?" he asked gently.

"I have to give you back to THEM when we get home," she cried. "I like having you all to myself. I guess I'm selfish." she sobbed harder.

"I like having you all to myself, too," he replied. They lay down in the bed and he held her until eventually her sobs dissipated.

"Fuck!" she shouted. "Who knew paradise would be so emotional?" She laughed exasperated. "I'm sorry. I must've filled up with saltwater and now it's all leaking out," she joked.

"It's been emotional for me, too," Cole confessed. "I have been working for this for years, I'm about to graduate and take it over on my own. It's what I thought I always wanted. It's been my goal. Then I meet you and you're so different than all those people."

"Ya, I'm no model and I'm a broke ass," Morgana jokingly interjected.

"No, you're grounded. You're easy-going."

"If you ignore all the blubbering," she interrupted again.

"Shut up!" He laughed. "You make me feel like I could be happy anywhere. Like, I don't need all this. You make me feel like I just want to give it up and just be with you."

Morgana sat up and looked at him. "No! I promised you I wouldn't take you away from your life. You have people depending on you. This is what you want."

"Is it though? I don't know anymore. I've been lost in the fantasy of it just being the two of us, too."

He looked at her with his big soft brown eyes. She melted into him with a long deep passionate kiss, and then laughingly cringed and covered her eyes when he reached into, yet another, nightstand drawer full of condoms.

After they made love, they had some lunch and swam in the pool. At 4 p.m., the man with the horses arrived at the veranda. They mounted up and trotted along the white sandy beaches next to the aqua blue water. They arrived back at their dock as the dinner boat coasted up.

"It's Mai Tai time!" Morgana giggled.

"You heard the lady. Two Mai Tai's, please. Oh, and I'll have one, too." Cole joked to the bartender. After a delicious meal and a gorgeous sunset cruise, the boat returned them to their private dock at the villa.

"Mai Tai me, please, dah-ling!" Morgana asked as she walked into the beach entry pool.

"As you wish, dah-ling!" Cole went over to the bar to make them some drinks, when he was slopped in the back by Morgana's soaking wet bathing suit.

"Oh, really?" he said as he turned to look at a giggling Morgana naked in the pool. He joined her delivering their drinks and removed his trunks, too.

"Do you want to come with me to Ostara at the lot this weekend?" Morgana asked.

"Of course," Cole answered. "What's Ostara?"

"It's the celebration of the Spring Equinox. Ostara and Eostre were ancient goddesses of the sun and fertility, and both were Goddesses of Dawn. The spring equinox is the time of full dawn, when from that day forward the days grow longer than the nights. It is a time of new beginnings, when the earth is freed from the constraints of winter. This equinox symbolizes a time of new life and fertility. It is also around the time of Easter, that celebrates Jesus's resurrection, also representative of new life and rebirth. The Easter customs of coloring eggs and bunny rabbits delivering sweets comes from this, with eggs symbolizing new life and rabbits denoting fertility."

"I always wondered why we hunted Easter eggs," he said with an interested laugh.

"It's a Saturday night dinner and a Sunday brunch. I can't imagine sleeping on those costs after being here all week." She laughed. "It's also going to be hard not sleeping next to you." With that realization, her eyes got all watery. "Oh, God, what are we gonna do when we get back?"

"Hey, hey." Cole wrapped her up in his arms. "Anam Cara. Soul friends, as long as we both agree, right?" He took her limp right hand and tried to fist bump their rings together. "Remember you said that whenever I need a break from all the fun, and all the money, and the glamorous lifestyle, I could always come slum it with you. Right?" Cole teased, making her laugh and playfully push him away.

"That's not quite what I said!" she shouted and splashed him.

"Oh well, it was something like that," he taunted. She tried to jump on him and dunk him under the water, but he overpowered her and kissed her instead. "We could always move here and sell beads on the beach. We probably wouldn't be able to live in this villa, but I'm sure we could find a box somewhere and be very happy together."

"I couldn't live with myself if I made you give up everything," Morgana said softly, and then added sarcastically, "You know, all the fun and all the money!" She splashed him again.

"Don't forget the glamorous lifestyle," he teased.

"You bastard!" She laughed and tried to splash him again but he pinned her arms and kissed her. "Oh no!" She wriggled out of his embrace. "No slumming for you tonight!" She laughed and ran out of the beach entry pool into the house. He found her washing off in his shower where he joined and started washing her back with a soapy loofah. They kissed and lathered each other up, eventually making their way to the bed where they fell asleep in each other's arms after making love.

She woke up the next day to the smell of coffee Cole was making for them. She put on her modest white nightgown and then curled up next to Cole who was on the lounge chair on the veranda. Neither of them spoke for a while, both knowing this was their last day as the only two people on the planet.

"I didn't schedule anything for today, but we can do whatever you want to," Cole finally broke the silence.

"I'm good with this," Morgana said tightening her hold around his amazing body. He held her in his arms and kissed her forehead. They lay there, afraid to move, listening to the sounds of the rolling ocean waves of paradise.

"What time do we leave tomorrow?" Morgana's tight throat barely let her speak.

"11."

"Exactly twenty-four hours left," she whispered, her eyes filling up. He rolled her on top of him and kissed her salty wet lips as the tears spilled down her face.

"Fuck it!" he shouted. "We're selling beads! I've decided! Let's go find some beads we can sell. I'm not letting us leave here."

"You know I won't let that happen," she said as the tears flooded down her face.

"No, you said you wouldn't take me away from my life. What if I want to spend my life with you?"

"I can't let you leave all those people that are depending on you and everything you've worked for," she sobbed.

"Then come with me," he asked.

"I can't. You know I can't fit in with that crowd."

"No, maybe you just don't want to!" He pulled her off him and stood up.

"Cole!" she pleaded.

"It's just money for fucksakes, Morgana!" He walked away to the kitchen leaving her alone on the lounge. She stared out at the crystal aqua blue water before walking into the kitchen where he was making Bloody Marys. She walked behind him and kissed his strong muscled shoulders.

"You know, I wouldn't feel right living off you and taking handouts."

"Je-sus!" He jerked away from her. "It wouldn't be handouts. I can help you get a job if that's you want," he snapped.

"And what if it didn't work out? What if you realize you don't want to be with me, and you finally figure out you want to be with a model?" She started crying again.

"Ah fuck! I've been with models. They're not anything special. They're human. Humans, that don't eat, but still human," he shouted.

"I don't deserve you, Cole. You're too good for me. Is that what you want to hear?" she screamed.

"That's bullshit, Morgana. And you know it. Maybe you're just holding out for Mr. Wonderful to finally acknowledge you. That's why you don't want to go with me. Isn't it? It's not about you not fitting in with my life. It's about you not wanting to leave him out of yours!"

"Fuck you!" she screeched and ran out the veranda down to the water's edge. She kept running along the beach kicking up the waves, soaking her white modest nightgown. She finally collapsed in the sand and sobbed with her head in her hands. A while later, she felt the towel being wrapped around her shoulders. Her white nightgown was completely soaked through and suctioned to her body.

"Come back to the house, Morgana," he said softly but sternly.

"Why? You don't want me there," her hoarse voice cracked back.

"Yes, I do," he sighed. "Please, come back."

She didn't move. After a few minutes she finally said quietly, "It's not about him. It's about me. I don't know who I am. You are offering me the world and it's a wonderful generous world, but I don't know if it's the world I want. I love you Cole, but I feel like I have to figure out who I am and what I want for my life. I don't know if I can do that if I get lost in your life."

Cole sighed. "And that's what I love so much about you. You say you don't know who you are, but I think you know more about yourself than most people know of themselves. You are strong and independent, and when you start believing in yourself, there's no telling how far you'll go." He paused. "I'm sorry for what I said, I shouldn't have yelled at you like that."

"I'm sorry, too," she said and he helped her up and kissed her forehead. They walked along the rolling shores together hand-in-hand back to the palatial vacation villa.

"Well," Cole announced. "This has been some week. We've laughed. We've cried. We've loved. We've yelled. What else shall we check off the 'ol list before we go?"

"I'm freaking emotionally exhausted. I think it's Mai Tai time," Morgana suggested. "Either that or I'm going to sleep 'til next week and miss the rest of our time here."

"Mai Tais it is," Cole declared. Morgana walked into the beach entry infinity edge pool still in her pasted on white night gown. Cole came in after with drinks in hand and they toasted their glasses before they drank. "To our last night as the only two people in paradise," he said.

"To us, dah-ling," she said.

After several hours and many Mai Tais later, "Well, it's 4:30. We skipped breakfast. Drank lunch. What do you say to some dinner?" Cole asked.

"Sounnnnds mah-ve-lous dah-linnnggg," Morgana slurred.

"Oh, great. You're drunk." He laughed at her.

"But not ooobliterrrrated." She gave him a sloppy wink and a trigger finger.

"Let's get some food in you before that happens." He shook his head with a smile and swam over to the pool bar to pick up the house phone and ordered some dinner. Morgana rolled herself onto the beach entry and acted like she was a beached whale.

"Come on Free Willy. Let's get you onto dry land for a while," he said, helping her onto the lounge chair then draped a towel over her. She dozed off, barely hearing the knock on the door.

"Hey, babe. Dinner's ready," Cole's soft voice rousted her.

"Already? That was fast." She stretched.

"It's been an hour. You fell asleep."

"Oh, wow! Sorry."

"No, it's fine. Let's eat. I'm famished."

"Me too!" The cooks had come to make them steak, sea bass, and sautéed shrimp. "Oh jeez, I'm not this hungry." Morgana surveyed the spread laid out on the dining table.

"I wasn't sure if you liked sea bass, so I had them make steak as an alternative."

"Good thinking!" She tasted a small sample with a grimace. "I think I'll enjoy the steak."

After their delicious dinner, Morgana was feeling full and refreshed. Cole laughed and pointed out she was still wearing her damp night gown. She stripped it off and playfully threw it in his face, then grabbed a towel and starting running down to the beach. He joined her where she stood nearly neck deep in the ocean, watching the sun near its watery grave.

"Still no mermaid tail," she announced sadly.

"I guess your destiny awaits you on dry land." Cole held her close, their bodies rolling in the waves, as they watched the ball of light deliquescent into the aqua blue tomb.

"Screw it. I wanna sell beads!" she said.

"Nope. I'm not going to let you run away. You're going to do great things."

"I really think you're giving me too much credit."

I'm giving you the credit you deserve. You're amazing. You just need to find your passion."

"Maybe beads are my passion," she said meekly. "You don't know."

"Maybe beads are your passion, but selling your life short isn't how I want you to do it. I know it's not how you want to, either." They exited the water and he wrapped a towel around her as they headed back to the villa. "Mai Tai, dah-ling?" Cole offered and headed into the kitchen.

Morgana sighed. "Yes, please. If it gets any more lively around here a funeral will break out." She laughed and dropped her towel as she walked into the pool.

"Hey, hey, now! That's not nice," Cole called out. "It's our last night here, we've still got exactly fifteen hours left. We need to blow this puppy up! We're going to rock this gnam gnam style!" He stood in the kitchen at the pool's edge in a proud cocky pose.

"What does that even mean?" She was laughing hysterically.

"I have no idea. I heard it somewhere once," he confessed as he handed down her drink. Then he dropped his shorts and playfully kicked them towards her snickering face before he cannon-balled into the pool. When he surfaced he swam back over to the pool bar and cranked up some local Caribbean music. "Damn, I meant to turn that on before I jumped in." He laughed.

"It was still quite dramatic." She laughed.

"Really? I just feel like it would have been better if the music had punctuated my entry. Should I do it again?"

"No!" she cried out laughing, then threw his wet shorts at him.

"Oh, see? I think you want me to do it again."

She swam over and grabbed his shoulder pulling him back before he could climb out, and wrapped her legs around his waist, and began kissing him. "Nope. No do-overs. You're stuck with your score."

"But can I get a different score if I try it with you on me!"

"No!" She tried to jump off but he grabbed her and kissed her.

"Fine. I'll keep my score. I'm still the winner of the night." He kissed her. "I have to admit." He kissed her again harder. "I don't think I'd like the mermaid tail too much." She laughed and wrapped her legs around him and he carried her out the beach entry, kissing her passionately. "Bedroom or lounge chair?" he asked between hard deep kisses.

"Lounge chair!" she answered still kissing his lips.

"Good, I don't think I could have waited til the bedroom." He quickly put on a condom and made her gasp with delight as he entered her. They made love on the veranda to the relaxing Caribbean steel drums on the radio and the crashing waves of the ocean just a few feet away. Afterwards, they lay there under a towel on the cushion lounge chair, holding each other, listening to the steel drums play to the rolling sea. Morgana felt like she wanted to cry, but instead wrapped the towel around her body and pulled Cole up. He wrapped a towel around his waist and they started dancing to the Caribbean beats.

"It's hard to be sad with this music playing," she said.

"I don't want you to be sad, Morgana." He pulled her to him. "This has been an amazing week between two soul friends. And you're right, who knows where our lives will take us, but we will always have this week. Plus, I don't leave for Paris for three months. Maybe I'll get fired or you'll be ready to move with me by then. Here's hoping." He laughed then twirled and dipped her.

They danced and swam to the Caribbean rhythms until dawn, laughing and planning what life would be like if they sold beads on the beach. "Let's file that under Plan B," Cole announced.

"I second!" Morgana said and they toasted their glasses.

When the first light broke through the darkness, Cole led her down to the water's edge. They sat holding each other watching the sun give life to the new day, and to the rest of the people on planet that would soon invade their tranquil paradise.

"Well, I guess we should pack up and then maybe have one last breakfast on the veranda," Cole suggested.

"I have four of my five things packed already. I just need to grab by nightgown off the bench," she softly joked. "Do we need to clean up or do laundry or anything?

"No, they'll come around."

The relaxing island music still played from the speakers as Morgana straightened up. Cole went into his room to pack. She stared out at the crystal aqua blue water then turned to go inside. She went into where Cole was packing up his shaving kit in his en suite. She walked past the long white double sink counter and directly into the open tiled shower.

She stood with her eyes closed, letting the hot water run down her head, over her shoulders and coat her body. Soon Cole's hands were stroking her arms and breasts. His lips pressed against hers, his soft tongue parted her lips. She savored his sweet flavor. Then he rolled his tongue down her neck, kissing and suckling her as he made his way down her body. He lifted her up and she wrapped her legs around his strong lean waist and he carried her to the bed where they made soft sweet love. They basked in the tranquility of sweeping ocean breezes blowing the white flowing sheer curtains through the open French doors as they nestled together until the house phone rang confirming their car would be there in thirty minutes. They gathered their bags by the door and took one last look around.

"You know, we haven't even had a frozen coffee in a week," Morgana pointed out.

"I think we supplemented it with a different kind of sweetness." Cole winked with an amorous smile.

"Ya, Mai Tais!" she teased.

"Oh, really!" He laughed.

There was a knock at the door, and then Cole helped the valet load the bags. Morgana took one last look around. She took a deep breath and tried holding on to the tranquil vibration of the wonderful week, the sounds of the waves, but tried to ignore the color of the crystal aqua blue ocean.

"Are you ready?" Cole called out.

"Yes, dah-ling."

$\mathcal{C}$hapter Fourteen

The Five Thousand Dollar Dress

THEY HAD RETURNED from their week in paradise the night before. Cole had offered to pick Morgana up today at 4 p.m. to head out to the lot for the Ostara celebration.

"I'm not sure if I can sleep on those cots," she had told him on the flight home. "Let's play it by ear. We'll pack to stay, but we can decide if we want to go. I do love how wonderful it feels out there. Last time I missed the feeling because I was so upset over you." She elbowed him.

"Don't blame me. You're the one who went AWOL." He laughed.

"Shut up. I wasn't blaming you. I was just so sad." She put her head on his shoulder in the business class seats. "I was sad because you hadn't bought me any frozen coffees," she teased.

"Oh, real nice!" He laughed and kissed her forehead. They napped a bit on the plane and got home around 1 a.m. Morgana slept until nearly 1 p.m. the next day.

When Cole came to pick her up, he met her at the door with a large sleek black gift box.

"What is it?" she asked suspiciously.

"Well, you know how you were telling me this would be the first celebration where you didn't have a new dress," he handed her the box.

"That's not what I meant!" She refused to take it.

"Really? I wanted to get you something," he insisted.

"Was it very expensive?" she interrogated.

"I got a really good deal on it. I swear!"

"Alright then." She was satisfied with his answer and finally let him in the house, where she opened the gift. "Oh Cole! It's so amazing! OH!

I love it! Thank you!" She pulled out a multilayer pink, purple, and beige ruffled dress with a corseted bodice, spaghetti straps, and a cropped A-line textured tulle skirt and a pair of nude sandals to match. "It's so beautiful and frilly. I look like a butterfly. Thank you!" She paused and stared at him sternly. "Are you sure it didn't cost you very much?" she confirmed threateningly.

"I promise!" He held his hands up in surrender.

With great relief, she hugged the dress and gave him a big kiss. "Thank you! I can't wait to wear it. It's so perfect."

He was really enjoying her excitement. "Alright, let's load up," he called out, still delighting in her happiness as she twirled around with her new present.

They headed out to the lot, stopping at the drive thru to get their frozen coffee fix. Cole refused her money to pay.

"Okay, meet back at the entrance?" Cole announced after they arrived and parked. He had walked her to the girls' tent where she could get ready in her new dress. He had to head over to the guys' tent to change, too.

"Yes, twenty minutes," Morgana agreed with a quick kiss and she went inside. She was so happy to be here. When they walked up to the entrance, the lot was decorated like a little wooded fairy glen. Pastel eggs and flowers adorned the mini kiosks, where people were decorating eggs, petting bunnies, and dancing to the live band playing happy whimsical music with flutes and lutes and harps.

Morgana quickly changed into her fanciful new dress. It fit perfectly. She loved the way it made her feel as she sashayed in the full tulle skirt. She had decided not to wear her amulet necklace this time and opted instead for a crystal butterfly pendant necklace. She added a touch of makeup and blended a braid in with her wavy hair and pinned it with a small crystal clip. She locked her bag in one of the available foot lockers as she looked at the hard flat cots with a sigh, and remembered the huge fluffy beds in St. Barth's and the sound of the rolling waves outside. Other than the cots, she was so excited to be here. She quickly headed to meet up with Cole.

He was standing at their meeting spot. He had changed out of his designer jeans and T-Shirt into a tan twill suit and white button down shirt. His suit coordinated with her dress and he looked as GQ as ever. He smiled as she approached, proudly fluffing her tulle skirt.

"You look like a fairy princess, dah-ling." He admired her.

"You look quite dapper yourself." He held out his right arm as an escort which she happily wrapped in her arm and they entered the enchanted fairy forest. The sun was setting, turning the sky brilliant shades of orange and pink as Morgana and Cole walked around the vendor kiosks looking at the handmade jewelry and trinkets. Mrs. Thompson was there with her dress shoppe. Morgana went in to say "Hi."

"Well, you look effervescent, Morgana! I might have to take some ideas from your fabulous dress," Mrs. Thompson said as she gave Morgana a big hug.

"Thank you. This is Cole. He got it for me." Morgana introduced her stylist of the evening.

"Very good taste, young man." Mrs. Thompson shook Cole's hand.

"I know it's not one of yours, Mrs. Thompson. But I knew how great it would look on her, so I couldn't pass it up." Cole was his charming self.

"You were so right!" Mrs. Thompson agreed and smiled with approval at Morgana.

"See you around, Mrs. Thompson." Morgana hugged her good-bye and they continued on their discovery walk of the charming little settlement.

"So, the story goes, Ostara is a fertility goddess. Her annual arrival in spring is heralded by the flowering of trees, plants, and the arrival of all the new animal babies. Ostara, along with the other goddess of spring, Persephone, Ishtar, and Eostre, bring us the message of awakening, renewal, and personal growth."

"And it's all represented by rabbits, cuz they like gettin' it on!" Cole added with hysterics.

As they strolled along, they passed a little petting zoo area with bunnies, baby lambs, and baby goats. The music was melodious and lured them to the dance floor.

"May I have this dance, dah-ling?" Cole asked.

"Why certainly, dah-ling." They joined in with the group on the dance floor and got lost together in the enchanting tune and the magic of the final moments of twilight. The music stopped as dinner was being served.

They went to find a table when Blake called out to them. "Hey, Morgana! Cole! Over here!"

"Hi, Blake!" Morgana waved back. She was secretly hoping not to see them all tonight, but since she was feeling so good and soaking in the elation of the night, she figured nothing could sully her mood. "Hi guys!" Morgana cheerfully greeted Blake and Jai, Brook and Tristan, and Mitchell and Trina. "You all remember Cole." Hugs and handshakes went around.

"You two look so tan and fabulous!" Trina complimented.

"Oh, thank you. We, uh, just got back from a week in the Caribbean," Morgana shared.

"Oh, lucky!" Trina and Blake exclaimed.

"Who's lucky?" Tiffany said as she came walking up from somewhere around the stage, just as Josef was returning from the bar. Morgana avoided looking at him.

"Morgana and Cole. They just spent a week in the Caribbean." Brook filled Tiffany in.

"Together? How wonderful," Tiffany said cheekily. "Oh, and look, you're wearing matching rings, too." Tiffany was quick to point out.

"Anam Cara rings." Morgana held up her right hand.

"Oooo soul mates!" Tiffany oozed.

"Well, um, actually, the literal translation is…" Morgana started to say.

"Soul friends," Josef interjected.

Morgana was surprised by Josef's response and finally looked at him. Butterflies fluttered in her stomach and she quickly took a drink of water from the goblet on the table.

"Wow, Morgana. That dress is amazing. It's a Marchesa, isn't it?" Tiffany declared.

"I. I don't know what that means." Morgana looked confused and turned to Cole.

"Oh, my God." Tiffany guffawed at her. "That's the Marchesa ruffled tulle cocktail dress! You can't even get that any more. How did you get it?" Tiffany questioned trying to cover her contempt.

"Um. Ah. Cole gave it to me." Morgana was starting to struggle to breathe wondering what that meant to have a dress with a name.

All eyes shifted to Cole. "We used it in a photo shoot. The designer let me have it," Cole explained calmly, as he searched for Morgana's hand under the table to try to soothe her. She was started to feel light headed.

"You are a lucky girl, Morgana. A five-thousand dollar dress and a week in the Caribbean. He's a keeper," Tiffany said haughtily.

"Tiffany!" Blake snapped. Tiffany gave an innocent look.

"Five…five…thou..sand. fi." Now Morgana really couldn't breathe. She tried to take a drink of water, but started to choke from it. She hurriedly got up from the table and ran towards the restrooms. Cole was close behind her.

"Morgana!" he yelled after her.

She stopped breathless. "I can't…I can't breathe," she cried. "You lied to me!" she shouted. "I feel like I'm going to throw up. Oh, my God, I'm going to throw up on a five thousand dollar dress." She shot him a look of anger and panic.

"Babe. Calm down. Breathe. I didn't lie to you. You asked me if it cost me a lot. It was given to me. For free!" Cole tried to comfort her, but she was flailing.

"I'm gonna pee my pants. I'm going to throw up and pee in a five thousand dollar dress. How could you do this to me?" she desperately implored as she paced back and forth holding her hand on her heaving chest.

"You look gorgeous. I knew you would love it. I also knew you wouldn't take it if you knew how much it was. But it was free to me. I didn't think anyone would call out a price check. She's got no class, that one." Cole shook his head as he helplessly watched the blood leaving Morgana's face. "Hey. You're okay. Take a breath," he tried to order her.

"I don't feel good." She was in full panic mode.

"Listen to me. Everything is fine. Go in and splash your face with some cold water. You're okay. I'll go to the bar and get you some water to drink. Okay?" Cole knew she wouldn't let him help her, but at least she listened.

"Okay." She slowed her pacing.

"Will you let me come with you into the restroom?" Cole's big soft brown eyes held her gaze.

"No," she slowly stated. "I'll be okay. You'll get me some water?"

"Yes." He helped her as far as she let him, then high tailed to get her a bottle of water back at the bar.

She went into the restroom, which was just a trailer with a small sink and a couple of stalls. She started to panic again and decided she really did want Cole. She slowly and carefully headed to the bar to find him, gasping the night air as she went. By the time she made it to the bar, she couldn't find him. She ordered a water and steadied herself on the bar top.

"Are you okay?" His silky voice ran chills up her spine, soothing her, and she was able to take her first full deep breathe again. She grasped at the water bottle the bartender gave her and thanked him as she ripped off the cap and took a giant drink. She turned to face Josef as she struggled swallowing but nodded that she was okay. His deep aqua blue eyes offered her comfort, and he put his hand on the small of her back helping to steady her. Her knees weakened at his touch and shivers ran all through her. Just his simple touch was calming her anxiety and she was starting to breathe normally.

"How was the Caribbean?" his smooth voice glided.

She quickly pulled away from him and looked at his deep aqua blue eyes. She felt betrayed by her body as her heart wanted to sing, but she shut it down and felt angry instead. "The water was the same color as your eyes, so I felt like you were watching me the whole time. Other than that, it was spectacular!" she declared. Out of the corner of her eye she saw Cole approaching with a bottle of water in his hands. He had witnessed their interaction. Morgana turned away from Josef and started walking to Cole.

Just then, Tiffany's voice came from the stage area. "Your attention everyone! Attention please. I would like to announce a very special birthday for a very special guy. Josef McClellan - Please come up here!"

Morgana met up with Cole. "I went back to..." he started to say tensely.

"Let's go. I want to go. Would it be okay if we go?" She was starting to lose it again and just wanted to get out of there as fast as possible.

"Sure." Cole accommodated. They went to the tents to grab their stuff and met back at the car. Morgana had taken off her five thousand dollar designer dress and put back on her five dollar leggings and sweatshirt. Cole was back in his designer jeans and T-shirt. He drove them out of there and they were both silent for an hour and a half until the turn off.

"I don't want to go home," she said quietly.

With a deep sigh, Cole responded, "Where do you want to go then?"

"I don't know." She started crying.

Cole was a pretty patient guy, but he was about to lose his patience now. He jerked his luxury car off to the side of the road and slammed it into park. "Stop crying, Morgana. Where do you want to go?" he said harshly as he stared out the windshield.

"I don't know!" She cried harder.

Cole glared straight ahead and snarled, "What did he say to you?"

"What?" Morgana was caught off guard.

"I saw him with his arm around you. What did he say?" Cole still didn't look at her and scowled straight forward.

Morgana wiped her tears. "He asked me how the Caribbean was," she shot back.

Cole's strong hands gripped tighter on the steering wheel. "And what did you tell him." His voice was eerily calm.

"I told him it was spectacular!" she shouted. "It was the best week of my life!" She hadn't said that part, but it was true.

Cole's white knuckles loosened their grip a bit. "Where do you want me to take you?" he asked again, his voice was still tight.

She started crying again. "I want to go back to St. Barth's! I want it to just be us again."

"We can't go back! That time is over."

That was like a dagger in her heart. "What? What are you saying?" She tried reaching for his arm but he pulled away.

"We're not the only two people on the fucking planet, Morgana. Where do you want to go?" he snapped.

"Can we go to your house?" she cried into her chest.

He didn't say anything, but started the car and drove to the wealthy side of town through the mansioned streets and into the long driveway

THE FIVE THOUSAND DOLLAR DRESS

back to his two-thousand square foot guest house with the million dollar skyline views of the city below. He pulled the car into the garage and got out to unload their bags. He slammed the trunk closed which startled Morgana who was still buckled into the passenger's seat.

"Get out of the car," he said sternly from the doorway to the house. She wiped her eyes and removed her seatbelt, cautiously exiting the fancy hi-performance vehicle. His hands were full of their bags, but he still held the door open for her as she meekly entered his house. She hadn't been back since the day she ran tearfully down the driveway and left him standing there. He threw their stuff down on the deluxe double tufted couch and went to pour himself a drink from his fully stocked bar.

"Can you make Mai Tais?" she asked sheepishly.

He didn't respond, but mixed up the drinks, but only after he took a shot of the rum straight. He handed her a glass then headed up to the roof top deck. She abjectly followed. She sat next to him on the gliding love seat and they sat in silence for a while staring at the city light below.

"I don't get you," he finally said. "We were having such a great time, then you let her or whatever, ruin it."

"You didn't tell me it was worth five thousand dollars," she said defensively.

"Really?" he snapped. "It wasn't. It was a prop from a photo shoot. I wanted you to have it." He was straining to keep his voice calm. "What difference does it make anyway? You loved it. You looked great in it. It made you light up." He stopped himself.

"I just wasn't...It's so much money...I just," Morgana stumbled. "It's just more than I make in a year practically. I just don't wear stuff that costs that much."

Cole's body hardened. She tried to reach for him but he stood up to get away and finished his drink in one last large swallow.

"How much do you think the amulet Mr. Wonderful gave you cost?" He looked at her with daggers in his eyes.

"What? I don't... I don't know. His dad, he made it."

"Well, he really knew was he was doing, because I bet you it's worth at least fifty thousand dollars." Cole took another swig from his already empty glass trying to get any remnants from the bottom of the glass.

Morgana froze. "Is that true?" Her head went reeling. "Why?...
What are you talking about?"

"Forget it," he snapped and headed back down to make another
drink.

Morgana sat stunned. She didn't understand. *Why would he say that?*
Why would he know that? She was trying to figure it out but it was all too
much. She took a big drink and headed downstairs, too. Cole was at the
bar, not making another Mai Tai, but drinking shots of rum. Morgana
had never seen this side of him and she was a little frightened.

"Do you want me to go?" she asked quietly.

"No, I don't. But that didn't stop you last time you were here. So do
whatever." He slammed another shot. She stood there not knowing what
to do. She knew he would never hurt her and clearly he was hurting. She
walked over to him and held on to his arm. He took another shot with
the other arm, but at least he didn't pull away this time. "I just wanted
to do something nice for you," he confessed.

"We just got back from a week in the Caribbean. You can't get any
nicer than that," she said trying to comfort him.

"I just wanted you to have something from me, and see you light up."
He took another shot, his fourth that she counted in the few minutes
since she came downstairs. His big brown eyes were a little red.

"Awe, babe," she cooed, moving herself between him and the bar,
and cupped his face in her hands and gave him a soft kiss. He didn't
respond but didn't pull away, either. She kissed his right cheek, then his
left, and this his lips again. This time he kissed her back passionately,
savoring her lips. She took him by the hand and led him to his bedroom
where they made love and fell asleep in each other's arms.

The next morning she felt him get up and heard him get in the
shower. She quickly ran out to the living room, grabbed her dress off
the couch, and then hid it back in the bedroom. She climbed into the
shower with him and soaped up his strong, defined, muscular back. He
reciprocated the favor, caressing her body.

"Do you want some breakfast?" he asked as he soaped up her body.

"Some coffee. And if you feel like making something, that would
be great, too." She turned to him and kissed him.

He kissed her back but then exited the shower. "I'll go see what I have." He wrapped a towel around his defined waist and headed into his closet to get dressed.

She finished her shower and put on her fabulous designer dress. She walked out into the kitchen to find him with his back to her, scrambling some eggs. She wrapped her arms around him from behind and kissed his back.

"I have eggs and toast. If you want something else, I'd have to call the main house."

"Eggs and toast are perfect," she said still nuzzling his back. The toaster popped and she went to grab the toasted bread, putting them on the plates Cole had set out. He finally looked at her as she swayed in her marvelous tulle skirt.

"What are you wearing?" he asked.

"The most beautiful dress I've ever had!" She smiled big and twirled in it. He tried not to smile but she just kept turning and dancing, trying to get him to respond. "I love it so much. I never, ever want to take it off," she gushed as she pranced around his kitchen.

His shoulders dropped. He was defenseless. "You are so adorable," he said finally cracking a smile to which she jumped into his arms and kissed all over his face. "You might have to take it off later," he said amorously in her ear.

She pulled back and looked at him with a big sultry smile. "Oh, really?" she cooed, biting her lip and batting her eyes. He pulled her to him and gave her a kiss.

They enjoyed their breakfast poolside in the fresh morning air.

"The main house seems quiet," she observed.

"They went to St. Barth's for the week," Cole explained.

"Oohh." Morgana sighed with envy. "I can't believe we have to go back to school and work tomorrow." Reality hit her. "It's been such a glorious week, dah-ling!" Then she reached for his hand and genuinely said, "Thank you for everything, Cole. This really has been the best week of my life."

He looked at her squarely and took a deep breath. "Mine, too." Then added, "Dah-ling."

They spent the day relaxing and watching movies, snuggling on the deep ultra-soft double tufted couch, and eating ice cream.

After the second movie, Morgana got up the courage and asked, "Cole, can I ask you why you were so upset last night?"

His body stiffened. "I just didn't like seeing him touch you."

He's totally jealous of Josef. "Awwwe babe," she cooed, then pulled herself up and straddled his lap, holding his face in her hands and kissed him. He responded to her touch and reached under her five thousand dollars' worth of multilayers of tulle and rubbed her smooth legs, kissing her lips, neck, and chest. They went into his bedroom and made love on his fluffy cloud-like bed with designer sheets.

They lay there together afterwards, Morgana stroking his perfect, muscular arm that was wrapped around her. "Do you think long distance relationships work?" she asked.

Cole perked up. "Well, I think if the people are committed to each other and the relationship, I think it could."

"Do you think you could be committed to a long distance relationship?" she asked softly.

He turned her to face him and looked at her with excitement in his big deep brown eyes. "Yes, I think I could. Do you?"

"How often could we see each other?"

"Well, I could fly you over during all your school breaks and long weekends. And after you get your associates degree next year, maybe you could transfer over there, or something. Or, after you graduate, maybe you could look for your career over there?" he said hopefully.

I didn't hear him say he would ever come here. "Ya, maybe," she said with a small smile.

"Really?" he asked.

"What do you think?" she said timidly. *Maybe it'll be okay.*

"I think I would really like that."

"Me too!" she said excitedly. And they hugged and kissed each other.

The next several weeks were wonderful for Morgana and Cole. They spent as much time as they could together. It was great. Cole rearranged his work schedule so they would work the same days and they would study together. They spent the weekends together at his house. Occasionally, Cole would have to work at the main house at one of Da-Veed and Pierre's garish galas. She still refused to go and would spend those times having dinner with Ms. Lane.

"Everything is so wonderful!" Morgana said romantically to Ms. Lane one evening. "He's so kind and smart and hardworking and so gorgeous," Morgana added. "I just wish…" She stopped.

"Go on, dear," Ms. Lane gently encouraged.

"Well, I just wish he wasn't moving away. And I wish he didn't have to work at those Godawful parties," she said into her chest. "He's so different when he's around those people like that."

"That's his job, isn't it?" Ms. Lane kindly asked.

"Well, yah. But why does it have to be like that?" Morgana questioned.

"Like what? Do you even know what goes on there?" Ms. Lane laughed at her young friend.

"I can only imagine." Morgana grunted.

"Imagination can be a dangerous thing. Maybe you should go just to see for yourself. Maybe it's not as bad as you think," Ms. Lane suggested.

"But, what if it's worse?" Morgana whined with an exasperated expression.

"You'll never know if you don't go. And you probably should know before he moves away and your imagination really plays tricks on you," the wise one pointed out.

Chapter Fifteen

A Garish Gala

"I THINK I need to go to your next event," Morgana admitted to Cole the next night when he brought her a frozen chocolate coffee to her kiosk.

"Really? Okay." Cole was accommodating. "I have one in two weeks."

"Will I hate it?" she asked fearfully.

"No, no. Yes! You will totally hate it. But I would love having you there with me." Cole flashed his perfect GQ smile. Morgana felt so lucky to be with him, but deep down her stomach was in knots.

The night of the party, Morgana was at Cole's to get ready. "Wear this." Cole held up a new, beautiful, one-shouldered red dress with an a-symmetrical ruffled hem and black sky high stiletto heels with red soles.

"What is it?" Morgana asked suspiciously.

"It's one of tonight's guest's designs that we're showcasing. Yes, it is every expensive," he stated in a matter-of-fact way. "But you'll look gorgeous in it and I want to show you off," he added and kissed her on the forehead. The knots in Morgana's stomach churned. There was a knock at the front door. "Oh, I asked one of my makeup artist friends to come help you with your makeup," he explained and left to let her in.

Morgana was leery. "Makeup artist?" she said to herself.

"Morgana, this is my good friend, Alexa." Cole introduced the tall, lean, blond that followed him back down the hall. Morgana extended her hand, but Alexa's hands were full of tackle boxes.

"Fabulous. Let's get to work shall we? Where can I set up?" She smiled at Cole.

"Why don't we go out to the kitchen? It's got better light," Cole suggested.

Morgana sat on the bar stool under the bright lights of the kitchen, feeling like a guinea pig while Alexa and Cole laughed it up like besties.

"First, we'll have to even out that skin tone," Alexa said digging through all her shades of makeup.

"Can I get either of you a drink?" Cole offered.

"Can I have a Mai Tai?" Morgana called out.

"Oh, my!" Alexa laughed condescendingly. "What is this Cancun?"

"Morgana likes the sweet drinks," Cole said. "Sweet just like her," he added and winked at Morgana. The knots in Morgana's stomach crushed her intestines.

"Ah, that's cute," Alexa replied derisively. "I'll have a double vodka neat," she ordered.

Cole brought over their drinks. Alexa slammed hers before Morgana could even take a sip of her own.

"Oh, honey, I need to work on your lips. Let's wait on that for now." Alexa took the glass away and proceeded to slather layers of make up on her uncomfortable living canvas. After two hours of blending and blotting, hair pulling and curling, Alexa presented her masterpiece to Cole.

"De toute beauté!" he cheered in French. "Go put on the gown then we can head over there," Cole ordered.

Morgana walked down the hall to Cole's room feeling queasy. She put on the beautiful red dress and slipped on the ultra-high heels. She looked in the mirror and couldn't even recognize herself. She had to do a double take. She looked glamorous and fancy, but nothing like herself at all. *Don't panic*, she ordered herself. *You wanted to do this. Everything will be fine.* She took a deep breath and grasped at her churning stomach.

"Everything all right back there?" Cole called from the living room. Alexa said something that Morgana couldn't make out, but she definitely heard Alexa's exaggerated laugh that followed. Morgana walked into the living room. Alexa had put away all her make up tools and was now at the bar leaning into Cole, who was on the other side pouring her another drink.

"Oh, babe! You look great!" he called out. "You do great work, Alexa," he complimented.

"I do what I can." She smiled at him. "Well, I guess my work here is done. I better let you go before Da-veed turns pink." They both laughed at clearly an inside joke. She gathered up all her gear and Cole walked her to the door. "See you later, doll." She kissed him on both cheeks, European style.

"Bye," an ignored Morgana said from where she stood in the living room.

Cole turned to Morgana who hadn't moved from her spot. "You hate it," he said.

"Well, I mean. Yes. I'm sorry," Morgana confessed, a little relieved that Cole knew she hated it.

"It's only for a few hours. You'll be great." He kissed her on the forehead.

That was less encouraging.

"Let me go change." He came back out within five minutes wearing a black tuxedo, crisp white shirt, and black bow tie. He looked amazing. Morgana was drinking her melted Mai Tai through the straw that Alexa had asked Cole for earlier so Morgana wouldn't "ruin her lips." Cole walked over to the glass slider. "Shall we?" he held out his arm. Morgana slowly walked over to him, getting used to the sky high heels. They walked a few feet across the patio, then Morgana stopped and took off her shoes.

"I'll put them back on when we get there." They made their way across the pool deck, along the slate path, through the garden, up the stairs to the huge patio deck and through giant double French doors of Pierre and Da-veed's immaculate part-time mansion home. It was ostentatious. Ten-foot gold statues of naked men adorned the doorways. Huge magnificent crystal chandeliers hung from the thirty-foot ceilings. Gold gilded mirrors lined the walls. Twenty-foot painted portraits of Pierre and Da-veed in various settings and locations, hung everywhere. Caterers and wait staff were scurrying about, setting up for the garishly splendid party.

"Will you be okay here for a minute? I need to go check in with Pierre."

"Um. Okay," Morgana said nervously.

"You'll be fine. You look amazing." He kissed her quickly on the cheek as to not "ruin her lips."

There was a string quartet set up by the twenty-five foot wrought iron front doors. Morgana found an out-of-the-way alcove and sat down to observe the chaotic display of gaudy opulence. Guests started arriving and Cole still hadn't come back out yet. He had been gone for nearly an hour and the house was full of "fab-u-lous" guests. Finally she saw him emerge from the back room, but instead of coming to her, he went to the front of the room.

"Ladies and gentlemen. Esteemed guests. It is my honor and privilege to announce our hosts of the evening, Pierre De La Cue and his partner, Da-veed!"

Two, tall, double wooden doors opened into the large formal living room, and the men emerged to much fanfare. Pierre was a distinguished looking gentleman with thick salt and pepper hair. He wore a dark tuxedo with a coral pocket square and matching bow tie. Da-veed was wearing a full coral tuxedo. He had dyed black hair and was wearing a diamond studded bow tie. Pierre gave a speech and introduced the guest designer of the night, who Morgana didn't recognize or know anything about. She stayed in the back of the crowd just trying to balance on her heels. Tuxedoed waiters carried dozens of silver trays full of champagne flutes through the crowd. Morgana accepted one that was offered. For about the next hour, Cole had to stay next to Pierre and Da-veed as they greeted all their guests. Then, Cole waved her over to introduce her to the hosts.

"Pierre. Da-veed. This is my girlfriend, Morgana." He smiled affectionately at her. She liked being introduced as his girlfriend and beamed at him.

"Very nice to meet you," she said graciously.

"Oh, mademoiselle. So great to finally meet you." Pierre grasped both her hands and kissed her cheeks, European style.

"Bonjour Chérie. So, this is the Morgana we've been hearing about," Da-veed said and also kissed both her cheeks. "Oh, is this our designer's gown? Turn around and let us see it." Da-veed fingered a twirl. Morgana obliged trying not to fall over in her shoes. "Look at how the fabric lays." Da-veed spoke to Pierre about the dress. "Merveilleux how it translates off the run way, and on someone short." Morgana now understood the sky high stilettos. She just burned a smile onto her face and hoped her reddening cheeks couldn't be seen under the thick layers of cake makeup. Pierre and Da-veed swiftly moved on to the next guest who squealed about the "fab-u-lous party!"

"Are you okay, babe? Sorry I got held up before. I just need to make sure they say hi to everyone and I'll be back for you. Okay?" He quickly explained and patted her shoulders.

"Ya, sure," Morgana replied. A waiter with a silver tray walked by and Morgana snagged herself another champagne flute.

Another hour, and three more champagne flutes later, and Cole was still stuck at his benefactors' sides. Women would come up to talk to the hosts, but they would paw at Cole, kissing his cheeks, pinching his chin or rubbing his arms. Morgana had made her way over to the buffet table overflowing with delicious foods that no one was eating. She helped herself as passerby'ers gave her odd looks. She would shove a cheese cube or something equally highly caloric in her mouth and just smile. Around 11:30 p.m., she wandered down the hall to find a restroom. She looked into an open doorway to see a sitting room full of models and girls. Some of them were talking. Some of them looked like they were doing drugs. None of them paid any attention to Morgana. Behind another door she heard screams and moans of way more than two people having sex. She gave up and headed back to the main room, afraid of what else she would discover. She came back to find Cole, who was surrounded by a bevy of women, all batting their eyes as he talked up his bosses. He saw her and excused himself to the dismay of the throng of fawning women and made his way to her.

"Hey, how are you? Can I get you a drink? Did you see the buffet?" he asked.

"How much longer do these things last?" Morgana looked down at a non-existent watch on her wrist.

"They go pretty late," he said.

"Do you have to stay the whole time?" she asked.

"It's only midnight, so probably a couple more hours, at least."

"Oh," she said dreadfully.

"Let me get you something to eat," he offered.

"No, I'm good. I've already eaten. Thank you."

"Well, come stand with me and meet some people."

Morgana shook her head. "Look, I know you have to do your job. I get it. I'm fine. But do you think it would be okay if I went back to your house?"

"You want to leave?" Cole sighed, he knew she had had enough. "Alright. I'll be back as soon as I can. Okay?"

"Okay." He gave her a quick kiss and she headed out the double French doors. The patio was filled with drunken invitees in designer gowns and tuxedos. Morgana made it down the steps then took off her painful stilettos and walked the path back to the guest house. She immediately showered and scrubbed her face as soon as she made it back. She carefully hung the fancy red gown in Cole's perfectly organized closet and put on her leggings and T-shirt. She helped herself to a bowl of ice cream and headed up to the upper deck. As she enjoyed her sweet frozen treat on the gliding love seat, she looked back over at the grandiose main house lit up like a Christmas tree with elaborate crystal chandeliers. She could still hear the high pitched laughter of drunken guests. She turned her attention to the city lights below and thought about the difference between this over-the-top flamboyant gala and the sweet celebrations she loved so much out at the lot.

She remembered a conversation she had with Ms. Lane one time.

"You mustn't judge people because they're on a different frequency than you, dear," Ms. Lane had advised. "There are trillions of vibrations available and every one of them is superb! You are on your own vibration based on your own experiences and thoughts. There are no rights or wrongs. We are all here to experience human nature. You can no more tell someone what makes them happy than you can tell them what their favorite flavor ice cream is. We are all just doing the best we can, and that's all we can do. Just listen to your heart. Stay true to yourself. All you can do is enjoy your own life and your own favorite ice cream."

So, that's what she did and she finished off her sweet mocha delicacy. Around 1 a.m., Morgana climbed into Cole's giant cloud bed and fell asleep watching a movie. It was almost 3:30 a.m. when he finally crawled in next to her and fell asleep.

She woke up at 9:30 a.m. and went into the kitchen to make them some breakfast. She remembered the last time she had made them omelettes while they were in St. Barth's, a world away from everyone. It was so good when it was just the two of them. He's so different when he has to be around the people he worked with. She wondered what it would be like when he moved to Paris as she made up a tray and brought him breakfast in bed.

"Wakey, wakey," she called out. He looked up at her with the tray and sat up.

"Smells delicious," he said sleepily. "So, how much did you hate it?" he asked between bites.

"Let's just say, it's definitely not in my vibration." She tried her best. "It was pretty much what I thought though, I guess. Drugs in the bathroom. Orgies in the bedroom." She shook her head. He just laughed. "I think the worst part though, was just the way the people treated me. Like an object or something?"

"Who? What do you mean?" Cole asked concerned.

"Well, umm, Alexa wasn't very nice. And Pierre and Da-veed just looked at the dress. It's like none of them looked at me."

"That's just how they are. They're used to busy fashions shows and all this is normal for them. Look, I can't defend them, they can be kind of rude," Cole confessed.

"And, well, umm. What about you?" Morgana said into her chest.

"Babe, I'm sorry I wasn't able to be with you more. I was working."

"No. I mean. When I was getting ready, the way you talked to me about the dress," she said cautiously.

"I didn't want you flipping out," he said tenderly.

"And all that makeup? Is that how you want me to look?" she said so low he could barely hear her.

"What? No babe. That's how I wanted you to look to go to that party so you would fit in." She shot him a look. "No, that's not what I mean. No. That's what I keep telling you. You're not like those people and that's what I love about you." He reached up to touch her face. "I'm sorry if you thought I was being rude. I just wanted to show you off, is all."

Morgana look into his big soft brown eyes and tried to ignore the little voice in her head that asked, *But is he really like those people? No!* she argued with herself. *He's kind. He's not like them. Right?*

The knots in her stomach tightened.

$\mathcal{C}$hapter Sixteen

Beltane and Breakups

"BELTANE IS COMING up May 1ˢᵗ," Morgana said one night at work over their chocolate frozen addictions.

"What's that?" Cole asked.

"Well, it's a celebration in honor of the union between the God and the Goddess. It's the last of the three spring fertility festivals."

"They sure liked gettin' it on in the olden days," Cole joked.

"Shut up!" She laughed. "It's a celebration of life and love," she said dramatically.

"Hey, you don't have to convince me. I'm down." He laughed. "So, what's the look for this occasion?"

"I don't know. I thought we could look up Mrs. Thompson's website for dress ideas."

Cole pulled out his phone and looked up the website. "Will you allow me to buy you one?" he asked sternly.

"Well, no...I can..." He shot her a look that stopped her from trying to make an excuse. "If we pick out one we agree upon."

"I can live with that," he approved. She picked one out that was on sale for ninety-nine dollars. He liked one that was three hundred. "Well, I guess the tie breaker is my credit card," he joked and bought the one he wanted.

"Hey! That wasn't the agreement!" She tried to grab away his phone.

"Too late. Already done." He laughed.

A couple of nights before Beltane, Cole came up to her at the kiosks with their favorite drinks. "Your dress arrived today," he announced.

"Oh, cool!" she cheered.

"I was thinking. Do you want to get a hotel out there? I know you don't like those cots and there's a hotel up the way. That way we could stay both days if you want. Of course, let me warn you, I looked up the hotels and they don't look much more comfortable than the cots."

"You never cease to amaze me," she said, wrapping her arms around him for a kiss. "If you don't mind, I think that would be great. I probably wouldn't mind the cots if it were just me, but how could I leave the sweetest guy in the world."

That's what I keep saying," he charmingly joked.

Morgana was feeling so comfortable in their relationship. He was so thoughtful and courteous, and as long as she didn't have to go to anymore of his so-called office parties, everything was great. She was so excited to go back to the lot. She loved her dress and there would be no unexpected price tag announcements. She told herself to not pay attention to the drama twins and just focus on the connection of the night, the night that represented the God and the Goddess coming together in union to create life for all of us. Beltane is the most joyful and frolicsome of the four fire festivals, most likely because its central premise was sexuality and fertility.

They checked into the modest hotel. It was a hotel like Morgana was used to, a little rundown but not too bad. Cole was not impressed. "What did you expect for the middle of nowhere?" She laughed.

"I guess. At least there aren't any bloodstains on the carpet, right?" He kidded.

Morgana was getting ready in the restroom putting on the white halter top chiffon Grecian style dress with an open back and gold belted empire waist. She entered the bedroom to find Cole wearing a white sleeveless shirt, leather cuffs on his wrists, and faux doe skin pants.

"Wow!" he said when she floated into the room.

"My thoughts, exactly!" she said, looking him over. "You look quite raw and virile!" she said biting at her lip.

"And you look like an ethereal goddess. Although, you're missing something." He held up a small gift box.

"What did you do?" she interrogated.

"It went with the dress. It's part of the ensemble," he professed. She opened the box to see a set of gold leaf jewelry that matched the gold leaf design on the belt. There was a gold circle necklace that came together at the nape of her neck with two gold leaves crisscrossing, and matching drop leaf earrings, and arm cuffs.

"Oh, they're beautiful," she said.

"I got you something else, too. I promise it wasn't expensive," he said sarcastically. On the long gold chain was a white iridescent polished stone. "It's a moonstone. So you can always carry the light of the moon everywhere you go."

"Oh, Cole! That is so sweet! You are so sweet! I love it!" She layered it with the gold leaf necklace and the length was perfect to sit right with the low-cut dress. "It protects travelers," Morgana explained. "It's also a lover's gift for passion," she added seductively.

"Really? Looks like I chose wisely." He grabbed her and pulled her to him, kissing her passionately. "Do we have time?" He kissed her neck.

"Uh-huh!" She swooned as he unzipped her dress and caressed her body.

"Wow! That thing really works!" Cole said when they finished making love.

"I guess so!" She giggled. "It is useless to resist me. I have all the power now," she said dramatically.

"You always did." He kissed her tenderly.

They left the hotel and headed to the lot. Morgana felt alive and impassioned.

"I feel electric," she said as they exited the car. "Oh, and it smells divine!" They entered to see five giant hay bales surrounding the camp set up to be lit in just under an hour. There were five tall May poles up on the dance floor and some people were dancing and laughing. Morgana felt rapturous. She felt so in love with Cole and in love with where they were. She felt so alive. Her whole body was tingling. She saw Trina dancing around one of the May poles. "Oh, let's go," she said dreamily as she softly stroked Cole's strong arms as they walked to the dance floor. Trina happily greeted Morgana with a hug and handed her one of the ribbons. Morgana felt euphoric and she danced and laughed with Trina and several other girls as they twirled around the May pole.

"Is it just me or do you feel...I don't even know how to explain it," Morgana whispered to Trina.

"I know it feels like every cell in my body is buzzing or something," Trina agreed. "Like I'm on some wonderful drug, but without the nasty side effects."

"Yeah, that's it." Morgana and Trina dropped their ribbons and started dancing with each other, giggling and delighting in the blissful feeling. Mitchell and Cole came over to join in. "Oh, Cole," Morgana cooed as the foursome danced together. "Do you feel it?" Morgana whispered into Cole's ear and then playfully nibbled it. "I feel euphoric and tipsy." She licked her lips. "I guess you could say, I just feel so turned on," she giggled delightfully.

"Yeah, I sort of feel tingling," Cole agreed. "Of course watching you is turning me on," he whispered into her ear. She rolled her head back with her arms around his neck, and he kissed her throat. Trina and Mitchell came back around and they all started dancing together again.

Over at each of the hay bales, cheers and roars sounded as the fires were started. Groups gathered and walked between the fires, a purification ritual of walking in the smoke. Some threw out sage or flowers, or different blossoms into the fires. A shirtless male dance troupe came out to perform various fire breathing, fire juggling, and other maneuvers of dancing with fire. Morgana watched in amazement as she stroked Cole's exposed arms and chest. She would alternate between watching the stunts and dancing with Trina. Her elated buzz lasted all through the night. The dancing ended at midnight, but Morgana called Cole to the hill so they could watch the fires burning out.

"God, I feel so amazing!" She rolled her head back and licked her lips. She looked at Cole and started kissing and licking his sexy muscular arms.

"Babe, I might have to take you right here if you don't stop that," he joked.

"I might have to let you," she said breathlessly.

"Okay, c'mon. Let's get you out of here." He helped her up, and as they headed to the car she was dancing and twirling along the way.

"Morgana?" His silky voice only enhanced her sensations more.

"Josef." As she said his name the feeling of ecstasy rolled through her. "Hi." She wrapped her arms around him and gave him a big breathy hug.

"We've got to go, Morgana," Cole demanded.

"Oh, yes, let's go," she ecstatically breathed and let go of Josef and grabbed on to Cole.

Cole could barely get the hotel door open fast enough. Morgana flopped on the bed, pulling him on top of her. "It's amazing," she said. "I don't know what it is, like the whole night, has been like one long orgasm." She giggled and kissed his lips. "I love your lips. I love your arms. I love these leather cuffs. I love you," she said as she stroked his arms that held him over her. When Cole entered her she screamed with ecstasy. She came again and again until he finished. "That was amazing!" she cried, before falling asleep in his arms.

She woke up the next morning feeling normal. "Oh, man. What was that?" she asked, stretching out in the bed. "Did I dream all that last night?" She rolled over and snuggled up under his arm. Cole was quiet.

"This place has a powerful effect on you," he finally said.

"Yah, I'll say! I love it so much when I'm connected."

"Do you think you'll be 'connected' like that when I'm not here?"

"Huh, what do you mean?"

"I mean, if I wasn't here last night would you have been in that mood, or whatever you want to call it?"

"Babe, I was in that mood because you were here. I had set my intention to be in love with you and with life, and clearly made the connection." She tried to kiss him but he pulled away and stood up. "Cole?" she said, sitting up in the bed.

"You hugged him like you wanted to go home with him," he snarled at her.

"What? What are you talking about? And besides, I've seen all the women throwing themselves at you. How is that any different?"

"Because I don't want to go home with them," he said coldly.

"I don't want to go home with him, either. I'm with you. I love you! I don't even know what his deal is." She shouldn't have said that. So, she quickly added, "He's nothing to me but an old crush, like Pa-tri-cia is to you."

"Do you think, maybe, you could not come out here anymore after I leave?" he asked softly.

How could he ask me not to come to my beloved lot? "Well, um, maybe we could work something out. Maybe you could come back and come with me. I would only go to the ones you could come to. There are only eight a year, you could make most of them. Plus, I guess, I'll probably be with you during summers and Christmas break, so that narrows it down to only five or six."

Cole stood there in front of her, his big brown eyes looking so sad.

"Or maybe," she paused and took a deep relenting breath, "maybe I could move to Paris with you?"

He quickly bent down on his knees in front of the bed to be eye to eye with her and held onto her waist. "Really?"

"Well, I mean, I love you. It seems like it would make sense, right?" She was nervous. "You said you could probably help me get a job. I mean, they make most perfumes in Paris, don't they?" she half-heartedly joked.

"Yes, sure. I can definitely help you get a job, if that's what you want."

"I just don't know about school. How could I pay for that?"

"I can help." She shot him a look. "I mean, I can help you get a loan, or something. Would you really go?" His big soft brown eyes looked so hopeful in his beautiful, perfect, excited face.

"Cole. I gotta ask, why do you love me? You can have anyone. And I can be a big pain in the ass," she joked. But then added, "I'm nothing special. I have nothing. I don't get it." Now, tears filled her eyes.

"I keep telling you, I love that you're a big pain in the ass. I love that you hold true to yourself. I love your magic. You keep me grounded. I need you to keep me from turning into one of them. I feel like myself when I'm with you, and I really like who I am when I'm with you." She was still sitting on the edge of the bed and he was in front of her on his knees. He wrapped his arms around her and put his head on her lap. "Just because you don't think you have anything, doesn't mean you're not special."

Tears flooded her eyes. She did love him. *The knots in my stomach must just be nerves,* she told herself. How would she tell her mom and

Ms. Lane that she was moving to Paris? And, she was about to put herself to the test when she faced Josef at breakfast.

"Oh, yah. Wear the cuffs," she said to Cole later as they were getting ready.

"You really like them. Good to know," he teased. "You're sure they go with jeans or should I wear the doe skins?"

"Jeans are fine. Besides, I think I remember us in the dirt last night, so the doe's are probably filthy. Look at my dress." She held up the brown dirt covered backside of her chiffon dress. Today she wore a short white strapless dress and put the gold leaf jewelry back on. "Should I attempt it and wear the moonstone again?" She laughed.

"Oh, yes! Tempt it!" he said amorously. She giggled and blushed remembering herself the night before.

They headed over to the lot and walked over to the brunch buffet. After they filled their plates, they found a table to themselves.

"I don't even remember eating last night," she said.

"That's because we danced through it." Cole laughed.

"Oh, no wonder I'm starving!" she exclaimed.

"Hey, good morning guys." It was Trina and Mitchell.

"Hi!" Morgana said.

"Can we join you?" asked Trina.

Morgana quickly looked at Cole, he nodded. "Oh, of course, please."

"Goodness, Morgana, you were in the zone last night. I thought I was the only one. I'm so glad you came to dance with us. That was so much fun."

"It was fun!" Morgana giggled.

"Hey, mates. Can we join ya?" Big Tristan had three plates in his hands and Brook was behind him with their drinks.

"Did you leave any food for the rest of the people?" Mitchell ribbed his friend and helped pull out the chairs. Morgana was getting nervous.

"There's a little bit left," Blake said coming up to the table with Jai in tow. "Good morning, Morgana, Cole."

"Hey, guys." Morgana scooted her chair closer to Cole and wrapped her foot around his.

"Luckily, they're making fresh crepes, otherwise they would

probably be out." Tiffany said as she and Josef brought up the rear and completed the gang.

"Are they serving crepes at the wedding?" Blake asked Brook.

"Not the night of the ceremony, but at brunch the next day like this," Brook answered.

"Oh, that's coming up quick. When is it?" Morgana asked.

"June 20th." Brook looked excited. "I have to send out the invitations as soon as we get home today. Don't let me forget," she told Tristan who was taking a massive bite of pancakes.

"Oh, wow. That's just next month." Morgana's stomach knots gripped her.

"Will you to be able to make it?" Brook asked.

"Um, I, I don't think so. Um, I might be moving to Paris with Cole." Morgana didn't look at Josef, but she swore she saw him choke a little on his breakfast.

"Paris, you're going? How exciting!" Brook exclaimed.

"Well, we just talked about it this morning. There's still a lot I have to figure out. Like how to tell my mom!" She laughed nervously.

"See, I told you he was a keeper," Tiffany piped in.

"Ah, anyone could clearly see that!" Blake snapped back.

"Please, you two," Brook said exasperatedly.

"Hey, I've gone along with everything she said when it comes to your wedding, but she doesn't have to be rude," Blake argued.

"I wasn't being rude. I was just stating that I told her so." Tiffany defended.

"Like you had anything to do with it!" Blake snarled.

In the midst of the back-and-forth, Morgana stole a glance at Josef, who was just staring at his plate, pushing at his eggs.

"Please, knock it off!" Brook barked.

"Would anyone like another drink?" Josef offered as he stood up from the table. Tristan and Mitchell said "yes" as Josef headed to the bar.

Cole tightened his hold on Morgana as she tried to figure out a way to talk to Josef. The knots in her stomach also tightened their grip. *I guess I'll have to wait,* she told herself and looked at Cole and smiled. She tried to ignore everyone and just feel for the connection. When Cole was done eating she leaned over to ask if he felt like dancing. He accepted.

They excused themselves. Trina asked if they were going dancing. "I want to go with you." The foursome made their way to the dance floor area. Blake and Jai joined shortly after.

"She just bugs the crap out of me, I can't stand her. I don't know why Brook puts up with her," Blake complained.

"Forget about her if you're going to dance with us. No negativity around the May pole," Trina said with a smile. "Grab a ribbon and join the fun."

"You're right!" Blake agreed. The three girls each grabbed a ribbon and danced in a circle to the right, entwining their ribbons with the other dancers. The guys all stood back and watched.

Morgana didn't let herself think about Josef, Cole, Paris or anything. *No negativity around the May pole.* She reached for the connection that she felt last night. When their ribbons reached the end, they all switched direction, and Morgana was starting to feel giggly again. She looked at Cole watching her with a smile. She felt love. He motioned that he was going to get a drink and she nodded, asking if it was okay that she stayed, he agreed. She was happy dancing, imagining being at the first Beltane of the God and Goddess's magical union. *Ahh,* she was starting to feel good, not like last night, but still happy and light. Next thing she knew, Josef was watching her. His deep aqua blue eyes met hers and the tingling started running through her body again. She looked away and kept dancing, laughing with Trina and Blake, but she felt his eyes on her and couldn't help but to stare at him again. Sweet chills ran up the back of her neck and she bit at her lip. She turned the circle and Cole was standing there on the other side.

Oh! How long had he been there? she wondered. The tingling stopped. She quickly dropped her ribbon and went over to him. He handed her a bottle of water. "Oh, thank you!" She gave him a kiss and took a big drink.

"How much longer do you want to stay?" he asked.

Oh, crap. Did he see me looking at Josef? she thought to herself. "I guess we can go whenever." She grabbed onto his arm. She had completely lost her connection. Now she was worried about Cole, and felt guilty over looking at Josef. "I'm ready when you are." She smiled at him.

"Okay, let's go."

She waved good-bye to the girls and they came running over.

"Will we see you before you leave?"

"Yeah, text me. Maybe we can all get together." She hugged them good-bye. Josef was nowhere to be seen, which was a relief.

They had already checked out of the hotel so they just headed home. Cole was quiet. "What do you think your mom will say?" he finally asked.

"Oh, um, I don't know." Morgana hoped that's why he was quiet.

"When are you going to tell her?"

"Um, I don't know. I've hardly seen her lately."

"I leave June 5th, will you be ready by then?"

"Um, ya, I guess. I don't know. There's so much to think about, right? Like do I need a visa and all that to move? Do you have a place lined up already? Is there room for me? Are you even sure you want me to go?" She tried to laugh.

"Yeah, there is a lot to think about," was all he said. Cole took her to her house instead of to his. "You should talk to your mom," he said and helped her get her bag out of the trunk. He walked her to the door, "I've got some work I need to take care of. Call you later." He kissed her quickly and got into his luxury car and drove away.

Her mom wasn't home and neither was Ms. Lane. Cole didn't call her that night. Nor did he answer any of her calls. She didn't see or hear from him for the next day. As soon as her schedule allowed, she drove over to his house. All the lights were on so she stopped and knocked on the front door. Alexa answered.

"Oh, hey, Alexa. Is Cole home?" Alexa didn't say anything but moved out of the way to let Morgana enter his house. Cole was in the kitchen cooking. "Well, I'm glad to see you're not dead or lying in a ditch somewhere," Morgana snapped, then ran back out the front door and drove away with tears streaming down her face.

She skipped her classes and called in sick to work the next day. Her doorbell rang at 7:30 that night. It was Cole.

"I don't want to come in," he replied angrily to her invitation. "I just want to know...what the fuck, Morgana!" He lost his composure and shouted. "You say you want to move with me, but that was just a lie wasn't it? You say there's nothing between you two, but that was just a lie, too! Wasn't it?" he screamed.

He most definitely saw her dancing for Josef around the May pole. She started crying. "Cole."

"I have done everything for you!" he shouted. "I love you. I need you. But you don't love me. Do you?"

"I do love you!" she implored. She tried to hold him but he turned away. "Cole, please!"

"Please, what? What do you want from me?"

"I just want you!" she cried.

"What does that even mean? You want me because you don't have him?"

"No, Cole!" She kept trying to reach for him, but he backed away pacing back and forth. "Cole, please, I'm sorry. I want to move with you. I'm just scared."

"Scared of what? It's not like you can never come back. So what is it? What are you so afraid of?" he shouted. "You're afraid you don't love me, aren't you? Just fucking admit it."

"Cole, I do. I do love you. I do!" she sobbed.

He stopped pacing and looked her, weeping in the inclined driveway. "You know," he said, "If you lit up half as much, fuck, even a fraction as much, when you say that to me as you do just looking at him, it would be enough for me. But by comparison, I'm not even a blip on your radar."

"What comparison? There is no comparison. I love you!" she cried.

"No, I think you are right the first time. There is no comparison." He took off his Anam Cara ring and shoved it at her. "I no longer agree!" he snapped.

"Cole! Please!" she begged. "No, I love you!" She tried to put the ring back in his hand but he pulled it away from her and walked off to his car.

He paused before getting in, and turned to her and said, "In case you don't know," he shook his head almost in disgust with himself for what he was about to say. "In case you don't know, he lights up when he sees you, too. Good luck to you, Morgana. I hope you find what you're looking for." He slammed the car door and screeched down the inclined driveway, scraping his luxury bumper at the end. She heard him swearing as he drove down the street leaving her sobbing in her driveway.

Chapter Seventeen

Buried Alive

IT HAD BEEN a month since Cole left her stranded in her driveway. She cried for weeks and had to force herself to take her finals. She didn't test very high, but still completed her classes with a B average. She only saw Ms. Lane a few times and told her all that happened.

"I tried so hard to love him!" She cried to her fairy godmother one night. "I was willing to give up everything and move with him. I mean, of course, it's scary, right? He had this all planned out for years. But it was all new to me. What a jerk!" Then she cried harder. "No, I'm the jerk, aren't I? What's wrong with me? He was perfect. He was kind. He was amazing," she cried. "He would have ended up leaving me. I know it. Everyone always leaves me!" She cried harder.

"Why do you say that, dear?" That phrase intrigued the consoling Ms. Lane.

"Because they do! I'm just unlovable, I guess. I'm too stubborn. I'm a mess," she cried. "I'm sorry…I don't mean to bother you with all this." Morgana got up and left Ms. Lane's house, crying all the way home.

The next time she saw Ms. Lane, Morgana didn't want to talk about Cole. All she said was, "It's June 6th. He's gone." At least she had stopped crying, but she was worried if she thought about it too much she would start all over.

Ms. Lane changed the subject and discussed Brook's upcoming wedding. "They're combining it with the Midsummer's celebration. Are you going?"

"Yes, I mailed my RSVP for one." Morgana's eyes started to fill with tears.

BELOVED GRACE ~ AWAKENING ~

"Midsummer's is a night of magic and miracles. Keep yourself open to possibilities, dear," Ms. Lane said in her whimsical way. Morgana tried to stay open, but she was emotionally exhausted. She hoped an evening at the lot would help, but she also knew if she didn't get her energies right, the energy of the lot would repel her like before. Ms. Lane gave her some meditations to listen to. Morgana tried a couple times to listen, but she just couldn't get into them. Instead of relaxing her, she felt irritated.

"That's because you're pinching yourself off, dear," Ms. Lane counseled. "You are rejecting the information. It's okay. It's okay to be sad when we feel loss. You just need to make sure you don't dwell in the sadness. Each day, try to hold a little better feeling, a little longer. You may only be able to hold a happy thought for five minutes today, but hopefully tomorrow it'll be six minutes, and then seven, and then eight, each day increasing. If that's all you can do, that's great. Just try not to get lost in the misery," Ms. Lane warned. "It feels bad to feel bad. That's how you know when you're out of alignment."

"But feeling good is too hard right now," Morgana whined.

"Feeling good is probably too far to reach, then. Just try to feel a little relief."

"How?" Morgana desperately begged.

"With baby steps and practice. Maybe you could tell yourself you won't always feel so sad, or maybe that you have years of love to look forward to."

Morgana shook her head.

Ms. Lane let out a hoot. "Oh dear. I believe you will get over this heartbreak one day. You will go on to live a happy and fulfilled life full of love, magic, and miracles," Ms. Lane stated in her whimsical way.

"I hope you're right," Morgana squeaked.

"Hope is a step in the right direction." Ms. Lane winked.

A couple weeks later, Morgana was driving herself out to the lot on Saturday for the Midsummer's celebration and Brook and Tristan's wedding. "Reach for the best feeling you can," she told herself. This had become her daily mantra ever since Cole left her bawling in the driveway. She hadn't heard anything from him. She tried calling and texting a couple times to wish him a safe trip but he didn't reply. She creeped on his social media page and saw the huge going-away party thrown for him. He looked fantastic and was smiling his gorgeous QG smile, surrounded by dozens of bikini-clad and body painted models. It hurt too much, she stopped looking.

As she drove, she said "My intention is to feel connected to spirit," tears filled her eyes. "Okay, maybe that's too far stretch, right. Let's try again. My intention is to share in the love of Brook and Tristan on their wedding day." No tears with that one. "Okay, good. I can feel happy for my friends. That's good. Focus on that. Don't think about how sad and alone you are." Tears surfaced. "No. Focus on how happy you are that they found each other. I can do this. I can do this. I can't do this!" She started crying. "Luckily, everyone cries at weddings so at least I'll blend in. They don't need to know I'm crying cuz I'm a loser and no one will ever love me." She wiped the tears away with disgust at herself. "I am such a loser," she said angrily.

When she pulled into the parking lot, she looked at her red eyes in the rearview mirror. "Oh, geez. Great! I am loser with big red puffy eyes." She took a deep breath and wiped her face with a handy wipe, then found her compact of translucent powder. "Oh great, I'm a loser with red puffy eyes and ghostly pale skin." She grabbed her sunglasses and her dress to go change in the tent. She figured she wouldn't stay the night, unless by the grace of God, she could connect to the wonderment of the surroundings. She walked to the entrance and in front of the High Council stage was a smaller raised stage surrounded by dozens of white cherry blossom trees. A white carpet runner separated rows of chairs that wrapped around forming a semi-circle around the stage. The rows of chairs were linked and tied off with a white silk sash adorned with bouquets of white, red and yellow flowers. Morgana headed to the girls' tent, trying to breathe, struggling for the connection. She found an empty corner and quickly changed into an aqua spaghetti strapped, short dress. She put on Josef's mother's necklace and the earrings that he'd given her for Christmas. Her intention was to pay homage to those who couldn't be here in person but were here in spirit.

"Morgana!" Trina called out from across the room. Morgana was happy to see her.

"Hi!" Morgana still had her sunglasses on inside. Trina came over and gave her a hug.

"What's wrong?" Trina saw tears from behind the shades as Morgana remembered the night of laughing and dancing with Trina, Mitchell, and Cole.

"We broke up. He moved without me," Morgana tearfully confessed, removing the sunglasses to wipe her eyes.

"Oh, honey." Trina hugged her.

Morgana shook her head. "It's been over a month and I can't stop crying," she said angrily.

"What happened?" Trina tried to console her friend.

"I just couldn't fit into his lifestyle. I guess." Morgana pulled out her phone to show off the images on the social media pages full of Cole surrounded by half naked women and elaborate parties. She didn't go into the part about Josef, she figured this would be enough.

"Oh, girl, not very many outsiders could fit into that."

"He was a rock star. I was just an adoring fan." Morgana tried to sum it up simply to avoid any further inquiries. She wiped away the tears. "I figured my tears would blend in with the wedding, but I need to pull myself together at least till it starts." She tried to joke. "Where is everyone?"

"Oh, that Tiffany has them cattle caged at the hotel up the road. She has been running them ragged with all her attention to detail," Trina said with sarcasm. "Josef has been a saint putting up with everything. You know he's the best man to her maid of honor. Mitchell and Blake are the other attendants. I don't know if Tiffany has been a help or not. Mitchell keeps telling me about all the stunts she's pulled, and honestly, I don't know how any of them have managed. Mitchell figures Tiffany is just practicing for her wedding to Josef, testing everything out on Brook's wedding for practice."

Morgana felt like she was punched in the gut! *Did she just say Tiffany and Josef were getting married?* "Oh, are they engaged or something?" she asked coyly.

"Who knows, but it's probably inevitable. Poor Josef doesn't have much of a choice with that one."

Morgana felt numb. *At least I stopped crying for the moment,* she thought to herself.

"Here, you want me to touch up your makeup?" Trina asked helpfully.

Morgana just stared at her bleakly and nodded.

"I'll use waterproof mascara," Trina said with a soft smile. Morgana just nodded again. It only took Trina ten minutes to add color to Morgana's cheeks and blend away her puffy eyes.

Morgana was still in disbelief. *He was getting married? Ms. Lane probably didn't have the heart to tell me.* Morgana had not given her much opportunity, either. If she wasn't crying over Cole, they were trying to practice happy thoughts.

"I get to join the wedding party for the dinner, but you and I can sit together during the ceremony. I always cry at weddings too, so we can blubber together," Trina chatted away.

"Okay," Morgana said listlessly.

"Boy, he really did a number on you," Trina said.

"What?" Morgana tried to focus on Trina, "Who?" she asked.

"Cole. How long did you date?"

"Oh, umm, I mean, unofficially for six months. I guess. But we were together for a while." Morgana didn't know if what she said made any sense, she couldn't think straight.

"Well, a rule of thumb is, it takes half the amount of time of the relationship to get over someone," Trina explained trying to offer solace.

"Oh, is that a rule?" Morgana tried to smile.

"Maybe if they're real jerks, it won't take as long." Trina smiled.

"Here's hoping," Morgana replied, more concerned about how long it would take her to get over Josef, now, too. "Thank you for helping with my makeup."

"Anytime. Are you ready to head out there? I'm guessing we should be starting soon."

"Um, Ya. Okay." Morgana just followed Trina in a fog.

Some people had already settled into the chairs. Jai waved to Trina. "Oh, there's Jai." Morgana just nodded and went along behind Trina and sat in the seats Jai saved for them.

"Hi, Morgana."

"Hi."

"She and Cole broke up," Trina whispered to Jai.

"Oh, hey, sorry to hear that. He was a really cool guy," Jai said. Trina elbowed him. "Oh, I mean, sorry."

Morgana didn't say anything, just nodded.

The four hundred seats filled up and the music started playing. The twelve council members came out and took their seats on the main stage. Tristan came out, escorting his parents to their seats. Then Mitchell came out, escorting Brook's mom to her seat.

"Please rise for the Honorable Grand High Chairman, Ms. Katherine Lane."

Morgana didn't know what was happening until Trina stood up. Morgana stood as Ms. Lane was escorted by Josef to her post at the altar on a small raised platform so all four hundred guests could see. Ms. Lane was wearing a buttery cream chiffon robe dress and looked so elegant standing there. Josef joined the line where the three men stood, all wearing formal kilts in Tristan's MacLeod tartan of yellow and black, with a red line accent. Morgana stared at Josef, so handsome, standing up there next to his friend, Tristan. This time her heart didn't sing when she looked at him, it ached. It hurt so badly it took her breath away.

"You may be seated."

Tristan walked up the platform to stand next to Ms. Lane. She was dwarfed by his huge frame. Mitchell and Josef left and walked around the back of the chairs to meet up with their counterparts and escort them up the white carpet aisle. Soft bagpipes played a sweet tune as Mitchell and Blake made their way up through the rows and took their place along the front. Josef and Tiffany soon followed. She looked so happy and proud on his arm in front of all the guests. She quickly kissed him on the cheek when they got to the front before she took her spot next to Blake. The girls wore corseted style bell skirt dresses with the yellow tartan sash as an accent piece. They carried yellow, red, and white bouquets that coordinated with the florals on chairs. The bagpipes stopped and the music changed to a sweet soft wedding march and everyone took the cue to stand for the bride. Brook was escorted by her father, her mother stood at the front wiping her eyes with a handkerchief as her daughter made her way up the aisle. The father and the bride stopped so she could give her mom a big hug before they finished the distance to the platform and Mr. Meadow handed off his little girl to the awaiting groom.

"My beloved friends," the Grand High Chairman, Ms. Lane greeted the crowd, motioning for everyone to take their seats. "Love is a special vibration that emanates at the highest of frequencies. When two people meet on that frequency, magic is made. I am honored and privileged to be here today, in the midst of the beautiful magic of Tristan MacLeod and my own, beautiful, great-niece, Brook Meadow. They stand before you, those of you here in body and those of you are who are here in spirit, to share their vows of love. Love is a glorious thing. When two people commit to each other in the frequency of love, their lives are enhanced, and the universe around us rejoices. May I have the rings, please?" Ms. Lane looked towards Josef, who handed over the bride's ring. And then to Tiffany, who handed over the one for the groom. Ms. Lane held them in her hand and walked up to three white candles with Tristan and Brook. Tristan lit one, Brook lit one, and then they let the center one. "Bless this union with love and light." They said as they lit each candle, and then said it together when they lit the third. Then Ms. Lane took their rings and waved them over the flame. "Bless these rings as a token that the bride and groom offer to each other to represent their unity." Ms. Lane handed Tristan the rings for his bride, and he carefully held them in his big fingers. "Tristan, please take Brook's hand and place the ring on her finger as an act to represent your commitment in this unity." He did. "Brook, please take Tristan's hand and place the ring on his finger as an act to represent your commitment to this unity." She did. "Please repeat after me, My love, I will always be there to hold your hand as we journey through this life together." They repeated. "May I please have the ribbon," Ms. Lane asked Tiffany, who brought it up and smiled in front of the crowd.

Trina whispered to Morgana, "Mitchell told me Tiffany insisted she hold the ribbon. Apparently, it is usually given with the rings."

"Mmm." Morgana motioned back not really having heard what Trina said. She hadn't heard much of what was being said at all, because she was focused on how it felt like her heart was being crushed in a vice. It was all she could do to not scream.

Ms. Lane waved the ribbon over the flame. "The promises made today, are bound together with blessings of love and light to greatly strengthen your union across the years as you encourage each other's lives and soul growth. Please hold left hands and look into each other's eyes." Ms. Lane wrapped the ribbon around their wrists. "Tristan, will you share in Brook's laughter, help her achieve her goals, and support her on her spiritual journey on this earth?"

"I willll," he rolled.

"Brook, will you share in Tristan's laughter, help him achieve his goals, and support him on his spiritual journey on this earth?"

"I will," she beamed.

"May the dreams that you share be fulfilled. May the hearts that you share be true. May the love that you share be unending. May this union be blessed in love and light."

Ms. Lane addressed the crowd. Servers had passed out champagne glasses. "You all have received a crystal champagne flute. Please raise your crystal as a sign of wealth, abundance, and grace to be bestowed on this couple. May their cup runneth over." Ms. Lane held up her goblet.

"May their cup runneth over," the crowd cheered.

"And by the power invested in me, I now pronounce you man and wife. And I hereby decree that so it is and so it shall be, for as long as you both agree."

"For as long as you both agree." Those words brought the tears back to Morgana's eyes. Ms. Lane had taught her those for the friendship circle when she gave Cole the Anam Cara rings that he threw back at her the night in her driveway. She didn't have Cole. She didn't have Josef. She didn't have anything.

Trina and Jai joined the wedding party at their table for dinner. Morgana avoided Josef at all costs. Of course, it was easy since Tiffany was dominating him. Morgana had enough. She headed back to grab her stuff so she could leave. As she passed the restrooms on her way to the tent, of all the people coming out, there was Tiffany.

"Oh, I see are you here. No Cole?"

"No, he's in Paris." Morgana just wanted to get past her.

"Well, I hope you end up going, because Brook and Tristan are now married, and Josef and I are practically engaged. So it would just be nice if everyone was as happy as me."

"Congratulations," Morgana uttered.

"Did you know Josef and I have been planning this for years? I used to sneak into his room when I would spend the night at Brook's house, and he and I would talk all night about our future together."

"That's nice." Morgana just wanted to get away.

"Oh, and Morgana. When I am his <u>wife</u>, I'll want that amulet back. It's a family heirloom and it belongs to our children." Tiffany gave a weak smile and turned away.

Morgana felt sick to her stomach. Her heart ached with the burning of a thousand hot knives being stabbed into her. She drove home and crawled into her bed. "We've been planning this for years." The words attacked her like piranhas biting and tearing away at her flesh. She finally fell asleep and slept through Sunday.

Without knowing what else to do with her life, Morgana had signed up for two summer classes. One was 8 a.m. to noon, and the other was 1 p.m. to 5 p.m. Then she went to work at the kiosk in the mall until 11 p.m. Without Cole visiting during his breaks and bringing her coffees, she loathed her position. She made an appointment with the career counselor at school, who said the only options that would possibly work around her heavy school schedule would be bartending, coffee barista, or a night job at the local factory on the assembly line. That last option was given as a joke by the counselor, but Morgana asked how she could get an interview there.

"Oh, honey. You're too pretty to work nights at a factory. Why don't you cut back on some classes and get a job more suited to your personality? I've got lots of office jobs."

"No, right now I need to finish school and make money," Morgana said with focused determination. The factory paid almost three times what she was making at the kiosk. The counselor obliged and gave her the contact information.

Several weeks went by, and then Ms. Lane texted:

ML: It's almost your birthday. Will I see you any time soon?

M: Sorry. Busy with school and work.

Was all she replied. She couldn't face her sweet fairy godmother right now. Morgana felt too down and didn't want to bother Ms. Lane. Her heart hurt every time she thought of Cole or Josef. She felt completely abandoned and just wanted to be alone.

It was her nineteenth birthday, and all she wanted to do was sleep through it. Her mom had tried to sing to her that morning. "I made you a cake!" But Morgana told her she didn't feel well.

"Are you okay? I haven't seen Cole around lately?"

"He moved to Paris last month."

"Oh!" Her mom was surprised. "Is that why you've been so mopey? Oh, my sweet girl. Boys are just heartbreakers. I'm sorry." Her mom hugged her but she just stood there limp.

"We'll talk tomorrow. I gotta go. Love you. Happy birthday!"

Morgana was curled up under her blankets, eating a solitary piece of birthday cake when the doorbell rang. She ignored it the first five times, but finally was annoyed enough to see who was so obnoxious to not get the hint she wasn't home.

Josef was standing there with a pink wrapped birthday gift. *From Ms. Lane no doubt.* She fought back the tears burning her eyes. *We've been planning this for years*, repeated itself incessantly in her head.

"Happy birthday!" he said in his silky voice.

Morgana waged a war within herself. The part of her that wanted to jump into his arms and get lost in his aqua blue eyes and sing and tingle, and the part that wanted to shut everyone out and silence the infuriating singing at all costs. She avoided his eyes and looked at the bubbly pink gift.

"I'm not feeling well," she replied.

"Oh, can I get you anything?" His concern gave power to the side of her that wanted to believe in love.

"No. I just want to be alone," she said still not looking at his face.

"This is from Aunt Katherine. She said she hasn't heard from you in a while."

"I figured it was a conflict of interest now, considering your engagement," Morgana said with more anger than she meant to let out.

"What?" Josef took a step back.

"You know, the engagement you've been planning for years with Tiffany. She told me all about your all night talks growing up together. Shall I assume you're here for the amulet? She said you would want it back," she hissed.

"When did she tell you all this?" He acted completely surprised.

She knew if she looked into his eyes she would lose her nerve. "At Brook's wedding. You're engagement was all anyone could talk about." The battle inside her raged on. "Wait here. I'll go get the necklace for you. Should I get the earrings, too?" Her heart shrieked in pain within her chest.

"No. Stop! Look, whatever you think about me right now, we will deal with later. I gave you that amulet because I wanted you to have it. You deserve it and I know you'll take care of it. It's yours. But don't ignore Aunt Katherine. She's eighty-three years old. She loves you and I don't want you to regret not spending time with her if anything were to ever happen."

Morgana felt a powerful surge of anger rush through her. *Regret!* she thought. *I regret ever laying eyes on you! I regret every minute of energy I wasted on you!* The part of her that believed in love was sorely losing the fight. Morgana gave all her energy to the winning side and she could feel her breaking heart being buried alive in stone. It flailed inside her chest, fighting frantically for its life.

"I don't need you to tell me about regret," she asserted through gritted teeth. Her wasted heart was nearly encased in a stony tomb. "I don't need Ms. Lane." Morgana could see in her mind's eye just the tiniest tip of her beating heart still exposed, desperately clinging to life and gasping for air.

"And I don't," Morgana looked dead into Josef's deep aqua blue eyes, "need you." She declared it with such intensity that her heart finally lost its battle and became entirely rock solid. The tears instantly dried up behind her eyes and she became completely emotionless.

Josef took another step back. He had witnessed the change in her right before his very eyes. "She would still want you to have this." He extended out the pink gift.

"Keep it. My wedding gift to you," she said dryly with complete detachment and closed the door.

She walked down her long tiled entry with the spindled half wall, back down the hall into her room, and called the contact at the factory. The school counselor had told her Morgana would be calling and the job was hers as soon as she could start. Morgana called her boss from the kiosk and gave her the news.

"We're sorry to lose you."

"Yes, thank you for the opportunity," Morgana replied in a monotone. Her new schedule would be brutal, but she didn't care.

She didn't care about anything anymore.

hapter Eighteen

The Rescue

FOR WEEKS MORGANA had been burning the candle at both ends. Fall semester started and she went to school from 10 a.m. to 5 p.m. during the day and then worked from 10 p.m. to 5 a.m. at the factory at night. She didn't talk to anyone. Her teacher would critique her on her non-participation but her grades were maintained. She worked on an assembly line at night with no one around which was perfect for her. She didn't need anyone. Even her mom would try to talk to her, but since she worked nights, too, as Morgana pointed out, it didn't give her any room to argue.

"I'm fine," was all she would say, then either head to bed, school, or the factory, depending on which time of day her mother tried to accost her. "If you have a problem with it, I'll move out," Morgana would say in her monotone, if her mom really got on her.

"What's wrong with you? Where are you?" Her mother would plead.

But Morgana would always just reply, "I'm fine."

"You're not fine."

"If you have a problem with it, I'll move out."

"One of these days I'm going to call your bluff," her mom called out behind her.

But Morgana didn't care. She had shut herself off from everything and everyone. She had no life left in her. She had turned her heart to stone and buried all her emotions with it. She would say to herself, "My frequency is flat lined."

She got an occasional text from Ms. Lane.

ML: We're celebrating Lammas at the lot, August 18th. Hope you can make it.
Delete.
ML: It's Mabon time. September 21st. Can you come?
Delete
ML: It's Samhain. What are your plans for Halloween?
Delete
Any free time she had, Morgana stayed locked in her room studying or sleeping. She slept through Halloween.

Around Thanksgiving, she couldn't concentrate on homework, and got a text from her mom asking if she wanted "to do a turkey this year?" Morgana got sidetracked and wandered onto her social media page. She had a thousand notifications, one of which caught her eye.

"Cole Williams has changed his relationship status."

She looked on his page to see him and some beautiful dark haired Parisian model gallivanting around Europe together with pictures of them in Paris, skiing in Zurich, and riding in the gondolas in Venice. He had posted pictures of her walking in fashion shows with captions like: "That's my girl." "So proud of my angel." "I'm the luckiest guy in the world." With her heart like petrified wood locked down in her chest, without any emotion Morgana deleted her account.

For Thanksgiving, Morgana tried to make dinner for her and her mom. She wasn't at all surprised when the turkey came out dry. "Didn't make this with love, that's for sure," she said humorlessly to herself.

"So, you're almost done with your associate's degree. You've been working so hard. I'm so proud of you," her mom said over dry turkey. "What colleges have you applied for to transfer to?"

"I figured I'm just going to stay here," Morgana shrugged.

"But I thought you wanted to move away from this one horse town? I thought that was your plan."

"I dunno. Plans change I guess."

"Morgana. What has gotten into you?"

"Nothing," she replied in her usual monotone.

"I figured you'd be over that boy by now."

"What?"

"You know. Cole. Mr. Paris. Isn't that why you've been upset?"

"I'm not upset. Did I ever tell you he wanted me to move with him?"

"He did?" Her mom was shocked. "To Paris?"

"Yup. Said he'd help me go to school over there and get a job."

"Well. What happened?"

"I was afraid, I guess," she said in a voice as dry as the turkey. "Would you have let me go?"

"Well, I mean. Let you? I guess, if you wanted to and felt safe. I would have needed to know when your first visit home would be. I guess so. How come you didn't ever ask?"

"I don't know. I didn't think I should abandon you."

"Abandon me?"

"Ya, you know, like everyone has abandoned us."

"No one has abandoned us, Morgana. People change. Life goes one. My parents died and I was an only child. They didn't mean to die."

"How come you don't have any friends?"

"I have lots of friends and all the people I work with."

"How come you never married?"

"Oh, I don't know. I guess I just didn't want to put you through my damaged relationships. Wait, is that what this is all about? Are you turning into me? Morgana, I've dated lots of guys. I've just never brought any of them home. I didn't want to uproot your life for some guy. I go out. I have friends. I guess I just go while you're at work or school. Plus, I know I'm always working but I was just trying to provide for us."

If Morgana had been able to feel emotions, she might have been pissed about now. Her mom would have let her move with Cole. She had a total social life Morgana never knew about. And her mom didn't feel the same abandonment and isolation Morgana felt her whole life. But such as it was, Morgana felt nothing as her heart was in its rock solid state, so all this new information was a moot point now.

"Are you okay?" her mom asked.

"Yes, I'm fine."

"Are you working tonight?"

"Yes, all weekend. Took some extra shifts."

"Just like your momma," her mom sighed and gave her a hug.

"I'll clean this up later," Morgana said as she walked out the door.

"I'll get it."

The month between Thanksgiving and Christmas always flies by. This year was no exception. Morgana was working extra shifts and studying for finals. She would earn her two-year degree in a year and a half, just like she planned. Starting January she'd be going to the university for more mind numbing courses in things she didn't care about, but she figured it was what she was supposed to do. She didn't care anymore whether she stayed in this one horse town or moved away. She didn't care about anything. She hadn't heard anything from Ms. Lane since October. She would occasionally wonder how she was doing, but she didn't let herself dwell on it too long.

Christmas night Morgana was working. Her job consisted of inserting tab 'A' into slot 'B' over and over for hours. When her shift was over at 5 a.m., she headed home like usual. But half way, she realized she had forgotten her phone. She never used it anymore but since she did finally have a day off the next night, she figured she better go back and get it. By the time she turned around, the morning traffic was heavy and she was delayed almost forty-five minutes. As she was finally heading up the street to her house, an ambulance and fire truck were leaving from Ms. Lane's house.

"Oh, God!" Morgana panicked, "Were those at her house?"

A text came in from her mom: There was a 911 call from Ms. Lane's address!

M: What did she say?

Mom: She fell and unable to get up.

M: Oh no! Which hospital are they taking her to?

Mom: St. Mary's

M: I'm going

Morgana ran into the emergency entrance of St. Mary's hospital trying to find Ms. Lane, but, because she wasn't family, no one would tell her anything. Morgana paced the hallways desperately searching for her sweet fairy godmother. *Oh, God. What if something happens to her?*

Fear and panic broke their way into Morgana's stone encased heart.

Finally, after an hour, a nurse took pity and let her know Ms. Lane was in surgery on the fourth floor. Morgana ran to the fourth floor. No one there would talk to her, either. She sat in the waiting room and fell asleep in an uncomfortable waiting room chair. A text from her mom startled her awake.

Mom: How is she?

M: IDK. No one will talk to me. I'm waiting in surgery.

Mom: Find Nurse Nancy. Let her know you're my daughter.

M: ok! I'll keep you posted.

Morgana went back to the surgical nurse's station. "Is Nurse Nancy working today?" she asked the busy nurse behind the counter.

"She's doing rounds. She'll be back," the hardworking nurse snapped.

"Okay, thank you." *Perfect*, Morgana thought. She started looking around trying not to be obtrusive.

"Do you know where I can find Nurse Nancy?" she asked a passerby in scrubs. He pointed down the hall. "Thank you." She headed down in the direction he pointed.

A tall statuesque nurse with dark grey streaked hair was closing a door on one of the rooms. Morgana tried to act causal as she peered for the name tag.

"Nurse Nancy?"

"Yes?"

"Hi, I'm Morgana Anderson. You know my mother."

"Oh, yes. My aren't we all grown up."

"Thank you, ma'am. I'm looking for a patient who came in this morning, Katherine Lane."

"Ah yes, she was here."

"Was here?" Morgana wanted to be sick.

"They've move her to recovery now. On the fifth floor."

"Oh." Morgana felt a little relief. "Would I be able to see her? No one is telling me anything because I'm not family, but she is family to me." Morgana's eyes filled with tears that she hadn't felt in nearly six months.

"Oh, there, there. You go on up. I'll let them know you are coming." Nurse Nancy gave her a wink.

"Oh! Thank you!" Morgana tearfully praised.

"Fifth floor. Take the elevator on the right." Nurse Nancy waved.

"Okay! Thank you!" Morgana walked as fast as she could to the elevator on the right, wiping off her wet cheeks. For months she had blocked all emotion but now was being flooded with fear, remorse, panic, and terror, over the status of her sweet fairy godmother.

The elevator felt like it took forever to finally open its door and release Morgana from its steel cage. She hurried to the nurse's station to find someone to help her. A little round nurse with little round glasses peeked her head up from behind stacks of papers.

"Can I help you?" her little voice squeaked.

"Um, I'm Morgana. Did Nurse Nancy happen to talk to you?"

"Nurse Nancy. Ah, yes. She said you were looking for your auntie."

"Yes, ma'am. Ms. Katherine Lane."

"She's in room 5036. Just down the hall on the right."

"Oh, thank you." Morgana took rapid steps until she reached room 5036. The door was open. It was dark inside except a small dim light in the corner. The room was filled with flowers, practically looked like a florist shop. She crept inside to see Ms. Lane's tiny little figure lying in the cold steel hospital bed. She had a cast on her foot and an ace bandage around her wrist. Her usually perfect silver ballerina bun pinned hair was down and matted to her head. Her eyes were closed and she looked eerily peaceful. Morgana just stared at her sweet face afraid to wake her. Morgana sniffed her runny nose and Ms. Lane's eyes opened. It took a second for them to focus.

"Morgana?" a soft whisper came out.

"Oh, I'm so sorry to wake you." Morgana didn't know if she should stay or go.

Ms. Lane cleared her throat. "Morgana, dear. It's good to see you." Her voice was normal.

Morgana raced to the side of the bed. "I'm so sorry. I'm so sorry I haven't spoken to you in so long. I understand if you don't want to see me. I just needed to make sure you were okay." Tears streaked down Morgana's face.

"Oh, dear. I'm fine. I'm so glad to see you. You know you're always welcome," she said with her sweet smile.

"I came home and saw the ambulance. I've been downstairs this whole time. They wouldn't tell me if you were okay," she cried.

"Oh come now, dry those tears. I'm perfectly fine." The strong old lady patted her young friend's hand.

"What happened?" Morgana said fearfully.

Ms. Lane let out her signature hoot. "Well, I was dancing and singing to my garden, using the hose nozzle as a microphone, when I somehow managed to kick one of the planters with my pinkie toe and then managed to get tangled up in the hose. I went down on my rear and the water shot straight in my face and up my nose. My hair must look atrocious!" Ms. Lane laughed at herself.

Morgana wiped her eyes, confused. "But, but they said you were in surgery."

"I ended up breaking my little toe again. I had broken it many times back when I was a dancer, so there was a lot of scar tissue. The good doctor said he could remove some of it with a quick surgery so it could heal up nicely," she quipped.

"And your wrist?" Morgana was relieved and still confused, but just so happy to hear Ms. Lane's sweet laughter again.

"It's got a good sprain to it. Got it twisted in my microphone nozzle. The real hero is Ol' Betsy here." Ms. Lane patted her rump. "Oh, I'm sure she's gonna be black and blue for a bit," she said with a laugh.

"I'm just so grateful you're alright," Morgana sighed and wiped her drippy nose. "I don't know what I would have done without you. I'm so sorry." Morgana hung her head.

"No need to be sorry, dear. It's good fortune that you happened to be home. I'm glad you came to see me." Ms. Lane patted Morgana on the head.

"Ya, good fortune." Morgana shook her head. "I forgot my cell phone and turned around to get it. There was more traffic than usual and it delayed me. I almost didn't go back for it," Morgana said shaking her head, thinking how if she would have come straight home she wouldn't have seen the emergency vehicles. If she hadn't retrieved her phone she wouldn't have gotten her mother's text.

"That's synchronicity, dear, powerful forces all aligning." Ms. Lane winked.

"But, I don't understand." She wiped her face. "How could you, Ms. Queen of Alignment, end up in the hospital?"

A big bright smile spread wide across Ms. Lane's face and in her whimsical voice she stated, "There are some universal forces even bigger than me."

Morgana was about to ask what she meant, when he walked into the room and turned on the bright light. "Okay, Aunt Katherine. The nurses are getting your discharge papers in order and we should be able to get you out of here in no time." He was surprised to see Morgana sitting there, but as soon as he realized who it was his whole face, eyes, and body lit up.

The emotions of panic and fear that Morgana had felt while searching for her sweet dear old friend had cracked the rock façade that encapsulated her heart, and when she heard his silky voice and saw him standing there beaming because of her, her heart shattered its rocky prison with the force of an atomic bomb. It nearly took her breath away and for the first time in months she took in a deep long breath, bringing the life back into her dormant cells. She felt energy rushing to every cell in her body, awakening them like a field of wild flowers dancing with new life in the first spring rain. She could smell all the sweet pungent aromas of the fresh bouquets that filled the hospital room satisfying her senses. She locked onto his deep aqua blue eyes and she felt endless in their reflection. He took a step back because of the electricity exchanging between them.

"Hi, Morgana," he said, stunned.

She just smiled. She knew he was with Tiffany and that was okay. She felt herself come alive and that's what was amazing.

"Listen," Ms. Lane said, "why don't you two take all these flowers to the children's wing while I have a nurse help me get myself together. Morgana, would you please open the curtains? Josef, why don't you ask if they can spare a trolley cart so you can take all these flowers?"

"Yes ma'am." Josef flashed a smile at his sweet aunt, then gave an even brighter one to Morgana, and then exited the room.

Morgana stood up from her chair at Ms. Lane's bedside and opened the heavy curtains, exposing a bright warm sun that flooded into the room with its golden rays. She closed her eyes and felt its warming kisses on her face. She took another long deep breath, savoring the sweet floral aromas and basking in the soft sunlight shining in through the window.

"Ah, there's my girl," Ms. Lane said as she could see Morgana's energetic pathways opening. "Feel better now?" Morgana turned and nodded with a new soft smile that she declared would be her permanent expression from now on. Josef returned with a cart and they loaded up as many of the beautiful arrangements that fit. "Save me the cards, please. I want to thank my well-wishers." Ms. Lane waved them off as the nurse came in to help her dress.

Morgana was in a calm state of euphoric peace as they walked to the elevators. When they loaded themselves and waited to reach their floor, Morgana said softly, "You were right. When I saw that ambulance leaving her house, it was like my life flashed before my eyes. I saw life without her in it and it was terrible. I'm sorry for what I said to you."

"There is no need for you to apologize. You had good reason to feel how you felt and say what you said," Josef replied gently.

The elevator doors opened at their floor. Josef explained to the nurses all the flowers and they happily accepted them. The elevator was full of patrons on the way back up to fifth floor and Ms. Lane was waiting in a wheelchair when they returned.

"They said I'm free to go," Ms. Lane declared with a bright smile and her hair back in its perfect ballerina bun.

"You're chariot awaits, my lady." Josef wheeled her around and headed back to the elevators.

"Oh, I'm parked over here." Morgana pointed to the opposite direction. "Can I grab us all some drive-thru and meet you back at the house?" she offered.

"That would be lovely, dear. Thank you. Let me give you some money." Ms. Lane tapped Josef to reach for her purse.

"No, my treat," Morgana said with a bright smile.

"Well, thank you, dear. That is very kind of you." Ms. Lane felt the sincerity in her energetic exchange and gratefully accepted it with a smile. "Can I get a big juicy cheeseburger?" Ms. Lane put in her order with big wide eyes.

"You got it!"

Josef said that sounded good, too. Morgana gave Ms. Lane a quick hug and then made it to her car. She drove with the windows down, feeling the cool winter wind on her face. The drive-thru was quick and the server was friendly, even gave her a free drink while she waited. She felt the connection with the universe again and it felt so good.

When she arrived at Ms. Lane's house, Josef was just wheeling her into the pink confectionary Christmas home. "Here, let me help." Morgana helped get Ms. Lane settled in on the couch and wrapped up in a soft pink blanket with her casted foot propped up on some pillows. Then she maneuvered her way through the kitchen, brewing a fresh pot of decaf coffee and served Ms. Lane her juicy cheeseburger and cup of decaf just like she liked it.

"Well, this is just lovely. Bless this day," Ms. Lane said as they all enjoyed their dinner next to a crackling fire and the sweet glow of Ms. Lane's twinkling lit pink Christmas tree.

"I have tomorrow off. I can come over in the morning if you would like. I make pretty good omelettes, and I can help you with whatever you need," Morgana suggested cheerfully.

"I'm going to take you up on that, dear. Thank you."

Morgana cleared everyone's plates and cleaned up the dishes. "Is there anything else I can do for you tonight?"

"No, I think we've got it from here. Thank you for dinner and taking such good care of us." Ms. Lane smiled.

"I would stay, but I've been awake for nearly twenty-four hours, if you don't count the two hours of sleep I think I got in the waiting room chair," Morgana jested.

"I don't think you can count those." Josef laughed.

"You're already in your house coat, so you're good for tonight. Josef, you can help her get to bed alright?"

"Yes, we'll manage." He smiled at her.

"Okay, I will be back when you get up at six then." She gave Ms. Lane a big long hug, careful not to squeeze too tightly to disturb Ol' bruised Betsy.

Josef walked her to the door. "You call me if she needs anything." She made him promise. "I'll be here at six. Good night."

"Merry Christmas, Morgana," his silky voice called out as she headed down the walkway.

"Merry Christmas," she said whimsically. She walked up her inclined driveway, exhausted from lack of sleep, but still feeling joyous and alive. Ms. Lane was fine and Morgana felt the connection again. She flopped into her bed and passed out, still with the sweet soft peaceful smile affixed to her lips.

Morgana arrived fresh the next morning promptly at 6 a.m. Josef let her in with a sleepy, "Hello."

"How is she?" Was the first thing out of her mouth.

"She's fine. Slept all night," he replied with a waking yawn.

"Can I make you some coffee?" Morgana offered.

"That would be great. I'm gonna jump into the shower." Josef's deep aqua blue eyes shined at her.

She embraced the tingles that ran all through her body and made her way to the kitchen to brew up some fresh java. She prepared a cup for Ms. Lane and went to check on her.

Ms. Lane was bright eyed and sitting up in her bed reading a book.

"Oh, thank you, dear. That smells delicious." Ms. Lane held the pleasant smelling, steaming hot beverage under her nose before she took a savoring sip.

"Would you like to come out into the living room?" Ms. Lane said yes, and Morgana expertly helped her up, put on her house coat, and then into the wheelchair. She stopped her in front of Ms. Lane's ivory vanity and brushed her hair, pinning it up in a perfect ballerina bun. She brought her a warm washcloth to freshen her face, and then wheeled her down the hall to the kitchen. She helped her step down into the sunken plush pink carpeted living room and settled her on the couch.

"Do you have any green candles?" Morgana inquired.

"Yes, my candles are in the chest on the shelf." Ms. Lane pointed. Morgana picked out a green pillar candle and placed it on the end table close to Ms. Lane's casted foot. She lit it and said with closed eyes, "Dear Archangel Raphael, please bless this foot with fast, healthy healing and make it strong once more."

Ms. Lane was impressed. "How did you know how to do that?"

"The thought came to me on my way over here. I heard the name Archangel Raphael and saw the color green."

Ms. Lane got a wide smile on her face. "Very good, dear. Thank you. Archangel Raphael has long been regarded as the angel of healing and emerald green is his color."

Morgana knew she was connected again. She went into the kitchen, lit a white candle, and proceeded to make everyone fresh, organic, and blessed, savory omelettes. Afterwards she cleaned up the dishes and wiped down the kitchen when everyone was done. She returned to the living room where Ms. Lane and Josef were having a discussion.

"Morgana, Josef and I were just talking about how well you are handling me and yourself and we would like to make you a proposition." Morgana looked back and forth between their smiling faces. "Would you be interested in being my personal assistant? I just want to stay off my foot for a couple of weeks and I know Ol' Betsy here is gonna take at least a week or two before she's ready to get back in the saddle." Ms. Lane laughed. "I have a nursemaid who will come twice a week to check on me and help me with all that, I'll just need some extra help for a few weeks to water the garden just until I'm nimble again, in addition to running some errands and things for me."

"Sure! Of course! Anything I can do!" Morgana was eager to help.

"I know you've got school and your job at the mall but maybe we could work something out." Ms. Lane was hopeful.

"Oh, totally. It's still winter break for a couple of weeks. I quit the kiosk and I work nights on the assembly line down at the factory." Ms. Lane and Josef exchanged stunned looks with each other. "I was going to school during the day, so I took the job at night. I make three times what I was making at the kiosk and I did just get my associates degree in a year and a half, as planned," she explained. "So, no, really, I'm available all day for the next couple of weeks. I can come over at six when I get off work and make your breakfasts and help out with your morning routine. Then, if you don't mind, I'd go home for a couple hours of sleep, but I would be back by, say one for afternoon errands, tea of course, and then make you dinner before I leave for work. It's perfect." Morgana was excited.

"That's not perfect. That's insane," Josef quipped.

"What? No! Please, I'd be happy to anything I can do to help. Just let me know. Really!" Morgana was completely optimistic about the opportunity to help her wonderful fairy godmother who had always been there for her. "It's the least I can do."

"This position I'm offering you would be a paid position," Ms. Lane tried to clarify.

"Oh, no! I couldn't take your money. It's my privilege to assist you." Morgana refused.

"Alright," the diplomatic Josef intervened. "Morgana, I don't think you understand. We are offering you a full time job as the Grand High Chairman's personal assistant. It's a salaried position that needs to be filled. If it's not you, we will have to find someone else. And Aunt Katherine really wants it to be you. Will you accept the position?"

"OH! Really?" Morgana was surprised by the employment opportunity. She looked at Ms. Lane's excited smile.

"Yes, dear. I think you're perfect for the job."

"Oh, Yes! Yes! I would love to!"

"Great!" Ms. Lane clapped her hands together, carefully because of her sprained wrist. "Josef has some paperwork for you to fill out so we can get you on payroll immediately. How much notice do you need to give to the factory?"

"I'll call them later today and find out!"

"Wonderful!" Ms. Lane was delighted.

Morgana was ecstatic!

Chapter Nineteen

The Energy of Abandonment

MORGANA SAT DOWN in one of the high-back floral chairs at the huge marble pedestal table in Ms. Lane's delightful dining room under the smiling faces of the adorable figurines, and watched Josef as he arranged all the documents for her to sign. In her connected state, she was now loving the tingles and buzz her whole body got from him. She knew she couldn't act on any of them, but she just allowed her butterflies and her energy flow. She felt like she was on a large swing, floating through the air, thrilling yet serene, and tummy tickling and safe. She hoped the he and Tiffany felt that way for each other. He looked up from the paper work.

"You okay?" he asked with a smile.

"This is such an honor. I feel so blessed," she replied. His smile sent her virtual swing higher.

"Listen," Morgana said to Josef after signing all the documents, "I don't know what your plans are. I'm assuming you probably need to get back home. But if you could just give me, like, an hour or two, to take care of some things, then I'll be back for the rest of day and then you can go. Would that be alright?"

"Oh, yah, sure. That would be fine," Josef agreed.

"Okay, thank you." She instinctively reached out and touched his hand. The energy shockwave was exhilarating. It bubbled like champagne within her and she couldn't help but let out the rolling giggle. "This is all just so exciting!" She tried to explain her joyful outburst and got up from the table to check on Ms. Lane, who was dozing on her Victorian-era silky cream rayon upholstered couch. "Ms.

Lane, are you comfortable out here or would you like to go back to your bed?" Morgana whispered.

"You know, I think I would like to go lay down. Thank you." Morgana carefully helped her up and wheeled her back to her room.

"I'm just going to take care of some things. I'll be back in an hour or so. You take it easy and get some rest. Can I get you some water?"

"That would be lovely, dear," a sleepy Ms. Lane responded. Morgana returned with the water and the green pillar candle, quietly setting them on the nightstand, as not to disturb Ms. Lane who was already back to sleep.

Morgana backed down her inclined driveway and headed to the factory to see what her options were. She went to talk with Keri, the HR Coordinator.

"Hi Morgana. Nice to you see. You look different. Did you change your hair or something?" Keri, a sweet and helpful lady, who was always available to listen, was the one who hired Morgana. Morgana didn't talk much to anyone at the factory, but Keri was always there with a cheerful smile. "You're not scheduled to work today. Is everything alright?"

"Well, I would like to give my two week notice and I wanted to talk with you about what my options are. You see, I have been blessed with the opportunity of a lifetime to work with someone I highly admire and I am just so honored to be asked to fill this position. But, I totally know and understand I have my responsibilities here. I was wondering if I could go part time for the next two weeks to finish out."

"You are a very dedicated employee and an honorable young lady, Morgana. We are sorry to see you go. Let me just pull you up in the system." Keri looked at her computer. "Well, it looks to me like you have some vacation time owed to you. And, wow, not one sick day taken. So, if I just do this." She clicked and clacked away on the keyboard. "Adjust that. Let me print off these. I have to click here. Did you bring your key card with you? Great, let me have that. I'll just sign here, here, and here. Can you sign there? And initial there. Perfect. Alright, Miss Anderson, it looks like we are all set. Here is your final check and you take care of yourself," Keri said with her wonderful cheery smile.

"What? That's it. But I wanted to be sure to give the proper notice," Morgana clarified.

"And we appreciate it. I've got you all taken care of and you are welcome back any time." Then she said in a sweet and sincere tone, "Go now. Follow those dreams. Good luck to you."

"Thank you, Mrs. Meyer. Thank you very much." Morgana was surprised and happy. "Awesome!" She cheered when she got back into her car.

When she returned, Josef was on the phone when he opened the heavy wooden door for her and waved her in.

"Si signore." (Pause) "Posso esser li. Quanto tempoche stato cosi?"(Pause) "Si."

Hearing Josef's silky voice speak Italian was almost more than Morgana could bear. She tried not to eavesdrop but couldn't help herself. She had no idea what he was saying, but it sounded heavenly dripping from his lips. She finally forced herself down the hall to check on Ms. Lane.

"How's the little patient?" Morgana asked Ms. Lane who was sitting up reading.

She let out a hoot. "I'm wonderful, dear," she said in her whimsical way.

"Are you okay or would you like to come out?"

"I would like to come out and have some tea," she decided. They loaded her up in the wheelchair and brought her out to the kitchen.

"Couch or gazebo?"

"I think outside is a marvelous idea." Morgana opened the huge glass slider. Josef was still on the phone on the patio.

"Okay. See you soon. Love you, too." He hung up the phone. Morgana wheeled Ms. Lane over the slider tracks and out into her secret garden.

"There's my girls." Josef smiled as they made their way outside.

Did he say girl or girls? Morgana thought to herself.

"Well, I just got off the phone with Grandma Lynetta," Josef said.

Grandma? Morgana was a little happier knowing she heard him saying "I love you" to his grandmother and not Tiffany. *I must stop thoughts like that,* she gently reminded herself.

"It looks like I have to leave earlier than expected. Adalberto was telling me the machine is still having that problem and I need to go before it shuts production down completely. Are you sure you don't want to recover in Italy?"

"No, I'm fine here. I've got the best nurse assistant ever taking care of me." She patted Morgana's hand. "Plus I just can't imagine sitting on a plane for thirteen hours with Ol' bruised Betsy here." She patted her bum.

"Well, Morgana." Josef looked directly at her with those amazing aqua blues. "I hate to do this to you, but do you think you'll be able to handle that schedule of working nights and helping Aunt Katherine during the day?"

"Oh, I talked to the factory today to give my two weeks and the HR Coordinator did something and said I was free and clear. I don't have to go back," Morgana explained.

"Oh! Sweet synchronicity," Ms. Lane cheered.

"Well, that's great! A valued asset to the team already." Josef gave her a big, beaming smile.

Morgana wondered to herself if the sun was jealous of how brightly she felt she was shining at that moment.

Morgana got Ms. Lane all tucked in and situated with a blanket in the wicker recliner in the gazebo under the smiling cherubs. As she was in the kitchen making tea, Josef came out from the back room with his bags all packed.

"All set then?" Morgana said from behind the large marble kitchen island.

"Yep, I'm just going to say good-bye to Aunt Katherine." He walked across the room to the large slider. Morgana was pretending to be preparing the tea tray, but she was really soaking in the elated feeling she got when she was around him.

This is how I want to feel when I'm with my true love, she told herself as she harnessed the vibration. When he came back in, she had just finished setting the tea tray. He came behind the island to where she was standing and wrapped his arms around her in an endearing embrace.

"It really means so much to us that you are here," he said softy in her ear.

She held on to him, breathing him in. Was he not letting go or was she not letting him let her go, she couldn't really tell. When they did finally separate, she felt like Velcro when it's being pulled apart.

"I really wish I didn't have to leave right now. You don't even know," he said looking directly into her eyes, then leaned down and brushed her cheek with his lips. "Call me, if you need anything."

"Have a safe trip." She smiled, turning to grab on to the tea tray to stop herself from jumping on him and taking him right there on Ms. Lane's large marble kitchen island.

"Here, let me get the door for you," he offered.

"Thank you."

She heard the door close behind her. She wanted to turn around to see if he was still there but she focused on cute little Ms. Lane at the end of the path, cuddled up in her gazebo surrounded by her enchanted garden and probably having a delightful conversation with all the fairies who dwelled there.

"He's such a good boy," the great-aunt proudly stated about her great-nephew. "Smart as a tack, loyal and dedicated."

"Yes." Morgana nodded as she poured the tea. "I heard him speaking Italian when I came in today."

"He speaks Italian, French, Spanish, and German, all fluently," his aunt boasted. "And some Gaelic, too, but I think that's just so he can understand Tristan," she added with a laugh.

"I found this tea in your cupboard labeled 'special healing blend.' I hope that was okay?" Morgana said changing the subject.

"Oh, I am so happy you are here!" Ms. Lane beamed at her.

"So, in addition to making tea, what are some of my other duties that I may personally assist you with, Madam Chair?"

"Now, this pampering me stuff is only for a few weeks. Doctor said to stay off of it for three to four weeks. Wouldn't be that big of a deal, but at my age, I want this little piggy to heal up properly so I can dance in my garden again."

"And, I will make a note to get you a cordless microphone so you don't get wrapped up in the hose again." They both laughed.

"Well, the first thing on the agenda is New Year's Eve. The council members will be here for our annual blessing ritual. Then we'll decide if I want to celebrate my birthday this year. I just don't think I can make it out at the lot in a wheel chair. January 9th is only two weeks away and I don't want to be walking in the dirt on my cast that soon. But then after that, we start planning for Imbolc on the 2nd of February. When does school start back up, dear?"

"January 15ᵗʰ. But I haven't decided if I want to go back."

"Why not?"

"Well, you know my plan had always just been to get out of here so I could start my real life. But I was numb for so long and now I feel so alive again. I just don't know if I can go back to those boring classes," Morgana admitted.

"Do you want to talk about the numb part?" Ms. Lane encouraged.

Morgana, now feeling great and connected, remembered shutting herself off six months ago. "I guess I got tired of feeling abandoned. I got tired of feeling alone." She took a deep sigh. "I guess I got tired of feeling, so I shut it off. I didn't allow myself to feel anything about anything. I was a walking zombie, just going through the motions of life. I was probably pretty sleep deprived too, so that helped a lot with my zombification." She chuckled. "You know, Josef once told me I brought him back to life. I was glad that I did, but I didn't really understand what he meant until I was with you two at the hospital yesterday. It's like all of a sudden I was resuscitated. I felt life surging back through me. I felt like I could breathe again, see colors again, and smell again." She closed her eyes and breathed in the delicious December air surrounded by flowers in Ms. Lane's secret enchanted green-house garden. "He told me I brought him back to life." She smiled. "I guess he just returned the favor."

"Come sit next to me, dear." Ms. Lane motioned for Morgana to scoot her chair closer. "You have mentioned abandonment before. Let's see if we can't get to the root of the emotion. Hold your arm out ninety degrees from your body and think about the feeling of abandonment." Morgana did. "Now try to resist me as I push on your arm. You're not going to lift up, just try to resist." Ms. Lane gave a little push down on Morgana's arm and it was strong. "Good. That means you've got a hold on the correct emotion. So now, we are all energy beings and when we form in the womb, as infants, and as children, we are pure energy soaking up the vibrations of the world around us. That's how we learn to adapt to being human, if you will. As we are forming, we are picking up frequencies from the world around us, and we are creating root emotions from the dominant energies that surround us. This is the basis of the lives we go on to live. Remember I showed you the tapping technique?" Morgana nodded, remembering when she used it to study for finals and get a date. "Well, this is another energy tool to help you root out vibrations that may no longer serve you, as you move towards living your highest and best life. Want to give it a try?"

"Of course!"

"Great! So, we have established that abandonment is the correct emotion that you are holding on to. So let's discover when you first got that, and from whom." Morgana looked intrigued. "You don't have to know the answers, per se. I mean, you know them, but your arm will tell us as we go. Remember, just resist when I push down on your arm."

"Got it."

"Okay, so how old were you when you first felt abandonment? Conception to birth?" Ms. Lane pushed on Morgana's arm. "Pretty strong. Let's check another. Birth to one?" Morgana felt no strength in her arm.

"Whoa! What happened?"

Ms. Lane laughed. "That means it wasn't true for you."

"What?" Morgana laughed. "Do another one."

"Okay. When you first felt abandonment you were one to three?" No resistance. "Three to five?" No resistance. "Okay, so let's circle back. Conception to birth?" Strong resistance.

Morgana laughed. "That's crazy!"

"Our bodies have a very smart bio-field around us. It will let you know anything you want to. What food is better than others. Which vitamins or medications work best for you. Even which shirt will empower you the most that day. You just have to practice listening."

"That's so cool. Now what?"

"Well, we've established the abandonment frequency was strong between your conception and your birth. So let's see whose frequency you picked up. Ready? Arm out. Okay, was it your mother's?" No resistance. "Was it your father's?" Strong.

"What?" Morgana was confused. "Do that again, please."

"Sure. Was it your mother's?" No resistance. "Was it your father's?" Strong.

"Wow! But, he's the one who left." Morgana sat back in her chair, with a sudden realization.

"I was tired of feeling abandoned, so I shut everyone out. I had decided if I didn't care about anyone, it wouldn't hurt so much to lose someone." She took a breath. "You know, all this time I thought my mom felt the same abandonment I felt. Then we had a conversation at Thanksgiving where she told me that's not what she felt. Now you're telling me, rather my arm is telling me, that I got this from my father. I don't know much about him, but I heard his parents had a bad divorce when he was a little child. I'm sure being seventeen and knocking up someone was probably a little freaky for him. Interesting. So, is there more?"

"Now we find out where you are storing this energy block. Remember the seven chakras?" Morgana remembered the beautiful set of chakra stones she got for her birthday. "Are you storing this emotion in your root chakra?" No resistance. "In your Sacral chakra?" No resistance. "Solar plexus?" No resistance. "Heart?" Strong. "Throat?" Some resistance. "Third eye?" No resistance. " Crown?" No resistance.

"Okay, looks like it's in your heart chakra mostly."

Morgana thought about how it was her heart that fought tooth and nail for life but lost its battle and was turned to stone. It was her heart that ultimately shattered through its rocky prison when she saw Josef yesterday. "Okay, that makes sense," Morgana agreed.

"Now, we want to remove that root emotion from your energy field. This is a personal experience for you. Close your eyes and think of your heart. See your heart in your mind's eye and picture what you think it might look like. We want to remove that root emotion of abandonment. You can picture a garden and you need to remove a weed. Or you can think of an energy grid and there's a broken panel. It can be a relaxing removal or it can be a rescue mission. Go with whatever feels good to you."

Morgana closed her eyes and took a deep breathe. She remembered scuba diving in St. Barth's. She loved that feeling of floating underwater and breathing in a liquid atmosphere. She pictured herself scuba diving in her heart. A red underwater sea, and instead of fish, there were blood platelets swimming around her. She imagined swimming through the heart ventricles like caves, as she explored an unknown frontier. Something grabbed her attention, so she swam over to a find a shiny reflective plate that clearly didn't belong there. She tried to grab it, but it was buried in. She was finally able to unwedge it from its burial ground and she held it in her hands. It was a large round gold dish, about the size of a large pizza. As she brushed at the surface, clearing away debris, she saw an image of her father as a young child, maybe two or three. He was crying in the corner as his parents fought. His father shouted at him, "Quit crying! Boys don't cry!" And she suddenly felt her dad shut off his emotions just like she had. He was just a baby. She then saw him at seventeen years old, holding her as a newborn. He struggled to feel emotion, but he didn't know what would happen if he let himself feel. Knowing that he couldn't be the loving father she deserved, he handed the baby to its mother and walked away, hoping her life would be better without him in it.

Morgana opened her eyes as tears of love and forgiveness streamed down her face, and she looked at Ms. Lane. "He didn't abandon me, he did what he thought was best," she said.

Ms. Lane nodded with a caring smile. "That's all any of us can do." Morgana sat still.

"Let's test to see if we got the root." Ms. Lane pushed on Morgana's extended arm. Strong. "There are possibly more aspects, but that, I'm sure was the biggest. So now, ask yourself, are you ready to let go of this root emotion that no longer serves your highest and best self?" Morgana held out her arm. Strong as a rock.

"So now, go back to your mind's eye and see a situation with your father that feels good. It could be something that actually happened or something you wish could happen."

Morgana closed her eyes again. This time, she saw herself at three years old having a tea party with her dad. He wouldn't have been much older than she was now. She witnessed their tea party as an unseen observer in the room. She didn't know if this was a memory or if she was making it up, but she was enjoying the innocent interaction between father and daughter sitting at a little round plastic pink table and drinking from plastic pink tea cups. She then watched as both of them aged about sixteen years, making it current times. She walked over to the table and sat in her counterpart, assuming its place across the table looking at the man who is her father. He smiled at her and said, "I love you." She said, "I love you, too." The feeling of love washed over Morgana. She felt such relief and release. She opened her eyes and looked at Ms. Lane's smiling face.

"Wow! That feels so good!" she said taking a deep breath. "That's amazing. Like, I literally feel lightness in my heart now. That's crazy!"

"Take a drink. You released some good stuff there," Ms. Lane instructed.

"So, what is that? Like was that real?" Morgana asked after taking a big drink of cool, refreshing water.

"Very real. Emotions are real. You feel real relief, don't you?"

"Yes. It's weird."

"It's energy work." Ms. Lane smiled.

"Well, like, do you think he felt it too?" Morgana inquired.

"Have you ever suddenly thought about someone and then they called you? Or have you ever smelled a scent that was out of place, like perfume when you're alone, or flowers that aren't there? Depending on how open or in alignment someone is, is how they receive the energy. He may have just smiled thinking about you. You may never know how it affected him, but know that you just sent a very strong signal of love his way and hopefully he was able to receive it. And finally, the last thing we want to do is lock in this new feeling. Hold out your arm." She pushed down on Morgana's arm. "Yes, nice and strong. We have successfully removed that particular emotional root. The next time, if there is a next time, you feel a feeling of abandonment, you can dismiss it with love and light. Remind yourself, that emotion no longer serves you. You can think of it like donating an old toy, you just don't need it anymore."

"Love it!" Morgana was giddy. "But like, so what, then? I'm cured?"

"Well, how do you feel about your father now?"

"Um, well. I guess I feel...I feel like I have a better understanding of why he did what he did. And I feel like I don't blame him because I recognize how he must have felt. And I shut down too, so I feel like we have a common connection. Or something. It's hard to explain." Morgana tried to pin point her feelings.

"Do you want to see him?"

"Ahh, probably not." Morgana made a face.

Ms. Lane let out her signature hoot. "Well, you might not be completely cured but at least you're feeling better. And really that's all that matters."

"What do you mean, feeling better is all that matters?"

"Well, do you feel better?"

"Yes."

"Then by feeling better, your vibrations have changed. And with that shift, you're now sending out higher vibrations to the world around you and your connection deepens. When you send out higher vibrations, you sync up with other things on that higher frequency, like the birds and flowers, and the furry little creatures of this delightful planet that we are blessed to exist on."

"I like that." Morgana smiled at the plants around her. "It's pretty weird to think I was closed off to all this."

"If you would, please, go into the guest room and grab the box off the nightstand."

"Of course." Morgana went down the hall to the guestroom. It still smelled like Josef. She filled her senses with his aroma as she looked for what Ms. Lane had sent her to retrieve. On the nightstand Morgana recognized the pink wrapped gift box that Josef tried to deliver to her on her birthday, the day that she had shut down. She carried it back outside to the gazebo and sat back down next to Ms. Lane.

"Go on. Open it." Ms. Lane encouraged.

Morgana unwrapped the most delicate and beautiful white winter fairy with glittery iridescent wings. The description read: "And winter came. It is the time we experience the greatest darkness, when the hours of dark are much greater than the hours of light. And yet, it is within this time of great darkness that the light of the world is reborn, for now the hours of daylight will begin to grow and the hours of darkness will lessen."

"Thank you," Morgana said to her fairy godmother, with all her heart.

Morgana went to sleep later that night after a delicious dinner and a wonderful first day at her new job. She was so grateful and felt so blessed.

That night she had a dream she went on a picnic with her dad. It was a really good dream.

*C*hapter Twenty

Feeling Hopeful

NEW YEAR'S EVE was upon them, and Morgana was preparing for her first meeting with the High Council. She helped Ms. Lane pin up her silver hair in its perfect ballerina bun and fasten a beautiful antique broach at her neck. Ms. Lane was dressed up in a white silk blouse and cashmere cardigan, with a long black skirt and one lace up Victorian kitten heel boot. Her wrist was still a bit sore and Ol' Betsy was all black and blue, but Ms. Lane was her happy Mary Poppins-Glinda the Good Witch self as Morgana wheeled her down the hallway and helped her get situated in her floral high-back chair at the huge round marble pedestal table under the adorable smiling faces of the figurines. Ms. Lane had Morgana clear off the Christmas floral centerpiece and place a large round silver tray, lined with wax paper, in the middle of the table. Morgana handed Ms. Lane two all-natural while pillar candles. One was a 4" x 2" and the smaller one was a 2"x 2". Then, Morgana set out the blessed cookies she made earlier that day, dancing and spinning with Ms. Lane in her wheelchair to the music as they baked. She set up silver snack trays and silver coffee decanters and tea pots out on the large marble kitchen island.

"Silver tea pots? That's new," Morgana commented.

Ms. Lane chuckled. "Those are about as new as I am. I use them on nights like this. Real silver has good frequencies." Then she smiled. "Not that my pink Royal Antoinette pots don't." She laughed.

"Everything in your house has very good frequencies. That's for sure," Morgana said.

The doorbell rang and Morgana went to open it. Her lace up

Victorian kitten heels clicked on the hardwood entry. She wore her hair up in a ballerina bun, showcasing her amulet necklace and earrings. She remembered Cole's argument that the necklace was worth fifty thousand dollars, but when she wore it she felt connected to those who had transitioned, and she felt connected to Josef, which was probably Cole's real problem with it. She didn't care what price tag a jeweler would place on it. To her it was powerful and priceless. She greeted the twelve council members as they entered the blessed home of the Grand High Chairman. Morgana took their coats or cloaks and showed them in. Six men and six women each took their seat around the huge round marble table.

"You've all met my new personal assistant, Morgana," Ms. Lane introduced her to the group, who all greeted her with smiles and welcomes. Then Morgana took a seat at the kitchen island and observed the annual New Year's Eve Blessing ritual.

Each member had brought a specific colored 2" x 2" candle with them, and placed it in front of them on the table. Ms. Lane lit the taller of her two white pillar candles and she degreed, "Bless this night with love and light." She handed the lit candle to the member on her right.

He lit a blue candle. "Bless this night with peace." He handed the white candle to the member to his right.

She lit a pink candle. "Bless this night with emotional well-being."

Around the large marble table the white candle went, lighting each member's designated candle in a specific color representing a blessed virtue. There was a red candle for love, yellow for success, green for prosperity, orange for creativity, purple for magic, grey for harmony, light blue for cleansing, turquoise for healing, lavender for friendship, and brown for grounding.

The tall white candle came back around to Ms. Lane, who lit her smaller white candle. "And bless all who share in this time space with abundance of all these virtues the whole year through."

They all held up their candles, as to toast, and then put them close together in the large silver tray in the center of the table, with the tall white original candle in the middle.

"Welcome, my beloved friends." And with that, the Grand High Chairman opened the meeting.

Earlier that night during dinner, Ms. Lane was explaining the night's procedures to Morgana.

"So are you, like, witches or something?" Morgana asked curiously.

Ms. Lane smiled. "Not exactly. We try not to label ourselves because it seems like once you label something people try to box it and add limits and rules. We are a group that believes that everything that exists is made up of the same energy and everyone on this earthly realm is an unlimited being of pure energy and we are all here on the leading edge of creation to play and to grow and to evolve. We believe there is great love in this universe available to help guide us to our highest and best selves, cheering us on, laughing with us, and, yes, sometimes probably laughing at us, but always supporting us in all our endeavors. We believe we are on this earth, we are not of it. We believe this is the kingdom of heaven and everything is available to all of us. We believe life is what you create it to be. We believe life is supposed to be fun. We believe everyone has a true heart's desire, a reason for being here. We believe everyone should be allowed to follow their bliss, find their passions, and do what feels right. We believe life is innately good. We believe in the laws of the universe, like the Law of Attraction and Law of Growth. We believe in vibrations and frequencies, and that we are made up of the same atoms that make up the stars and everything that exits. We believe we are all connected. We believe we are all one. We are each parts of the whole. Each of us on our own journey of self-discovery and to experience this wonderful life. We believe everything is magic and miracles. We believe in synchronicity. We believe feeling good feels so good and believe we should always try to feel the best we can and do the best we can. We believe total well-being is our natural state and we have the power to heal ourselves and our lives by tuning within, finding our alignment and connecting to All That Is. We believe there is an awakening happening on this planet and people are realizing how powerful they actually are. We believe in helping those who seek it. We believe in delighting in everything. We believe in keeping our energies high. We believe this planet is alive and marvelous. We believe we are eternal beings. We believe the universe and All That Exists is infinite and ever expanding. We believe in true love. We believe in happiness, joy, abundance, and prosperity, and we believe that these are everyone's inalienable rights. We believe in connection. We believe in the delicious flavors and enjoying being in these magnificent bodies and savoring the tactile use of this life. Yes, there are terrible things that happen here, atrocities and terror. But if you dwell on them, it's like throwing fuel on the fire. So you keep your focus on the good things as much as you can. It's not ignoring the bad, but it's giving your energy to the good. Instead of thinking what's wrong with this planet, you think, 'How can I make this a better place for all?' And when bad things happen, try to take the lesson and grow from it. We mustn't live in fear, for fear takes our power and can make us feel powerless. But fear can also give you strength that you didn't know you had. And if you can find your strength in the bad times, you can use it to do great things. There will always be contrasts. You have to take those contrasts and use them as catalysts to create a better world for all of us. We focus on sending love and light and blessings to all," Ms. Lane explained in her whimsical way.

"That's really lovely." Morgana smiled at her sweet mentor, friend, and real life fairy godmother.

As Morgana sat and listened to the night's meeting, Ms. Lane announced that she didn't think she wanted to go to the lot this year for her birthday and therefore was going to cancel the party. The group objected.

"But we all love you and love celebrating you," one said.

"I'm humbled by that, grateful and honored. I just don't know how we can do it this year," Ms. Lane replied.

One suggested finding a different location, like a hotel or convention room. They all laughed.

"Um, what if we had, like, a Cleopatra theme party and Ms. Lane was carried in by a chariot or something?" Morgana called out from her seat at the kitchen island. The group all exchanged excited looks and smiled at each other.

Ms. Lane let out her signature hoot. "What a fabulous idea! It's hilarious and fun and I love it! I think that might work." Ms. Lane beamed proudly at her assistant as the group listened and discussed the details as Morgana described her idea.

Morgana spent the next week working with council members and event planners getting everything ready for Ms. Lane's Cleopatra inspired eighty-fourth birthday celebration out at the magical lot.

On the day of the party, a driver came to pick up Morgana and Ms. "Cleopatra" Lane. While on the way Ms. Lane's phone rang.

"Hello, Josef."

"Happy birthday, Aunt Katherine!" Even through the phone, his silky voice charged Morgana's energy.

"Thank you, Josef, dear."

"I really wish I could be there. I wanted to fly in today, but I just couldn't get the machine to stop sputtering. We might have to replace it. And that's going to be a huge ordeal," he explained.

"Well, I would love to see you but I know you need to do what you need to do. Thank you for handling everything for us. It's very important work, and we all appreciate you. Here, Morgana wants to say hi." Ms. Lane passed the phone to a surprised Morgana, who was shaking her head 'no,' as Ms. Lane put the phone in her hand.

"Hey, Josef." Morgana shot her beloved old friend the stink eye.

"Hi, Morgana." It was like a flurry of butterflies was released in her stomach.

"I'm going to send you a picture of Ms. Cleopatra. We got her a gorgeous gold dress and she's even wearing a black wig and everything. I swear I am sitting here with the Queen of the Nile herself."

Now, Josef's boisterous laughter was like catnip for her stomach butterflies and sent them all reeling.

"Oh, I can't wait to see that! Be sure to include yourself, I want to see you, too. I heard this whole birthday celebration was saved by you and your great idea. Awesome job! I really wish I could be there with you."

Morgana about dropped the phone. "Um, yah. We would love to have you here, too. Anyway. Here's your aunt. Talk to you later." Morgana hurriedly gave back the offending device that kept exciting the butterflies inside her. She felt like they were either going to take flight and fly her to Italy, or burst out of her chest and fly to him themselves.

"Well, you take care my sweet nephew," Ms. Lane said back into the phone. "Thank you for thinking of me on my birthday."

"Of course! Send me those pictures. Love you!"

"We love you, too. Bye-bye."

Ms. Lane and Morgana took a couple pictures and sent them to Josef. He sent them one back of him and Adalberto working on the machine.

When they arrived at the lot, instead of pulling into the regular parking lot, they went to a second driveway that took them through to the back that delivered them to the meeting spot where a group awaited their arrival. Since this was a birthday party and not a solstice celebration, it was informal. Morgana remembered last year when she was so upset over Cole. She sat in the back witnessing Ms. Lane's family, and beloved friends honoring her on the special day. Last year, Morgana felt isolated and alone. This year, she not only felt a part of the family but she was with the birthday girl herself and it was Morgana's idea that made this night happen. She felt so honored and included. The whole family, besides Josef, was there: Ms. Lane's sister, Lynetta and Henry, her husband, Jackson and Cindy, Brook and Tristan, and Blake and Jai. They were happy and excited to see Ms. Lane and Morgana.

Brook and Blake came over to Morgana and gave her a huge hug.

"This is so awesome!" a costumed Blake cried out to Morgana. "I can't believe you got her to wear a wig!"

"I had to wear one, too." Morgana laughed thinking about the conversation with Ms. Lane earlier in the week.

"I just don't know if I can wear a wig," Ms. Lane protested with a laugh to Morgana.

"Well, if you wear one, so will I." Morgana had to barter.

"Agreed!" Ms. Lane cheered.

Morgana helped Ms. Lane settle into a golden cushioned box chair, and four very strong men picked up the rails, hoisting Ms. Cleopatra. Drums started pounding and the strong men carried the honored birthday queen to her Egyptian theme party, flanked by her family members and led by Morgana. The party was a huge golden success.

Ms. Lane established long ago that instead of gifts she would only take donations, and those went to help fund the solstice celebrations. For party favors, everyone received a heart-shaped tealight-sized candle made from the melted remains of the New Year's blessing ritual candles. On New Year's Day, Ms. Lane had shown Morgana how to take the melted blob from the silver tray in the middle of the large marble table and melt it down completely in a large stock pot. Ms. Lane added several more large white pillar candles to make sure there was enough wax to make over two hundred tea lights. She showed Morgana how to fish out the old wicks and add in the extra wax slowly. They poured them in to the prepared heart-shaped molds with new wicks, and after the candles set they wrapped each one in a black favor box with gold ribbon to coordinate with the colors of tonight's theme party.

"Now we have 216 candles for the people to light in their homes and release the blessings from last night's ritual," Ms. Lane delightfully explained.

"Love it!" Morgana applauded.

Ms. Lane had decided she wanted to go home after the party and sleep in her own bed, instead of the hotel like she usually did. On the way home she thanked Morgana.

"That was the best birthday ever!" She patted Morgana's hand.

"I know tomorrow is your day off, but the family is coming over for brunch. We would love to have you."

"Thank you, Ms. Lane. I think I'm going to have brunch with my mom. I haven't seen her lately and I would like to spend some time with her."

"That's lovely, dear. I know she would like that."

Morgana helped Ms. Lane get all tucked in once they returned home.

"I'll see you Monday, then. Happy birthday, Cleopatra!" Morgana said.

Ms. Lane let out a hoot.

Morgana woke up the next day and made delicious omelettes for her mother and her. They had a great talk and her mother was so happy to hear about her new job working for Ms. Lane, and even more happy to see her daughter smiling again.

"What class do you think you're going to take this semester? You should probably go into culinary school. These omelettes are to die for!"

"Well, I think I might take an international business course and Italian."

"Ooooh Italian, Cara Mia!" her mom said and they both laughed. "I think those sound great."

Morgana sent her mom off to work later that day with a big hug, and then enjoyed her day off.

She sent a text to Ms. Lane that evening:

M: Can I come over to help with anything?

ML: Nope, all set. Jackson, Cindy, my sister, and Henry are all still here.

M: What time tomorrow?

ML: Noon, would be great.

M: Awesome. See you then!

ML: Good night.

Ms. Lane's sister, Lynetta Meadow, and her husband stayed for a week. The sisters would spend time holding hands while meditating together in the gazebo.

"Come, Morgana, join hands with us," Mrs. Meadow said.

"What do I do?" Morgana joined in a circle with the sisters.

"Focus on health, vitality, love. Whatever feels good. We want happy, light, vibrations. Picture Katherine dancing again, and you want to focus on it as if it has already happened," she explained.

Morgana closed her eyes and thought about Ms. Lane's casted foot and Ol' bruised Betsy. *Picture her dancing again as if it's already happened,* Morgana repeated to herself. *Okay, umm...* She remembered the first time Ms. Lane showed her how to do the ritual baking blessing. They danced together in the kitchen. She remembered them laughing and having such a good time. Then she thought about how Ms. Lane loved to dance in her garden. She imagined her dancing with the garden fairies in the moonlight. She added herself and Mrs. Meadow into the mix with the three of them wearing white flowing dresses, dancing, laughing, and basking under the smiling moon, serenaded by the sweet singing flowers and surrounded by beautiful and powerful fae. She saw them all dancing around a tall May pole, entwining the long silky colorful ribbons. Her thoughts shifted and she saw Josef watching her dance, like he did at Beltane, when she was so connected with the night, and the lot, and every breath that rolled through her was ecstasy. Next thing she knew she was dancing with Josef, locked in his eyes, and his lips so close to hers. Everything faded away. All she saw was his face looking into her soul with those deep aqua blue eyes. He leaned in to kiss her lips and as she was about to feel his soft touch, when Ms. Lane let out a loud hoot.

Morgana felt like she was being pulled through thick heavy atmospheric layers as she was lugged back into the reality of sitting in the gazebo with the sisters. "What? What happened?" She tried to bring back her hazed focus. "What is it? Are you okay?" Morgana asked Ms. Lane.

"Oh, my! That was some good energy! Thank you, ladies!" Ms. Lane popped.

"I felt that, too. You are very powerful, Morgana. What were you thinking about?" The sisters' four eyes were all gaping at Morgana with supreme interest.

"Oh. Um. Lots of stuff. I guess. I pictured the three of us dancing around a May pole being sung to by the flowers and surrounded by cheerful fairies and powerful Fae."

Ms. Lane squeezed her hand. "That's so lovely, dear. I felt the joy in your heart." Ms. Lane beamed.

Morgana blushed. "So what did we do there?" she asked.

"Our bodies are miracles and know how to heal themselves. We just have to get out of their way. When you feel high vibrations, it gives your body a chance to do what it needs to do to keep you healthy. If you dwell in lower frequencies, it can't do its job very well. That's why we get tired when we're sick, it's our body's way of saying, get out of the way and let me do my job!" Ms. Lane let out a hoot and laughed at herself.

"If you think 'healing' thoughts," Mrs. Meadow added, "you are still sort of interfering because you're telling yourself that something is wrong and needs to be healed. It still kind of pinches off the energy flow. But, if you think of yourself as if already healed, then you have left the door wide open for the energy to flow freely. Feeling good, happy, lighthearted, thoughts, like dancing with fairies, are all perfect, fun, high frequencies. And having the three of us linked through holding our hands and sharing those high frequencies magnifies them exponentially. For instance, say one person on a high-frequency radiates at a thousand. When three people get together like this, it takes it to the third power, which radiates at a billion. And we focused those one billion good feeling thoughts of life, health and love at our dear Katherine. Really good job, Morgana!" Mrs. Meadow complemented her.

"That's a lot of healing power!" Ms. Lane exclaimed and winked proudly at her assistant. Morgana was still a bit flushed with the image of his deep aqua blue eyes.

It was an amazing week with Mrs. Meadow, the younger of the two sisters, and her husband there. Morgana loved hearing the sisters' stories about growing up together. Mrs. Meadow had brought some different fresh tea leaves and herbs and the foursome would spend tea time creating new special blends for the company. Morgana learned about the different healing properties of flowers, herbs and other holistic medicines. By the time Mrs. Meadow and her husband were leaving, Ms. Lane's wrist was better and she was walking like a pro on her booted cast. Morgana loved every minute of time learning from the two sisters. She may have especially loved the daily healing meditations in the gazebo with the ladies. She would try not to think of gazing into his deep aqua blue eyes and dancing together in the moonlight, but she convinced herself it was for Ms. Lane's benefit. She couldn't very well stop the flow of energy, could she? *No,* she said rolling her eyes and laughing at herself. *Only until Mrs. Meadow leaves, then I will stop.* She shook her head at her attempt for justification.

School started back up and Morgana only had two and a half hours of classes on Tuesdays and Thursdays. Barely a blip in her day compared to the brutal schedule she had last semester. She also felt like she was learning more being with Ms. Lane than in school anyway. However, she was enjoying learning Italian and tried not to picture herself having romantic conversations with a certain deep aqua blue eyed someone. "Remember, he's taken." She would remind herself. "Okay, well, it's not him then. It's someone else who makes me feel the way he makes me feel." She gently corrected herself. "That's right. For now he's the only one who makes me feel like this, so I'll just think about him as a substitute until the real one comes along. Ya, that's it." She practiced convincing herself.

The next couple of weeks flew by as Morgana helped Ms. Lane plan for the Imbolc celebration. Ms. Lane explained, "Imbolc marks the halfway point through the dark half of the year. The term means 'in the belly,' referring to the first stirrings of spring in the womb of Mother Earth. It is the time to give thanks and celebrate the new fertility, new life, and new beginnings that lay ahead. It is a time of hope and expectation. It invokes the gentleness and mothering needed in our first years on Earth. Our Imbolc celebration is a gentle beautiful festival where we light candles and float them in water in the center of a ceremonial circle. We honor the Goddess Bridhid, the fertility mother and goddess of poets, healers and midwives. Consequently, poetry and songs are often part of the ritual with great bonfires lit in her honor and to also impart the extra energy to God, so he will continue to increase the light. Candlemas, a feast day dedicated to the Virgin Mary, is another way of celebrating Imbolc. Today, both Imbolc and Candlemas are viewed as a time for dedications and initiations of a new beginning and the freshness of a new coming season."

The night of the celebration Ms. Lane was able to walk herself up to the High Council's table and enjoyed the night's festivities. Morgana loved talking with the event planners, caters, and vendors getting everything all set up. She liked being a part of the crew and making sure dinner was served on time, that the vendors had what they needed, and that everything ran smoothly.

When she was satisfied that everything was humming along, Morgana went up the hill and watched from afar. She enjoyed the night air, hearing the laughter and the music. She was quite content focusing on her connection with the stars. Morgana and Ms. Lane stayed at the local hotel and went back for brunch the next morning. Morgana busied herself chatting with the merchants as they closed up their trailers.

When she got home later that afternoon, she caught her mom just as she was leaving for work.

"Morgana, are you available next Friday night for dinner?" her mom asked nervously.

"Sure, what's the occasion?"

"Um, I want you to meet someone, my friend...oh, my boyfriend," she sputtered out fretfully. "What do you think?"

"I think that's fantastic! When and where?"

"Oh, God. I didn't think about that part. I'll figure it out and let you know. Oh, I'm late. We'll talk later." She ran out the door.

The next Friday night, Morgana met Jeff, her mother's forty-five year old boyfriend and the local fire chief. He brought Chinese take-out to their house.

"My wife died two years ago from cancer," he explained during dinner.

"Wow, she was so young," Morgana said softly.

"She was my friend from work. She's the one who introduced us," Morgana's mother explained.

"Any children?" Morgana inquired.

"No, ah, she wasn't able to conceive," Jeff said. "Tell me about you, Morgana. Your mother says you're the personal assistant to your elderly neighbor. What does she do?"

"Oh, many things. She and her sister started a family business, it's mostly run by the children and grandchildren now, but they do herbal teas and essential oils and things. She's a very busy eighty-four year-old." Morgana laughed.

"And, you're going to school, too?"

"Yes, studying business for now."

"That's great."

Jeff was nice. Dinner went well and Morgana helped her mother clear the dishes.

"He's really great," Morgana said to her mom over a sudsy sink full of dishes.

"Do you think so? I really like him," her mother confessed. "He's quite foxy, wouldn't you say?"

"Foxy?" Morgana laughed. "What? Who says foxy?"

"A super nervous thirty-seven year old mother to her nineteen year old daughter, that's who." She laughed tensely.

"OH! Then yes, I agree. He is quite foxy!" Morgana teased. "How long have you two been seeing each other behind my back!" Morgana really teased.

"Oh!" Her mother looked frightful.

"I'm only joking. It's all good. I'm really happy for you!" Morgana assured her.

"Um, about a year."

"Really? Good for you!" Morgana patted her mom on the back. "Well, listen. I'm going to let you and Mr. Foxy enjoy your evening. I'll go see Ms. Lane and be home about ten. Sound good?"

"Yes, thank you." Her mom gave her a hug.

She texted Ms. Lane as she walked down the inclined driveway.

M: Mind if I crash the party?

ML: My dear, you are the party.

Morgana knocked, and then let herself in, opening the heavy wooden door. Ms. Lane was reading alone on the couch.

"So how was dinner?" Ms. Lane inquired.

"He's really nice. Young, fit, attractive. Mom called him foxy!" Morgana chuckled, but then added more seriously. "He said his wife died two years ago from cancer. She would have barely been forty. I don't understand. If our bodies can heal themselves, then why do people die like that?" Morgana asked distraughtly.

Ms. Lane set her book down and offered to make some tea. "I'll make it." Morgana got up and boiled the water, then brought back the pink Royal Antoinette tea set.

"It's hard to say what a person's life journey entails, Morgana," a soothing voiced Ms. Lane started. "We each have a plan that we picked before we got here. We picked our parents, knowing everything about them. We picked siblings, our goals, everything, all based on what we thought we might like to experience here on this earthly plane. And they're not the same kind of human earthly goals, they're more experience expansion goals. And even then, it's not serious. It's kind of more like picking out what kind of movie you feel like watching during the short time we're here. Whether it be a few seconds or a hundred years, it's still barely a blip on the time space continuum. We are infinite spiritual beings. That's hard to even fathom, in-fin-it-e. So, when we come here, it's to learn, play, experience, share, love, hate, all of it. When we transition we get to see our lives over again and watch ourselves and laugh at how close, or how far as the case may be, we came to accomplishing our goals. As you've been learning, this life is all about alignment. Lining up with the source energy that we truly are – then getting into, then out of, then back into alignment. Diseases are usually caused because we are out of alignment. But as soon as we die, we transition right back into perfect alignment."

"But, she was so young. How could she be that far out of alignment to cause cancer?" Morgana was visibly upset.

"Well, as you've discovered, sometimes we take on the energies of those around us. If they are negative energies that keep us in the lower vibrations and we let them compound as we go through life, then we are continuing to feed the misalignment. If we don't pay attention to the signs and try to get ourselves back into alignment, the signs get bigger and louder, and those blocked energies become diseases. Do you know what kind of cancer she had?"

"No, but he mentioned she couldn't conceive children. I don't know if that had anything to do with it."

"Well, that could be ovarian or cervical cancer, amongst others.

Our ovaries represent a point of creation, the ultimate creation for some women. If she couldn't have children she may have built up a resentment for that. Cancer usually represents deep hurts and longstanding resentments. It sometimes is caused by a deep secret or grief that literally eats away at the self. Burying anger or carrying hatreds are all blocked energies. The universe is trying to tell us what our blocks are, so we can learn and release them. It's a mirror constantly reflecting the emotions we emit. As do our bodies," she explained. "And in addition to all that, each of us has a mission, a purpose for being here. And sometimes it takes a special person to leave early, as some may see it. But that person's energy and message is carried on by the people whose lives they touched. His wife has moved on, but maybe he can find happiness and bring happiness to another, like your mom. You said the wife was the one who introduced them to each other," Ms. Lane said gently.

Morgana sipped her tea and let the words soak in. "I want my mom to be happy, of course. But she could have healed herself," Morgana said desperately.

"Maybe, maybe not. We have spiritual tools like energy medicine, mediation, teas, food, and western medicine. But sometimes a person just can't let go of the block because that is their path. We try. We do our best. That's all we can do."

Morgana sat quietly. "My grandpa died four years ago. He was only fifty-five. And then grandma died just two years later, from cancer. But I think it was a broken heart, he was her everything."

"How did he die?"

"He had a heart attack. It was sudden, a complete surprise to everyone. He was healthy, ran every day. He ate right. He did everything right!" Morgana felt a little angry. She took a deep breath, trying to calm down. "Why don't more people know how to heal themselves?" she whispered through her tight throat.

"Oh, my dear child," Ms. Lane sympathetically sighed. "We knew this long ago. Then we forget. Then we remember. Then it's forgotten again. But the signs are always there for those who are open to them. We have unseen helpers guiding us, encouraging us, but we have to be open and listening. They can't interfere. They can only guide us to what we choose to put our focus on."

Morgana didn't know what to feel. She looked at Ms. Lane in her pink housecoat, in her pink house, drinking from her favorite pink tea cup. "You once said, we can't be sick enough to make someone well. Or poor enough to make someone rich…"

"All we can do is focus on feeling good and being happy, to try to be a good example to help others find their own happiness." Ms. Lane helped complete her sentence.

"I think I get that now. Because if I'm upset, that takes me out of my alignment. It puts me on lower frequencies, just adding to lower frequencies overall, and possibly even risking getting a disease myself. But if I can keep my vibrations high, then I'm able to help others better, and I'm adding to the overall higher vibrations. I think that makes sense." Morgana felt some relief.

"And, you have just been given a sign." Ms. Lane pointed out.

"Huh?" Morgana was confused again.

"When something matters to us we feel emotions. That's our guidance system telling us something. That's our angels and helpers trying to get our attention. So, what was upsetting you a moment ago?"

"Um, that everyone dies," Morgana guessed.

"A little more specific." Ms. Lane encouraged her to really think.

"Oh! That more people don't know how to heal themselves."

"Is that right?" Ms. Lane verified.

"Ya. I felt bad because grandpa thought he was doing everything right, but then he still died young. And then grandma lost her true love, so then she transitioned to join him. And, Jeff's wife died way too young. If they knew how to connect within themselves then maybe they'd still all be here."

"So, now you have a piece to your puzzle. You want to help people learn how to help heal themselves. But, helping people can be tricky. You can lead a horse to water, but you can't make him drink. That's why I say focus on feeling good. Be a good example, then those who seek will be drawn to you. 'Seek and ye shall find.' And you'll be available to guide them to follow their own bliss and find what matters to them."

"Oh! I get it!" Morgana clapped happily. Then she remembered. "Your husband died, umm, transitioned, too early, too. That's why you founded an organic tea and essential oil company," Morgana suddenly realized.

"Yes." Ms. Lane nodded. "Lynetta used those oils and teas on Henry to help save him. We wanted to provide the best quality products we could find to help those who sought it. But," Ms. Lane added, "keep in mind, emotions are the key. The best medicines in the world can't help you if you don't get your emotions in alignment."

"Well, it's late. I will let you go to sleep and get some alignment," Morgana lightly teased. She helped clean up and said goodnight. It was 10:30 p.m. when Morgana walked up the inclined driveway. Jeff's lifted Ford pickup truck was still there but the house was quiet. *Spending the night, I see. You go, Jeff with your foxy self,* Morgana laughed to herself.

It was Valentine's Day. Morgana and Ms. Lane were going over some paperwork when the doorbell rang with a delivery of a huge floral arrangement and some imported chocolates. Morgana set them in front of Ms. Lane.

"Looks like you've got a secret admirer," she taunted her old friend.

"Let me see that." Ms. Lane reached for the card and let out a hoot. "Looks like we both do!" she taunted right back. "To my favorite girls. Happy Valentines Days. Love Josef."

"He shouldn't have done that," Morgana stated, her voice a little tense. She hoped Ms. Lane didn't notice.

"No, that little turkey. Let's call him!" Ms. Lane laughed. Morgana walked into the kitchen away from the phone call.

"Hey, Aunt Katherine. How's my girl?"

"I'm looking at a huge bouquet of flowers and some delicious looking chocolates."

"Oh, good!"

"You shouldn't have. That was so sweet."

"I know you have your own flowers, but what do you get the sweetest aunt who has everything? It's hard." He laughed. Morgana busied herself in the kitchen. She had been trying so hard to let him go.

"Morgana, come say hi!" Ms. Lane called to her.

"Hi, Josef! Thank you for the wonderful stuff. I'm doing dishes right now. Can't talk!" she yelled from the sink.

"Well, anyway," Ms. Lane got back on the phone. "When are you coming home?" Morgana couldn't hear him and that's what she wanted. "Really? That long? (Pause) Not even for your birthday? That's a shame. But I guess that is a lot of back and forth. Might as well stay until it's all done. (Pause) Well, I think my sister just might be taking advantage of having her grandson there. I know she loves it. (Pause) Thank you very much for the beautiful flowers. We love them. And we love you. Morgana, would you like to say good-by?"

"Good-bye. Thank you!" she yelled with soapy dish hands in the sink.

"Okay, bye-bye." Ms. Lane hung up the phone, and gave her a look, but only said, "He's so thoughtful. Such a good boy."

"Yes." Morgana agreed, trying not to think about the house filled full of roses she was sure he gifted to Tiffany. *Being gone this long…of course, he's probably flown her over there every weekend, romantic weekends in Italy. She's probably there now. Valentine's Day together. He's probably going to take her to Paris. At least he had time to think of his sweet aunt. Damn him! He really is such a good guy,* she argued internally.

"What are you doing over there?" Ms. Lane interrupted Morgana's deep thoughts.

"Huh? Oh, um, I was just, um, rinsing our lunch plates, so they didn't, get stuck on." *That was terrible,* Morgana shook her head to herself. "Can I get you anything?" she offered.

"No thank you, dear."

When Morgana got home that night, Jeff's truck was in the driveway. She walked in to find them sitting close together at the dining table. "Hey, guys!" Morgana greeted them. "Watcha doing?"

"Hi, honey. Could you sit down for a minute?" her mom asked.

"Okaaay?" Morgana sat down and looked at their bright smiling faces.

"We have some news. We're engaged!" her mother squealed and held out her hand to show off a nice sparkling diamond ring.

"Oh, my God! That's so great! Congratulations!" Morgana was so happy for them.

"Is it? Is it okay with you?" her mom asked nervously.

"Totally! Of course. I'm so glad. Good job, Jeff!"

Morgana's mom jumped up from the table and ran to hug her. She was giddy and bouncy. Morgana had never, ever, seen her like that. She had to laugh.

"Is there a date yet?" she asked as she was appraising the rock on her mom's finger with approval.

"No, no. We are just going to get used to being engaged for a while. No one even knows we've been dating. So, we're just going to take it slow."

Jeff got up and Morgana congratulated him with a hug. "The sooner the better, in my book. But I can wait for as long as she wants." He kissed her mother.

"Awe, that's so sweet," her mom said, kissing him back. "Isn't he so sweet?"

"Yes, very sweet." Morgana was truly happy for her mother. She never saw this side of her and she was glad her mom had found someone that made her feel that way. As for herself, Morgana went into her room and ate the whole box of chocolates Mr. Wonderful had sent to his favorite great-aunt and her assistant.

By March, Ms. Lane's cast was off and she was her ol' dancing self again. She took Morgana to the farmers' market and showed her all the different organic fruits and vegetables, whole spices, and loose leaf teas. Morgana loved learning and listening to Ms. Lane explain the healing properties of each. Her favorite was, of course, learning that dark chocolate is really good for you, and they took several samples from the vendor just to be sure they understood all its healing effects. It was such a wonderful time, meandering outside through aisles and aisles of delicious foods and organic options in the fresh air.

On the way home, in Ms. Lane's big old, deep maroon Cadillac Deville, Morgana pondered out loud, "Why don't more people live like this?"

"Like what, dear?"

"Well, I think about how I spent all that time working on an assembly line in a factory, and even at the mall at a job I hated, when I could have been out here living."

"You were going to school, too, a pretty heavy schedule, if I recall," Ms. Lane remembered.

"I know. And I did that to myself. I didn't have to take that many classes. I was just so focused on 'getting out.' But, that didn't make sense did it? Why didn't you tell me?" Morgana demanded jokingly.

Ms. Lane let out her signature hoot. "You wouldn't have heard me if I did, dear. Everyone has to come to their own awareness in their own time. My mother tried and tried to tell me, but I was too headstrong. You would have thought I would have gotten the message when I broke toes, time and time again. But it's not important when we get the message. What's important is that we get it, eventually. When we wake up and realize the beauty in the world around us. When we discover there's more to life than traffic and devices. When we open ourselves to the love that is constantly surrounding us. But no matter where you are, or what you are doing, if you can just take a moment to feel appreciation for everything right then and there, that will make all the difference in your life."

"I really appreciate you," Morgana said to her fairy godmother.

"And I really appreciate you, dear!"

"So, how do they get out?"

"By finding something that feels good and putting all their attention on it. Then following their emotions, if it feels right, do it. If it feels wrong, don't. Learning step by step how to heed the calling of their true heart's desires."

"What if their desires are unavailable?"

"Hold on to the feeling of what you want. Never doubt that it will come. Doubt and worry block the energy flow. You just have to practice feeling as good as you can, like it's already yours, and soon enough you'll be matched up with what you desire or something even better. The universe is wise and unlimited, and it knows more than we do. Trust. Believe. Relish. Savor. Appreciate. And know that the universe is lining you up with everything you can possibly imagine, and then get yourself ready to receive it," Ms. Lane said in her whimsical way.

Morgana tried not to, but she imagined losing herself in his deep aqua blue eyes, his silky voice, and the way he made every cell in her body come alive. *If the universe can do better than that, I can't wait to see it!* she said to herself.

Morgana loved every minute working for Ms. Lane. They laughed and talked. They would meditate together and Ms. Lane showed her stretching and yoga exercises. She explained to Morgana that all these modalities: meditation, stretching, healing teas, blessed organic foods, and the like, were all about building a foundation for an aligned life.

"Stretching and yoga are another way of connecting to our bodies, opening our channels to let energy flow. Pay attention to what your body is telling you. It will give you messages to let you know where and what your blocks are. Every minute you are interacting with life, you are interacting with energy. That's how life is. It's a constant interaction and reaction with the contrasts around us. And as we make our way through each day, taking in the opportunities for expansion, sometimes we might get a little block. But if you are aware of it, and use the tools for connecting to yourself, then those blocks are easily released. Like brushing your teeth after eating, sometimes, we can get a little piece of energy stuck in our teeth and you just have to brush it out." Ms. Land pretended to pick at her teeth. They both laughed. "But most of all, have as much fun as possible! Life is a game of alignment."

It was almost Ostara again. Morgana and Ms. Lane had been working with an event crew, lining up volunteers and getting everything ready.

"I can't believe it's been a whole year already," Morgana said one day. "Last year at this time I was headed to the Caribbean with Cole. It feels like a lifetime ago. God, who was that girl? I don't even recognize her at all. I felt so scared all the time. Cole probably thought I was nuts. One minute I was laughing, the next minute crying." Morgana laughed at herself shaking her head. "The Caribbean was fun, though. The beach was beautiful. The house was practically isolated at the end of the cove. It felt like we had the world to ourselves." She paused. "Do you think I should have moved to Paris with Cole? I mean, of course, he took away that option in the end, but what do you think would have happened? You say there are no wrong decisions." Morgana tried to put her fairy godmother's philosophy to the test.

"There are no wrong choices because ultimately everything is an experience. Every experience is an opportunity for expansion. It's all about discovering more about who we really are. That we are part of 'All That Is.' That life flows to us and through us. There are lessons we learn in harder ways than others, but every lesson is a miracle. And understanding that lesson is magic," Ms. Lane explained it in her whimsical way.

"You have all the answers," Morgana teased.

"There is only one answer, get into alignment. By listening to your heart, you didn't go to Paris with Cole."

"Well, he ultimately dumped me in the end," Morgana interjected.

"Yes, but only because you didn't conform to him. And you didn't conform because your heart didn't let you," Ms. Lane pointed out.

"Was that stupid? Cole was perfect." Morgana questioned herself.

"Was he perfect for you, though?"

"Well, I really liked it when we were alone. He was different when it was just the two of us. He was perfect for me then, but I guess, that's not reality. The reality was he had a job and a life controlled by other people. It was almost more like he had to do it, rather than he wanted to. He once told me he needed me to keep him from turning into those people. I really did love him and I tried so hard to be in his life, but I couldn't allow myself to conform, as you said, and he wanted me to. He even asked me not to go to the lot! It never wouldn't have worked, would it? He wanted me to give up everything and he wasn't willing to give up anything. Of course, maybe that's me thinking he should have conformed to me. Hmmm. Interesting."

"When you have to 'try hard' at something, especially love, that's the universe letting you know you're going against the current. And, that just means that you're not clear on what you want. Have you heard from him?"

"No!' Morgana laughed. "He made it pretty clear he was done with me." She took a deep breath. "I hope he's happy in love. He deserves to be happy."

"And what about you?"

"Oh, well. I don't know about me. I guess I deserve to be happy in love, too. My problem is," she paused and thought about how magnificent Josef made her feel, "I think my expectations are too high."

"High expectations are a good thing, as long as you're in alignment on the receiving side."

"Meaning?"

"If we set the bar high and then we feel we can't achieve it, it puts us in negative vibrations. But if we set the bar high and feel inspired, excited, and challenged in a good way, then the universe can bring it to you. That's how you communicate your desires, through your feelings. Feel good and you'll get good things. Feel bad and you'll get bad things." And then she added with deep feeling in her whimsical way, "Feel amazing and get ready to be amazed!"

"I'm going to hold you to that!" Morgana laughed.

"Don't hold me to it. Hold yourself to it and then watch the universe respond."

"Well, I still think it would have been wrong if I moved to Paris, because then I wouldn't have been here to work for you," Morgana stated.

"And that's how the universe works."

"What?" Morgana questioned.

"Well, you had an internal conflict about moving to Paris, right?"

"Ya, I guess. I mean, I was nervous, scared, worried about what I would do, worried about Cole."

"Right. If moving had been in your highest and best interest, then it would have all worked itself out, Cole or no Cole. But the bigger conflict was the move, would you agree?"

"Okay, yes."

"And that's because moving there, while not a wrong thing, per se, wasn't in alignment with your true heart's desire. So, your broader self let you know, through uneasy emotions, that moving away wasn't the best choice. There aren't wrong choices, but there are better choices in regards to what you desire most. And then that's when sweet synchronicity takes place. And here you are."

Morgana was about to ponder that when Ms. Lane's phone rang. "Helllooo, Josef," she sang out.

"Hi, Aunt Katherine. Sorry I missed your call earlier. I was under the machine and didn't hear my phone."

"Your timing is perfect dear. Sweet synchronicity is always at work," she said with a wink. Morgana turned red and gave her dear old friend the stink eye. "Morgana and I were just wanting to wish you a very happy birthday!"

"Happy Birthday!" Morgana called out.

"Hey, thanks, girls. I wish I was there with you. That's for sure!"

His voice sent tingles up her spine. She started to fight it off but then she reminded herself, *This is how I want to feel when I am in love.*

"Is that machine still giving you grief?" Ms. Lane carried on her conversation.

"Yeah, we tried to rebuild it, but I think it's going to need to be completely replaced. It's just not compatible with the newer parts and no one makes them for this anymore."

"How much longer do you think?"

"I'm hoping June at the latest."

"You'll miss Beltane?"

"Fraid so."

"Well, I know everything will work out for the best," Ms. Lane assured.

"I know you're right, Aunt Katherine. Love you guys."

"We love you, too. Happy birthday!"

"Thank you. Bye," he said and hung up.

After the call ended, Morgana asked for more verification, "So you say, I'm just supposed to hold on to the feeling I want, and the universe will bring me what I want, or better?"

"Yes, that's right."

"How do I know if it's the right vibration?"

"Because it feels good," Ms. Lane said whimsically.

"So, if it doesn't feel good, then it's not right?"

"There are no right or wrong vibrations. If you feel for what you desire, but it doesn't feel good to you then it means you're not in alignment with your desires. And it's letting you know you have a block."

Yeah, a big block named Tiffany! Morgana thought to herself. "What if something feels good, but you don't want to?" she asked sheepishly.

"Do you want to explain that?" Ms. Lane inquired with a confused look.

Morgana didn't want to detail to her fairy godmother how she was still in love with Josef, even though he was engaged to someone else. So, she just said, "Well, I'm just trying to figure out how to hold the vibration of what I want without really knowing what I want."

Ms. Lane gave her an inquisitive look, but then said, "You might be focusing on the how instead of the emotion. Sometimes we get ourselves out of alignment because we are trying to figure out too many details. Let the universe handle the details. You don't know how many pieces are going to fit together and there's no possible way you can, but the universe knows. So trust it. Dream about what you think is the best case scenario. When you feel good and are in alignment, you are open to all possibilities. Believe in the feelings. Enjoy feeling good."

Morgana took a deep breath and thought to herself, *Well, I guess he is in Italy, so when I feel happy hearing his voice it's not hurting anyone. And if I hold onto the vibration of what I want to feel, than eventually the universe will match up to it and bring me someone, available, who matches. If I try to block my emotions, than I'm blocking the flow and pinching myself off from possibilities. I definitely don't want to do that again.* "Okay, I think that makes sense," Morgana said.

"And sometimes old vibrational patterns try to make their way back in. If you are feeling good but then you feel bad about feeling good, that is just an indication of an old vibration that no longer serves you. You can do tapping or meditate or we can do muscle testing, if you'd like."

"How?"

"Think about what you want. Feel good. Think of the best case scenario," Ms. Lane instructed.

Morgana closed her eyes and pictured his smile, getting lost in his deep aqua blue eyes, and how elated she felt when she was close to him. The tingles ran up her spine and she couldn't help but smile.

"Hold out your arm so we can lock that in," said Ms. Lane. Morgana held out her arm ninety degrees from her body and it was strong. "Good. Now on a scale from one to ten, let's see how close you are to that vibration. Are you in the range zero to five? Are you in the range of six to ten? Which one felt stronger to you?" Ms. Lane had pushed down on her extended arm.

"Umm, I guess zero to five," Morgana answered.

"Okay, let's narrowing down some more. Are you at a zero? One? Two? Three? Four? Five?" Ms. Lane pushed down with each number. "Which one do you think felt the strongest or had the most resistance?"

"I think five," Morgana answered.

"Good. Ask yourself, what does being a five feel like to you."

"Um, a little hopeless, I guess," Morgana said a little quietly.

"That's alright. Let's find out when you first acquired that vibration. Hold out your arm. Was it during conception to birth? Zero to one? One to five? Six to eight? Eight to Eleven? It's during conception to about the age of eleven that we are most susceptible to the vibrations of those around us. It's during these years we form our basis for how we view life. Which one felt the strongest or had the most resistance?"

"Can we try two to five again?"

"Were you two? Three? Four? Five?" Ms. Lane tested for each age.

"I think two or three were the strongest."

"Okay. Can you think of anything that happened when you are two or three? Is there a memory or story that you heard that comes up for you?"

"I think that was the last time my mom saw my dad. I don't know if she was trying to get him back or trying to get money from him."

"Well, let's see. Hold out your arm. This memory is the first time you picked up on the hopeless frequency?" She tested. "That was pretty strong. Do you agree?"

"Yes."

"Alright. Let's see whose emotion it was. Was it your dad's? Was it your mom's?" Ms. Lane pushed on Morgana's arm.

"Ha! They're both strong." Morgana laughed.

"Alright, let's do one parent at the time. So, where are you holding onto your dad's feeling of hopelessness? In your first chakra? Second? Third? Fourth? Fifth? Sixth? Seventh?"

"I think in the first?"

"Let's verify. You're holding onto your dad's vibration of hopelessness in your first chakra? In the second?"

"First, for sure," Morgana confirmed.

"Okay, so close your eyes. The root chakra is located at the base of our spine. It provides the foundation of survival and safety on which we build our life. Picture in your mind's eye what a block might look like and how you'd like to remove it. You can picture something like white light filling in from the top your head and lighting any dark spots. Just close your eyes and allow a picture to form."

All of a sudden Morgana pictured a bunch of cute fluffy puppies licking her legs. She giggled at the thought. The puppies were so cute and soft and their little tails were wagging. They licked and licked at her shins and knees with their little soft tongues. She couldn't help but laugh and after a bit, opened her eyes. "Does it count if I saw puppies licking me?" she asked.

"Let's check. Do you feel like you've released your dad's feelings of hopelessness." Strong resistance. "Very good. Now, let's work on your mom. Where do you feel you're holding in your mom's feelings of hopelessness? In your first chakra? Second? Third? Fourth? Fifth? Sixth? Seventh?"

"I think it was my fifth," Morgana answered.

"The fifth is the throat chakra. Our throat is our voice, our willpower, and it's also the link between our heart's fourth chakra and our head's sixth and seventh chakras. If you have a block here you can have a hard time voicing your opinions or speaking up for yourself. So, close your eyes and see in your mind's eye how you'd like to remove your mother's vibration of hopelessness."

Morgana took a deep breath and what came to mind was the part in the movie where the mermaid has to sing to get her voice back, and golden light illuminates her throat. Morgana pictured that golden light in her own throat opening the flow between her heart and her head. After a few minutes, she held out her arm. There was strong resistance.

"Looks like you got it. Now, we go back to the original question. Think about what you want, the best case scenario that you can feel."

This time, Morgana felt strong arms wrapped around from behind her. She couldn't see a face but she felt the blissful serendipitous love and the tingles running up her spine and her soul coming alive. She felt safe, secure and desired. It felt transcendent and magical. She felt sure about this feeling and held out her arm to lock it in place.

"How do you feel?" Ms. Lane asked.

"Hopeful! Like, it's Christmas Eve and tomorrow I get to unwrap the most perfect present." And she couldn't stop smiling.

$\mathcal{C}$hapter Twenty-One

You Had the Power All Along

WHILE GETTING READY for Ostara, Morgana pulled out the five thousand dollar Marchesa dress from the back of her closet. She had buried it back there when she had buried all of her feelings. It was a beautiful dress and she loved how it twirled. She remembered the panic attack she had when she found out how much it cost, and had to laugh at herself.

"Maybe, Cole was right. It is just money."

Ever since she got the job at the factory and then of course, the awesome salary Ms. Lane was paying her, her money fears had subsided. Or more accurately stated, she had release some of her old money fear-based vibrations, opening herself up to the awesome salary she was now receiving.

"I probably still wouldn't pay five thousand bucks for a dress, but at least I can wear this one!" she said to herself. "Okay, maybe I still have a few more money blocks to let go of." She laughed.

Morgana worked Ostara, chatting up the vendors, working with the caterers, and enjoying the celebration from afar. She loved seeing how it all comes together, from the theme, to the bands, and the vendors, and she had helped with all of it. It made her feel good. A little part of her may have been avoiding the group, not necessarily wanting to hear all Tiffany's love stories, but she hadn't seen any of them so she wasn't even sure who was there. She was still enjoying the connection of the night. She spent her time focusing on the magical feeling of her mystery man with his loving arms wrapped around her. They would dance, and laugh, and make wonderful love. The world around them would fade into the background when they were together because they were so in love and in sync, and in alignment with each other and the universe. They would love being together and encourage each other's dreams.

"Maybe we can work together? Oh, but how could that happen?" Morgana asked herself, and then quickly realized as she felt the energy flow stop, "Oh – wait! Too much details. Back it up! Back to feeling wonderful when we're together." So, she started over. They would laugh and dance and make love, and it would be blissful and magical. "There we go. Back on track," she said as the tingles resumed tickling up her spine.

On a lovely April day during her international business class, Morgana had an idea flash in her mind. She couldn't wait to get home and tell Ms. Lane all about it.

"So, I have an idea," she said later over tea.

"Yes, dear?"

"I want to design a line of products with you that we can sell in kiosks in the mall. I want it to be a 'healing cart.' It would look like a cute farm stand cart and we would arrange the products, like candles, oils, lotions and teas in a color code, corresponding to the chakra colors. Then we would have a website that would give more information on chakras and information on how to allow the body to do its job of keeping us healthy. What do you think?"

"I think it's a marvelous idea! Can you come up with the presentation that we can present to the board?"

Morgana was nervous but totally excited. "Yeah, I can do that!"

She set to work. She asked her professor to help her make a business plan. She designed a kiosk cart shaped like a farm stand cart and spoke with several malls in the area, gathering information on prices, fees, measurements and limitations. She worked with Ms. Lane and they chose aromas, colors, and flavors that she felt coordinated with the chakras.

"I want the focus to be on enhancing feelings," Morgana explained to Ms. Lane. "Like you say, focus on feeling good. I want our products to speak to the higher frequencies. And of course, they have to be fun!" she said in a whimsical way.

She spent weeks gathering and collecting information and putting it all together. She had a blast doing it too. She was really feeling the flow of energy moving through her. During her business class she would get ideas and her teacher was excited because she was helping apply the information from the book and making class more interactive.

The last week before finals, Morgana's professor came up to her and said, "I had you in class last year and I marked you down for not participating enough." Morgana remembered. "I'm really impressed with the change in you. Plus, it's exciting to see your enthusiasm for your product. I really hope you are successful with this enterprise."

"Oh! Enterprise? Love the sound of that! Thank you so much for all your help. I'm so excited!" Morgana exclaimed.

"When do you present to the board?"

"The week after finals. Oh geez, that's only two weeks away."

"I think you're definitely ready. I am looking forward to the final presentation as part of your finals."

Along with all her work on this project, Morgana and Ms. Lane were setting up for Beltane. Morgana giggled, "Last year at Beltane, it was like I was drunk on love. It was euphoric. I just felt alive and..." She stopped herself. "How do I put this?"

"Frisky?" Ms. Lane provided the perfect emotion.

"Yes! Very frisky!" Morgana laughed hysterically. "It was amazing. But I was with Cole and this year I'm all alone. No excitement feelings for me."

"Why not?"

"Well, um, you know," she said blushing.

"What was the intention you set up last year?"

"Um." She tried to remember. "I guess it was to be in love, to celebrate with the God and the Goddess and life. I felt comfortable in my relationship at the time, ironically, considering it was right after that I got the boot." She laughed.

"So really, you felt comfortable with yourself. You set the intention to enjoy the night of love and magic and possibilities. You were grateful and in the flow with the energy of the night. That is what created the euphoric feelings. Cole was just the delicious icing on the cake." Ms. Lane winked. Morgana turned red.

When they arrived at the lot for Beltane, Morgana did busy herself with the vendors and caterers. But around 9 p.m. she decided she would stop hiding and open herself up to the possibilities of the universe. She loved dancing around the May pole last year, so she made her way to the dance floor. She was a little relieved when she didn't see anyone from the group.

"I guess I still have a block there," she said to herself. But set the intention to enjoy the reason for celebration, the union of the God and Goddess, life, love, fun, connection, joy, laughter, and bliss. She allowed herself to fill in with all the higher frequencies she could think of as she circled around the May pole entwining the long flowing colorful silk ribbons with the other dancers. She started to feel the buzz. She slightly closed her eyes and pictured dancing with her anonymous lover. She felt herself awaken and she felt like she was floating. She danced for hours having a wonderful time. She could tell she still had a little resistance, and she didn't let herself completely go like she did last year, but she did enjoy herself immensely.

At brunch the next morning she saw the gang all eating at the table, no Tiffany in sight. *Stop that!* she reminded herself as she made her way over to say hello to everyone. "Hey, guys! Are you having a good time?" Morgana greeted them.

"Morgana! It's so good to see you!" They all jumped up to give her hugs.

"We hear you are putting together a presentation for the board next week. Are you super excited?" Brook asked.

"Yes! I've been working a lot on it, still putting on some final touches. I'm totally nervous, but definitely hopeful." Morgana gave an anxious smile.

"Oh, you'll do great. I'm looking forward to hearing all about it." Brook said eager enthusiasm.

"And don't let Mr. Finds scare you. He's all guff," Blake added.

"Who's Mr. Finds?" Morgana asked.

"Oh, he's on the board," Brook answered.

Morgana never thought about guff board members. She always just pictured Ms. Lane's little fairy friends having tea parties. "How many board members are there?"

"Twenty-three, as of right now. I've been working with them as I'm learning the biz," Brook explained. "Mr. Finds isn't that bad, but he can be quite intimidating. Don't let him scare you."

"How come we didn't see you last night?" Trina asked. "I missed my dance partner!"

"I was there! I was on the far left May pole," Morgana explained.

"Ah! We were on the front right. Totally missed you. Bummer!" Trina said with a hug. "Beltane is my favorite night. Last year you were completely buzzing. I was hoping to get a contact high again." They all laughed.

Morgana felt really accepted by them. She laughed at herself for hiding. "I have to run for now, but I'll see you guys later!" She actually did have to go. She had set up a meeting with a vendor who offered an alternative to the cots. Hopefully, she could figure out a better solution.

As they were being driven home, she went over the options with Ms. Lane. "You have been such a great help to me, Morgana. You have done so much. I'm so pleased," Ms. Lane sincerely complimented her.

"I love my job so much, it's wonderful. I love being a part of all of this. Thank you. I feel so blessed."

The following week Morgana got a standing ovation from her classmates for her presentation. A lot of them had questions about if it really worked. "Yes, definitely!" Many of them had questions about healing because so many had family and friends dealing with illnesses. She did a couple of muscle testing demonstrations on some volunteers in front of the class, and everyone could see the instant effects on each person. "This stuff is amazing!" The group all expressed their excitement.

"I hope it goes as well in front of the board as it did today!" Morgana relayed the details of class to Ms. Lane. "I mean, I don't expect a standing ovation." Morgana laughed.

"I'm sure it will, dear." Ms. Lane gave her a big smile. "Our flight leaves Tuesday and you'll present Wednesday morning."

"Flight?" Morgana questioned.

"Yes, dear. We have to fly to New York."

"New York? What? But that's not where everyone lives. They're only an hour or two away from here. I thought we just were going to drive down the hill?"

"Oh, no, dear. We have to meet before all the board members at headquarters in New York."

"Ms. Laaaaaane!" Morgana whined. "You didn't tell me that! OH NO! What? I don't know..." She started to panic.

"Don't worry, dear. You'll be great. I'm so excited. You've put a lot of work into this. I believe in it and, even more, I believe in you. You just have to believe in yourself."

"Haha." Morgana laughed nervously. "You're not the first person who's said that to me."

"Really? Do we have a vibrational pattern that no longer serves you?"

"Umm, ya. I guess I do."

"Would you like to remove it?"

"Yes!"

"Start tapping on your karate chop point. It's the point on your hand where you would chop wood if you were a Kung Fu master," Ms. Lane explained with a wink, "and state, even though I am nervous, I still love and accept myself."

Morgana repeated the phrase.

"It works best if you are honest. Go on, state your personal truth."

"Okay, even though my fairy godmother just dropped a bomb on me and I don't think I'm good enough, I still love and accept myself."

"That's good. Is that how you feel?"

"Yes!" Morgana laughed, giving her mentor the stink eye.

"The part about not thinking you're good enough," Ms. Lane specified with a laugh.

"Alright. Yes, that's how I feel. I mean, I just don't think people will take me seriously, like they don't care what I have to say. I guess maybe, I don't take myself seriously. I'm doing much better. You've helped me so much. But I'm just stuck, kind of, you know? Am I supposed to keep tapping?"

"Yes, keep tapping as you feel around to find your sweet spot, your truth. Why do you feel stuck? Keep tapping."

"I've always felt stuck. That's been my whole thing. Trying to get out."

"Okay, let's put it in more of a set up statement. Even though…."

"Even though I'm stuck. I'm…ah, holding myself back. Umm, I'm not good enough. Even though I don't think I can do this on my own, I still love and accept myself."

"Do what on your own?" Ms. Lane encouraged her to reach for the deeper feeling.

Morgana sighed deeply. "I wanted to shut everyone out because I felt alone and abandoned all my life. But really, I don't want to be alone. I want somebody to love me. I want to share my life with someone."

"I think we found your truth." Ms. Lane nurtured her young friend's emotional honesty.

"Ya, I think so." Morgana softly admitted. "So, now what?"

"Tap on your inner brow and just repeat a word or phrase that encompasses your truth."

"I don't want to be alone," she said with some sadness.

"Tap on your outer eye and say it again or another truth."

"I want to be loved," she finally admitted to herself.

"Under the eye."

"I want to love."

"Under the nose, on your lip."

"Love"

"On the chin."

"Love. I want love."

"On your chest, just below the collar bone."

"I want to love and to be loved."

"Under the arm."

"I am ready to be truly loved."

"Top of the head."

"Why would anyone love me if my own father didn't love me?" A fretful Morgana looked for advice from her mentor.

"Continue through the points. Talk yourself through until you find the relief."

Inner brow: "Well, I guess I kinda know the answer. Right? It's not that he didn't love me, he couldn't love me."

Outer eye: "I don't know if that feels any better. Didn't. Couldn't."

Under eye: "Is that why I've always had such crappy boyfriends?"

Lip: "Cole was definitely the best, the rest were abusive and awful."

Chin: "Cole is one who said I needed to believe in myself."

Collar bone: "He was right, I guess. I probably pushed him away because I didn't think I deserved him."

Underarm: "I attracted all those abusive relationships because I didn't think I deserved better."

Top of head: "The Law of Attraction was just being a mirror to show me that I didn't love me, so I attracted guys that didn't love me."

Brow: "I need to love me. Cole told me he needed me, but he then also tried to change and control me."

Outer eye: "I need to love and accept myself as I am."

Under eye: "That's hard."

Lip: "Why is it so hard? I'm a good person. I try my best."

Chin: "I really do try my best. And that's all any of us can do, right?"

Collarbone: "I can accept that. I can accept that I do my best. And, I mean, you like me. And you're awesome!"

Underarm: "And if someone like you can like me, I can't be all that bad. Can I?"

Top of head: (a deep sigh) "If you can like me, then I can like me. And I guess I can accept myself because I'm trying. I'm learning. I'm growing. I am an evolving being, here for the life experience."

Brow: "And life is supposed to be fun."

Outer eye: "Life is what I make it. And if I pay attention to what life is trying to tell me and I work with it, there's nothing I can't do."

Under eye: "I am an unlimited being."

Lip: "There's nothing I can't be, do, or have. All I have to do is focus on what I want to feel, then reach for the alignment."

Chin: "That's pretty cool."

Collarbone: "Being human is pretty cool!"

Underarm: "I can love myself for being human."

Top of head: "I love and accept myself because I am an unlimited being with a life of possibilities that await me. And the higher my frequencies, the better my life can be. I can believe in myself because I understand it's all about my vibrations. I can love myself because I am an eternal being in the constant state of growing and evolving."

"Deep breath," Ms. Lane advised. Morgana took a deep breath in. "How do you feel?"

Morgana paused and thought about it. "I feel good. I feel like I understand myself differently. I feel relieved. Like I got this, ya know?"

"Very good." Ms. Lane smiled.

"What's the difference between tapping and the arm testing thing?"

"Both are equally good. You can use either one or both anytime. I just wanted you to use tapping now to remind you that you are in control. You have the tools and know how to get yourself through any situation. Just find your truth and then work through it until you find the feeling of relief."

Morgana got really excited listening to Ms. Lane and moved to the edge of her chair. "OH! Are you going to say it? Oh, please say it!" she requested with much giddy enthusiasm.

"Say what?"

"Say, you had the power all long!"

Ms. Lane let out her signature hoot. "It's true."

Morgana leaned in and sat on the tip of her chair, as Ms. Lane indulged her. "Yes, my dear. You had the power all along. You just had to learn it for yourself."

"Ahhhhhhhh!!!" Morgana squealed and clapped at her very own real life 'Glinda the Good Witch' fairy godmother, who was now laughing hysterically at Morgana.

The next Tuesday, they retrieved their luggage from the baggage terminal of JFK airport in New York City. A private car took them to the Waldorf Astoria hotel. Ms. Lane was greeted by name and attended to like a celebrity. "Do you come here often?" Morgana asked.

"Well, yes, I've been staying here for decades, but they treat everyone wonderfully here."

They were shown to their double suite and Morgana was blown away by the beauty and opulence of the historic hotel. She twirled around their room and then stared out the window at the enormous city outside.

"You know, it's funny. The old me would have had a panic attack flying first class and then I probably wouldn't have made it into this building. I would have spontaneously combusted right out there on the sidewalk. I guess that means I'm making progress, right?"

"Well, it means you are allowing more energy to flow. But you still get to choose how it makes you feel. How do you feel?"

"I feel proud of myself for not combusting. I'm honored that I get to be here with you. I'm grateful for the experience of being here, in this hotel, in New York. I'm excited about the possibilities of tomorrow's presentation. And I'm really enjoying the spectacular view from this window. And this is super fun!"

Ms. Lane smiled. "Those are lovely high frequencies, dear."

Morgana laughed at her little fairy godmother then flopped on the ultra-luxurious marvelously comfortable bed. A little later, they freshened up and got ready for the night to see a Broadway show and dinner.

It was a lovely evening. Morgana thought, *Lovely frequencies = lovely time.* As she drifted off to sleep that night in her luxury suite, sending out positive vibes for tomorrow and her presentation, her last thought before she succumbed to the night was of her mystery man standing behind her, loving her, supporting her, and filling her internal butterflies with magic.

The next morning over breakfast, Ms. Lane went over the day's schedule. "Your presentation is at noon. I will have to stay with the board for our annual meeting. You have your list of things you wanted to see and do?"

"Yes ma'am!" Morgana replied with eagerness.

"Very good. I'll be tied up the rest of the day in the meeting, but we'll meet back here at 6 p.m. and head to the airport to fly back home."

"Sounds good. I'm so excited!"

A car delivered them to corporate headquarters, a very formal business building. In the elevator to their floor of the sky scraper, Morgana was a little disappointed. "I had hoped it would look like Willy Wonka's Chocolate Factory," she shared with her fairy godmother.

Ms. Lane let out a hoot. "This isn't the factory. This is just headquarters," she said with a wink, making Morgana giggle.

The elevator doors pinged open and they stepped into an opulent cream, brown, and beige decorated entry, with live plants and a water feature to sooth the atmosphere. Ms. Lane's Victorian lace up boots clicked on the smooth tile floors. The sweet familiar sound made Morgana smile to herself.

"Good morning, Ms. Lane. Good morning, Miss Anderson." The receptionist greeted them. "You will be meeting in Boardroom Three, in thirty minutes. Ms. Lane, Mr. King is waiting for you in his office. I will bring your tea in there. Miss Anderson, you may set up if you would like in the boardroom. Can I bring you a beverage?" Morgana looked to Ms. Lane.

"She'll have one of mine. Thank you so much, Kendra. You are looking lovely, dear."

"Thank you Ms. Lane. As are you."

Kendra was friendly and professional. Morgana guessed Kendra wasn't much older than herself, and she admired how well the young professional carried herself in the big business office building. Ms. Lane took Morgana to Boardroom Three on her way to Mr. King's office.

Morgana walked into the huge windowed room with the long dark mahogany wood conference table that had eleven chairs on each side and two head chairs at the far end. A young man named Aiden came in with Morgana's tea and showed her how to sync up with the multimedia screens. She stood staring out the massive glass that overlooked the sky line of New York and tapped out some last minute nerves using the EFT points on her fingertips.

Thumb: "I am so blessed to be here.

Index: I am so thankful to be here.

Middle: I can't believe I'm here.

Pinky: How did I get here?

Thumb: I am so excited to be here.

Index: This is amazing to be here.

Middle: I can't believe I'm here.

Pinky: I can do this."

She took a sip of her tea and enjoyed the view, and then walked over to the computer to make sure everything was set up and ready to go.

She was reviewing her notes, with her back to the door, when an arm stealthily wrapped around her waist on the right side and his silky voice whispered into her left ear, "I'm so proud of you. You are amazing."

Before she could even breathe he was already gone and heading to take his seat at the long wooden table. It was like a drive-by boosting. By the time she turned around to search for her covert complimentor, he was engaged in a conversation with another board member. He looked away from his discussion for split second and locked those deep aqua blue eyes onto hers. She got lost in his eyes, and felt time stop for that second and all the cells in her body came alive. He returned to his dialog with a small smile on his lips and she turned back around to her notes.

I didn't know he was on the board, she thought to herself taking in a long slow breath.

The two dozen chairs were filling in and the buzz of interchanges filled the room. A tall ominous looking older gentleman came in. *Must be Mr. Finds*, Morgana surmised. She stood by witnessing the scene almost in an out of body way. She was soaking it all in, filling herself with the joy of the experience. She was nervous, but she and Ms. Lane had talked about what would happen.

"After you give your presentation, the board members will discuss their take and vote on it. Then, we'll submit the presentation and your notes to legal to see what it will take to make it happen. That will probably take several weeks. There may be more questions and more meetings amongst the members, but today is just about you sharing your idea with the group. This is your idea and it's a good one. So just have fun with it."

Finally, Ms. Lane and her sister, Mrs. Meadow, with Mr. Meadow and Mr. King came into the room. Ms. Lane came up to Morgana, "Are you all set?" she asked with a wink.

"Yes, ma'am," Morgana smiled proudly.

The sisters took their seats at the head of the table on the far end. The room quieted and Ms. Lane spoke, "I would like to start this meeting by welcoming our newest board member, Josef McClellan. Welcome to the team." Josef accepted the acknowledgement and the accompanying claps. "Today we are here to listen to Miss Morgana Anderson present her business proposal. You may begin, Miss Anderson."

"Ladies and gentlemen. My name is Morgana Anderson. I am here today to share with you, The Healing Cart." Morgana started flipping through the coordinating slides. "The Healing Cart, is a mall kiosk that is designed to look like a fresh fruit market cart. The layout of the products will be color coordinated with the seven colors of the seven chakras. Each color will have two sizes of candles, essential oils that come as pure oils, in room diffusers, in a perfume roller ball or spray, bath bombs, and in a car fresher option. Finally, each will have its own special blend of teas. Each color product is designed to enhance specific emotional frequencies.

"For the first chakra, the color is red the flavor aroma I chose to represent this chakra is strawberry pomegranate. I chose these flavors because the first chakra is the root chakra. It's our primal instinct for survival, our foundation, our history, and our grounding. The red strawberries grow from roots in the ground and blossom their fruits for us to see. Strawberries are very antioxidant and full of nutrients and vitamins and minerals for our overall health. The red pomegranate represents our blood. When you open a pomegranate, its seeds even look like blood capillaries. The blood flowing through our bodies brings us life, keeps our systems clean and functioning. The emotional frequency of the color red represents power, love, and passion.

"The second chakra is represented by the color orange. For this chakra, I chose the flavor aroma of spiced tangelo. A tangelo itself is a cross between a grapefruit and a tangerine, and mixing the antioxidant, anti-inflammatory and heart protecting properties of cinnamon with the rich dietary fiber essential vitamins and minerals of the citrus family is a perfect blend of sweet and spicy. This sacral chakra impacts our creativity and sexuality. The emotional frequency of the color orange evokes ambition and creativity.

"We move to the third chakra, the solar plexus. Yellow is the color of this chakra, and the flavor I chose is banana-lemon. Bananas have great benefits for digestion, heart health, and they have lots of fiber, which is good for the solar plexus that is responsible for our gut instincts and our personal power. The tart lemon awakens the adrenal glands also associated with the third chakra. The emotional frequency of yellow is focus and intuition.

"Our fourth chakra is the heart, represented by green. I chose green apple-lime as the flavor aroma. Green apples are rich in dietary fiber. They lower cholesterol, ease digestion, and are full of vitamins including riboflavin and B6. Limes help with weight loss, skin care, eye care and respiratory disorders. The two tart flavors mix together well to keep the heart strong and pumping. The emotional frequency of green is abundance, prosperity, and luck.

"Next we move to the fifth chakra, in our throat. This is our voice. Our voice we use to speak up for ourselves. The throat chakra is the channel between the heart and the head that allows us to express ourselves artistically from our hearts and spiritually from our higher chakras. The flavor aroma I chose is blueberry cream pie, a combination of blueberry and soft vanilla. Blueberries contain antioxidants which are very helpful for supporting healthy cellular functions. Vanilla includes antioxidant and anti-inflammation abilities. The throat color is blue. I chose light blue for its calming healing and cleansing energetic frequencies. The emotional frequencies of blues are peace, patience, and healing.

"Our sixth chakra is the third eye chakra. The 'Ajne Chakra' literally translates to 'center of knowing or monitoring.' The opening of your third eye is an opening to your intuition and cosmic power. I chose the flavor aroma of lavender dreams. A blend of lavender's ability to eliminate nervous tension, relieve pain and enhance blood circulation with chamomile used for its calming and overall soothing health properties. The color of the third eye is purple or light purple. Purple is the color of mystery and magic. I chose light purple, as it combines the innocence of white with the spirituality and passion of purple. The emotional frequency is well-wishes and friendship.

"And finally, we come to the seventh chakra, the crown. This chakra can also be associated with a light lavender color, but it can be iridescent. The crown chakra is the connection to that which is beyond. It is our pipeline to the universe. I chose the color white as its pure representational color. White is purity and new beginnings. And the flavor aroma I chose is coconut almond. Coconuts have many vitamins, minerals, as well as plenty of electrolytes. Almonds help promote healthy blood sugar levels and have fiber and magnesium. The emotional frequency of white is purity, clarity and connection.

"When someone comes to 'The Healing Cart' they have several different ways of picking the product that is right for them.

Sight- they are attracted to the color as the optical sensory is attracted to what it needs.

Smell- each flavor aroma will connect the person with what they need.

Emotional frequency- each product lists properties for promoting its emotional frequency of their needs.

Taste- the teas coordinate with each flavor aroma, speaking to the person's needs.

Energetically- the fun happy fruit cart look is quaint and accessible. They will be open to looking and smelling.

Healing- the term itself speaks to their heart, grabbing their attention.

"And every product will have a page on the website that gives more insights to keeping your total well-being, allowing good health to flourish by explaining that our bodies know how to keep us healthy and it's our job to keep ourselves happy.

"In your packets I'm handing out I have detailed the combination of flavor aromas based on what your company currently already has. These are just new combinations, so it won't take extra resources to make any of the new flavors. Sort of like more recipes with the same ingredients. I have also detailed employee profit sharing. I spent most of my time that I worked at the perfume kiosk doing my homework and collecting my minimum-wage, but if I had some incentive in profit sharing, I would have been more inclined to address customers. Plus, we want to promote total wellness, and happy employees make for better representatives of the product.

"What it all comes down to is promoting happiness. Some may just look at the simple happy fruit cart and smile for a split second. Some may be inspired to eat a piece of fruit that day. Better yet, some will come over and learn that adding an herbal tea blend to their daily routine could lead to a healthier lifestyle. Some will be surprised to find out that adding pure essential oils to their house or car or even wearing it on their person, will have dramatic healing effects on their lives as our sensory glands are some of the strongest brain waves we have.

"In conclusion, there is an awakening happening. People are connecting to their power. We are on the leading edge of evolution, and I want people to know they can be, do, and have anything they want, but really what we are searching for is connection. The connection to the Beloved Grace that unifies us all. We are all One. The only separation is the imaginary boundaries and walls we put up to keep people away, to keep our dreams away, and keep away the Great Love that is out there helping us and lining things up for us along our way. We have the power to be happy, healthy, and prosperous. Not just for one- but for all. There is more than enough of everything to go around. Total well-being is our natural state. We are eternal beings here to learn experience and evolve, and life is supposed to be fun. It all starts with learning to listen to yourself using your emotions as your guidance system and following your intuition to your true heart's desires.

"Ladies and gentlemen, I really appreciate your time today. Thank you very much."

"Thank you, Miss Anderson. It was very informative and creative. We will discuss this and look over your handouts and get back to you." Ms. Lane said from the end of the long wooden conference table with a wink and a smile. That was the cue they had set up so Morgana would gather her things and then go play in New York until it was time to meet up and fly home.

She hadn't looked at him the whole time, but she felt him looking at her, feeding her positive energy. As she picked up her notecards, she had to look. He was watching her. Their eyes locked again and time stood still. She quickly looked around seeing if anyone noticed. She couldn't tell how long they had been staring at each other- was it tenth of a second or two hours, she didn't know, she just got lost in his face, his smile, and those deep aqua blue eyes.

She got out of there as fast as she could without running. Was she even walking? She felt like she was soaring. She went back to the Waldorf to change clothes and then spent the rest of the afternoon blissfully seeing the sights in New York on her agenda.

$\mathcal{C}$hapter Twenty-Two

A Life Full of Love, Magic, and Miracles

IT WAS ONLY a few days later that the phone rang while Morgana and Ms. Lane were having a discussion about next month's Midsummer's celebration.

"Hello, David," Ms. Lane answered her phone. (Pause) "Yes, she's here with me now. Shall I put you on speaker?" Ms. Lane heard his reply and then adjusted her phone. "Okay, you're on."

"Miss Anderson?"

"Yes?"

"This is David King. I am the Executive Vice President of Beloved Grace Organics."

"Hello, sir." Morgana looked at Ms. Lane with big excited eyes.

"The board was pleased with your presentation and has voted to move forward with implementation. There were concerns about your young age, so we would like to assign a senior mentor to your team. We have not decided who that will be yet."

"Okay, that's fine."

"There will be paperwork involved in setting up your company, licensing, and trademarking, so I will send a courier with the contracts for you to review. Do we have your address on file?"

"Yes sir, I believe so."

"Okay, good. Well, congratulations. I look forward to working with you. Have a great day, Miss Anderson. Good-bye, Katherine."

"Good-bye, David," Ms. Lane said and hung up.

Morgana let out a loud squeal! "Oh, my God! What! What? What!"

Morgana got up and started dancing around the kitchen and into the sunken pink carpeted living room.

Ms. Lane's phone rang again in the dining room. "Hello, Josef!" Morgana slowed her dancing and looked through the open white bookcase that separated the living room from the dining room. "We did. David just called. Yes, she is so excited." (Pause) "Well, bless me. That is wonderful news, too! Of course, I would be honored to officiate. Just try and stop me!" (Pause)

Morgana's heart stopped. *Did she just say officiate? Josef is finally back from Italy and they must've set a date.* Morgana couldn't breathe. She immediately felt sick. All the joy and excitement drained from her so quickly she felt faint. She couldn't let Ms. Lane see her like this. She quickly gathered up her stuff while Ms. Lane finished up her phone call.

"Are you leaving?" Ms. Lane called to Morgana.

"Um, yes. I'm sorry. I don't feel good all of a sudden. Umm, too much excitement for one day." Morgana was scurrying to the heavy wooden door as fast as she could. Ms. Lane got up from the huge round marble table. "No. No. Don't get up. I'll be fine. I just need to go lie down," Morgana said. She could barely keep her eyes open.

"Did you hear Josef's news?" Ms. Lane asked but then noticed Morgana's pale face. "Dear? You look like you've seen a ghost. If you did it was probably just my Richard. He loves weddings." Ms. Lane tried to make a joke. Morgana had her hand on the door and her foot out through the threshold.

"Um, yes. I'm so happy for him. I really just am not feeling well. So, I'm going to go now. Please tell Josef congratulations for me," Morgana called back from the sidewalk. Ms. Lane said something, but Morgana couldn't hear what she said. All she could hear was her heart pounding so loudly in her ears as she ran across the street up the inclined driveway and into her house. She barely made it inside the door before she started sobbing. She had to feel her way down the hall into her bedroom because her eyes were welded shut from the flood of tearful howls. She collapsed on her bed and buried her head in her pillow to muffle her bemoaning wails of agony as her heart was being ripped to shreds.

After about thirty solid minutes her sobs finally slowed. She came out from underneath the pillow and lay on her back. She stared blankly at the ceiling for at least another thirty minutes, just trying to breathe. Finally she thought to herself, *I knew it was only a matter of time. This shouldn't be a surprise.* She tried convincing herself for another twenty minutes as she stared bleakly at the ceiling, hoping it would collapse on her and end her miserable suffering. She closed her eyes and they burned. She opened her eyes and they burned. She finally mustered all of her strength to grab a warm washcloth and wiped her face. She barely made it back to her bed before her legs gave out. She lay there with the wet rag on her eyes when the doorbell rang.

By the fifth ring, she knew he wasn't going to go away.

She dragged herself to the door, not knowing if she had the strength to see him right now. Her hoarse voice called out, "I'm not home."

"Morgana, please let me in," Josef's smooth silky voice said through the closed door. His sound depleted the little resources she was using to stand and she dropped to the cold floor.

"I'm not feeling well right now. I don't want to see anyone. Can you come back later?" she weakly called out.

"Morgana, let me in," he commanded.

"I really..." Her throat closed off as she struggled to speak. Then she heard a key enter the locked door.

"Then, I'm coming in," he announced. She found a surge of energy and jumped up as he let himself in the front door to her utter shock. "Your mom gave us a key for emergencies."

"Of course she did." Morgana shook her head as she desperately clung to the half wall and its open spindles of her long entry way. He walked past her and went into the living room. She stood by the front door, still holding on to the half wall for stability, looking at him through the spindles and watched him perch himself in her house.

"I owe you an explanation," he stated, looking directly at her.

"You really don't." She closed her eyes to break the contact.

"Please," he insisted gently.

She took a deep relenting breath and slowly walked down the tiled entry, around the back of the couch, past him and sat down, avoiding looking at him the whole way.

"This really isn't necessary. I don't know what Ms. Lane told you to make you come all this way today. I'm really very happy for you. I promise. Really, I am. I just need a little time," she said, tearing up again.

"Morgana," he said in his silky voice. "Please, look at me."

"I can't," she said into her chest. He sat down next to her on the couch.

"Morgana," he said softly. "I love you."

"Oh, please don't say that!" she said still avoiding looking at him. He reached out to touch her chin, turning her face towards his. Those deep aqua blue eyes penetrated her soul.

"I love you," he repeated earnestly.

"Then why are you marrying Tiffany?" Morgana took all of her strength and snatched herself away from him.

He immediately let out his boisterous laugh and said, "No! No! No! You don't understand. Mitchell and Trina are getting married." That got her attention and she finally looked at him.

"What?" she said desperately hoping she didn't make up what she just heard.

"Mitchell and Trina are getting married. I am not marrying Tiffany. I have never been engaged to Tiffany. I've never even really dated Tiffany."

Morgana jumped up from the couch as if it was burning her. "What?" she demanded as she was trying to make sense of what was happening. "Last year! She said!" Morgana remembered Tiffany in her face, and then remembered herself shutting the door in his face. *What did he say? Didn't he confirm it?* She searched her memory.

"When I was, like, sixteen and seventeen, she would sneak into my room sometimes when she spent the night with Brook and we messed around. She would talk about the future, but it wasn't my future. At the time I was going through a dark period after my parents died. I didn't care about the future. I didn't think I had a future," he confessed.

Morgana just stood there frozen, trying to process what was happening. Josef stood up and approached her, cautiously and carefully, like trying to tame a wild animal.

"I confronted her after what she said to you last year, and made it clear there was nothing between she and I. When I explained to Brook that I didn't really want Tiffany around me anymore, Brook wasn't very pleased with Tiffany's behavior either. I can't be sure, but I don't think they talk very much anymore."

"But..." Morgana was still not sure what was happening. He gently reached out and took her right hand in his. Confused and perplexed, she looked at him. "But you never said anything?"

"Well, that's what I'm trying to explain."

Morgana cut him off, "But, all those celebrations, she was all over you. What about all that?"

He smiled with care. "Which celebrations, exactly? Mabon, where you and I danced all night? Samhain, when we talked all night with my parents? Are you talking about Aunt Katherine's birthday when you ran away from me?"

"But...I...she." Morgana tried to come up with all the reasons why she had thought he was with her. She was trying to remember as his gentle smile was wearing her down and his deep aqua blue eyes held her spirit. He was still holding her hand and stroking her fingers. She finally realized that she was the one who had put up a wall around herself just because she knew Tiffany liked him. Morgana had been the one to assume so much, but Josef never really did anything but be cordial to Tiffany. Morgana was the one who made it all up in her mind. Even Cole knew Josef liked Morgana. She just couldn't see it for herself. Thoughts flashed in her mind over all the times he was there. Starting at her eighteenth birthday when he gave her a priceless family heirloom. Then, they danced all night at her first celebration out at the lot when she felt the magic of the connection. He found her at Samhain and they talked all night about his parents and true love. She was the one who brought Cole to the winter solstice dance and the rest of the events. She was also the one who shut the door in Josef's face not giving him any chance to explain himself. And, she was the one who shut herself off from everyone.

"I will admit, I did let her run interference..." Josef offered apologetically.

"Interference?" she interrupted with a gasp. "That was torture for me!"

"Yes, you looked so tortured while you were with the coffee guy, the Anam Cara guy, the Caribbean guy, the..." he gently listed with an endearing little laugh as he was still softly twirling with her fingers.

She cracked a smile but tried to hide it. "That was all the same guy."

"Ya, like, the best looking guy ever! Where did you find him, perfectly chiseled dot com?" Josef joked.

She was trying really hard not laugh and poked him in the chest with her free hand, "Ya, and he dumped my ass because of you!"

Josef caught her hand. "I am so sorry to hear that," he said tenderly, but with some irony, as he softly kissed her fingertips.

Josef had her right hand laced with his and he was lightly kissing the fingers on her left hand. Morgana's tough exterior was starting to melt and her breath was starting to quicken.

"He said...I didn't light up for him...the way I light up for you," she confessed as the tingles started running up her spine.

"Good looking and smart. He was a real catch," Josef noted, as he delicately kissed the interior of her wrist.

"He said you...you lit up for me too," she softly uttered as she felt the butterflies starting to swirl. Then she remembered, she saw Josef light up for her that day in Ms. Lane's hospital room when he brought her back to life, and there were other times too. She remembered he told her he didn't want to leave her to go to Italy and all the times he called he always said he wished he was there with her. She had a block up and never let him explain.

Josef looked at her. "A year and a half ago we stood right here and I stopped myself from kissing you and I promised you an explanation." (He lightly paused.) "Morgana, I have loved you since the day I first met you. I told you that you brought me back to life, but I didn't tell you that I also fell in love with you that day. I have spent the last seven years trying to prove to myself that I could be the man you deserve. I'm sorry if it was torture. I'm sorry you were dumped. I had a lot of damage I had to let go of. I'm not perfect, but I don't want to go any further in my life without you. I've done all I can on my own and now I'm hoping we can help each other grow together."

Tears of love were filling Morgana's eyes. It was like he was reading her private thoughts of what she imagined true love to be. She thought about how much she had changed in the last year and a half since they stood on this spot. She felt like she was a completely different person. Ms. Lane had taught her so much and she had learned so much about herself. And then she thought about Ms. Lane, her fairy godmother, who had been mentoring her since she turned eighteen, to let go of the negative vibrations so she would be open to the higher frequencies. "You will go on to live a happy and fulfilled life full of love, magic, and miracles," she had once told Morgana.

Ms. Lane, Josef's favorite aunt, the one who sent him to Morgana's house that day to mow her yard, the one who came and got Morgana that wonderful fateful day that changed her life forever. Was she the orchestrator of all this? *That little witch!* Morgana thought with a smile. She thought about all the growth and changes she had made in the past two years and she completely understood what Ms. Lane meant by "sweet synchronicity." The timing was lined up perfectly and here they both were, ready to move forward, together.

"I promise that it will be you and me together forever, no matter what." Josef looked deeply at her. "I beg you, please tell me now if you need more time. Because I swear, that when I do kiss you- I will never let you go."

She looked into his deep aqua blue eyes and saw her future reflecting back at her. With all her heart and soul, she said to him, "Then kiss me, and never let me go!"

With great resounding relief and deep loving desire, he passionately pulled her to him. When he finally pressed his delicious lips to hers, it was like every cell in both of their bodies exploded into fireworks.

It was amazing.

It was electrifying.

It was true love.

It was magic!

Epilogue

IT WAS THE eightieth birthday of Morgana, the beloved Grand High Chairman.

She sat in front of her vanity mirror pinning up her silver hair into a perfect ballerina bun. She clasped the aqua blue diamond amulet around her neck that was showcased by her long black velvet dress. She fastened the matching heart diamond earrings in her ears and laced up her black Victorian boots with the kitten heels that clicked their way down the hall as she made her way to the kitchen.

And there he was, standing in the kitchen, illuminated by a single candle in her birthday cake. His sun-kissed blond hair was now white. His golden tan skin a little paler, but that exquisite smile and those deep aqua blue eyes still sent tingles up her spine.

For the last sixty years they had been in love together, traveling the world, working side-by-side. Together, they kept the magic alive.

"Happy Birthday, Lady Morgana. Make a wish," Josef said. His silky voice stirred her internal butterflies. She smiled at him as she walked around the kitchen island and softly kissed his sweet lips.

She didn't have to make a wish – he had already made all her wishes come true.

And with a slight wave of her hand, the candle flame went out.

Printed in the United States
By Bookmasters